EDITH'S WAR

EDITH'S WAR

•

ANDREW SMITH

Andrew Smith

AXIOM

Edith's War
Copyright © 2010 Andrew Smith
Front cover photograph: ©iStockphoto.com/eliandric
Back cover photograph: ©iStockphoto.com/gwarrington

Library and Archives Canada Cataloguing in Publication

Smith, Andrew, 1947-
Edith's war / Andrew Smith.

ISBN 978-0-9864962-0-2

I. Title.

PS8637.M553E45   2010 C813'.6   C2010-901072-8

Published by Axiom Publishing Inc.
533 College Street, Suite 402, Toronto, Ontario M6G 1A8
Telephone: 647-343-0230   e-mail@axiompublishing.com
www.axiompublishing.com

Visit the *Edith's War* web site for e-trailers featuring live footage overlaid with spoken
readings, photo albums, interviews with the author, and other content related to events
and locations featured in this book. **www.edithswar.com**

Printed and bound in Canada

1 2 3 4 5 6 7 8 9 TCP 17 16 15 14 13 12 11 10 09

IN MEMORIAM

•

The hundreds of men and boys of Italian heritage
living in Britain during World War II who lost their lives as a
result of the British government's internment policy of 1940.

•

Winston Collins

•

Barbara Sears

This is a work of fiction based on actual events, only the characters are imagined.

ITALY

"Ma fai attenzione! Madonna!"

Will Maguire had run slap bang into a burly young man who was letting it be known he considered the collision to be entirely Will's fault.

In fact, the hefty Venetian had stopped abruptly, just past the crest of a narrow bridge that spanned the Rio di San Barnaba, while Will and his brother, Shamus, had been walking immediately behind him. Admittedly, Will had been admiring the sparkling canal and ancient edifices off to his right, but there was nothing he could have done to prevent himself from crashing into the Italian even if he'd been looking straight ahead.

Thrown off balance by the impact, Will staggered sideways, caught a heel on the edge of a paving stone, and fell to the ground. The guidebook he'd been holding flew into the air and landed with a loud slap an inch from one of the man's huge feet.

"Guarda cosa hai fatto alla mia scarpa!" the man bellowed, pointing down at his shoe. A smear of dirt, clearly caused by Will's foot as he'd stumbled, marred the pristine leather. The tall Italian appeared to be in his late twenties, with a huge head of vigorous, coal-black hair. Now he glared at Shamus accusingly, completely ignoring Will, who lay sprawled on the ground at his side.

Shamus's immediate concern was that his brother may have broken something; at sixty-one, Will's bones probably weren't as strong as they had been. Shamus stepped toward Will and bent to help him to his feet.

Having received no apology, the young Italian lifted both hands in a dramatic gesture of exasperation and gazed, his substantial eyebrows raised, toward a couple of passersby as though appealing for their support. The bystanders, two girls walking arm in arm, rolled their eyes and shook their heads. Shamus was left with the distinct impression the young man was known to them, and his operatic behaviour was all too familiar.

Appearing unsurprised with any lack of sympathy from his fellow Venetians, the sturdy Italian squatted and licked one large thumb. With a single swipe, he erased the muddy mark on his shoe, then retrieved a handkerchief from his jacket pocket and scrubbed his thumb. It was only after the gleaming leather was restored to perfection and his thumb clean that the young man paid any attention to Will, who was struggling to stand with the help of Shamus's hand under one of his elbows.

"Scusa," declared the Italian, "spero che non ti sia fatto male." His tantrum seemed to have dissipated as quickly as it had erupted. He frowned, but more as an expression of sympathetic regret at Will's clumsiness than from any remorse for his outburst. Nevertheless, he stooped to take Will's other elbow while deftly retrieving the guidebook with his free hand.

As he bent over, a metal object slid out of an inside pocket and tumbled to the ground with a clatter. The thought flitted across Shamus's mind that it might be a gun. But it was a silver cigarette case. Shamus couldn't recall having seen one of the rectangular, hinged cases since he and Will had been boys, in the '50s and early '60s. Once a small clasp was released, the case could be opened like a slim, hollow book to reveal a single layer of ten or fifteen cigarettes held in place by a narrow elastic strap.

Once Will was safely on his feet, the man released him and picked up his cigarette case. Will and Shamus watched as he polished each shiny surface with the grey woollen fabric of his jacket sleeve. He examined it for damage and then, satisfied that there were no dents, returned the cigarette case to his inside pocket. Shamus noted that the olive-skinned Italian was handsome in a brutish way.

"You are American," said the man, studying the cover of the English-language guidebook.

"British," said Will, brushing some dust from his trouser leg while scrutinizing the man's face.

Shamus wouldn't have been surprised by an angry explosion from Will. The slightness of his brother's frame — almost half the size of the Italian's — had never held him back from confrontation in the past. And the whole brouhaha had been the young man's fault in the first place. But instead, while clearly unhurt by his fall, Will appeared more confused than angry. He was staring at the man and frowning, as though trying to work out how, and from where, the young Italian had materialized.

"British!" exclaimed the Italian. "From London perhaps? I lived there for two years when I was a student. Very nice."

To Shamus's astonishment, Will merely nodded his head and continued to stare at the man. Shamus wondered if perhaps his brother was in shock; normally quite vocal, it wasn't Will's style to be so tight-lipped.

"I live in London, but we're from Liverpool originally," Will finally blurted, shaking himself out of his trance. He smiled at the man.

"Liverpool!" exclaimed the man. "Good football. Very tough fans. Maybe you want to fight?" He beamed at Will, who grinned back in return. If Shamus hadn't known his brother better, he'd have thought Will had taken a liking to the temperamental young Italian.

Then the man, with the illuminated expression of someone who's been hit by a brainwave, his dark eyes flashing mischievously, thrust Will's guidebook into Shamus's hands and took two strides to the very crest of the hump-backed bridge that spanned the narrow canal.

"Come. Look." He beckoned for the brothers to join him.

A greengrocer's barge was moored to one side of the bridge, stacked high with piles of fruit and vegetables glowing in the brilliant morning sun. Shamus followed the scent of apples on the damp Venetian air toward where the Italian gestured excitedly for the two brothers to examine something on the stones at his feet. When Shamus and Will stepped closer, they saw four white marble footprints embedded in the paving stones. The two sets of prints, like fossilized insoles, were facing each other.

The man carefully placed his feet into one pair and adopted the pose of a boxer, holding up two fists. "You stand there," he ordered Will.

Like a small child eager to play, Will stepped up to the opposing set of footprints and stood toe to toe with the young man, who indicated, by re-establishing his pose and nodding vigorously, that Will should follow suit. Shamus was amazed when Will immediately took the same pugilistic stance as the Italian. His brother could be playful, but his suspicious nature usually inhibited him from acting the fool with anyone but a proven friend and ally.

"*Bravo!*" cried the Italian. He furrowed his forehead into an exaggerated frown, trying his best to appear fierce, but the corners of his lips twitched as he suppressed a smile.

The sight of his lightweight, sixty-one-year-old brother fist to fist against a lusty heavyweight in his twenties was so comical that Shamus laughed out loud. In part, Shamus's laughter was nervous; he wouldn't have been at all surprised if Will took it into his head to take a swing at the Italian. His abdomen tightened, as it always did when there was any danger of argument or conflict.

A passing woman wearing a bright blue headscarf and clutching a plastic carrier bag bulging with fruit appeared to know the young man — she smiled and made a comment. Judging by her tone and her expression, Shamus guessed it to be a sarcastic remark. Whatever the woman said, it put paid to the young man's ferocity. He collapsed with laughter and slapped Will playfully on the back. Will dropped his fists, his cheeks glowing pink, and he smirked like a teacher's pet with a new gold star. If he had a tail he'd be wagging it, thought Shamus.

"These footmarks are hundreds of years old," said the Italian. "There were once gangs, yes?"

"Yes," said Will, nodding his head to reassure the young man he was understood.

"One gang lived over there." The Italian indicated one side of the canal with a sweep of his long arm. "The other lived on the other side. They met here to settle the arguments. The two *capi*, they would fight to settle the arguments between the gangs. Very bloody fights. Sometimes, one of them died."

"Fantastic," said Will, eyes shining.

His comment coincided with the sound of a bell ringing the hour.

"*Madonna!* I'm very late," exclaimed the man, glancing at his watch. "When you bump me, I was returning to fetch my briefcase. I forgot it at my house, just over there." He gestured toward the street that led to Campo Santa Margherita. Then he took Will's hand and pumped his arm a couple of times. "Nice to meet you," he cried as he strode away. "*Arrivederci.* Good holiday in *Venezia.*" Will stood gazing after the young man. A bemused smile played across his lips until the Italian disappeared into a doorway. Then he shook his head as though to wake himself.

"Are you okay?" Shamus asked. Although five years younger than Will, it wasn't unusual for Shamus to feel responsible for his elder brother's welfare.

"Fine," Will assured him. "No harm done. Quite the reverse, in fact."

"Yes, you seemed to enjoy yourself immensely," said Shamus.

Will muttered, "There's something about that young man . . ." He stared after the Italian for a few seconds, frowning. The he shook his head again. "Sod him. Let's find that coffee."

The two brothers turned and crossed the bridge that led them into the open space of Campo San Barnaba. The yellow-ochre reflection of a row of handsome, sunlit façades glowed on the rippling surface of the canal, which ran along one side of the campo. The scene couldn't have been more idyllic. The row of burnished buildings bathed in sunlight was in perfect proportion to the surrounding square. Weathered wooden shutters and doors complemented golden stucco walls. It was easy to imagine a feeling of contentment in anyone who might inhabit the spacious rooms behind such sturdy walls, their lofty ceilings measured by the height of tall, light-flooded windows. Shamus was filled with envy for the inhabitants, who emerged every day to find such humane surroundings as Venice's pedestrian-only streets, squares, and canal-side walks. And the air was alive with the invigorating tang of a fresh maritime breeze — a far cry from Shamus's smog-choked hometown of Toronto, where the summer had been unusually hot and oppressive.

"In fact, it looked like you and the Italian stallion were enjoying a positive love fest." Shamus nudged Will's arm.

"That's more your bailiwick," snarled Will, his good humour evaporating.

"All right, no need for unpleasantness," said Shamus. He was taller and broader by far than his brother, but Shamus had to hurry to keep up as Will strode toward the tables of one of the outdoor cafés that lined the square.

"It's just that when I banged into that young man, I was deep in thought about something else entirely, that's all," said Will, once they were sitting at one of the small round tables.

When Shamus asked what could possibly have been so distracting, Will muttered something about having been preoccupied with a property deal, a house he was trying to buy. But as he spoke, instead of looking Shamus in the eye, Will made a point of twisting around in his chair to see if a waiter had emerged from the café behind them. "Who the hell do you have to bribe to get served around here?" he growled.

"What house? Where?" Shamus persisted.

"None of your business," retorted Will. "It'll probably come to nothing anyway."

It wasn't unusual for Will to appear annoyed with Shamus for no apparent reason. When they were children, Will had sometimes become so irritated with Shamus that he'd throw a punch in his brother's direction. Once Shamus had outgrown him, Will didn't dare continue with the thumpings, but the sniping continued. True, Will had mellowed a little since they'd both left home. In fact, there were a number of years, before Will was married, when they got along well, more like friends than brothers. But since their late twenties, when Shamus went to Canada, they'd seen little of each other. On the dozen or so occasions in the past three decades when they'd been together, Shamus had always supposed they'd assume the amiable relations they'd enjoyed before he left England. There was certainly deep familiarity whenever they met; how could there not be? They'd grown up together. But Will often exhibited a stiffness bordering on hostility. It never occurred to Shamus that perhaps it was he who'd changed, or that Will's animosity might be a reaction to something he'd done. He assumed Will's strained manner had something to do with his marital problems, and the fact that the two of them were always in the company of other people: their parents; Will's wife, Mary; Shamus's partner, Luke.

At the thought of Luke, Shamus experienced such acute yearning that his body shuddered, as though someone had walked over his grave, as his grandmother used to say. If only it were affable Luke and not peevish Will who was sitting across the café table. Shamus stared at the stone columns topped by bulging capitals that embellished San Barnaba church, across the square from where they were sitting. They were probably fine examples of some architectural period or other, but in Shamus's present mood, the masonry decorations seemed grossly overwrought. He should have known better than to agree to this lunatic weekend in Venice.

A few days earlier, Shamus had returned to his hotel in Verona to find a message demanding that he phone Will urgently. Shamus immediately jumped to the conclusion that their mother, Edith, had died, even though there was no good reason for Shamus to fear her demise; she'd been sick barely a day in her life. But when Shamus saw that Will had left a number with a German dial code, indicating that his brother was obviously not at home in England, he realized his fears for his mother were probably unfounded. Would he always assume — since Luke — an unexpected phone call to bring news of illness or death, he wondered.

"What do you want?" asked Shamus when he reached Will in Germany.

"A young wife with ample breasts," replied Will.

"Aren't you forgetting you already have a wife somewhere?"

"Not true, kiddo," said Will. "The divorce finally came through — signed, sealed and delivered."

"Wonders will never cease," said Shamus. "It's only been fifteen years since you separated."

"Best years of my life," declared Will. Shamus was reminded of people who claimed the same thing about being at school — he didn't believe them either.

"You'd better sit, if you aren't already," Will continued in a bossy, older-brother tone of voice that immediately irritated Shamus. "Edith has decided it's time she did a little travelling, namely a sojourn in Venice with her darling sons."

Shamus and Will had addressed their parents by their first names ever since they'd reached their late teens. Neither brother could remember exactly how Mum turned into Edith, nor how Dad became Joe. But at some point Edith and Joe had stopped referring to each other as Mum and Dad, and the brothers had simply followed suit. Will claimed that their parents had relinquished their parenthood.

"Let's face it, they were never very good at it anyway," he'd said.

"Us? In Venice? With *Edith?* You're joking. She never goes anywhere!" Shamus said, incredulous.

"Well she's going places now, honey," said Will. "When I told her I was off to Dresden on business, she said you were working in Verona for a few days and asked if Verona was near Venice. When I said yes, she claimed she'd always wanted to go to Venice and went on at some length about what a shame it would be not to take the opportunity for all of us to be together there for a long weekend."

"I'm not sure I have time for any sojourns in Venice, mother or no mother."

"I'm afraid it's a done deal," Will's disembodied voice reverberated slightly in Shamus's ear. "I told Edith I was sure you'd delay your trip back to Toronto for a couple of days. She arrives in Venice on Saturday morning and is expecting us to meet her."

"Trust her to start flying around the world post-9/11. Why didn't she do her air travel when it was glamorous and safe? And isn't she a little old? She just turned eighty-three, for Christ's sake!" Shamus exclaimed.

"She's probably chosen to start flying precisely because of 9/11; you know how contrary she can be if she gets a whiff of any chipping away at civil liberties," said Will. "And she's in perfect health, as you well know. Now that's it's a *fait accompli*, I'm rather looking forward to being in the bosom of my family in beautiful *La Serenissima.*"

Shamus, glancing through the window, was momentarily distracted by the sight of hundreds of specks swooping above the terracotta tile roofs of Verona. Swallows, preparing for migration to Africa. He'd migrate to Africa himself, he thought wryly, if it would get him out of this trip to Venice. He stared silently at a forest of ceramic chimney pots as he shifted the telephone from one ear to the other. He could only remember one other occasion when Edith had travelled any distance outside of Liverpool. He and Will had been sharing a flat in Notting Hill. They'd entered into the arrangement more out of necessity than desire. But they were both revelling in their independence from their parents and excited to be living in London. The years the two brothers had spent cohabiting was a period of pleasant amiability and peace between them. As far as

Shamus could remember, it was the only period during which Will seemed to do more than merely tolerate him. Except for one occasion when Edith and Joe travelled down from Liverpool by train to visit them. It was only a matter of hours before Will and their father got into a ferocious row. Then, when Shamus attempted his usual role as peacemaker, Will had turned his ire on his brother. Edith burst into tears, and she and Joe had returned to Liverpool two days early.

"Don't be such a wet blanket!" Will's voice was almost a welcome interruption to Shamus's recollections. "All you have to do is change your return flight back to Canadian Bleak House until Monday or Tuesday. I'll motor down and meet you in Venice. We'll have the whole day on Friday to catch up before Edith arrives on Saturday morning."

"There's nothing to catch up on," said Shamus, resentful of Will's manipulations. "Anyway, isn't Dresden to Venice rather a long drive? And what do you mean by Canadian Bleak House, for Christ's sake?"

"You've lived in Canada for too long; we don't cross the Alps by elephant any more," Will sneered. "Europe has tunnels and highways. Autobahn and autostrada. It'll take me less than a day to drive down there."

"And what did you mean by Bleak House?" repeated Shamus.

"Well let's face it, since Luke died, you have no reason to go home, do you?" asked Will. "Don't you get lonely in that empty pile of bricks, curled up in the fetal position with your thumb in your mouth?"

Shamus said nothing.

"Look," said Will. The change in the timbre of his voice was a signal of a halt in his harangue. A huskiness that, despite the imperfect phone connection, Shamus recognized — remembered — as the white flag of a temporary ceasefire. "For some reason unknown to man or beast, this trip seems to matter to Edith. I'd like you and me to do this together, that's all," concluded Will.

"Are you sure she hasn't gone gaga?" Shamus asked, aware that Will's appeal had weakened his resistance.

"Not at all. In fact she seems more lucid than ever. And now that there's no paterfamilias to fuck everything up, how bad could it be?" said Will.

A couple of days might not be so bad, thought Shamus grudgingly. Maybe Will was right; they might actually get along without Joe to put them all on edge.

After hanging up the phone, Shamus stood for a moment and stared out again at the rooftops of Verona lit by late afternoon sun, their west slopes glowing with golden light, their shadowy east sides assuming the purple tinges of evening. He watched the swallows outside his hotel window as they continued to dart and dive. Strange, he thought, how they managed never to collide.

Will had been right, of course. It was no problem for Shamus to change his flight. He'd finished work at the printing plant late on Thursday and travelled the short distance from Verona to Venice by train that evening. Despite Will's protestations of its being an easy drive, Shamus had turned in for the night before his brother arrived around midnight. And now here they were, sitting in a Venetian piazza, twenty-four long hours stretching ahead of them until their mother arrived. Shamus wondered what in God's name they were going to talk about.

"*Prego, signore,*" said the waiter, placing small white paper mats in front of them with the words "Caffé Lavazza: ricco e morbido" printed in lurid red letters.

"Not a moment too soon," Will's exaggeratedly cheery tone was rife with sarcasm. The waiter eyed Will suspiciously. Shamus felt a contraction in his intestines, which only relaxed a little when the waiter dismissed Will with the kind of disdainful shrug that Italian shoulders seem to perform so expressively.

"*Due cappuccini, per favore,*" said Shamus.

"Would a croissant be too much to ask for?" asked Will curtly, squinting in the sunlight as he looked up at the waiter. The waiter glanced at Will's guidebook, lying on the table. He made a show of not understanding the question; he frowned, shook his head, and scowled down at Will.

Will put his hand to his forehead — ostensibly an innocent move to shield his eyes from the sun, but Shamus recognized it as a defensive gesture, which prompted another turn of the screw in Shamus's intestines. It was as though his stomach remembered more clearly than he the unbearable tension at the family dining table, which would invariably erupt into a vicious battle between Will and Joe. Despite deep lines at his brow and the worn texture of his sixty-one-year-old skin, Will's expression of vulnerability, a scuffed-suede quality in his blue irises, was as obvious to Shamus as it had been during family meals when they were boys, their father simmering with rage at the head of the table. Shamus's annoyance with Will drained away, to be replaced by a sympathy so intense his eyes stung. Shamus couldn't help becoming indignant at the waiter for so obviously dismissing his brother as nothing more than an annoying tourist.

"*Dolci,*" snapped Shamus. "Do you have *dolci?*" His rudimentary Italian abandoned him in the wake of his irritation.

"*Si,* we have," replied the waiter, "Chocolate or . . ." he hesitated, "*albicocca.*"

"Apricot," Shamus translated for his brother.

"Chocolate for me," said Will.

"*Vorrei albicocca, per favore,*" said Shamus.

The waiter nodded and disappeared as brusquely as he'd arrived. Shamus wondered at the force of emotion he'd felt as a result of Will's little spat with the waiter. And why did he feel as though he were somehow responsible?

"Try not to make a fuss if it isn't a croissant," Shamus said.

"What?" asked Will, remnants of uncertainty flickering in his eyes.

"You asked for croissant. But they're French. The Italian equivalent, *dolci*, are usually more like bread, sweet rolls kind of thing."

"I have actually been to Italy before," said Will with a scowl.

Shamus suddenly became aware of the irony — the hypocrisy — of his annoyance with the waiter for harbouring exactly the same low opinion of his brother that he himself had felt minutes before. Shamus wished that he, like the waiter, were unfamiliar with the formative experiences of his brother's childhood. It'd be so much easier to simply dislike Will. He watched idly as a bookseller who had set up a folding table in the middle of the square arranged ancient volumes, some with torn jackets, in neat rows.

"*Prego,*" said the waiter as he placed a cup and saucer on each paper mat, then whisked two plates onto the table, quickly followed by the tab. "*Otto euro, per favore,*" he demanded, one hand thrust in his apron pocket in anticipation of making change. Shamus, unfamiliar with the etiquette of tourist establishments and accustomed to paying when ready to leave, was flustered. He fished for his wallet in a back pocket, muttering "eight euros" for Will's benefit. Will promptly produced two 5-euro notes, handed them to the waiter, and said, with a wave of his hand, "Keep the change."

"Grazie, signore," intoned the waiter, appearing less hostile now that negotiations had come to a satisfactory conclusion. He ambled over to a man and woman a couple of tables away who were arguing in German, fingers stabbing at a map spread out on the table in front of them.

"If I'd noticed the bastard hadn't brought real croissants I wouldn't have tipped him," said Will, looking at the *dolci* with mock horror.

"Very funny," said Shamus. "We'll be lucky if he didn't spit in our cappuccinos."

Will ignored him. He was staring at the German couple whose argument had escalated; their strident voices could be heard quite clearly.

"God but Kraut is an ugly language," Will said loudly.

ENGLAND

Friday, April 26, 1940

It wasn't the bloodshed that sickened Edith; she'd seen worse brawls. What repulsed her was the expression of sheer hatred that had transformed Liam's normally placid, boyish features into a grotesque agglomeration of convulsive muscle and quivering flesh.

"You're a bunch of Nazi wops," he'd screamed. "Why don't you clear off back to Italy before we lock you all up."

Liam was standing nose to nose with Domenico Baccanello, the youngest son of the Italian family who lived in the bungalow next door. He gripped the front of Domenico's shirt so tightly his knuckles were white with tension.

"You and whose army," Domenico had yelled. Edith saw a spray of spittle fly a few short inches from Domenico's mouth to land on Liam's cheek. At that, Liam butted Domenico's nose with his head and a stream of crimson blood burst from Domenico's nostrils. Undaunted, the Italian boy managed to land a hefty punch on Liam's left eye. Edith was doubly shocked, as the two boys had always been such fast friends.

"Stop it," shouted Mrs. Maguire from the open doorway behind Edith. "Liam, for God's sake, stop fighting." She hurried down the couple of steps from the porch to the lawn. Before she could reach the two boys, they'd dragged each other to the ground, where they flailed at each other, punching and kicking as hard as they could. Although slight, Mrs. Maguire was always energetic and full of purpose. As she hovered, bird-like, above the brawling boys her frustration at not being able to separate them was obvious.

Despite Edith's diminutive size — she matched the description in the popular song, "five foot two, eyes of blue" — she would normally have waded in and helped pull them apart, but she wasn't going to risk harming her unborn baby for the sake of her brother-in-law. In an attempt to assuage the guilt she felt for not helping her mother-in-law prise the scrapping boys apart, Edith tried to tell herself it would serve Liam right if he got a good thrashing. But she didn't really believe it, and Edith was relieved when a burly figure appeared from a row of conifers that separated Mrs. Maguire's garden from Anna and Gianni Baccanello's property.

The strange man appeared to be older than Edith, twenty-five perhaps. He strode purposefully towards the boys, who were still scrabbling at each other on the grass, Mrs. Maguire hovering fretfully above them. Judging from his luxuriant black hair and tawny skin, the newcomer belonged to the Baccanello family. But Edith was sure she'd never seen him before — she would have remembered.

"Now you two, that's enough," he said, grasping each boy by an upper arm and yanking them to their feet as effortlessly as if they were pint-sized dolls instead of two lusty teenagers. The boys practically dangled from the man's gargantuan hands, their shirts streaked with grass stains and spotted with bright circles of blood. "Domenico, apologize to Liam and to Mrs. Maguire."

"But it was his fault," spluttered Domenico, wiping his nose with one hand, smearing blood across his cheek in the process. "He called me a wop."

"*Basta,*" barked the man.

"There's really no need," insisted Mrs. Maguire. "Liam was as much to blame." As much to blame, thought Edith — her keen sense of fairness filled her with indignation. It was entirely Liam's fault, the little bugger.

Despite Mrs. Maguire's protestation, Domenico muttered a perfunctory apology, eyes lowered.

"Now go back to the house," ordered the stranger. Domenico slunk across the expanse of grass, compliant as a well-trained dog, and vanished through a gap in the line of fir trees.

"And you, my lad," Mrs. Maguire addressed Liam. "Up those steps and into your room. And stay there until I say so."

"I'm sorry, Mrs. Maguire," the man said as soon as Liam had disappeared through the front door.

Edith's mother-in-law frowned slightly. "Carlo?" she asked.

"But of course," the man said. "Didn't you recognize me?"

"Good heavens," cried Mrs. Maguire. "You look so . . ." she cast around for the right word — "mature."

Edith could contain herself no longer. "But it was all Liam's fault," she spluttered. "You needn't apologize."

"Well, we don't know everything that was said before we heard them out here shouting, do we?" Mrs. Maguire interjected. Then, in an obvious attempt to change the subject, she introduced Edith to Carlo. "This is my daughter-in-law, Edith." She turned to Edith. "Carlo is Anna's oldest son," she explained. "But I haven't seen him since he was married. Was it four or five years ago?" she asked.

"Six," said Carlo, smiling. "Pleased to meet you." He extended one of his giant mitts to Edith. Once her fingers were released from his enveloping grip, Edith unconsciously cradled her swollen abdomen in the palm of her hand.

"How far along are you?" asked Carlo. The question took Edith by surprise; she wasn't showing much and it was unusual for a man to ask, even if he were sensitive enough to be curious.

"Five months," she replied.

"Pregnancy obviously suits you," said Carlo. His brown eyes held an expression of amused curiosity.

"She does look well, doesn't she?" chimed in Mrs. Maguire.

"Yes indeed," said Carlo, smiling. "Beautiful as the Madonna." He pronounced the last word in an unusual way, elongating the o and lingering on the n's.

"Nonsense. I look like a beer barrel," Edith muttered, averting her eyes from his. She was sure Carlo must be teasing her. Nevertheless, she couldn't help feeling flattered; he was the first person ever to call her beautiful.

"Edith's staying with us for the duration. Liverpool's much too dangerous; the bombs could start dropping any day now," said Mrs. Maguire. "And Joe's off in God-knows-where fighting for King and country."

"Yes, my mother told me he was called up," said Carlo.

"Joe and Carlo were quite chummy when they were younger," explained Mrs. Maguire. Edith found it hard to imagine the two together. While both were dark-featured and good-looking, her husband, with his short, wiry figure, must have looked like a lepre-chaun in comparison to Carlo's massive frame.

"Isobel and I have moved here to escape from Liverpool too," said Carlo. "That, and because of her illness."

"Goodness, where will you all sleep?" asked Mrs. Maguire.

"Oh, we've squeezed into a lot less space before now," said Carlo, laughing. "Well, I must be off. If Domenico misbehaves again, you let me know." He grinned at Edith and gave a little nod of his impressive head as he turned to leave.

After he'd disappeared between the firs Edith gazed across the lawn and beyond the lane to the fields that dipped down toward the Dee estuary. A line of low dunes, their sandy flanks held in place by grey sea grass, separated farmland from a ribbon of beach. The tide was in, and Edith took in the white-flecked, bottle-green expanse of seawater stretching to the hazy coastline of Wales, which hovered on the far side of the river's mouth. It was a commanding view, refreshing after the grime and monotony of the crowded Liverpool neighbourhood where Edith and Joe had lived since they were married.

* * *

"What on earth got into you?" asked Mrs. Maguire. She held a com-press, a wad of old cotton sheet soaked in cold water, to Liam's swollen eye. "You and Domenico have been friends since you were babies."

"Things have changed," said Liam darkly. "There's a war on now, and Dom and his brothers are sure to be fifth columnists."

"That seems very unlikely," said Edith, lighting a cigarette and carefully shaking the match out before placing it in a nearby ashtray. She wasn't entirely sure what fifth columnists were, but she suspected the term implied traitorous behaviour. And it was ludicrous to think of the Baccanellos as anything but innocent, hard-working immigrants. She'd come to know the family well in the eight weeks since she'd moved from the flat over a chemist's shop in Liverpool that she and Joe had rented after they were married. On three occasions in the last couple of months, they'd all, Liam included, had supper next door with the Baccanello family. Anna Baccanello, who was plump and motherly, liked nothing better than to feed people.

"It says so right here," said Liam, grabbing the *Daily Mirror* from the sofa cushion next to him. "In black and white."

"Sit still," said Mrs. Maguire. "Better yet, you hold this on your eye while I soak another in cold water." She bustled off to the kitchen.

"Let me see the paper," said Edith. Instead of handing it to her, Liam held up the newspaper with his free hand and peered at it with his good eye. He quoted line by line in an exaggeratedly dramatic voice:

> There is a stinking wind from the Mediterranean which bodes no good,
> Yet we still tolerate Mussolini's henchmen in this country!
> The government of Italy has thousands of loyal followers here,
> Italians by birth, Fascists by breeding.

"You're making it up," exclaimed Edith. "They'd never print such rot in a national newspaper."

"Here, read it for yourself," said Liam, thrusting the crumpled copy of the *Daily Mirror* in her direction. Liam was absolutely right; he'd quoted the lines verbatim. Edith skimmed the rest. The phrase "'fifth columns" was there in the sixth line. The writer, a John Boswell, estimated that there were twenty thousand Italians living in Britain, describing them as "brown-eyed Francescas and Marias, beetle-browed Ginos, Titos and Marios . . . " He portrayed them as being "usually inoffensive, decent and likeable, BUT . . . " and claimed that they'd formed fascist clubs. Then, in an indulgent use of bold type, came the statement **"every Italian colony in Great Britain and America is a seething cauldron of smoking politics, Black Fascism. Hot as hell."**

"The bungalow next door doesn't seem like a seething cauldron of smoking politics or Black Fascism to me," said Edith, tossing the newspaper back to Liam. "It's sometimes warm, but nothing like as hot as hell."

"You can joke all you want," pronounced Liam. "But you'll be laughing on the other side of your face when we all wake up with our throats slit."

Edith wished Liam hadn't brought her attention to the article. She liked the Baccanellos tremendously, and she was sure that none of them had a fascist bone in their body. After all, it wasn't as if they'd just arrived in England; in fact, she remembered Anna saying that Domenico and Paolo had been born in Liverpool. Paolo must be around twenty years old, the same age as herself.

Edith remembered some mention of an older son, but she hadn't paid much attention. It was typical of Joe not to have mentioned Carlo. She found herself idly wondering what might have happened if she'd met someone like Carlo before she married Joe. But then she exhaled her last drag of cigarette and stubbed it out, shredding the remaining nub of tobacco into a mess of tiny golden strands.

"It looks like they're going to cancel the Olympics," said Liam, who'd moved on to another page of the *Daily Mirror*. He'd dropped the compress from his eye; Edith could see that his upper and lower lids and part of his cheek had turned an alarming shade of purple. The white of his eye was bloodshot. "That's a shame. Jack Beresford would have cleaned up in the rowing. Britain was guaranteed a few medals there. Damn nuisance."

"Watch your language, young man," said Mrs. Maguire, who appeared from the kitchen clutching another wad of wet fabric. "I'm not sure this compress is doing any good. You've got a real shiner and no mistake."

"Really?" exclaimed Liam. He jumped up to inspect himself in the mirror above the fireplace.

"Black eye or not, you're still helping me build that henhouse tomorrow," said Mrs. Maguire. "So don't think you can wriggle out of it."

Saturday, April 27, 1940

From inside the wooden shed, where she was clearing shelves of seed boxes, some packed with sprouting potatoes and others bristling with vegetable seedlings, Edith could hear Mrs. Maguire and Liam bickering outside.

"Hold it straight, Liam. You're more hindrance than help," exclaimed Mrs. Maguire.

"I don't know why you don't take the stake and let me do the hammering," grumbled Liam. "It's more of a man's job anyway."

Edith carried a couple of boxes out of the shed in time to see Mrs. Maguire swing the mallet with gusto, bringing it down squarely on top of the wooden stake that Liam was grasping. The stake sank a good six inches into the earth.

"I heard hammering and came over to see if you needed help, but it looks like you have everything under control." Carlo smiled at them from the shadows of the back wall of Mrs. Maguire's bungalow. He was wearing an old tan corduroy jacket with leather patches on the elbows that gave him a slightly raffish air.

The garden shed where Mrs. Maguire and Liam were working stood atop an incline that rose steeply at the rear of the house. Just beyond the shed lay the unfenced boundary of Shrimpley Heath, a few hundred acres of gorse, heather, bracken, and birch trees that blanketed the hills above the houses.

"Not so much under control that we couldn't use another pair of hands," Mrs. Maguire called down to Carlo, giving Liam a meaningful look.

Carlo took off his corduroy jacket, laid it on a nearby window ledge, and clambered up the slope, rolling up his shirtsleeves. "Since I'm to be one of your crew, perhaps you'd tell me exactly what it is you're up to," he smiled.

"We're turning the shed into a henhouse, and these posts are to make a run," explained Mrs. Maguire. Then, with a nod of her head, she indicated a large roll of chicken wire lying nearby. "We'll be thankful for the eggs when food gets scarce. The Great War will seem like a picnic compared to this one; you mark my words."

When World War I began, Mrs. Maguire was newly wed, and she experienced first-hand the results of war when her young husband was granted a medical discharge in 1918, two months before hostilities ceased. Mr. Maguire was sent home from the battlefields of France suffering from the effects of gas poisoning; his lungs were covered in scar tissue. Despite chronic shortness of breath, his matinee idol exterior was unblemished. He was a popular guest at New Year's Eve parties, where he was given a lump of coal and sent outside so that he could return, clutching the coal, as soon as midnight had struck.

It was considered good luck for a dark-haired, handsome man to be the first to cross the threshold. Mrs. Maguire couldn't remember the significance of the coal but thought it had something to do with assuring a bountiful year to come. At thirty-four, Mr. Maguire died of a heart attack, a result of his gas-damaged lungs.

Carlo picked up a stake and examined it. "When are the hens arriving?" he asked.

When Mrs. Maguire explained that the farmer down the lane was due to deliver them the following Monday, Carlo relieved Mrs. Maguire of her large hammer. "Well let's get to it, then," he exclaimed. He steadied the stake with one hand and used his other to wield the mallet.

"It doesn't look like you'll be needing me any more," said Liam.

"Oh but we do," retorted Mrs. Maguire. "You and I can start nailing the wire to the posts."

"And what's your contribution to the war effort?" Carlo asked Edith once he'd driven in his first stake.

"I'm off to plant these," she said, holding up some boxes of sprouting potatoes and trying to appear as if he'd interrupted her in her activities, when in fact she'd been staring at him, admiring his dexterity with stake and mallet. "We need to empty the trays to make nesting boxes out of them."

"I'm already beginning to detest the expression 'war effort,'" complained Liam. It struck Edith as ironic that Liam, who only the day before had been viciously attacking Domenico for imaginary unpatriotic activities, would much rather be lying on his bed sneaking cigarettes and reading *Picture Show* magazine, hoping the war would be over before he turned eighteen and was old enough to fight.

* * *

"Well I think we all deserve a cup of tea," declared Mrs. Maguire two hours later. She took a final admiring glance at the transformed shed with its hen run securely enclosed in gleaming chicken wire. Carlo had carved out a couple of openings at the base of the shed wall, inside the run, for the hens to go in and out. Edith had planted sprouting potatoes and vegetable seedlings — Brussels sprouts, cabbage, and lettuce — in the bed that Mrs. Maguire had prepared to one side of the front lawn. Liam had disappeared into the house the minute the last section of chicken wire had been secured. Carlo retrieved his jacket from the window ledge and swung it over one shoulder.

"You two go and sit on the front porch," suggested Mrs. Maguire to Carlo and Edith. "I'll bring the tea out in a minute."

Why Mrs. Maguire called it a porch Edith couldn't imagine, as it wasn't enclosed in glass. It consisted of a wooden platform sheltered by a shingle roof that was supported by four sturdy wooden pillars covered in peeling, cream-colored paint. When Edith had once referred to it as the "verandah," Mrs. Maguire laughed out loud. "Where do you think we are, Memsahib?" she asked. "This isn't a posh bungalow in the Punjab, you know."

Half a dozen other residences were dotted along the length of Sandy Lane, a mile-long, unpaved cul-de-sac that ended at a gate to a grassy meadow. Mrs. Maguire's house and the Baccanello property were the only ones to sit cheek by jowl; the rest were separated from each other by fields and hedgerows. Most were identical. Their bulging bay windows and exteriors of pebbledash stucco in pastel shades, typical of seaside residences constructed in England during the early 1900s, appeared incongruous, a misguided attempt to recreate a rash of Indian-style bungalows in the lush English countryside. To Edith, who'd never undertaken a longer journey than the hour-and-a-half-long trip from Liverpool to Shrimpley, their names — Resthaven, Namaskar, Longview— were suggestive of the exotic romance of the Indian Raj. She couldn't think why her mother-in-law was so clearly embarrassed when she had to give her address as Shambhala, the name inscribed in faded, swooping script on the sagging front gate. "Anybody would think we lived in a heathen temple," muttered Mrs. Maguire. "Numbers would be far more sensible." The Baccanello bungalow was called Annapurna, but nobody called it that. It was alluded to by one and all as "the Italians' house."

"It's a fine view from here," commented Carlo, settling onto one of the porch chairs. Edith sank into the chair beside him and surveyed the scene before them.

The topography provided Mrs. Maguire's porch with an unobstructed panorama of the estuary's tidal flats, a vast expanse of sand and water stretching inland to the east and westward toward the Irish Sea. The red roof of the Shrimpley Yacht Club could be glimpsed among the dunes below. Edith thought the term "Yacht Club" was rather grand for the barn-like building next to an unkempt boatyard that housed a motley collection of old dinghies with paint peeling and rigging in need of repair. A few sailboats in better condition were anchored in the estuary. They floundered on the sands when the water was low, but now that it was high tide, they bobbed jauntily among the whitecaps.

"Here we are," sang Mrs. Maguire as she emerged from the front door carrying a tray with a blue milk jug, a teapot engulfed by a pink crocheted cosy, and a plate with four plain digestive biscuits. Carlo jumped up to take the tray from her and placed it safely on a small table between his chair and Edith's. Edith noticed there were only two cups.

"Aren't you joining us?" she asked, suddenly and inexplicably nervous.

"If you don't mind, I'll have mine inside," said Mrs. Maguire. "*ITMA* will be on the wireless soon, and I'd rather not miss the beginning."

ITMA was short for a radio program called *It's That Man Again.* The star of the show was Liverpool-born comedian Tommy Handley, much loved by Mrs. Maguire for his local roots. The title came from a newspaper headline reprinted whenever Hitler made yet another outrageous territorial claim during the months leading up to the war, when more than one newspaper developed the habit of proclaiming "It's That Man Again" on their front page.

"Sorry there aren't more biscuits, but Liam seems to have eaten our quota for the week," explained Mrs. Maguire. "Dreadful boy doesn't seem to understand the concept of rationing. I suppose he'll learn soon enough when we have nothing left to eat," she muttered darkly before disappearing inside.

"I get so sick of all the doom and gloom," said Edith crossly. "Can you honestly believe there'll be no food in the shops?" Then, without waiting for an answer, she found herself launching into a tirade. "Mind you, no wonder everybody's on edge. It was bad enough when they were handing out gas masks willy-nilly before war was even declared. A mere whiff of floor polish or bleach was enough to put the fear of God into people and send them fumbling for the darn things. It might not be so bad if they didn't look so horrific, all these grisly black-rubber snouts roaming the streets. And now they're forcing everyone to carry identity cards. It's no wonder everyone's so glum."

"Such passion," Carlo said, an amused expression on his face.

Edith felt her face flush. She looked away, toward the estuary.

"Sorry," said Carlo. "I shouldn't tease you."

"No, it's I who should apologise, ranting on like that," she said. "My father always said I take things too seriously. Not that he was exactly a barrel of laughs himself."

"He's dead?" Carlo asked.

"God no," exclaimed Edith. "It's just that I haven't seen much of my parents since I was married."

"Oh?" said Carlo.

"A silly row between Joe and my dad about religion," explained Edith. "The ridiculous thing is that Joe hasn't stepped into a church — Catholic or otherwise — since he left school. And my dad is an indifferent Protestant at best. He hasn't marched in the Orange Day parade since my granddad died ten years ago. But that didn't stop him and Joe from going at it. It got so heated I began to wonder if they weren't fighting about something else entirely."

"Joe always was high-strung," said Carlo.

"I keep forgetting you know him."

"I'm a couple of years older than Joe; I think I was twelve when we moved here. He must have been nine or ten. But with no other kids of our age to play with — Domenico was a baby and Paolo had only just started school — Joe and I knocked around together. I was in and out of this house; Mrs. Maguire was always so welcoming."

"She's been generous to me too," said Edith.

After Edith's parents told her never to darken their door again, following her father's argument with Joe, Mrs. Maguire had told Edith, "Well you're always welcome in *our* house." At the time, Edith thought it sounded more like a criticism of her parents than a genuine invitation, but her mother-in-law had proved true to her word.

As soon as she heard she was to be a grandmother, Mrs. Maguire had insisted Edith come and live with her and Liam. Edith was hesitant. After Joe had gone into the army, her solitary life in their furnished flat was comfortable enough. Ironically, her days were considerably more peaceful than before the war, when she'd lived with her parents. Once Edith realized that she and her sister had been living under her father's thumb rather than under his wing, she couldn't help wondering if perhaps she'd married Joe just to escape. The seventeen shillings a week that Edith received from the government as the wife of a serviceman, plus the seven shillings a week that Joe was required by the army to send her — which, as he was quick to point out, only left him with a measly shilling for the whole week — supplied all her basic needs. It wasn't as much as she'd earned as a filing clerk for the Mersey Docks and Harbour Board, but she'd rather have things a little tight than have to work in a dreary office, being leered at by accounting clerks with ink-stained fingers.

Edith had to admit that the winter, the coldest in forty-five years, had been hard on her. She was at too much of a loose end in the gloomy city, where air raid shelters and barrage balloons lent a pervasive atmosphere of impending doom. But with no tangible evidence of war — the press dubbed the first months after war was declared "The Bore War" — Edith felt like a fraud for fleeing Liverpool. A few days after she'd arrived in Shrimpley, she secretly welcomed the news that Germany had invaded Norway and Denmark. Although Edith still couldn't imagine such a thing, the eventuality of bombers over England was deemed more likely, making her exit from the city appear less premature.

Now she looked around at the expansive lawn, its herbaceous borders colourful with early-flowering blooms. At least I chose a man whose family wasn't stuck in dreary old Liverpool, she thought.

"How on earth did you meet Joe anyway?" asked Carlo.

"You sound surprised that he met me at all," said Edith.

Carlo was clearly nonplussed by her accusation. "I didn't mean to sound rude, but you have to admit you and he are . . . different."

"I suppose we are," Edith said. She assumed Carlo was referring to their religious backgrounds. He couldn't know about the other disparities — her private schooling, her upbringing in a house rife with middle-class pretensions. Normally she might have tried to elucidate, but with Carlo she found she didn't feel any need to explain herself.

"We met last year, four or five months before war was declared," Edith said "And in November we were married — obviously," she laughed, patting her swollen belly. "But this was May, a little less than a year ago. My sister, Agnes, and I had gone to the Grafton ballroom. You know, on West Derby Road?"

"Yes, I know the place," said Carlo, impatient to hear more.

"It was the day that conscription was announced. My dad went on about how it was the first time in British history that compulsory military enlistment had happened during peacetime. The Grafton was full to bursting despite all the pessimism about war being inevitable. Joe and I literally stumbled across one another. We'd been standing back to back when I turned to see what was keeping my sister, who'd gone off to the Ladies. Joe turned around at the same time and we almost banged heads; I had to grab hold of him to stop myself from coming a cropper."

Edith paused for a moment and gazed across the estuary. The Welsh hills were clearly visible on the far side. It was an unusually clear day; she could make out a patchwork pattern of fields and hedges spread out across the hillsides. The Grafton dance hall seemed worlds away. Nevertheless, she could picture herself there, being forced to hold on to a handsome stranger to prevent herself from falling, one hand on his shoulder, the other grasping his arm. Afterwards, Joe enjoyed telling people that Edith had "thrown herself at him" on the night they met, then he'd wink at Edith and give her a little nudge. Edith would try not to appear ticked off, but later, as it became more and more obvious that she would never have "thrown" herself at him, she found it hard not to scowl.

"He asked me to dance, and the rest is history," concluded Edith, turning to look at Carlo.

"Joe's a lucky man."

"Do you always flirt with your friends' pregnant wives?" asked Edith.

"I'd never do that," Carlo retorted, straight-faced.

They both laughed.

"And anyway, Joe's not my friend." said Carlo. "I haven't seen hide nor hair of him for years, especially since I left school and started working with my father." He leaned over and lifted the teapot. "We'd better drink this tea before it gets cold. Shall I be mother?"

Edith couldn't help smiling — anybody less like a homely housewife was impossible to imagine.

Once he'd poured their tea, Carlo fished a cigarette case and a lighter from the pocket of his corduroy jacket. He snapped open the case and offered a cigarette to Edith. Then he flipped open the top of his lighter and lit it with a flick of one thumb. Carlo held it out for Edith, cradling the flame from the breeze with both hands.

"Maybe Joe felt I'd deserted him when I got married and moved to Liverpool to work in my father's fish and chip shops."

"I wouldn't worry about Joe. He's a bit needy sometimes," said Edith. She took a drag of her cigarette.

"Working in a chippie must be hard work — long days and all that," she said.

"But it's steady — even in the Depression we did well. You wouldn't believe how many people will readily spend their last few pennies on a helping of cod and chips. The worst part of working in the middle of Liverpool is the trek back and forth from here each day."

Edith had always enjoyed the trip back and forth from Shrimpley to the city centre, but she could see how onerous the journey would be as a daily trek to work. After reaching Shrimpley village in the twenty-seater local bus or by foot across the heath, Carlo would have to take a larger, double-decker bus the six or seven miles across the peninsula that separated the estuaries of the River Dee and the River Mersey. The bus terminated at the Mersey ferry dock in Birkenhead, where boats regularly crossed the river to Liverpool on the opposite shore. No wonder Carlo had moved at the first opportunity.

It must be wearisome to have to resume such a tiresome daily trek now that he'd moved back to Sandy Lane. But he wasn't alone, thousands of people in Britain had relocated even though it meant travelling longer distances to work every day. It was preferable to being in a city overnight, with the threat of German bomber attacks imminent. Everybody assumed that central Liverpool, with its docks and factories, was likely to be a prime target. But nothing had happened so far, and Edith had trouble believing that bombers would ever venture that far.

"Isobel will be wondering where I am," pronounced Carlo. "I must get back and finish building her ramp. That's what I was doing when I heard you lot hammering."

"Ramp?" queried Edith.

"Isobel has multiple sclerosis and she has to use a wheelchair more and more these days. So I'm building a ramp at the back door so she can get out in the garden when the weather's fine."

"I'm so sorry," said Edith. The fact of Carlo's wife leapt into the realms of reality. Up until then, Edith had unwittingly swept Isobel to the edge of her consciousness.

"We must get you two together. I think you'd like each other," said Carlo.

Not knowing how to react, Edith said nothing. She looked toward the estuary. The tide was retreating. Islands of wet sand had appeared, surrounded by channels of turbulent water rushing toward a ragged line of distant breakers that marked the fringes of the sea proper, a few miles to the west. She looked up to see Carlo unfolding himself from the wicker porch chair. As he passed behind Edith's chair, he reached down and gripped one of her shoulders lightly. Surprised by his touch, Edith tilted her head back to look up at him. For a split second, Carlo's expression was thoughtful, almost grave. But then he smiled, and before he released her shoulder, he gave it a gentle shake. He jumped down the couple of steps to the grass, calling goodbye as he crossed the lawn.

After Carlo disappeared, Edith reached for a digestive biscuit. She could smell the honeyed scent of blossom from a nearby hawthorn bush recently come into bloom. Any initial fears she may have had about being alone with Carlo had proven completely unfounded. There'd been none of that circling around, sizing each other up, trying to decide who stood where on the social ladder. She'd noticed the same thing when she first met Anna and the rest of the Baccanello family. Edith put it down to their not being English. The tide was almost at its lowest. Edith could see that the wind had dried the peaks of sea-drenched sandbars to the colour of pale eggshells. The soporific cooing of a wood pigeon drifted down from gorse-covered slopes above the house. The exertions of the day had tired Edith; she closed her eyes and fell contentedly to sleep.

ITALY

As the cool shadow of the façade of San Barnaba retreated across the campo, Will and Shamus drank their coffee and ate their *dolci* at a leisurely pace. Creamy cappuccino and sweet pastry comforted Shamus and calmed his rebellious digestion. He allowed himself to think how pleasant it was to bask in the warmth of autumnal sunshine, watching the world pass by.

Sounds were more harmonious now that the German couple seemed to have settled their differences; they were conversing in a low murmur.

"I take it back," said Will.

"Take what back?" asked Shamus.

"German," pronounced Will, "is perhaps only ugly when people are shouting." Shamus was glad Will spoke out of the side of his mouth so there was little chance anybody else could hear.

"Maybe we presume it is always ugly because we were swayed by all those newsreels and recordings we were subjected to when we were kids," suggested Shamus.

Will raised an eyebrow. "You mean all the World War II Hitlerish stuff?"

"Yes, those harsh jingoistic speeches. And old movies haven't exactly portrayed the softer side of the language, have they?"

"The evil POW camp commander yelling, "*Heraus, schnell*," mused Will. "But is there a softer side to the language?"

Shamus leaned forward in his chair, put his elbows on the table, hands clasped, and looked into Will's eyes. He recited in as melodious a voice as he could muster:

Frühling, frühling, tanzen und springen.
Alles die Vögel im Baumen singen.

"Bugger me," said Will. "I didn't know you could converse in Kraut."

Shamus glanced at the Germans, but they seemed completely preoccupied with each other. "You've obviously forgotten that I took German at school," said Shamus, feeling superior, although secretly he doubted if he could muster up more than a few phrases. "Not exactly a classic, but I like that little verse because you don't have to understand German to guess what it's all about. You can almost hear a warm spring breeze ruffling newly formed leaves, don't you think?"

"It's certainly mellifluous, especially the way you play it," said Will. "I bet you've ruffled more than a few leaves with that rendition. It must make you very popular with the Manfreds, if you know what I mean."

Shamus gave Will what he hoped was a withering look.

"I get your drift, though," said Will. "*Das Deutsch* doesn't have to sound like the guttural über-lingua of the world."

The German couple stood and wandered hand in hand across the campo in the direction of the Grand Canal. Shamus leaned back in his chair to watch them, then looked across to where the greengrocer's barge was moored. He could make out piles of fruits and vegetables on the deck, gleaming in the sun. The hustle and bustle of early morning had subsided. The crowds of students and dozen or so grandmothers laden with shopping who'd criss-crossed the square earlier had disappeared. Shamus presumed that classes had started for the day and all the *nonne* were at home unloading their groceries. A couple of tourists wandered by, scanning the sides of buildings for signs directing them to the Accademia or Piazzale Roma.

The waiter came and whisked away the Germans' dirty dishes. As he passed Will and Shamus, he cheerily asked if they'd like anything more.

"*No, grazie,*" Shamus answered.

"*Prego,*" said the waiter as he sauntered away, leaving the magnanimous impression that the brothers could linger as long as they wished.

Will shifted his chair so he could stretch his legs out in front of him. Shamus watched the greengrocer polish red apples before adding them, one by one, to a pyramid of fruit glowing in the sun at the front of his barge.

Suddenly, out of nowhere, desolation swept over him, as it had with unsettling regularity during the last two months. How was it possible that apples were shining in sunlight if Luke was dead?

Shamus blinked back tears as he watched the floating greengrocer. He remembered his first foray out of the house after Luke's death.

Two interminable days had passed, and a friend had gently suggested that perhaps it was time for Shamus, as executor of Luke's estate, to visit a lawyer.

Shamus was early for his appointment at the law office. He went into a nearby café to pass some time more than from any particular desire for coffee. Shamus was incredulous that the people behind the counter were smiling genially at customers, who chatted mindlessly about cappuccinos, muffins, and the unbearably hot, humid weather. How could they behave so normally? It was all he could do to restrain himself from shouting it out. From letting the terrible news be known that, after being together for more than a quarter of a century, his boyfriend, his partner, his lover, his spouse — all infuriatingly inadequate words — had died.

"When did you first come to Europe?" Will's voice yanked Shamus back to the present.

He swallowed and forced himself to look away from the green-grocer's barge. "I think a school trip to Germany was the first time."

"Oh yes," Will mumbled. "I seem to remember you abandoning me to Joe and Edith's clutches when you took that holiday to Deutschland."

"I was only fourteen," exclaimed Shamus, immediately wondering why it sounded like an excuse. "It was the first time I ever got drunk, must have been 1958 or '59. A few of us went on a day cruise down the Rhine without the teachers. The hotel owner's nephew was supposed to be in charge. He wasn't much older than us, but old enough to order beer. Huge steins of the stuff. I was sitting next to him, and I remember flirting with him. The more beer I drank, the harder I pressed my thigh up against his. He didn't seem to mind."

"Well you're not drunk now, so spare me the sordid reminiscences," said Will.

"Nothing happened. When we got back to the hotel, I threw up in the sink in my room."

"Lovely," said Will.

"Joe was a bit weird about it, I remember."

"About your beery, queery behaviour?" asked Will.

"No, stupid. About paying for me to go to Germany," said Shamus. "Something about not wanting his hard-earned wages to shore up the German economy. Edith prevailed, as usual — I think she thought it would widen my horizons."

"Well she had that right," snorted Will.

"I remember her saying that if more people had visited Germany in the '30s, there might not have been a world war."

"What twaddle. With parents like that, it's a bloody miracle we grew up to be pragmatic, reasonable people," said Will. He smirked and added, "Well I did anyway."

"Maybe she had a point," said Shamus, ignoring Will's dig. "Look at the way people travel around Europe these days. Last time I was in Liverpool, all I heard about was this person going off to the Italian lakes or that person to the Algarve. Liverpool Airport must be busier than Chicago O'Hare."

"Do try to keep up. It's called John Lennon Airport now. 'Above us only sky' and all that. And what are you trying to say? That we'd revolt if our leaders threatened to invade Majorca? Sorry, bad example. We Brits overran that unfortunate island years ago."

"Well you have to admit travel promotes understanding of different cultures," Shamus reasoned.

"Hitler's sojourn in Liverpool before World War I didn't stop him bombing the shit out of it thirty years later, did it?" said Will.

"You don't really believe that old chestnut about Hitler living in Liverpool, do you?" Shamus scoffed. "The geriatric ramblings of his Irish sister-in-law. Half-sister-in-law, to be accurate."

"Nobody's ever proved her wrong," said Will. "And it's not beyond the realms of possibility that a German lad would come to visit his half-brother and wife in England. You know the Hitlers lived in Toxteth, don't you? And I seem to remember that particular part of the city was pretty well annihilated during World War II. It's probably precisely *because* little Adolf lived there that he had the place bombed so thoroughly. It's not exactly pretty now. It must have been hellacious when the Führer-to-be was there."

"Well anyway," said Shamus. "A war happening in Europe is inconceivable these days."

Will screwed up his face in incredulity. "Last time I looked, Serbia, Croatia, and Bosnia were all west of the Bosphorus," he scoffed. "There was war in Europe less than seven years ago."

"But that's localized; it's not what I meant."

"Germany invading Poland wasn't exactly global, was it?" said Will. "Most wars start with next-door neighbours."

"But Western Europe is like one big family now," reasoned Shamus. "Slightly dysfunctional, but a family nevertheless."

"Even if I were to grant you that, what's your point?" asked Will.

"Well there's more understanding," said Shamus lamely.

"Dream on, kiddo. Since when did being a family mean increased understanding? I mean, look at us. Two generations of raging hostility and simmering resentment."

Shamus glanced at Will apprehensively before responding. "You may have ruined any chance of an idyllic childhood for both of us with your battles with Joe, but I don't think I harbour any raging hostility or simmering resentment."

"Well I bloody well do," said Will, glaring at Shamus. But then he appeared to relent. "Okay, maybe not between us so much. But look at Edith and Joe. Edith barely spoke to her parents or her sister all the time we were growing up, and Joe didn't have anything to do with Uncle Liam after that big row that Christmas, do you remember, when we were both still living at home?"

They were interrupted by a loud cracking noise. The brothers' heads snapped around in unison as, with a noisy fluttering and flapping of wings, a ragtag flock of terrified pigeons flew up from under a nearby table.

"Ho spaventato gli uccelli," shouted the waiter by way of an explanation for the commotion. He held up a tablecloth and gave it a sharp shake, demonstrating the cracking sound again, and pointed with his other hand at the retreating pigeons.

"Never mind the birds; he certainly scared the shit out of me," said Shamus, nodding at the waiter and forcing a smile. "I thought it was a bloody gunshot. It's weird how you never think you're particularly affected by news reports, but then they're the first thing you think of when something like that happens. Terrorist attacks. Al-Qaeda. They explode into your consciousness from some hidden recess of your brain you didn't know you had."

Will grinned. "I just saw a headline in my mind — 'Bloodbath on the Piazza: Vengeful Waiter Massacres Tourist Brothers.'"

"It serves us right for having a ridiculous conversation about war," said Shamus.

"Only your side was ridiculous," said Will.

"Let's not start again," said Shamus.

ENGLAND

Edith was woken by the sound of her mother-in-law browbeating the hens, telling them in no uncertain terms that there'd be roast chicken for Sunday lunch if they didn't produce some eggs lickety-split. At first, Mrs. Maguire had attributed the bird's lack of production to their "settling in," but as one eggless day followed another, she'd begun to despair of their ever laying. Lately she'd taken to threatening the recalcitrant birds each morning as she fed them. Edith, whose open bedroom window was close to the henhouse, grinned. Her mother-in-law's threats grew more dire by the day.

It looked like they were in for another day of perfect weather. Two sharp-edged slivers of sunshine fell from either side of Edith's blackout curtains across a frayed oriental rug on the bedroom floor. Although faded from its former glory, the rug's worn pile of mellow oranges, rusty reds, and royal blues glowed luminously along each slice of sunlight. Spring had glided into summer in an endless procession of sunny days.

Edith lay back in bed and thought dreamily about a day a couple of weeks before when she and Carlo had been sitting in canvas deck chairs on the Baccanellos' dandelion-dotted lawn. Carlo's wife, Isobel, was positioned between them in her wheelchair.

The first thing that struck Edith when she eventually met Isobel was her fragility. Her skin appeared almost translucent. It seemed particularly delicate in comparison to the vigour of her hair. Isobel's dark mane appeared impenetrable. Her pink-flowered sleeveless dress revealed graceful arms as she sat in her wheelchair with her hands resting in her lap, palms upwards. Isobel reminded Edith of the white marble statues whose smooth, shapely surfaces had impressed her whenever she visited the Walker Art Gallery in Liverpool. If it hadn't been for an occasional involuntary quaver of Isobel's fingers, Edith wouldn't have known there was anything amiss.

The newspaper on the day they'd been sitting on the lawn basking in May sunshine had been filled with dark dispatches describing the retreat of thousands of Allied troops who were stranded on the beaches of Dunkirk; they appeared to be sitting targets for an advancing German army. Edith had visualized details of the accounts as if they were from a novel or film — dishevelled soldiers huddled on damp beaches, fearful faces betraying their desperate situation — but she couldn't grasp the reality of it. What was real to Edith were the sensations of warm air, soft as chamois leather on her skin and redolent with the scent of blossom, the reassuring buzz of worker bees speeding from one flower to another.

Carlo's two brothers, Domenico and Paolo, were sprawled on the grass laughing at an account of some German saboteurs who'd been captured in Ireland in possession of bombs disguised as cans of French peas.

"Listen to this," exclaimed Paolo. "They were going to ask the Irish Republican Army to help them blow up Buckingham Palace. So after they landed by dinghy, they asked the first person they met to direct them to the IRA. Turns out the man was pro-British and took them straight to the nearest police station." He collapsed into gusts of laughter.

"'MI5 dismissed their plan as amateurish,'" crowed Domenico. He gave Paolo a nudge of delight and rolled over on his back, giggling.

Edith smiled and sipped her tea. Despite the four-year disparity in age, the two brothers seemed to get along like a house on fire. The only thing Edith and her sister, Agnes, had in common was a loathing of their father, which wasn't enough to keep them particularly close. Edith had only seen her sister once since she and Joe were married. Agnes had joined the Women's Land Army soon after Edith's wedding and been shipped off to work on a farm in Lancashire, somewhere near Bolton.

"Isn't the blossom lovely?" Isobel had asked, her head and neck trembling more than usual from the effort of leaning back in her wheelchair to admire the blooms of a nearby apple tree flowering so profusely that clots of white petals coated every limb.

"Spectacular," said Carlo. "But such a flashy display doesn't seem right on such a dark day in history." At that, Isobel frowned and slumped a little in her wheelchair. Her husband's pronouncement seemed to have robbed her of the will to sit up and appreciate the tree.

"Nonsense," Edith remembered saying. "Why deny ourselves the simple pleasures of life just because there's a war on?"

Carlo stared at Edith, who, conscious of his gaze, kept her eyes glued on the flower-laden tree. Eventually he'd said, "You're absolutely right. If we let things get us down and we don't enjoy — how did you say it — the simple pleasures of life, then the enemy has won. Forgive me; I swear this war is making me insane."

Edith had been relieved to make her point without any wedge being driven between them — she liked Carlo all the more for it. Not many men would have conceded that she was right. Joe certainly wouldn't have. She had watched as Carlo reached up from his low-slung deck chair to put his hand on his wife's forearm. "Sorry to be such a wet blanket," Carlo said. "I didn't mean to spoil your enjoyment."

Isobel reached across her wheelchair to rest a hand on his. Displays of tenderness, physical or spoken, were rare in Edith's family; as a child she'd been discouraged from any show of affection, especially in public. Whenever Joe attempted more than an arm around her shoulder while they were out, she resisted with a "Don't be daft." Carlo and Isobel's intimate exchange had unsettled her; nevertheless, she was unable to look away. She watched as Isobel's pallid thumb twitched against her husband's darker skin, and she thought how insubstantial Isobel's hand appeared next to his. Edith's eye had been caught by a golden gleam of sunlight reflecting off Isobel's wedding ring. It flashed regularly with each tremor of her finger, rhythmic as one of the beacons at the mouth of the estuary that alerted ships to the presence of perilous sand shoals. When Edith looked up, she caught Carlo watching her with a smile. Edith averted her eyes.

"All I know is, we're going to have a lot of apples this year," Paolo announced.

"Ma will be pleased," Domenico had said. "She makes the best applesauce."

Edith was brought abruptly back to earth by the sound of Anna Baccanello's raised voice coming through her open bedroom window. At first, Edith thought her neighbour must have joined Mrs. Maguire in terrorizing the hens. If so, Anna clearly thought it more effective to shout loudly in Italian. But then she switched to an anguished English as she called desperately to Mrs. Maguire, "My friend, come quickly. They're taking Gianni and the boys. Come help us, please."

Edith threw back the covers and swung her legs over the side of the bed. As Anna's beseeching cries continued, Edith cursed herself for being slow, but she'd grown considerably bigger in the previous month and a half. She found it impossible to move any faster. She pulled on her dressing gown over her cumbersome belly, and to save herself the trouble of tying shoelaces, she slipped her feet into a pair of Wellington boots. By the time Edith reached the porch, nobody was in sight, but beyond the conifers dividing the two properties, Edith could hear a babble of voices, male and female, English and Italian. As she hurried across the lawn, she glimpsed the shiny sides of a black van that was parked in the lane immediately outside the Baccanellos' gate.

When she pushed her way through the conifers, Edith was confronted by a scene so extraordinary that it took her a few seconds to take it in. The tableau of figures clustered on the Baccanellos' front path reminded her of a reproduction of a grim Victorian painting that her father had owned, a graphic illustration of a gang of bailiffs evicting a destitute family from their humble cottage.

Four policemen in uniform and domed helmets gripped a Baccanello male each by the arm. Anna was remonstrating wildly with the officer who was holding her husband. He seemed to be the oldest and had sergeant stripes on his sleeve, while the other three were barely old enough to shave. Mrs. Maguire held Anna by the shoulders, as though afraid her friend would attack the officers at any moment. Carlo seemed to be trying to placate his mother. A few yards away, Isobel sat in her wheelchair, head in hands. The older policeman was trying to reason with Anna.

"Look," he said. "Strictly between you and me, I'm more sympathetic to you Italians than most. Why, I was sent out last night to arrest a man I've known for almost twenty years. A barman at the

Adelphi Hotel — Enrico Bertucci. Hardworking as all hell. Trouble was, he owned a bit of land back home, and because he had to pay taxes on it, he was in and out of the Italian Consulate. And of course he was a member of the local Fascio. But he's more loyal to this country than some Britons I could name. It broke me up to have to take him in."

"Fascio?" asked Edith, struggling to understand the situation. Everybody turned to look at her. She must have been quite a sight, a pregnant woman in a pink dressing gown and black rubber boots, her hair dishevelled.

"You must all know it," answered the sergeant in an accusatory tone. "It's that Italian club. I told the inspector that Enrico posed no threat whatsoever, but it didn't do no good. The command came down from Churchill himself."

At the evocation of Winston Churchill's name, everybody fell silent, looking perplexed. Edith's head was filled with so much confusion she didn't know what to do. Then the sergeant barked an order. "All right, look smart, you lot. Let's get them in the van." His words set off another storm of objection from Anna, who, had it not been for Mrs. Maguire's grip, would have launched herself at the policemen. Carlo, who could easily have torn himself away from the skinny constable holding his arm, turned in an effort to calm his mother. "Mama, it's not as if we didn't expect it. Don't worry; we'll be home in no time — once everybody realizes we're no threat."

Gianni glanced up at Carlo as the sergeant led them down the path to the gate. Edith could see the scepticism on the older man's face. It was obvious Gianni Baccanello was of the opinion that they wouldn't be returning any time soon. But Carlo's words seemed to have brought Anna around to a state of resentful resignation. The women watched as Gianni, Carlo, Paolo, and Domenico were led out of the gate and bundled into the back of the police van. Paolo's face was pale, his jaw clenched. When Domenico looked back fearfully at the women before the doors to the van were slammed shut, Edith was struck by how young he appeared. What in God's name was the point of carting a child off to jail, let alone the rest of them? Edith felt stunned, wishing she'd wake up in bed any minute and realize this had all been just a nightmare. Isobel dropped her hands to her lap and gazed disconsolately at the open gate as the van lumbered away, down the lane.

Liam's voice disturbed the ensuing stillness. "Why didn't anybody wake me up?" he yelled as he strode across the garden, a look of glee on his face. "I just heard about the internment order on the wireless. Are they in that Black Maria I saw driving away? Have I missed all the fun?" Mrs. Maguire dropped her hands from Anna's shoulders, took one or two vigorous strides toward Liam, and landed a hearty smack on the side of his head. Liam recoiled, a look of pain and disbelief on his face.

"What was that for?" he complained, holding his head.

"Get to school right now," ordered Mrs. Maguire, fury in her voice. "We'll talk about this tonight." Liam sloped off toward his mother's house, swiping at the conifers in frustration as he pushed his way past them.

"What did Carlo mean?" asked Edith, still trying to comprehend. "What did he mean by it not being unexpected?"

"Because of Mussolini, that *stronzo,*" Anna spat out the last word and shook her fist at the sky.

"We always knew, since war broke out, there was a chance Italians might be interned," explained Isobel in an exhausted tone. "We have some German friends who were put in an internment camp on the Isle of Man for the whole of the last war. But since yesterday, when Mussolini declared war on Britain, the mere fact of having an Italian name seems to be enough to get you arrested."

At last Edith began to understand. The idea that Carlo and his father and brothers could be of any harm to England seemed preposterous, but she remembered the hysterical tone of the anti-Italian article in the *Daily Mirror* that Liam had quoted aloud from a couple of months before. And then she remembered something Mrs. Maguire had once said about the outset of World War I: "People were stoning dachshund dogs in the street because they were German."

"Paolo and Domenico were born in this country, for God's sake! How could they arrest them?" Anna groaned. She covered her eyes with the palms of her hands and doubled over at the waist. Mrs. Maguire went to her side and pulled her gently upright again. For a few long minutes, they stood motionless — Anna wringing her hands, Mrs. Maguire with an arm around her shoulder, Isobel gazing at the open gate. Edith felt the heat of the sun on her shoulders. In the distance, they could hear the noise of an automobile, perhaps the police van, changing gears as it ground up the steep hill to Shrimpley village.

"Our only crime is our Italian roots," Anna eventually said, dropping her hands to her sides.

Edith was alarmed by a tinge of defeat in Anna's voice. "There must be something someone can do," she cried. She was overwhelmed by a desperate desire to maintain the comfortable status quo of the last couple of months spent with Carlo and the Baccanello family. She was already mourning the loss of harmless chitchat over languid teas on warm afternoons. She couldn't believe that the rug could be pulled out from under them all so abruptly. Just fifteen minutes before, she'd been happily contemplating a morning of housekeeping and anticipating — she had to admit — the strong possibility of encountering Carlo at some point in the day. She was miserable at the thought of his being incarcerated somewhere as distant as the Isle of Man for the rest of the war.

A huge bumblebee was buzzing loudly around their heads. Mrs. Maguire tried to wave it away, but it persisted. Eventually, Anna wheeled Isobel up the ramp that Carlo had built and they retreated into the house. Mrs. Maguire and Edith slowly made their way through the conifers and across the front lawn to the porch.

Edith spent the rest of the morning working busily in the kitchen, trying to take her mind off the arrests. The supplies were dwindling; all they had left was one precious can of condensed milk and some sardines. Edith decided to take the sad situation as an opportunity to give the near-empty shelves a good washing and a fresh lining of greaseproof paper in anticipation of more abundant days ahead. She refused to believe that rationing would continue for much longer. But she performed the task in a daze, barely aware of her actions. Edith's thoughts kept returning to the Baccanello men. She ran through the scene of their arrest again and again in her head. Sometimes she concluded that what Carlo had said was doubtless true and they'd be home again as soon as it became evident that they posed no threat. At other times, Edith's heart sank when she remembered the expression of hopelessness on Gianni's face, and she kept thinking about Isobel's story of German friends who were interned on the Isle of Man for the duration of World War I.

Wednesday, June 12, 1940

The memory of the previous morning's events inundated Edith as soon as she woke. Over breakfast, her spirits were raised a little by a sympathetic article in the late edition of the previous day's *Liverpool Echo*. Its commiserative tone gave Edith a glimmer of hope that the men might be released sooner rather than later. The report described how "Italians who have lived among English people for years have been taken aback by the sudden turn of events." The newspaper continued:

> Following a Home Office decision thousands of Italians throughout the country are being apprehended in the little shops and businesses where many have made their homes. Measures were enacted within a quarter of an hour of Mussolini's speech and are proceeding on lines prepared days ago.
>
> Initial action has been taken only against male Italians, both aliens and British-born, and over 160 men between the ages of 16 and 70 have been arrested in Liverpool alone.

Edith glared at Liam, who was sitting across from her, noisily crunching a slice of toast. It didn't seem fair that, just because of the circumstances of his birth, he was sitting at home enjoying his breakfast. If he'd been Anna's son, he'd be languishing in prison, even if he'd been born in England or the last thing he'd consider would be siding with the enemy in the event of an invasion.

In an attempt to calm herself and to avoid needling Liam, Edith got up and moved over to the window. The tide was on the turn; she watched the white-flecked expanse of sea as it began to flow out of the estuary. But, unable to distract herself, Edith finally turned back to her brother-in-law. "If you'd had an Italian father, you'd have been arrested too, just like Domenico," she said.

"Well I didn't have an Italian father, did I?" said Liam belligerently, waving his toast at her. "I'm British through and through, like Blackpool rock. I told you we had to keep our eye on those fascists next door. I don't know why the government didn't round them all up sooner."

Edith was taken aback by the force of her anger. She was afraid of what she might say or do to Liam. She sat down and reached for the last round of toast even though she wasn't at all hungry. She struggled to control her emotions as she spread a thin smear of butter; there was no point in picking a fight with her young brother-in-law. And it wasn't as if she hadn't heard the same, or worse, before — her father's odious condemnation of Catholics, for instance. She'd experienced that particular brand of acrimony since she was born. But until the fuss over her marriage to Joe, she'd never thought much about it, merely accepted it as a fact of life. How differently she saw things now. And what made matters worse was that she was finding it difficult to separate the outrage she felt at the injustice of the situation in general from her selfish concerns in relation to Carlo. Edith let out a frustrated breath; suddenly the war didn't seem to be quite as straightforward as she'd imagined.

"Now what did I tell you last night, my lad?" said Mrs. Maguire, who'd appeared from the kitchen holding a bowl of brown eggs. She'd obviously overheard their exchange. "We'll have no more of that kind of talk, thank you very much."

Liam peered into the bowl, ignoring his mother's scolding. "I see the hens finally delivered, then," he said. "Wonders will never cease."

"I knew they'd come through in the end," said Mrs. Maguire, sitting herself down to wipe green and yellow muck from the gleaming tan surfaces of fifteen eggs. "We'll take a half-dozen next door in a minute and see if there's any news," she announced to Edith. "And you, young man, get off to school or you'll be late — again," she ordered Liam.

When Mrs. Maguire and Edith dropped by with the eggs, Anna insisted on serving them coffee. She also produced a plate of diminutive, almond-flavoured biscuits. Edith hadn't tasted anything so delicious for months; they had a crisp outer coating but were slightly chewy in the centre. The Baccanello bungalow seemed larger, and a great deal emptier, without the presence of Gianni and the boys.

"Our old friend, Bob MacDonald, phoned this morning to tell us they've arrested Italians all over Liverpool. Apparently there's been looting, too; God knows if our properties are all in one piece," said Anna. Edith marvelled at Anna's equanimity, although she noticed the skin under Anna's eyes was slack and sallow; it was obvious she hadn't slept.

"How on earth did the police know where to find all of these Italian men all over the country, I wonder," mused Mrs. Maguire

"Since we arrived in England, we have to carry alien registration certificates, with our photo and address," answered Anna. "We have to go to the police if we move. So they have it written where everybody lives. For almost twenty years, we carried our damned registration with us everywhere, thinking it would protect us better than any patron saint."

"But the government probably had records from the Fascio too," said Isobel, who looked unusually unkempt. Edith wondered if she had trouble dressing without Carlo to help her. "They wouldn't have been so inclined to arrest everybody had it not been for the Fascio."

"Are you members of this Fascio club?" asked Edith.

"Yes, of course. Everybody is," said Anna, obviously seeing no reason to deny it. "But I doubt if we're there more than a dozen times a year, and then it's only for a dance or a wedding. Sometimes the boys go there to play football. It's crazy to think that everybody who belongs to the Fascio is loyal to Mussolini, especially now that he's fallen in with Hitler."

She held out the plate of biscuits. Although she would have liked another, Edith refused. She knew how precious they were; God only knew when Anna would find more ingredients in the village shops.

"Just because people go to the Fascio doesn't mean they don't love this country, doesn't mean they don't want to stay," insisted Anna. "Imagine if you live in some other country for a long time. You miss things about your old country: music, food, language. If you can go somewhere in your new country that reminds you, that has those things that are familiar, that you enjoy, wouldn't you go?" The answer seemed too obvious to warrant a reply.

"It's just that we never expected . . . so many so soon," Isobel groaned. "We hoped internment would be only for those idiots who wore black shirts and went around spouting bits and pieces of Mussolini's speeches."

"*Il Duce* meant little to me and Gianni, and even less to my boys," interjected Anna. "Paolo and Domenico have never even set foot in Italy, for God's sake." She bit her lower lip, obviously struggling to control her emotions. "But I understand. We're caught in a web." She looked around distractedly, as though unfamiliar with her own living room. "I just hope no spider eats us up before this war finishes," she concluded in a tremulous voice.

"Did your friend Bob have any idea where Gianni and the boys were taken?" asked Edith.

"It's hard to get any facts, but the rumour is that a lot of them are at Walton Lane Police Station in Liverpool," said Isobel. "My sister and some other women were there yesterday afternoon, but they couldn't get anything out of the desk sergeant. Nobody would confirm if any Italians were there or not."

"Isobel, I'm so sorry," said Edith, "I never thought to ask if any of your family was arrested."

"That's all right," said Isobel. "It's difficult to take in the scale of it. My dad died a couple of years ago and I don't have any brothers, thank heaven. But my brother-in-law was arrested."

"I'm really sorry," said Mrs. Maguire with such feeling that it sounded as though she was apologising on behalf of the entire country.

"Bob MacDonald is going to try and find out more today," announced Anna. "It's his half-day off tomorrow, so he said he'd come over here in the afternoon and let us know. He doesn't think we should say too much on the phone; it's a party line. You never know who's listening."

Edith stifled the impulse to look over her shoulder. The complacency she'd felt just a few days before had been replaced by a sense of unease and foreboding. She stroked her pregnant abdomen distractedly.

Thursday, June 13, 1940

"Johnny and the boys are there all right," insisted Bob MacDonald, who was a wiry man, bristling with energy, his movements as exuberant as his strongly accented Liverpool voice. He'd lived in Toxteth all his life and worked in the docks nearby, but he'd gone out of his way to make the detour up to Walton Lane Police Station on his way to work that morning. "Nobody let on officially, but the desk sergeant made it obvious. He said he wasn't free to divulge the names of prisoners, but when I asked point-blank if he had Gianni Baccanello and his sons locked up, he gave me a look that could only have meant yes."

The four women, Edith, Mrs. Maguire, Anna Baccanello, and Isobel, watched as Bob sipped his tea. They were sitting in Anna's living room. The stretch of warm weather had been broken by a cool wind that blew up overnight; they could hear gusts buffeting the windowpanes.

"They can't keep them there forever," said Edith, a note of desperation in her voice.

"Remember that Maltese feller you know, name of Cassar?" Bob asked Anna. "I met him once or twice with Johnny."

"The solicitor," said Anna. "We know him from when we bought our shops. He speaks Italian. You think he can help us?"

"Hold your horses," said Bob. "No point in getting anybody's hopes up. I phoned your Mr. Cassar. He said he'd been inundated by Italians looking for help, but there was nothing he could do. He told me about some regulation or other that the government passed last August, just before war was declared. That's how they're able to arrest people without any proper charges. I must say, Mr. Cassar sounded really ticked off about it all; he said that at least prisoners of war have the Geneva Convention to protect them. I put the phone down pretty quick when he said that, I can tell you. Next thing you know, they'll be arresting me if I'm not careful."

Edith's tea was getting cold, but she was too dismayed by Bob's report to drink. "Why did they have to arrest so many?"

"After Quisling's shenanigans in Norway, the government's probably scared witless that if the Huns manage to invade, any non-

Briton will immediately side with the Germans," concluded Bob.

"Who is this Quisling?" asked Anna. "How can he have anything to do with us?"

"Quisling is a Norwegian politician," volunteered Isobel. "He was put at the head of the government after the Nazis occupied Norway. Some people say that Quisling and others had been secretly working for Hitler from within the country for months before the invasion. I read somewhere that it was as if Germany had built a kind of Trojan horse inside Norway."

"But a family of fish and chip shop owners — it's ridiculous! They'd make a pretty poor excuse for a secret army," cried Edith in exasperation.

There was an awkward silence. Mrs. Maguire looked down at her lap.

"I'm sorry," said Edith. "I didn't mean . . ."

"No, you're right," remonstrated Anna. "We're just ordinary people. What do they think, my Gianni will suddenly pick up a gun and become a Nazi overnight?"

"Of course he would never do that," said Bob. "But look at it through Churchill's eyes. All he sees are several thousand men who could potentially be disloyal to Britain. He obviously believes they could form a considerable army."

"An army?" said Edith. "They're dotted all over the country. Who would organize them? How could they arm themselves? It's too ridiculous."

"That's unfortunately where the Fascio comes in," said Bob. "We might think of it as a social club, but to Churchill it's an organization with a fishy-sounding name whose members are linked by a network of clubs all over Britain. Presumably, they could all be called to arms at the drop of a hat through the Fascio."

"You sound like you're defending the government," accused Edith.

"Not in a million years," insisted Bob. "But I can see their reasoning."

"It's a shame someone had to come up with that name," said Isobel. "But 'Fascist Party' never used to mean what it does now. Before Mussolini, life in Italy was terrible. That's why my parents left — they'd have starved if they'd stayed. You'd have had to grow up there to realize what Mussolini means to Italians.

"They say he put a stop to corruption," Isobel continued. "No more bribes when you need a marriage licence or a driving permit. He built better roads and made the trains run on time. And he built a dam that's made life a lot easier for poor farmers in the north. Everybody here believed that the changes he made would benefit their family and friends in Italy." Isobel smiled wanly. "And what's more, there's even a priest in London, Padre Barbera, who's a big fan of Il Duce. I personally think Barbera is a little crazy, obsessed with warning everybody, especially young girls, of the dangers of dancing the foxtrot. And he hates the tango too. But that's a priest for you. The point is, many Italians wonder how Mussolini could be so bad when the church supports him."

"And on the English side, the newspapers don't help," said Bob. "They've been stirring up bad blood against Italians ever since the war began."

They sat quietly for several minutes, each preoccupied with his or her thoughts. A branch of a lilac tree outside the living room window was being blown against the glass, making a scratchy rhythmic tapping on the windowpane. Edith managed a sip of her lukewarm tea. Even though she'd known Carlo for less than two months, she felt a keen sense of loss. It was as if she'd found an aspect of herself — a confident, self-assured facet that she hadn't known existed — when she met Carlo. As well as feeling bereft, she harboured smouldering anger at the gross injustice of the arrests. The image of Domenico's face in the back of the Black Maria flashed across her mind; he was no more than a boy, for God's sake.

"It's a crime," she blurted out.

The others were startled, but before anyone could react, the phone started ringing in the hall. Anna hurried to answer it.

"Isobel, it's for you," she called after a minute or so. Isobel wheeled her chair slowly across the carpet and out into the hall.

"It's her sister," explained Anna to the others as she started clearing the cups and saucers. Edith pulled herself up to help. Just as they were about to carry the dirty crockery into the kitchen, Isobel appeared in the doorway.

"They're all being moved tomorrow," she announced, her voice quavering with excitement.

"How did your sister find out?" asked Anna.

"She was at Walton Lane Police Station this afternoon, and they told her they'd been instructed to tell the families."

"Where are they being taken?" asked Edith.

"A place in Lancashire — Warth Mills. It's an old cotton mill. The sergeant told my sister that families were to be informed, so it was all right for him to let her know. He told her a visit will be organized for relatives in the next week or so."

"An old cotton mill," said Mrs. Maguire. "Why on earth would they be taken there?"

"My guess is it'll be a holding place," said Bob. "To collect the lot of them before they're shipped off somewhere else."

"You make them sound like bloody cattle," erupted Edith.

"Edith," said Mrs. Maguire sharply. "There's no call for that kind of talk."

"I'm really sorry," said Edith, instantly contrite. "It's just all so unfair."

"That's all right, love," said Bob. "We're all upset." He stood up and patted her shoulder. "I should be going or it'll be dark before I get to Liverpool. It's no fun getting around in the blackout, I can tell you. They've even taken the lamps out of the inside of the trams. They've stuck in some blue lights that they say can't be seen from the air, but they're no good at all. I sat on a woman's lap the other night, by accident of course." Bob winked broadly at Mrs. Maguire, who smiled and looked away.

"I'll walk out with you," offered Edith in an attempt to make amends for her earlier outburst.

The sky outside was leaden. Colourless countryside merged with lowering clouds that obscured hilltops on the other side of the estuary. Edith tugged at her coat in an effort to close it across her belly as she accompanied Bob down the path.

"I didn't want to tell Anna," said Bob, "but that lawyer fellow, Cassar, told me he was sure they'll all be interned for the rest of the war. Probably on the Isle of Man; there was a big internment camp over there in the last war."

Edith paused, her hand on the latch of the gate. "Do you think they'll be . . . okay?"

"You know, I hate to say this," said Bob. "But they may be better off. At least they'll get fed, and there's little likelihood of bombers over there."

"I suppose so," said Edith. But she couldn't see how anyone — especially a sixteen-year-old boy like Domenico — could be better off in what was for all intents and purposes a prison.

Shamus and Will lingered for a few more minutes at the table in Campo San Barnaba, but the waiter's shenanigans with the tablecloth seemed to signal that breakfast had run its course. They stood and, in unspoken agreement, wandered in the direction of the Giudecca Canal.

Shamus allowed himself a glow of triumph in the sibling rivalry stakes when he, a full head taller than Will, noticed scalp showing through thinning hair on top of his brother's head. His own hair was as thick as it had ever been, but he knew better than to crow about it to Will. He remembered how in their teens Will had compensated for being overtaken in height by taunting his overgrown brother with names like "freak" and "Frankenstein." Shamus had occasionally made a feeble attempt to retaliate, calling Will "shrimp" or "weed," but his heart wasn't in it.

Shamus had soon learned to keep quiet, but it still rankled with Will. He blamed Edith's smoking during pregnancy and the scarcity of food during the war for stunting his growth, claiming that Shamus had benefited from free orange juice, cod liver oil, and a better diet during the postwar years. Shamus had known better than to point out that Will's build could be explained simply by looking at their father. Will would never admit to any similarities to "that bastard."

But what on earth was he doing in the middle of Venice obsessing about Will's hangups, thought Shamus. Eager for distraction, he examined the buildings around him. He marvelled at light reflecting off water that illuminated etched edges of ivy leaves sprouting between ancient stones. At the turn of a corner, he stopped to point out a distant dome framed by water, stucco, and sky, looking to Will for a nod of shared appreciation.

As they explored the twists and turns of Dorsoduro's *fondamente,*

Shamus remembered how as a small boy he'd begged to accompany Will on any forays his brother took out of the house. It was hard to believe now that he'd wanted to be with Will so badly that he'd cried shamelessly if he was left behind. Shamus glanced at Will, recalling with some surprise how often his brother had relented despite the groans of his friends when Will showed up with Shamus lumbering behind yet again. Maybe Will had cared more than Shamus remembered.

Will poked his arm and pointed toward a working boatyard, clearly visible on the other side of Rio di San Trovaso. The two-storey, barn-like structures that lined one side of the yard appeared more rustic than most Venetian buildings. Their incongruity lent them an air of artificiality; they reminded Shamus of a pantomime, *Jack and the Beanstalk*, that he'd once been taken to by the parents of a childhood friend. He could imagine actors playing peasants in medieval dress milling around in front of the wooden edifices. The yard itself was littered with gondolas at various stages of completion. Will and Shamus stood admiring the craftsmanship that went into the building of each wooden boat.

"Why do you think we liked construction sites so much when we were kids?" Shamus asked Will as they stared at the graceful curves of the exposed wooden ribs of an unfinished gondola.

"Actually, they're called building sites in England," said Will, as though explaining a difficult language to a small child. "And I'm not sure we were particularly fond of them, were we?"

"We loved them," declared Shamus. "Don't you remember how we used to climb all over the scaffolds and explore the half-built houses after the workmen had left for the day? I think those incomplete houses were a symbol of hope. They represented possibility, a better way of living than we were accustomed to."

Will rolled his eyes. "We liked to play on bomb sites, too, heaps of rubble on top of shattered furniture. All evidence of lives destroyed," said Will. "What does *that* say about us, Mr. Psychotherapist?"

"I'm not sure it says anything about *us*," said Shamus. "But the fact that you mention it now says a lot about *you*."

Will gave his brother a withering look and turned to continue along the quay that led to the Giudecca Canal. "But you're right about 'construction sites' versus 'building sites,'" Shamus said in a conciliatory tone as he drew level with Will. "I'm always confusing which term is British and which is Canadian."

"It can't be easy, having to remember whether to say elevator or lift, garbage or rubbish," said Will sarcastically.

"They're just the easy ones. You'd be surprised how many come up. And then there's all the cultural references."

"Like what?" Will demanded.

"Things like ice hockey teams, the names of candies people ate when they were kids, TV programmes, winter clothing. For instance, do you know what a toque is?"

"First of all, we say sweets, not candies," said Will. "And, secondly, I've no idea what this tuke thing is, but I bet you're about to tell me."

"You see? You have no experience of it, but every Canadian kid wore one growing up. It's a woolly tam-o'-shanter kind of thing. And in reverse, I miss not being connected to some of the English stuff. Even the most committed immigrant likes to be reminded of things from home."

"I never think of you as an immigrant, but I suppose you are," said Will.

"Of course I am," said Shamus. "And Canada's home for me now, but I still miss some of the British things, especially from when I was growing up."

"Like what — sweets and tam-o'-shanters?"

"I can't think of specific examples," shrugged Shamus. "It's just that one feels left out when Canadians start talking about TV programmes or comics that were around when they were kids, things that don't mean anything to me. It would be the same if I started talking about *The Flowerpot Men* or *The Beano* — nobody would know what I was talking about. But they're the things that have informed me, and I miss not having them around, consciously or not."

"Well I still live in England," said Will. "And I don't chat to friends about comics or kids' television programmes. They'd think I had a screw loose."

"I'll bet the references come up more often than you think. There are tons of cultural touchstones in the place where you grew up that help define who you are. They're so familiar that you take them for granted. But you miss them when you emigrate; you always feel incomplete somehow."

"Is that why you're a slave to *Coronation Street* every Sunday morning on Canadian TV?" said Will, giving Shamus an unnecessarily hard dig with his elbow.

"Sometimes I wonder why I ever tell you anything," said Shamus.

They'd almost reached the Giudecca Canal, its wide expanse visible beyond the next bridge, when Will moved to one side of the narrow quay to make room for a young man who was so preoccupied with examining the buildings that he was paying little attention to where he was walking.

"*Scusi, signore,*" said the young man, hitching up his capacious knapsack and holding out a piece of paper. "*Sa dove posse trovare Fondamenta delle Zattere ai Gesuati?*"

The boy had a regional accent that was beyond Shamus's limited comprehension, so he opted for ignorance.

"*Scusa, no,*" he replied. "*Non sono Veneziano.*"

The young man narrowed his eyes and switched to English. "You're American?" he asked, appearing confused.

"Canadian," said Shamus. "Well, English actually, but Canadian . . . lately."

"My brother suffers from nationality confusion," interjected Will. "Among other things."

The young man frowned and said to Shamus in an irritated tone of voice, "It's just that I thought perhaps you were Italian American. One of those who were born over there, whose parents emigrated years ago."

"Good Lord no," said Will. "We're bog Irish from way back."

The young man explained that he was looking for his hotel, which was located on the Fondamenta delle Zattere. Shamus pointed out Le Zattere, just beyond the next bridge. As they walked in that direction, the Italian explained in impeccable English that he was moving to Venice from his home in Rome to do graduate studies at the university. He'd once lived in Oxford, studying medieval history.

"Ah, the Dark Ages," said Will.

"I could never understand why the British call it that," said the young man.

"All that ignorance and brutality, I suppose," said Will.

"There was undoubtedly widespread ignorance, as you call it," said the young man. "A great deal of violence, yes. But I'm not convinced it was *darker* than any other period."

Will turned to look sceptically at the boy, eyebrows raised.

The young Italian persevered, "Like now, for example? The twin towers attack in New York and the inevitable consequences?" His voice rose emphatically on the last word of each sentence.

Will scowled. Shamus knew how his brother loathed that particular, smug speech pattern. He hoped Will didn't decide to make some snide remark. While he too found the boy's tone irritating, Shamus didn't see the point of causing any trouble.

"I think my hotel must be this way," said the young man, obviously keen to leave the brothers behind. *"Arrivederci."*

"Goodbye," said Shamus.

"Uppity little prick," said Will before the boy was barely out of earshot. "He'll make a fine academic."

"You can take the man out of Liverpool, but you can't take Liverpool out of the man," ventured Shamus.

"Even you would have to admit the lad was a complete tosser," Will argued.

"Maybe, but do you have to be quite so judgmental?"

"I don't know if it's your university degree or indoctrination by liberal Canadians, but you've become a prissy, politically correct pain in the arse."

Shamus could feel his anger rising. "Do you know, the first time I took Luke to Liverpool, he thought all the men were about to whack each other," he said, in as breezy a tone as he could muster, not wanting his irritation to show. "And they were just having what to them was an everyday, amicable chat. Why do they have to sound like they're spoiling for a fight all the time?"

"You sound like one of those people who are astonished by soccer hooliganism. Why are they so surprised? Didn't they study English history? Centuries of bloody battles at every turn. Us Brits have always been the most warlike mob in the world."

Shamus was frustrated by his lack of a compelling rebuttal. For want of anything else, he retorted, "What do you know about academics anyway?"

"I've met a few in my time," said Will. "And why are you getting your knickers in such a knot?"

Shamus said nothing. He was thrown off balance by his sudden irritation toward Will. Shamus's own anger disturbed him as much anyone else's — he never knew what to do with it.

They emerged onto the broad quay that made up Le Zattere, and he looked across the expansive Giudecca Canal for some kind of solace. The large church, Il Redentore, sat on the far shore, its beautifully proportioned dome sitting majestically between two miniature, matching spires. A salty breeze enlivened the wide, olive green surface of the canal, throwing up foam-fringed waves. Shamus, skin tingling from the gusts of fresh air against his face, realized he was thinking of Luke again. Perhaps the boy's mention of university life had reminded him. Shamus had been living in London when he met Luke, who'd just arrived for a yearlong sabbatical from the University of Toronto. Mere months after they'd met, Shamus and Luke had agreed that Shamus would move to Canada with Luke at the end of Luke's year in London. Shamus, having never discussed his sexual orientation with his parents, had decided not to tell them the full extent of his and Luke's "friendship." Will, who had known for years that Shamus was gay, had phoned as soon as he heard the news of the move. "I wish you'd tell them you're queer," Will told Shamus. "It'd drive Joe up the wall." But Shamus had been adamant; Will's misadventures with their father had taught Shamus to give his parents just enough information to keep relations cordial, and nothing more.

"Look," said Will. "If it's Luke you're thinking about, I know he wasn't like that. He may have had his faults, but he wasn't pompous or stuck up like a lot of academics."

Caught off guard by Will second-guessing his preoccupation with Luke — he hadn't credited his brother for having such insight — Shamus's ire was immediately overwhelmed by an irresistible impulse to sob.

After a few deep breaths, Shamus managed to blink back all but a couple of tears, which he surreptitiously wiped from his cheek with one finger. "No, he wasn't," he agreed. Luke had loved teaching but held a healthy disdain for the more self-important of his university colleagues.

The brothers stood watching crowded waterbuses chugging backwards and forwards across the foam-flecked canal, from the quayside to the island of Giudecca.

"Stupid little twat," said Will. "Taking you for an Italian American."

ENGLAND

Monday, June 24, 1940

Anna begged Edith to accompany her on the trip to Warth Mills. "But the bus is for Italian families of men from Liverpool," argued Edith. "Surely you'll know people on it."

"Maybe not," said Anna. "And Isobel can't go in her condition."

"But I'm not a relative," Edith reasoned.

"If anyone asks, you can say you're Carlo's wife," countered Anna.

* * *

"Easy, love," said the white-haired conductor as he grasped Edith's elbow to guide her safely from the bus she and Anna took on the first leg of their journey. Edith was sometimes bemused when people were deferential to her; it took her a second or two to realize that her pregnant state was the reason for their thoughtfulness. As she thanked him, she noted the conductor seemed a bit old to be offering a helping hand — it seemed that every day there were fewer young men in evidence.

The tide was out when they reached the Mersey ferry dock. As a result, the boat floated considerably lower than the concrete rim of the riverbank quay and Edith and Anna manoeuvred the steep incline of the wide gangplank carefully. The low water level revealed thick mud on rocks at the water's edge. To Edith, recently frustrated by unfulfilled food cravings, they appeared to be coated in molten milk chocolate. But the odour, rancid seaweed with a hint of decaying fish, wasn't the least bit appetizing. It was a sultry, sunny day, so Anna and Edith hoisted themselves up a short flight of stairs to the slatted wooden benches on an open-air upper deck rather than travel in the airless indoor saloon.

Edith looked across the River Mersey toward Liverpool, less than a mile away. The limestone of the palatial Dock Office, where Edith used to work, gleamed in the sunlight. Edith could see the huge clock faces on the darker Royal Liver Building. I wonder why we pronounce it like alive and not like Liverpool, mused Edith to herself. She supposed it sounded better than pronouncing it like the organ, which they'd been eating a bit too often since the war started — even if it was smothered in fried onions, which Edith adored. She admired the winged statues of two mythical Liver birds, one atop each gothic tower of the building. They hovered even higher than the lofty copper dome on the massive Dock Office. Between these two imposing edifices sat the Cunard Building, elegant and substantial but a plain cousin compared to the grace of its neighbours. Barrage balloons wallowed in the sky above both banks of the river. Despite their size — sixty-two feet long, almost as big as the ferry boat — the balloons were tethered so high that they looked more like New Year's Eve party balloons trapped in invisible baskets hung from the sky blue ceiling of a ballroom in anticipation of a midnight release. They appeared so festive it was hard for Edith to believe they and the wires that trailed below them were there to deter enemy airplanes.

Edith was so intent on taking in the sights that she was startled when the ferry abruptly sounded its foghorn to announce their departure. Tugboats and dredgers plied up and down the river, and a couple of large cargo ships were being skilfully manoeuvred between dock gates. A sleek grey battleship, with its multiple gun turrets, was moored at the opposite bank.

As soon as Edith and Anna reached the top of the gangway from the ferry and stepped onto dry land, Edith noticed a marked contrast to the listless Liverpool landscape of the Bore War winter months. Some of the disparity was the result of summer sunlight, the assertiveness of sharp-edged shadows against sunlit walls, but the greatest difference lay in the amount of human activity she observed all around her.

Groups of soldiers hefting cylindrical kit bags on their shoulders strode past, talking loudly in regional accents that were unfamiliar to her. She'd never seen so many cars and vans in one place as on the wide expanse of road in front of the Liver Building. Edith watched as a black car stopped in front of the Port of Liverpool building to disgorge two men in suits who were carrying briefcases.

A khaki-coloured jeep driven by an efficient-looking woman in military uniform immediately followed the car. But most people still travelled by bus or electric tram, whose overhead cables stretched like cobwebs above the main thoroughfares.

As Edith and Anna's tram ground its way past both the James Street and Central stations toward Lime Street, where they were to board the bus for Warth Mills, Edith could see large signs directing people to use underground railway platforms as air raid shelters. Almost all the windows on every building along their route were criss-crossed with tape like latticework pastry on a pie, a pattern designed to minimize flying glass in the event of a bomb blast. Some shop windows were boarded over, and a few were protected by walls of sandbags. Edith had heard that Middlesbrough and parts of southern England had suffered bombing in the last month or so. That fact, coupled with the impressive scale of precautionary measures all around her, made it impossible for Edith to summon up her old scepticism that the German Luftwaffe would ever reach this far. She was left with the uneasy impression that bombers could arrive momentarily.

During the bus trip to Warth Mills, Edith tried her best to appear optimistic. Despite what Bob had said about the Maltese lawyer's belief that Gianni and his sons would be held for the rest of the war, she told Anna that the place they'd been taken was obviously a transit camp and that the men were doubtless being interviewed and assessed. "Surely they'll be released as soon as the authorities discover that they pose no threat," she said encouragingly. Anna turned and put her warm hand on top of Edith's and said simply, "We're in a war, Edith. We don't know what's going to happen." They rode the rest of the way in silence, each deep in her own thoughts, gazing through the windows at small towns and lush countryside.

The words from a hymn she'd sung as a girl at school echoed in Edith's head when the bus shuddered to a halt outside the derelict cotton mill.

> And was Jerusalem builded here,
> Among these dark satanic mills.

"Il mio Dio," said Anna as she stepped from the bus. A double chain-link fence, seven feet high and topped by swathes of barbed

wire, formed a compound in front of the entrance to the mill. Hundreds of men stood or squatted on the ground behind the wire mesh fence. Armed soldiers walked or stood among them, their neat uniforms a stark contrast to the grimy civilian clothes worn by the internees. Beyond them, the massive, decaying building was a grotesque relic of the Industrial Revolution. Weeds and small trees grew at the base of its smoke-stained walls. The only windows appeared to be a series of cracked or broken panes that formed part of the roof. It was obvious that the mill had lain derelict for years, probably since the Depression. Despite the brightness of the day, Edith had the impression the scene was bleached of colour; apart from the odd tuft of green leaves, everything seemed to be shades of grey with an occasional patch of dull khaki.

"Mama, over here. We're here," a voice shouted. A soldier indicated a ragtag group of men pressed up against a section of the outer wire fence — men from Liverpool, clearly herded there to receive their visitors. There was a crush of bodies as the women scurried toward the internees. Edith stood aside to protect her abdomen — her baby — from being jostled by the crowd. Shouts of *"Papa," "Gino," "Sono qui,"* quieted gradually as people found their loved ones and each group established an island of intimacy. At first, little was said. Sobs could be heard up and down the line. By the time Edith spied Anna at the fence, Anna had located Gianni and the boys.

Gianni, his white shirt deeply creased, with black smudges that appeared to be engine oil, held up both hands and pressed his forehead against the wire. Anna immediately did the same. Their palms and forehead would have come into contact were it not for the mesh of metal separating them. As it was, the fence only allowed their fingertips to touch. Carlo, Paolo, and Domenico stood quietly watching their parents.

"What on earth are you doing here?" asked Carlo, obviously astonished when Edith approached.

"She's your wife," mouthed Anna, nodding her head emphatically to hint that Carlo shut up and act along with them. Carlo coloured visibly. He couldn't suppress a sheepish grin.

Suddenly, a commotion could be heard a few yards along the fence. One of the visitors, a young man in a British Army uniform who Edith had seen boarding the bus in Liverpool, was cursing and crying with rage. An unshaven and dishevelled older man, obviously the soldier's father, stood weeping inside the fence. The soldier tore off his army tunic and threw it onto the barbed wire. Then he started yanking his jacket against the spikes, ripping it to shreds, howling an obscenity with each wrench. Brass buttons glinted in the sunlight as they flew through the air, severed from the khaki fabric. The older man stood with his hands covering his eyes, shoulders heaving, while the soldier son bellowed in anger and frustration.

"It's Emilio Rota's son," said Paolo. "Emilio has been telling everyone how his son fought for the British Army in France and only escaped death at Dunkirk by the skin of his teeth."

"Doesn't look like he'll be fighting for England anymore," said Carlo as two soldiers pulled the young man aside and roughly restrained him.

"What he must have been through, and then to find his father in this hell hole," whispered Anna, eyes wide with consternation.

As suddenly as the fracas had erupted, it was forgotten as people turned back to their relatives. Questions were fervently asked up and down both sides of the fence. "Where do you sleep?" "Is the shop okay?" "Can you eat the food?" "How's *Nonna?*"

The difference in age between Gianni and his two younger sons became obvious from the contrasting stories they told.

Gianni recounted the horrors. "The place is filthy, grease from the old machinery everywhere and rotting cotton rags lying all over the place. We have to sleep on dirty straw mattresses on the floor with only one thin, filthy blanket each. The noise is unbelievable; three thousand men coughing and moaning all night long. And the lavatories . . ." He'd begun by speaking in English out of respect for Edith but lapsed into Italian to describe the frightfulness of the toilet facilities. "Forty cold-water taps for washing; we have to queue for hours," he concluded in English.

"The soldiers don't treat us badly," interrupted Paolo.

"They call us young ones the Dead End Kids," said Domenico. "We keep together, sunbathe on the roof. We've even managed to organize a couple of football games."

"Sometimes we help the soldiers, gathering blankets and stuffing straw mattresses for the newcomers. They give us candles in return," said Paolo. "Then we can play cards in the evenings."

"*È terribile,* no gas, no electric light either!" said Gianni. "And what a noise these boys make, with their candles and card games, when we're all trying to sleep."

Paolo and Domenico grinned.

Edith edged as close to the fence as her pregnant belly would allow. "Have any of you been interviewed?" she asked Carlo.

Carlo shook his head. "Interviewed?" asked Paolo.

"Well presumably you're here to be assessed, to see if you'd be a threat in the event of an invasion," said Edith.

"I wish it were so," said Carlo. "Ninety per cent of us would be released right away. Most are waiters, tailors, or shopkeepers like us, who couldn't care less about politics and are willing to swear by all that's holy that we'd never do anything to harm this country. There's only a handful of troublemakers who are a little overzealous when it comes to Mussolini. I suppose they might pose some kind of threat."

"Nobody is being assessed. No government people here to do it — there's just the guards and the camp commander," said Paolo. "He's got his hands full, I can tell you. Some blokes kick up an awful fuss. But he does his best. He's organized a sick bay, and he keeps telling us that this is just temporary."

"There you are," said Edith encouragingly. "You'll soon be out of here."

"Yes, but we're told the next move will be to more permanent quarters," said Domenico.

"Maybe the Isle of Man," said Gianni, obviously despondent.

"*Madonna,*" said Anna.

Now that the first flurry of emotion and the excitement of seeing loved ones had diminished, Edith noticed a change on both sides of the fence. An air of resignation hung over the scene. Anna and Gianni started to murmur to each other in Italian. Paolo and Domenico even looked a little bored.

Carlo elbowed Domenico to one side and hooked his thick fingers around a length of wire in the chain-link fence in front of Edith. "I worry about Isobel," he said in a low voice. "How is she faring? I think about her all the time."

"She's holding up all right," said Edith. "Try not to worry; we'll look after her."

"You've been so kind, you and Mrs. Maguire," said Carlo. Edith was amazed and perturbed to see tears appear in Carlo's eyes. She'd never seen a man cry before.

"It's such a shame we can't leave you anything," said Edith hastily. "Cigarettes or something, but we were told nothing could be given."

"Yes, they told us the same thing when we heard we were getting visitors," said Domenico.

"I wish you hadn't mentioned cigarettes," said Paolo.

"Sorry," said Edith. She glanced at Carlo, who seemed to have recovered; the only evidence of his show of emotion was some moisture glistening on one of his cheekbones.

"I didn't have time to grab my case and lighter before they arrested us," he sighed. "I've been dying for a cigarette ever since we arrived."

"Listen, I have a packet of Players," whispered Edith, glancing at two listless soldiers who stood a few yards away. "Here, take them," she muttered. Turning to shield her hands from the soldiers' view, she opened her pack and pushed half a dozen cigarettes one by one through the wire mesh. Paolo and Carlo pocketed them surreptitiously, beaming at her like mischievous schoolboys.

At that moment, Edith felt an urgent need to urinate. There was nothing for it but to find a bush to squat behind before the bus journey back to Liverpool.

"Nature is calling me," she said shyly, looking about for a private spot.

Paolo and Domenico looked mystified, but Carlo, eager to be helpful, pointed to a copse of trees about a hundred yards down the road that encircled the mill.

"That's probably your best bet," he smiled.

As she slowly made her way toward the trees, Edith thought how youthful Paolo and Domenico looked. If she could disregard the incongruity of the hellish building, armed guards, and barbed wire,

Edith could almost imagine the brothers to be two schoolboys behind a schoolyard fence. Despite a juvenile haze of beard on their jaws, there was a boyish air of innocence about them. They appeared to see this momentous turn of events in their lives as an adventure. Perhaps it's just as well, Edith reflected. As long as they were fed adequately and weren't physically harmed, to them this must seem more like a lark than a huge hardship. Edith prayed there'd be no reason for their outlook to change.

"Where do you think you're going, then, luv?" a voice said. Edith could barely understand the soldier's broad London accent.

"I'm just going over there to spend a penny," said Edith, colouring slightly.

"Okey-dokey, but don't hang about," said the soldier, cockney vowels twanging. "The bus is leaving soon."

Edith found a suitable spot without nettles and hidden from the mill, where she managed to relieve herself without mishap. She felt like a child at school, having to explain herself and her actions. How quickly one's dignity can be taken away, she thought. On the walk back to the bus, she could see soldiers ushering visitors away from the fence. She was anticipating an emotional outburst from Anna, but an atmosphere of compliance persisted and farewells, although tearful, were subdued.

"Goodbye, wife," whispered Carlo. Edith's cheeks grew warm. Flustered, she mumbled goodbye and turned away. When she glanced back, Carlo smiled — somewhat ruefully. Edith managed an answering smile, which she found difficult to lose as she pulled herself up the steps to the bus and plonked herself down on the seat next to Anna.

As they drove away from the mill, Gianni stood motionless, one hand raised, his eyes fixed on Anna's face, which was pressed to the bus window. Once the mill was out of sight, Anna reached over and grasped Edith's hand. She stared blindly at the passing countryside for the entire return journey without uttering a word, but she kept her fingers entwined in Edith's until the bus ground to a halt outside Lime Street station in the centre of Liverpool.

Edith noticed that Emilio Rota's soldier son hadn't returned on the bus; he must have been detained at the mill. At least he's with his father now, she told herself in a feeble attempt to find a silver lining.

* * *

For supper that evening, Mrs. Maguire served a ham, a rare treat even though the entire roast was no bigger than a grapefruit. But the day's events had robbed Edith of the taste for food and she felt guilty for not being able to summon up much of an appetite. Meat was becoming scarcer; she ought to enjoy it while it was available. It was difficult for Edith and Mrs. Maguire to get to Shrimpley before dawn to be at the head of the queue when the shops opened. As a consequence, all the stock was often sold before they reached the counter.

After the ham, served with young lettuce leaves from the garden and a few dabs of Colman's mustard, they tried their first taste of Edith's rhubarb jam. They smeared it onto homemade bread thinly spread with butter. Edith didn't think she'd ever tasted jam so sour. Liam, who often switched the initial letters of words so he could use unacceptable language in respectable company, pronounced the jam "pumhole buckering." Edith had been so eager to be doing something that she'd picked the rhubarb before it was completely ripe. And now that sugar was rationed to a mere twelve-ounce bag a week, there wasn't a lot left over for making jam, especially after Liam had filched enough for his usual three teaspoons in every cup of tea.

"We'll give it another boil next week with a bit more sugar," said Mrs. Maguire.

Fat chance I'll be able to do any more cooking now, thought Edith. It was with some reluctance that Mrs. Maguire had allowed Edith to make the jam, having made it quite clear from the first day that she didn't want Edith "messing around" in the kitchen. "No fancy dishes now there's a war on and three mouths to feed," she had said. "We'll all have to pull in our belts." Mrs. Maguire controlled the meal planning and cooking. It was Edith and Liam's job to wash and dry the dirty dishes and put them away, but Liam, after drying a few plates, invariably muttered, "Nature calls," and disappeared into the lavatory for as long as it took Edith to finish everything.

But that evening, in his eagerness to tell Edith all the news from his latest issue of *Picture Show*, Liam forgot his usual ploy of excusing himself. He dried all the dishes and put them away, chattering non-stop about Greer Garson and Laurence Olivier making a film of *Pride and Prejudice*. "With Olivier playing Mr. Darcy, it's bound to be good," he pronounced. "It seems like sacrilege to make a film from a Jane Austen novel," Edith muttered.

When the kitchen was shipshape, Liam took himself off to his bedroom to finish reading his magazine. Edith, rather than sit in the living room, where Mrs. Maguire sat darning Liam's socks, carried the Agatha Christie she'd borrowed from the village library onto the porch, where there was still plenty of daylight. But despite her book's promising title, *Appointment with Death,* she found it impossible to concentrate. Miss Christie's descriptions were vivid enough, but Edith had trouble imagining the towering cliffs of Petra. Every time the Arabian cliffs were mentioned, all she could envision were the sheer walls of a sandstone quarry she'd glimpsed from the top of a double-decker bus a mile or so outside Shrimpley. Edith wasn't sure if the carved cliffs of Petra might resemble a quarry face in northern England, but somehow she doubted it.

She closed her book and gazed at a pink halo of light above the mouth of the estuary to the west, unable to imagine such peace ever being shattered by the noise of hostile aircraft or the sound of exploding bombs. Even when Germany had invaded Belgium and Holland a few weeks earlier, combined with the subsequent reports of the Allied retreat in France, Edith had found it difficult to believe that the war would be more than a minor inconvenience for England. She couldn't conceive of stranded soldiers on the beaches of Dunkirk being left to their fate; she assumed that the authorities would find a way to rescue them. It came as no surprise to Edith when they did. She remembered the government leaping into action as soon as war was declared, sending home 140,000 hospital patients to make room for casualties from non-existent air raids. Thousands of petty criminals were released from jail so they'd be available to join the forces. One day, Liam had regaled them with a newspaper account of snakes in London Zoo being put to death in case they escaped during an air raid.

"Isn't that taking things a bit far?" Edith had asked.

"Can you imagine how annoyed you'd be?" said Liam. "Surviving a barrage of Adolf's bombs and then being bitten to death in the middle of London by a black mamba!"

Despite all the madness, Mrs. Maguire had been thankful that things weren't as hysterical as the last time war was declared. "At least there's none of that silliness that happened in 1914," she had said. "People were stoning dachshund dogs in the street because they were German." Edith had never imagined that those words foreshadowed such an unthinkable event as the arrest of the Baccanello men.

Liam had gone on to recite a statistic that the autumn months of 1939 had seen "the greatest flood of marriages ever counted in British statistics."

"We don't need to read a newspaper to know that," said Mrs. Maguire without looking up from her knitting. Edith had glanced at her mother-in-law and shifted uneasily in her chair.

Now, as the garden grew shadowy and dusk fell, Edith could smell a dewy fragrance rising up the porch steps — the sweetness of grass cuttings sharpened by an undertone of pine needles. The sky arched above Edith's head, a robin's egg blue toward Ireland in the west darkening to indigo in the east. As she watched, couple of stars appeared, almost as though a switch had been flicked. The pointed crowns of the half a dozen fir trees that separated Mrs. Maguire's property from the Baccanellos' bungalow next door were black silhouettes against the sky. Edith couldn't make out any lights next door on account of blackout curtains at every window, but she guessed that Anna and Isobel were still up. They weren't sleeping much these days. Although they appeared stoic, Edith could tell they were both beside themselves with worry.

How could she have been so complacent when war was declared? Why had she found it so difficult to imagine the consequences that were predicted daily by everyone from shopkeepers to faceless radio announcers — deprivations, starving? And now this inhumane roundup of Italians. What next, she wondered.

Night was falling fast. Edith supposed it was time for her last chore of the day, to boil a ration of milk diluted with water for her and Mrs. Maguire's bedtime drinks. She pulled herself out of her chair with some effort. Reluctant to leave, she stood at the top of the porch steps, one hand holding her book, the other cupped around the swell of her abdomen. Edith couldn't help admiring the brightness of emerging stars and savouring the smells of the garden. She lingered for several minutes in the gathering darkness. As she turned to go inside, the screech of an owl signalled a night of hunting mice and voles up on the heath.

ITALY

Reluctant to prolong their spat — Shamus wasn't sure if it had been about the young student, academics in general, or merely their usual discord — the two brothers walked the length of Le Zattere to its easternmost limit in silence. Outside the old customs house of Dogana di Mare, they sat on a bench facing a panorama of water and sky. Crowds thronged the San Marco vaporetto stop to their left. To the right, the spires and dome of the church of San Giorgio Maggiore appeared peaceful and dreamlike. The expanse of water that separated Will and Shamus from the church and its island was teeming with reflections; wavelets created thousands of watery prisms that caught the sun to form a glittering expanse. Shamus had the impression that San Giorgio Maggiore was hovering above the tremulous surface of Bacino di San Marco. He leaned back, crossed his arms, closed his eyes, and basked like a bear in the warmth of the sun.

Will finally broke the silence. "You can see why the Brits were always so enamoured of Italy, can't you? There's an 18th-century garden in Wiltshire, near my darling ex-wife's parents, that's totally modelled on Italian landscapes. The original owner got the idea for the garden's design on one of those Grand Tours the wealthy were so fond of taking back then."

"Look at Forster," Shamus said to Will. "He used the Italians' passion for food and their overt sexuality in his books as a contrast to the prudish narrow-mindedness of the English middle class." Shamus was spouting a theory he'd learned in a course he'd once taken at university. "I think the infatuation with things Italian allowed a bit of sensuality into straight-laced British propriety."

"Talking of pretentious academics," said Will, glancing in Shamus's direction. "But let's not get into all that again. I remember some Italians living next door to us in Shrimpley during the war. I don't remember anything particularly sensual about them, although I remember liking them. But even if they were hedonistic, I doubt very much whether Edith and Joe would have noticed. Joe wouldn't have recognized eroticism if it stared him in the face."

Shamus resumed his bear-like pose, legs spread apart and stretched out in front of him. He was surprised by Will's mention of Italian neighbours during the war; it was the first time he'd heard of them. Shamus concluded that Edith and Joe couldn't have been very friendly with any Italian neighbours or they'd surely have been mentioned.

Shamus enjoyed the warmth of sunlight on his face and the intense scarlet that flooded his retina as the sun illuminated the blood coursing through his eyelids. He thought about a British woman he'd met on his first business trip to Verona, six or seven years before. She was an interpreter, and he'd noticed how her face seemed transformed when speaking Italian — as if it changed her character in some way. She admitted that perhaps she felt less inhibited in what she called her "Italian mode." After that, he made it a habit to study people as they switched languages. He was fascinated by the idea of being liberated from a lifetime's "Englishness" by a mere change of language.

Later, Shamus had jokingly mentioned to an Italo-Canadian friend of his, Vince, that he was an Italian wannabe. "Believe me, you don't want to be Italian," Vince replied. "Italian families are relentless. Your business is never your own; everything you do is under scrutiny. And the stereotype of the outgoing, demonstrative Italian is a load of bullshit. They sometimes put on a good act, but they're as uptight as anyone else." That hadn't stopped Shamus from taking Italian lessons.

The warmth of the September sun was making Shamus drowsy and he shifted further down on the wooden bench to get comfortable.

"You mentioned Forster in your dissertation just now. Wasn't he one of your mob?" asked Will.

Shamus opened his eyes to take the measure of Will's self-satisfied expression. "If you are referring to his sexual orientation, then, yes, I believe you're correct," said Shamus and closed his eyes again.

"I suppose we ought to be grateful to you homos," said Will. "Introducing us philistine heterosexuals to the sensual things of life. Hedonism and interior design. Kudos should go to you lot for the popularization of fellatio and the revitalization of acres of urban neighbourhoods."

"Thank you," said Shamus.

"The Brits weren't so enamoured of Italy when it came to Mussolini, though, were they?" Will commented.

"Oh I don't know," replied Shamus. "Edith used to say he made the trains run on time."

"How in God's name would Edith know that? She's just parroting what everybody always says. Like they claim Hitler built the autobahns. As though that made him less evil."

"I took a train from Milan to Verona recently. You should see the train station in Milan. One bloody great monument to fascism, but it's quite magnificent in a brutal kind of way. I suppose Mussolini was responsible for that too."

The two brothers sat, soaking up the sun and listening to the sound of seagulls screaming and water lapping.

"Do you remember cousin Susan?" asked Will.

"What you're really asking is, do I remember when she asked me that question at your wedding," said Shamus.

"Well you have to admit it was pretty funny," said Will. "'Aren't you too big to be a queer?'" he paraphrased in a squeaky, girlish voice.

"You didn't think it was so funny when she said she'd always thought *you* looked more like the gay one," said Shamus, trying to appear unruffled. But despite himself, he launched into his usual diatribe about the vicissitudes of growing up gay in Liverpool.

"Save the hard-done-by-victim speech for someone who cares," groaned Will, settling back on the bench. "You were too big to get beaten up anyway."

Shamus closed his eyes again, refraining from pointing out to Will that his size may have cut down on the bullying, but it hadn't stopped snide remarks and cold shoulders from classmates. He'd quickly learned to hide his sexuality so successfully that sometimes even he had wondered what it was.

A few minutes later, when Shamus opened his eyes, he noticed Will was ogling a passing woman. Before he could stop himself, he remarked, "She looks a bit like Mary, don't you think?"

Will frowned and shrugged. He stared moodily across the wide stretch of shimmering water. Shamus was struggling for something to say to placate Will when his brother erupted.

"You know what started it all, don't you. She began going to a so-called psychotherapist. I'm sure that kind of thing is fine with a qualified practitioner, but she began seeing this radical feminist quack that some New Age idiot friend of hers recommended. She got so she hated all men, including me. Eventually, I had to tell her, 'I'm not your sodding father.' But it didn't do any good. That was at the root of it, you know — she began to confuse me with her shit of a father. Me, of all people! And then, to add injury to insult, she walked out on me."

"Isn't it insult to injury?" questioned Shamus.

"In this case, it was definitely the other way round; I was fucking devastated!"

Shamus was surprised by Will's admission of vulnerability. "Sorry," he murmured in what he hoped was noncommittal sympathy. He nervously eyed a small mole of a man with a long nose and brown suit, sitting on the next bench to them, who had turned to examine Will through thick spectacles.

"What are you apologising for? You sound so bloody Canadian," said Will. "Even the buses in Toronto say sorry, for Christ's sake."

"What?" said Shamus, trying to ignore the mole-like man, who was by now staring unabashedly.

"When I was there, I saw a bus with its sign flashing, 'Sorry, out of service.' I couldn't believe it."

Shamus was about to suggest that a considerate Canadian style might be better than the selfish manner so prevalent in Britain since the greed of the Thatcher era, but before he could get into it, Will stood and abruptly walked away. By the time he caught up with him, it seemed pointless to continue the conversation.

ENGLAND

"It was Bob MacDonald," said Isobel as she wheeled herself down the ramp and onto the lawn, where Edith and Anna were sitting in deck chairs. They'd heard the phone ring five or ten minutes earlier, just a couple of rings. Isobel had obviously been close enough to answer it. "He met a man in a pub at lunchtime and thought we should hear what he had to say," said Isobel.

"Something to do with Gianni and the boys?" asked Edith.

Since her visit to Warth Mills, Edith had taken to affectionately describing Carlo, Paolo, and Domenico as the boys, as though they were her brothers. Paolo and Domenico's grinning faces had a habit of popping into her head completely unbidden. She often thought too of their father, Gianni, especially at night, when she imagined him stretched out on a dirty, straw-filled mattress trying to sleep. But most of all she thought about Carlo; she wished with all her being that they could all return to the pleasant days, before the arrests, of tea on the lawn and walks on the heath.

"Bob said the man was a steward on a day's shore leave. Apparently he'd had a few beers and was shooting his mouth off, complaining that his beautiful cruise ship had been turned into a ferry for refugees."

"Which ship is it?" asked Edith. Her father, like many Liverpool people, took an avid interest in the ships that sailed in and out of the port. Every night he would read out loud from the newspaper the names of ships that were reported as having arrived or departed that day. He'd comment on each ship. "She's a lovely vessel," he sometimes said. "I'm not familiar with her," he'd say of a ship whose name he didn't recognize.

"Bob told me the name, but I can't remember," said Isobel. "He thought it was a Southampton boat. The man in the pub said it had been a luxury cruiser before the war, only first-class passengers. The man had been all over the world with her."

"Why did Bob think we'd care about that?" asked Anna. "But go on about the refugees," she added impatiently.

"Bob said this man claimed a cannon and anti-aircraft gun had been put on the ship. He told some story of how they picked up a shipload of Polish troops from somewhere in France," said Isobel. "Fifteen hundred of them, according to the man. He was complaining about passengers sleeping on mattresses on the floor of the dining room. He went on about what a shame it was that such a beautiful ship had to have its rich fittings removed for the sake of a bunch of dirty soldiers."

"This is all very well, but what on earth does it have to do with Gianni and the boys?" asked Edith.

"As he was leaving the pub, the man told Bob that they'd be loading a pile of aliens on board tomorrow. When Bob asked the man what kind of aliens, the man said he'd heard they would be Italians and Germans."

Edith and Anna looked at each other; Anna raised her eyebrows and nodded her head slightly. Agitated by the implications of the news, Edith looked away and scanned the hazy silhouette of hills on the far shore, indistinct and wavering against a pallid sky. She involuntarily took a sharp breath and turned to Isobel.

"Do you think they may be taking them to the Isle of Man?"

"You'd think those bastards would let us know," Isobel replied.

"If they're over there, we won't see them until the end of the war," said Edith.

The meaning of that phrase — "the end of the war" — had changed so much in the last few months that it was difficult to believe it was made up of the same five words. There'd been a time when most people, Edith included, believed the end of the war would automatically involve a speedy victory and a resumption of life as it had been before Neville Chamberlain had broken the news that they were at war with Germany. But now everybody referred to life before that announcement as happening "before the war," the phrase now unmistakably implying a lengthy period before peace would return. Recent developments in Europe made victory seem not only less imminent but less certain. People could no longer imagine what the end of the war might bring or how long they'd be forced to wait to find out. And Edith wasn't sure how much of her recent ambivalence about a conclusion to the war was a result of her desire for change — perhaps she didn't want the war to finish if it meant a return to her former, so-called normal, life. But if it meant the safe return of Carlo and the others, she'd welcome war's end with open arms.

"They could be there for years," said Anna.

Monday, July 1, 1940

"Edith, will you sit with Isobel while we go into the village?" Anna asked when she called for Mrs. Maguire. The woman from the farm along the lane had told Mrs. Maguire there'd been a delivery of tinned goods at the Co-op grocery shop so the two women were making an early start to beat the crowds. The warm dry weather of June had broken. The morning was as gloomy as a day in November and almost as cold. There was little doubt there'd be rain before the day was out.

"I just had a call from my sister," announced Isobel, who was sitting in front of a coal fire when Edith arrived at the Baccanello bungalow. Anna had gone to the extravagant length of lighting a fire to fend off the chill of the day. Isobel's profusion of ringlets, which Edith had often admired for their gleam and bounce, appeared lank and dull. "She went to see Jimmy Roberts about her husband being interned; can you believe it?"

"The member of Parliament?" asked Edith, full of admiration for the nerve of Isobel's sister. "That was a good idea. He should be able to help. Isn't he supposed to be the voice of the underprivileged? Representative of the working stiff and all that?"

Jimmy Roberts was legendary in Liverpool. He was illegitimate, brought up by his widowed grandmother, who kept house and home together by taking in washing from officers and crew off ships at the docks. He left school at fourteen to work on the railways, where he became a full-time union man before entering politics.

"Well it turns out he's just like all the others," snapped Isobel, sounding disgusted. "Politicians are all the same — they keep two different faces. One for making speeches and getting elected and another for dealing with people like us after we've voted them in."

"Oh dear," said Edith. "I gather he was a washout."

"He told my sister that during such tumultuous times as these, hasty decisions have to be made, sometimes with unfortunate results, blah, blah, blah."

"Unfortunate results!" Edith was beginning to share Isobel's disgust.

"Apparently he maintained that Mr. Anderson, the Home Secretary, had been against the indiscriminate internment of aliens but that Churchill had overruled him when it came to the Italians. Then our man in Westminster concluded by telling my sister that it was 'regrettable' but that there was nothing he could do to intervene. He was sure — how he can be so certain, God only knows — that internees will be well cared for until they can all be assessed, and the chances were that most would be released before too long." Isobel slumped in her wheelchair. "I think it's more likely hell will freeze over first, don't you?" she muttered. "Poor Carlo. It's bad enough he married me. When he vowed to keep me 'in sickness,' he had no idea what he was in for."

"It's not your fault," said Edith.

"There was a lot of pressure on him to marry me," Isobel sighed. "You don't know what it's like. The minute an Italian turns eighteen, the campaign begins. Every wedding, christening, or family celebration — and there are a lot of them — it's always the same question. 'When are you going to find someone and settle down?' But the matchmakers are worse. They never let up. 'You couldn't do better than so-and-so,' or 'You should meet my cousin,' or 'I'm going to introduce you to what's-his-name; you and he will really hit if off.'" She put her slender hands on the arms of her wheelchair and shifted her weight. "I love Carlo's mother, but she was relentless. 'What are you two waiting for? If you don't hurry up, I'll die without seeing my grandchildren.' Sometimes I wonder if we married just to shut her up. Well she probably regrets it now."

"I shouldn't think so," said Edith reassuringly. "Anna's obviously very fond of you."

"Maybe," mumbled Isobel. "Anyway, if people were honest, I think most would admit they didn't marry for love. It's more often than not a matter of convenience."

Edith thought back to the night Joe had asked her to marry him.

He'd just received his call-up papers. She'd been unsure how to react when he told her, so she said nothing. When he suggested they return to the Grafton to "cheer themselves up," Edith realized Joe must have mistaken her silence for distress.

"You watch out," Edith's father had told them as they left the house. "There's more people being killed by cars in this blackout than anything else." Not one bomb had fallen yet, but with the precaution of extinguished street and traffic lights in force, the number of road accidents after dark had increased. Edith and Joe had walked to the Grafton with the aid of a battery-powered hand torch, wrapped with the mandatory two layers of white tissue paper to dull the light.

Joe asked Edith to marry him later that evening. Her first thought had been how romantic he was to bring her back to the place they met to pop the question. And his intense blue eyes, which had attracted her to him in the first place, couldn't have been more imploring. But when he ended his proposal by announcing that he wanted "someone" to come back to once the war was over, Edith felt obliged to point out that he made it sound as if anyone would fit the bill. Joe insisted that there was "more to it than that." Since the word "love" hadn't crossed his lips, Edith told him she needed to think about it.

Edith had missed Joe when he was away at training camp. Perhaps it was a case of absence making the heart grow fonder, but she found herself wishing his leave would arrive sooner. Most of all, Edith missed coming over to Shrimpley and seeing Mrs. Maguire and the Baccanello family. Anna was round, jolly, and always welcoming. Gianni was a gentle giant — tall for an Italian. Anna said it was because he'd been born in the mountains north of Venice. "In the north, they have to grow high to reach the sun," she often joked. Joe wrote regularly and always expressed the fervent hope that Edith would accept his marriage proposal. Edith began to picture herself as one of the wives who were often portrayed in magazines and newspapers, stoically keeping the home fires burning for their men fighting the evil Axis overseas. Finally, it seemed downright unpatriotic not to marry him. And it wasn't as if she was an oddity — lots of her acquaintances had taken the plunge and married a serviceman without necessarily being madly in love.

There was just enough time for a marriage licence to be issued before Joe's embarkation leave at Christmas. Edith didn't mind that there was no time for a proper ceremony; somehow a registry office seemed fitting. "At least you won't be married in a papist temple," Edith's father had muttered.

For a while after the wedding, Edith luxuriated in a glow of self-righteousness. She thought wistfully how short-lived her feelings of usefulness had been after Joe was sent abroad and life took on the tedious routine of the first uneventful months of war.

"I think I married Joe more for his mother than anything else," confessed Edith to Isobel. "She's been so much kinder to me than my own parents."

Isobel let out a feeble laugh. "That's as good a reason as any, I suppose."

"Tell you what," Edith suggested, changing the subject. "There must be lots of hot water in the boiler with the fire lit. Let's give your hair a wash. That might perk you up a bit."

"That's a strange idea for a tonic," said Isobel. Nevertheless, she laboriously pivoted her wheelchair around. "Come on, then," she said, "I think the kitchen sink would be better than the bathroom."

The diversion did cheer them up a little, and they laughed as Edith did her best to towel Isobel's hair. It was so thick that it was impossible to dry completely.

"Best sit in front of the fire," said Edith. "You don't want to catch cold." Just as she was stoking the fire, feeling vaguely guilty for using a whole shovelful of coal, the phone rang.

"I'll go," offered Edith. She didn't want Isobel sitting in the draughty hall with wet hair.

"I'm glad it's you," allowed Bob MacDonald when he heard Edith on the other end of the line. "It's not good news, I'm afraid. I went down to the docks to see that ship I told Anna about."

"The one that was supposed to be taking on aliens?" asked Edith.

"The very one," confirmed Bob. "I got a good vantage point from a window in one of the loading sheds. There must have been almost a thousand men on the dockside waiting to board, but they all seemed to be prisoners of war, most of them in uniform. Some poor blighters were in bad shape, bandaged and too weak to stand."

"But no Italians," Edith butted in, ever hopeful.

"After about half an hour, a train pulled up in the siding behind the loading sheds," explained Bob, taking no notice of her interruption. "Streams of men came off the train. And this lot were in civvies — a bit dishevelled, but ordinary trousers and shirts, with jackets on most of them. They were clearly internees, Italian by the look of them."

Edith took a sharp intake of breath. "Were Gianni and the boys among them?" she asked.

"There must have been more than fifteen hundred men crammed onto the quay. There were at least a hundred soldiers with rifles at the ready. What they thought those poor buggers, excuse my French, would do, or where they'd run to, is beyond me."

"So how could you know if Gianni and the boys were there with so many men?" asked Edith.

"You know what bothered me most?" asked Bob, ignoring Edith once more. "How pathetic they all seemed. Not a word out of any of them. It was eerie, how quiet they were. All you could hear were seagulls screeching and the occasional yell from a soldier or the blast of a ship's siren on the river. But hardly a peep out of all those men. I thought to myself, if Paolo and Domenico had been there, they'd have been messing about, kicking up a bit of noise at least. So I thought maybe they weren't. But then the soldiers began to herd the poor beggars onto the ship like they were so many cattle."

"And did you see them then?" asked Edith, exasperated with his evasiveness.

"First of all, I thought I saw Johnny's white hair. He stopped halfway up the gangplank to catch his breath, and one of the soldiers shouted at him to keep going. The man in front turned round to see what was happening and I could see it was Carlo. You can't miss Carlo, the size of him, even from a distance. Then I realized it was all four of them, Paolo and Domenico too; they were right behind Johnny and Carlo."

He fell silent. Edith could hear a slight hiss on the line but couldn't conjure up a single word to fill the eerie sound of emptiness.

"Are you still there?" asked Bob.

"Yes, I'm here," she replied.

"You know, seeing them being loaded onto that ship reminded me of all those stories you've heard about the old slave ships that used to sail out of Liverpool," said Bob.

"Except people valued the slaves," said Edith bitterly.

Bob cleared his throat. "They're on a ship called the *Arandora Star*," he continued. "And I heard this morning there's another boat, the *Ettrick,* slated to be loaded up with more of the unfortunate beggars later on today. It's a troop carrier designed to carry more than two thousand men."

"But how can they possibly accommodate all those men on the Isle of Man?" And how was she going to break the news to Isobel and Anna that Gianni and the boys had been shipped off to God knows where?

ITALY

After Will's outburst about his wife, the brothers walked in silence along the wide Fondamenta delle Zattere, past the imposing façade of the Chiesa dei Gesuati, until they approached some tables and chairs belonging to one of the quayside restaurants.

"Let's have another coffee," suggested Will.

"Don't you think we're hyper enough as it is?" said Shamus.

"Speak for yourself," said Will, sitting at a table near the water next to Le Zattere vaporetto stop. "I'm serenity itself." It was true that Will seemed to have calmed down. That was the deceptive thing about Will. He always appeared to assuage his demons in outpourings of vituperation, but Shamus knew very well there'd been no resolution. Which meant Will was likely to blow up again at any time. And more often than not, Shamus was left feeling guilty, as though he were somehow to blame.

When the waiter arrived, the brothers asked for cappuccinos.

"Decaffeinato per me," added Shamus. Will rolled his eyes.

A vaporetto arrived at the dock. The engine huffed and puffed as the boat was manoeuvred into position. Eventually, a rope was secured and a gate retracted to allow a crush of passengers to disembark as others waited to board.

"Do you ever remember Edith and Joe quarrelling?"

"What's that got to do with anything?" exclaimed Shamus. He had to raise his voice to make himself heard above the grating noise of the vaporetto gate as it was closed in preparation for departure.

"It's just that I actually can't remember any interaction at all between them apart from the 'Shall we have beef or lamb on Sunday?' kind of thing," said Will. "I have to admit that often, after Mary and I had one of our humdingers of a battle, I asked myself how come Joe and Edith never quarrelled."

Shamus scoured his brain for any memory of skirmishes between his parents. The noise of the vaporetto's engine revving up made it hard to concentrate. A cloud of grey smoke lingered above the water as the boat glided away from the quay and sailed off across the Giudecca Canal. The ensuing quiet was a relief.

"I suppose it's a bit difficult to quarrel when you hardly talk to each other. I remember the way Edith and Joe could put each other down with just a dirty look, but you're right, they never actually engaged in battle," concluded Shamus. "They bickered a bit about dates, what happened when and so forth."

"But it was never an argument," said Will. "Only wrangling about whether something happened 'before the war,' 'during the war,' or 'after the war.' And don't you remember that 'after the war' didn't encompass many years? I used to think life stopped for them around the time of the Coronation. And that was 1953, wasn't it? They didn't seem to consider anything after that worth discussing. And they definitely talked about before the war in a different way than they did about during and after."

"What do you mean?" asked Shamus.

"When they talked about during and after, it was always in a stilted, constipated way, as though they were being really careful what they said. And they only mentioned other people, friends or acquaintances, whereas before the war was all about themselves. Christ, that ridiculous story about how they met. How pathetic is that?"

"'She threw herself at me in the Grafton ballroom,'" quoted the brothers in unison. Shamus laughed and Will shook his head.

"You know, I always thought Joe sometimes gave that line a bit of an edge," said Shamus, "depending on how many snifters he'd drunk. And Edith always looked pained when he said it, like she wanted to be anywhere but where she was."

"Who cares anyway?" said Will abruptly, eyes narrowed in a sullen frown. "Ridiculous people."

"You're the one who asked," said Shamus indignantly. He pointedly shifted his chair to look across the water toward the hulk of Molino Stucky, the neo-Gothic flour mill whose menacing 19th-century bulk crouched like a sulky teenager next to its older and more graceful neighbours. He should have known Will would revert to his normal scathing style. Not that there was anything normal about it, thought Shamus. The waiter arrived with their coffee and placed it with a small flourish before them on the table. A small, empty envelope of Hag espresso, proof of his cappuccino's decaffeinated status, was perched on Shamus's saucer.

"That's what I love about Italians," said Shamus, unconsciously making an effort to brighten Will's mood, unaware that he was reverting to his usual fence-mending tactics. "Who else would take the trouble to reassure you that your coffee really is decaffeinated by showing you the empty packet?"

But Will remained distracted. Another vaporetto had announced its arrival with a loud thud as its bow hit the floating wooden dock. Will watched the boat ready itself to disgorge its passengers onto the nearby quayside. It wasn't until the gate finally opened that he turned his head in Shamus's direction. "What are you on about?" he asked.

"This. Look!" said Shamus, holding up the small paper sachet.

"And your point is?" asked Will. "Apart from forcing me to ask the question, 'Why bother?'"

"Why bother what?" asked Shamus.

"Drinking decaffeinated coffee," said Will. "Why bother?"

Shamus sighed loudly. "I think it's courteous and thoughtful of them to put one's mind at rest that it really is decaffeinated," he said. "But perhaps that's a principle you find difficult to understand."

"The fact that producing the so-called evidence is common practice here only means that Italians are considered untrustworthy, even by other Italians," said Will.

"What did an Italian ever do to you?" asked Shamus.

Will's attention had returned to the vaporetto stop. There were five or six people waiting to get on. They were jostling each other, inching forward before the last person to disembark had stepped ashore. A bulky male won the competition to be first on board. His persistence was rewarded with one of only two vacant places to sit. He was so large — not fat, but tall and heavily built — that a single seat was barely wide enough to accommodate him. The man sat facing the quay. He was swarthy, with dark eyebrows so defined they could have been drawn with charcoal.

"Nothing that I can remember," replied Will, staring at the man.

"Yeah, well, it seems to me there are two types of people in this world," said Shamus. "Those who mistrust everyone right off the bat, and the other half, who trust everybody until proven wrong."

"And which half are disappointed most?" asked Will.

Shamus, refusing to be drawn in by Will's rhetorical question, sipped his coffee. He wondered why Italian cappuccino was more delicious than Starbucks' and then realized it was probably because it was made with full-fat milk. He usually only drank skim milk, even in his coffee. Should he be concerned, he wondered.

"You know, I've been thinking about that Italian bruiser's cigarette case. It sounds odd, but it reminds me of learning the alphabet, or how to read . . . or something," Will added lamely.

It took Shamus a moment to figure out that Will was talking about the melodramatic young man he'd bumped into on the bridge earlier that morning. "That's not just odd, it's downright weird," he said.

"Some help you are," snapped Will.

"How am I supposed to remember what happened to you before I was born?" asked Shamus, desperately racking his brains for some memory that might appease Will.

"Who said it was before you were born?"

"Wait, I remember now!" exclaimed Shamus. "Maybe you're not weird after all. You must be remembering that joke that Joe used to make about Players cigarettes."

"What joke?" demanded Will.

"You remember. They had the slogan 'It's the tobacco that counts' printed on the inside flap. You know, to boast about the fine Virginia tobacco their cigarettes were made of. Joe would lift up the closed pack, put it to his ear, and start counting out loud, 1-2-3-4-5-6. Then he'd slowly slide open the flap to reveal the words and read in that idiotically dramatic voice, 'It's the tobacco that counts.'"

"Christ, how could I forget that?" Will sneered. "He really was a fool, wasn't he?"

"Well it was probably funny the first time," allowed Shamus.

"Yeah, well, that wasn't what I was thinking of anyway," said Will, still frustrated that he couldn't remember.

Will watched as the departing vaporetto slid away from the quay. The crowded boat picked up speed and laboured toward the Stazione Marittima, leaving in its wake a churning of foam-topped eddies that marked its path through the jade-coloured waters of the Giudecca Canal. Will was frowning slightly, as if struggling to recall something at the edge of consciousness, like a familiar word on the tip of his tongue. Curious, Shamus followed his gaze and found it was directed at the Italian with the suitcase and coal-black eyebrows, who, thanks to his size, stood out from the other passengers as the boat receded into the distance. Puzzled, Shamus looked back questioningly at Will, but his brother just continued to stare at the retreating boat, his brow wrinkled and his eyes narrowed.

ENGLAND

"Why would they be taking *all* of them to the Isle of Man?" asked Mrs. Maguire.

"I don't think they've released a single man. According to Bob, there were about fifteen hundred being put on the *Arandora Star* alone," said Edith. She imagined a continuous file of mute figures trudging silently up a gangway and disappearing, one by one, into the shadowy bowels of the ship.

Her musing was interrupted by the sound of Isobel's cry wafting through the crack of a barely open window. "Edith, come quickly. For God's sake."

Mrs. Maguire ran for the door. Edith lumbered after her as quickly as she could, her back aching from the weight of her seven-month pregnancy. Isobel was obviously in some distress; perhaps she'd fallen out of her wheelchair in the garden. Carlo had often told her to be careful on the uneven surface of the lawn. But why would Isobel be wheeling around the garden in the rain?

When Edith and Mrs. Maguire reached Isobel, she was sitting safely in her chair between the two conifers nearest to Mrs. Maguire's property. But it was clear from her damp hair and dark water stains on the shoulders of her blouse that she'd been outside for some time.

"I thought you'd never hear me," Isobel moaned.

"Whatever's the matter?" asked Edith, chest heaving from the exertion of hurrying to Isobel's side.

"It's dreadful news," she said. "Anna's gone into the village, but I just had to tell someone."

"Tell what?" asked Mrs. Maguire, her face glistening with rainwater.

"Bob telephoned to tell us. The *Arandora . . .*" Isobel started to cry.

Edith knew immediately that some disaster had befallen Gianni and the boys. She put her arm around Isobel's wet shoulders.

"The *Arandora Star*," she began again. "It was torpedoed and sunk yesterday." Her voice quivered, but she continued. "Bob heard the news at the docks this morning."

Edith was stunned. "Yesterday? But they would have told us sooner. Maybe it's a mistake; perhaps it was the other ship," she spluttered, her voice strangled as though somebody's fingers were tightening around her throat. Isobel shook her head mutely.

Mrs. Maguire took in a breath to steady herself. "Were there any survivors?" she asked gently. Isobel dropped her head and sobbed. Edith clutched Isobel's shoulders more tightly. Rain fell in a slow but steady stream, and rivulets of water dribbled unimpeded down the back of Edith's scalp.

Mrs. Maguire wheeled Isobel inside, where Edith helped her change her wet blouse. When confronted by Isobel's naked shoulders Edith was struck by the pallid colour of her skin. Then she remembered how she'd once compared it to fine marble. But that had been on a sunny day in the garden, not in the murk of Isobel's darkened bedroom, its window turned gunmetal grey, the glass made opaque by lashings of rainwater. Edith was struck by the enormity of what had happened. Up until then, she'd held on to the fragile belief that the war wouldn't — couldn't — be so bad. She liked to think that one day in the near future, she'd wake up and find Gianni, Carlo, and the boys returned home. Now those hopes were completely crushed. She was conscious of every ounce of optimism being sucked out of her; as a result, she felt a constriction of her chest she knew might never leave her.

"Edith, I can't get my hand in," Isobel complained.

"Sorry," said Edith, forcing herself back into the moment and holding the blouse in a better position for Isobel to slide her arm into her sleeve.

Mrs. Maguire's voice rose, excited, from down the hall and they heard the phone being slammed down and the sound of hurried footsteps. "There are survivors," shouted Mrs. Maguire, bursting through the doorway. Even in the dim light of the bedroom, her eyes shone. "Bob didn't know how many, but quite a number apparently. They arrived in Greenock safe and sound earlier this morning."

Isobel and Edith stared at her.

"The boys? And Gianni, Carlo — are they safe?" Isobel demanded. "I don't know, he didn't know, we just have to . . ." Mrs. Maguire's voice trailed away. "We just have to hope for the best," she concluded. Isobel shook her head and started to silently cry, whether from relief or disbelief Edith didn't know. Edith remembered the grins on the faces of Paolo and Domenico when she'd seen them last at Warth Mills, describing their shenanigans with candlelit card games, and football. She remembered Carlo's rueful smile as she left him. Don't let them be gone, she prayed. Not the boys. A thought leapt into her head. If somebody has to be dead, let it be Gianni; he's had a life. Their father, but not the boys, please God. She was immediately swamped by horror and disgust that she could have conjured such a monstrous bargain. She closed her eyes as tightly as she could in an effort to excise the idea from her brain. Just then, as if to torture Edith's conscience even more, the woman on whom she'd mentally inflicted widowhood arrived home, exuberant, from shopping in Shrimpley village.

"You should see the scrag end I managed to find at the butcher's," Anna called as she walked down the hall toward them. Her jubilation at finding some mutton was short-lived. The moment she heard the news about the *Arandora Star*, she paled and looked as if she might buckle at the knees. Edith steered her to a seat in the living room while Mrs. Maguire picked up the butcher's package from the floor where Anna had dropped it and deposited it in the meat safe. Mrs. Maguire, always one to rise to the occasion, bustled around Anna's kitchen as if it were her own, making cups of sweet tea without regard for the scarcity of sugar or the threatened rationing of tea leaves.

Around three o'clock a telegram arrived for Anna, who read it silently and let out an anguished wail. Isobel wheeled to Anna's side and wrested the telegram from her hand. She read it out loud, almost shouting, as though willing the volume of her voice to carry her through to the end, "Sorry to inform you STOP following sinking of *Arandora Star* STOP Gianni Baccanello and Paolo Baccanello missing, presumed dead STOP Carlo Baccanello and Domenico Baccanello rescued and uninjured STOP."

Isobel took in a great quivering heave after the word "dead," as if *she* were the drowning one. At that point, Anna began rocking in her chair, arms crossed and pulled tightly to her abdomen as though she were in terrible agony. She whimpered, a heartwrenching sound more appropriate to a young animal than a human being. Then, when Isobel read the good news about Carlo and Domenico, how could she possibly express any joy or relief?

Isobel threw the telegram violently to one side as though rejecting it utterly. She wheeled closer to Anna's chair and leaned over as far as she could. Isobel wasn't able to reach far enough to hug Anna, but she clutched at the back of her neck with one hand and held on to Anna's arm with the other. Her touch seemed to supply Anna with the release she needed to howl in Italian and beat the arms of her chair with her fists. Edith could make out Gianni's name as Anna shrieked it time and again among a string of curses. Isobel sobbed loudly, knuckles white as she clenched the back of Anna's woollen cardigan.

Mrs. Maguire caught Edith's eye and jerked her head toward the door. Realizing there was nothing they could do to relieve Anna and Isobel's anguish, they quietly left. On her way out, Edith picked the telegram up from the floor and placed it carefully on top of Anna's sideboard.

* * *

For the rest of the day, Edith felt so conflicted she thought she might go out of her mind. Every time she allowed herself a frisson of happiness about Carlo's survival, she was overcome by guilt, given the death of Gianni and Paolo. Unable to feel happy or sad, she seesawed from one emotion to the other without fully embracing either. She stroked and held her swollen belly in an attempt to comfort herself. But eventually she couldn't escape from the image of Gianni and Paolo behind the barbed-wire-topped fence at Warth Mills. The only people she'd ever known who had died were her grandparents and some ancient neighbours from her childhood. How was it possible that someone as young as Paolo, so vital and real, could be gone, never to return? She couldn't help wondering about his last minutes, hoping against hope it had been quick, a fatal blow to the head by flying debris perhaps. But she didn't believe it.

Any joy she might have felt about Carlo was completely eclipsed by the idea that Paolo was more likely to have drowned slowly, trapped in the pitch-black interior of the *Arandora Star* while frigid ocean water relentlessly displaced every pocket of available air.

Thursday, July 4, 1940

"It sounds like the Germans and Italians behaved like total cads," Edith overheard Liam say as she stepped into the front hall. Edith was returning from looking in on Anna.

She'd felt totally ineffectual. Every word that came out of Edith's mouth sounded inane and completely inappropriate. At one point, Anna had turned to Edith. "How come the government was so quick to send us that terrible telegram?" she pleaded, looking at Edith with such perplexity that her eyes could have been those of someone suffering from dementia. "They didn't tell us a thing about Gianni and the boys for weeks before that. Not since they were taken." Anna's complexion was sallow. The olive skin under her eyes was so dark it appeared tinged with green, as if bruised by grief. Edith couldn't supply any answer to Anna's question, clearly born out of a desperate attempt to comprehend what had happened. Instead, Edith had reached for her hand. Normally warm and dry, Anna's fingers were icy and her palm cold and clammy. Isobel had barely spoken. Edith could imagine, judging by her own conflicting reactions, how split Isobel must be by the shock of Anna's sudden widowhood in contrast to the relief she must be experiencing at the survival of Carlo. Edith felt guilty for not staying longer, but she couldn't bear the fact that there was absolutely nothing she could do to help.

Liam and Mrs. Maguire were sitting in the living room with the door open wide. Edith stood in the hallway out of sight, waiting to hear a response from Mrs. Maguire.

"Don't believe everything you read in the newspaper, Liam," she said.

"It's not the newspaper that's saying it," retorted Liam. "It's this steward chap, one of the crew who was rescued. He maintains the Germans and Italians were out of control. He says they were beating and biting each other to be the first to get on the lifeboats."

"I'm sure people were panicking. Who wouldn't under the circumstances?" asked Mrs. Maguire. "But I read that article too, and what that young man said, well I thought there was something a bit too pat about the way he described things. He sounds too clever by far for an eighteen-year-old steward."

"But it's a first-hand account by an eyewitness," insisted Liam.

"Yes, but an eyewitness who's travelled to London and been interviewed by the authorities before he's been allowed to talk to the news reporters," retorted Mrs. Maguire.

Edith's curiosity got the better of her. She walked into the living room, behaving as though she hadn't heard a word they'd been saying. She sat next to Liam on the overstuffed couch, an estate-sale bargain that had necessitated the removal of a doorframe as well as the door for them to coax the monster into Mrs. Maguire's modest living room. She glanced at the front of the newspaper Liam was holding. "The Aliens Were Frightful," trumpeted the headline.

"It's an account of the sinking of the *Arandora Star*," said Liam, holding out the newspaper. "See for yourself."

The more she read, the more affronted she became. She wasn't sure whether it was because Mrs. Maguire had suggested some kind of collusion, but the crewman's account of misconduct by the internees did seem improbably damning. He went so far as to suggest that, were it not for the Germans' and Italians' selfish acts, more men would have been saved.

"I don't see any mention of any blame," said Edith, once she'd finished reading the article.

"A U-boat was to blame," Liam smirked. "A bit of a joke that it was a Nazi torpedo that put paid to so many of their own."

"No, I mean who was to blame for putting them in the ship in the first place? Why were they there, like sitting ducks, in the middle of the Atlantic?" asked Edith.

"They were taking them to Canada," said Liam. "Didn't you just read the article?"

"But why?" demanded Edith impatiently. "There's nothing about why hundreds of innocent men were being transported halfway across the world."

"How many times do I have to tell you?" said Liam. "Because they're fifth columnists. We were putting them safely where they couldn't do any harm."

"What a lot of rot," exclaimed Edith. "And it didn't turn out to be very safely, did it?"

Nobody spoke for a few seconds. The sound of birds chirping furiously from the garden signalled that the rain had finally eased off, even if the sky was still overcast and the room murky.

"How do you know it's rot?" asked Liam.

"It's patently obvious to anybody with half a brain that these men are no threat to anyone," said Edith.

"Well I think I have a whole working brain and I don't see it," sneered Liam. He turned to his mother. "And why on earth would the government bother to tell this steward what to say?"

"To take the focus away from themselves, of course," said Mrs. Maguire.

"It's the government's fault that innocent men and boys have been killed for no good reason," chimed in Edith.

"The trouble with you," snapped Liam, "is that you've been consorting with the enemy. If you stayed home and waited for your husband — who, in case you've forgotten, is fighting for King and country — it'd be better for you and for Britain."

"All right, my boy," said Mrs. Maguire, "that's quite enough."

"You're as bad," cried Liam, turning to his mother. "Hobnobbing with aliens and fifth columnists." He jumped up. "It's times like these that call for duty to country above loyalty to family. I should report you both." With that, he ran from the room, and a few seconds later, Mrs. Maguire and Edith heard the sound of the back door slamming.

"What on earth's got into him, rushing off like that?" said Edith.

"You can't blame the lad for being upset," replied Mrs. Maguire. "And he might be right. Maybe we can't see the wood for the trees."

"What's that supposed to mean?" asked Edith.

"You know how fond I am of Anna and the Baccanellos," said Mrs. Maguire, ignoring Edith's question. "But maybe we should be looking more to our own. You should be thinking of Joe."

"I can't do a thing about Joe," said Edith. "He's beyond my help. And anyway, I do think about him," she added as an afterthought.

Mrs. Maguire was clearly not convinced.

"I know it's difficult," she said, her voice tinged with genuine sympathy. "Mr. Maguire and I were separated just a few months after we were married. He was off fighting in France and I didn't know if he'd ever come back. It was three years until I laid eyes on him again. There were times when I thought I'd dreamt him," she said. "He came home damaged in body and mind, but he was still my husband. I was glad then that I hadn't given in to temptation."

"Temptation?" asked Edith.

"I'll say no more, but I'd advise you to think on it," said Mrs. Maguire.

Edith could hardly believe her ears. Mrs. Maguire's prim insinuations that Edith may have been tempted by some kind of hanky-panky with Carlo enraged her. She was seven months pregnant, for God's sake. But more importantly, Edith believed unwaveringly that she and Carlo would never act on any attraction they might have for each other. She *was* willing to concede that if she'd never met the Baccanello clan, she might not be quite so appalled by the gross miscarriage of justice that had happened to the Italians. But she had met them — all of them, not just Carlo — and seen first-hand the pain and misery the internment order had caused. Was it any wonder she felt so strongly?

"If even one innocent person is maltreated, injured, or killed, isn't that one too many?" asked Edith, hardly able to string the words together, she was so frustrated.

"In normal times, maybe. But there's a war on," said Mrs. Maguire.

"That's no excuse," snapped Edith.

"In wartime, bad things sometimes happen that can't be helped," insisted Mrs. Maguire.

"Gianni and Paolo certainly can't be helped, can they?" Edith fumed. "It's too late for them."

"I'm going to see to the hens," said Mrs. Maguire, stalking out of the living room.

Edith was left languishing on the sofa, too exhausted by their spat to struggle to her feet. She realized she was trembling. She couldn't remember when she'd ever felt so passionate about anything. If she'd argued as fiercely with her father, he'd have slapped her down at the first hint of contradiction. She was sorry it had to be Mrs. Maguire who had born the brunt of her fury, but she didn't regret a word she'd said. Her eye was caught by a silver-framed photo of Joe that stood among some other family portraits on the Welsh dresser. His gleaming hair was slicked back from his smooth forehead. She could almost imagine that his curved eyebrows — so distinct in the black and white picture — were raised and that his piercing blue eyes were looking directly, accusingly, at her.

When Liam didn't return in time for tea that evening, Edith was surprised at how concerned she was. Anxiety was an unfamiliar emotion to her. Now that she was aware how easily a person — even someone as young and healthy as Liam — could permanently disappear, Edith felt apprehension bordering on dread when he hadn't appeared in time to eat with her and Mrs. Maguire. She'd always thought that fearfulness must be a result of ignorance. How naïve she'd been, when the opposite was surely true. The more you experience, the more there is to fear, she thought. The recent and unbearable realization that even the most robust of lives was woefully fragile had instilled a general unease in Edith for everyone's safety, even her brat of a brother-in-law.

"I hope he's all right; it's turned very cool outside," she said to Mrs. Maguire. "And it's not like Liam to miss a meal."

"He'll be moping around the heath," said Mrs. Maguire, who'd behaved as though their little contretemps had never happened since she returned from shutting up the hens for the night. She helped herself to another slice of bread. "I can't get used to margarine. It wouldn't be so bad if it was the colour of butter, but it looks more like lard. He's more sensitive than he looks, you know."

"Who is?" asked Edith, startled by Mrs. Maguire's abrupt change of subject.

"Liam, of course," said Mrs. Maguire. "Oh he'd like you to think he's as cool as a cucumber, but he's easily bothered. You should have seen him on his first day at school. The teacher had to hold on to him when I dropped him off, he was that upset. When she lifted him up to prevent him running after me, he kicked off his Wellington boots and screamed blue murder. But Joe was a different kettle of fish entirely. He strolled into his infant school without so much as a glance back in my direction. Quite hurt, I was, at the time."

After tea, Mrs. Maguire announced she was just popping along the lane to see if the farmer would be willing to sell her a carrot or two to go with some neck of lamb and a couple of kidneys she'd managed to cajole out of the butcher for a Lancashire hotpot. Edith sat in the living room, trying to concentrate on a Daphne du Maurier book she'd borrowed from the library, but her thoughts kept slithering away from the page and finding Gianni and the boys. The text she stared at might as well have been double Dutch, as instead of scenes from the novel, her brain presented her with a snapshot of Gianni and the boys waving goodbye from behind the criss-cross pattern of the wire enclosure at Warth Mills. Not dissimilar to the mesh of a trawler's net, she thought with a shudder.

She'd just given up on the book when she heard the back door open and close. Liam appeared at the living room doorway a few seconds later.

"Look," he said awkwardly. "I'm sorry I flew off the handle earlier."

"That's all right," said Edith. "I'm just relieved you're home in one piece."

"You make me sound like a baby who can't look after himself," said Liam, flopping into the chair opposite her.

"I didn't mean to," said Edith.

"It's just that I don't think you understand," said Liam.

"Understand what?" said Edith.

"War," said Liam. "I don't think you realize how it works."

"Why don't you tell me?" suggested Edith, trying her best to remain calm.

"You can't afford to be sentimental," said Liam. "You can't let personal likes and dislikes get in the way of the country's interest and the national good."

"All right," said Edith, beginning to wonder why she'd bothered to be concerned about him. "But let's suppose we'd never met the Baccanello family. Don't you think it was wrong that more than a thousand innocent men, some of them British citizens, were put in mortal danger by the government and that hundreds of those men — hundreds," she repeated, "died as a result?"

"Sometimes somebody gets hurt, it's unavoidable," said Liam flatly.

"Unavoidable," repeated Edith. "Why is that, Liam? What terrible disaster was thwarted? What catastrophe was averted by packing a thousand waiters, shopkeepers, and tailors into a ship and putting them at risk by hauling them across an ocean crawling with German submarines, torpedoes at the ready?"

"There was another ship that left at the same time. It obviously made it to Canada safe and sound or we would have heard. It was just the luck of the draw as to who was on which ship, that's all."

"But you're not answering my question. Why did they have to go in the first place? Why separate them from friends and family?"

"They posed too great a threat in the event of an invasion," said Liam smugly. "And let's face it, they were just a bunch of Italian peasants after all." He glared at Edith defiantly, chin raised and blue eyes glittering.

Neither of them heard Mrs. Maguire return home. She pushed open the door that led from the kitchen to the living room just as Edith reached the end of her tether.

"You stupid, despicable little idiot," Edith screamed at Liam.

Mrs. Maguire stopped in her tracks.

"I think it's time I went to bed," Liam announced, after giving Mrs. Maguire a meaningful glance, and left the room looking smugger than ever.

"Any more of this, my girl, and I'll pack you off back to Liverpool, baby or no baby, bombs or no bombs," said Mrs. Maguire, index finger stabbing the air in front of Edith's swollen abdomen.

* * *

Later that evening, Edith lay in bed listening to the wind in the trees up on the heath. After the warm days of early summer, July was turning out to be positively frigid. The rain, which had begun again as she was filling her hot-water bottle, lashed against the roof and walls of the house. She abandoned the idea of sleep half an hour after turning off her bedside lamp.

Edith asked herself over and again how Liam could possibly say, let alone believe, the statements that had fallen so glibly from his lips. Not even her father had displayed such heartless contempt toward his hated Catholics. He might well have thought their lives worthless, but, to her knowledge, he'd never gone so far as to say it out loud. And it wasn't as if Liam was talking about abstract individuals, but people as real as the neighbours he'd known his whole life.

Not long after she'd managed to fall asleep, the wind gathered strength and roared out of the east. Outside, the weighty boughs of an ancient English oak thrashed violently in the gusts, strewing leaves and immature acorns up and down the lane.

ITALY

27-09-2002 **11:52**

"Bugger it!" Will exclaimed.

"Bugger what?" demanded Shamus, startled.

"I can't remember what the hell that damn cigarette case reminds me of."

"Maybe you're suffering amnesia from when the Italian studmuffin threw you to the ground," suggested Shamus. "Why is it that you remember things from when you were little and I don't?"

"Do I?" Shamus asked.

"You're always banging on about something or other from when you were at infant school. I have no memory at all of my early years — not at home or at school." He looked at Shamus suspiciously. "I think you make it up most of the time."

"That's the kind of stupid theory abusers use to deny accusations of molestation," countered Shamus.

"Piss off," Will growled.

Shamus looked down at his empty coffee cup, where remnants of foam clung to the inside surfaces. No wonder Will's company caused him to miss Luke so keenly. Shamus and Luke had never fought. They had managed to resolve any disagreements with quiet acquiescence on the part of one or the other of them, usually Shamus. There had been times over the years, however, when Shamus had questioned the unrelieved constancy of his and Luke's relationship. There'd been passion enough when they first met, and an intensity in their lovemaking that had persevered. But Shamus was often left wondering whether there wasn't some intangible element lacking. It's not as though Shamus could identify the missing component from past experience; Luke had been his first and only live-in partner. Shamus didn't know why he'd expected more.

Shamus's doubts about Luke had always been dismissed after spending time with his brother and he became immensely grateful for the calm simplicity of his and Luke's relationship. Now, thought Shamus, being with Will only emphasized his loss of Luke, like shining a spotlight on an empty stage. He was suddenly engulfed with a yearning to be home; he ached to turn the key in the lock of his own front door. Shamus couldn't believe — as undeniable as he knew it to be — that Luke wouldn't be indoors waiting for him, eager, as he always was, to hear about Shamus's travels.

"What the hell are we doing here?" he moaned.

"What's your problem?" retorted Will. "Some people would give their eye teeth to be sitting at an outdoor café in Venice on a beautiful day like today, and in the company of such an engaging travelling companion as myself."

Shamus refused to respond. He stared across the broad canal to the uneven line of assorted buildings on the opposite bank.

"Come on, our kid, buck up. Your Mam will be here tomorrow," coaxed Will, mimicking a Liverpool accent.

"Why is it that when I'm with you, I always feel as though I'm waiting for the other shoe to drop?" asked Shamus, referring to the undeniable element of danger he always felt in Will's company.

"Probably because I'm a complex, creative character," said Will. "Multidimensional individuals are often fascinatingly mercurial."

"So are most psychopaths," muttered Shamus.

"Oh for God's sake, stop whining," said Will, an edge of irritation to his voice that caused Shamus's intestines to tighten. "You and Mary. You're one of a kind."

"I'm nothing like her," Shamus protested.

"It's funny how, according to Mary, before we were married, I was 'exciting.' After a few years of marriage, I became 'unpredictable.' And then it changed to 'volatile' and we were in the downward spiral until we hit rock bottom and I'd become 'psychotic.'"

"You have to admit you're sometimes a bit extreme," said Shamus.

"Extreme?" questioned Will.

"Yes, you know. Over-the-top engaged one minute, distant and unfathomable the next," said Shamus.

"Whatever," said Will.

"There you go, you see?" said Shamus. "Suddenly disconnecting, totally pulling the rug out from under me."

"I should have married Mary's sister," said Will, ignoring Shamus's protestations. He gulped the last of his coffee. "She always professed to find me interesting."

"Last time her name came up, you said she was a left-wing loony. Look what she did to Edith."

"Edith went to Greenham Common of her own free will," contended Will. "One of the rare occasions she actually acted on her 'bolshie beliefs,' as Uncle Liam always called them."

"Janey browbeat Edith into going down there in the middle of winter, dumped her in a draughty tent with a group of hairy-arsed amazons, then took off to the wilds of Scotland to protest some nuclear submarine or other," cried Shamus. "Is it any wonder Edith caught pneumonia?"

"Careful, bro. Your politically correct veneer is cracking," replied Will, smiling smugly. But Shamus was in such a hurry to make his case that Will's taunt didn't register.

"Then Edith had to find her own way home because Joe wouldn't drive down to collect her," Shamus continued excitedly. "To use Joe's words, 'She'd made her bed and got above herself,' or some such mixed metaphor."

"What did she expect?" said Will. "By then, Joe was spouting all that Thatcher rhetoric about a crime being a crime being a crime. The thing that always amazed me was that he and Edith never exchanged words about any of it, ever. Talk about two ships passing in a marriage!"

"Maybe not, but Granny Maguire certainly tore Joe's balls off a time or two back then about his infatuation with Thatcher," said Shamus.

Will grunted and then laughed in agreement.

Joe's mother was the one person toward whom Will had shown no antipathy; he'd never disguised his fondness for her. Shamus wondered if all siblings trod the line between enmity and alliance in quite the same way as he and Will. Occasionally, Shamus could manipulate Will from one side of the line to the other with rewarding alacrity. He'd known that mentioning their grandmother would change his brother's mood.

"And anyway, Edith loved it when the Yanks were eventually forced to slink off home with their cruise missiles between their legs," said Will. "To hear her crow about it, you'd have thought she was a permanent Greenham Common protestor instead of just a one-weekend visitor."

"She did have weird flashes of agitprop activism," said Shamus. "Remember, early on, she had us all making red paper flowers for the Labour Club May Day parade when Harold Wilson was campaigning for member of Parliament?"

"There you are, you see! Yet another false memory — you were only about five years old, for God's sake," Will insisted.

"Well maybe I was told about it," said Shamus. "But I'm sure I remember red paper flowers all over the house, and being on a float in the parade."

"On the big day, when the future prime minister actually patted me on the head, Edith was over the moon," groaned Will. "I swear it's the only time she's ever looked at me with any sense of pride at all."

"And yet she was often so timid," said Shamus. "Remember how frightened she used to be of old Briggs when we were at grammar school?"

"Well he was the headmaster from hell," said Will. "And the number of times she and Joe were hauled in to see him about your shenanigans."

"Me!" protested Shamus. "You were the one letting off fireworks in the playground."

"Maybe, but I didn't get caught pleasuring a sixth-former in the biology lab."

"It was an anatomical experiment," said Shamus, primly.

"Too bad it wasn't part of the curriculum," said Will. "I can't believe Edith and Joe didn't clue in to you back then. You always got off easy."

"They were too worn out from fighting with you to bother about me," said Shamus. "If you'd eased up a bit, I might have got some of the flak."

"You were so much more interesting in those days," commented Will in a deliberately wistful tone of voice.

"More irresponsible, you mean," countered Shamus.

"That response is exactly the kind of thing I'm talking about," muttered Will.

ENGLAND

Saturday, July 6, 1940

"You shouldn't be gallivanting all over the place — you're the size of a house," said Mrs. Maguire.

"You exaggerate. I'm more the size of a small bungalow," said Edith. "And it's only a bus ride away. Isobel can't go, and Anna shouldn't have to go alone."

They'd been told that all the survivors of the *Arandora Star* disaster had been brought down from Greenock to a camp not far from Shrimpley. Edith was determined to see Carlo and to hear first-hand what he and Domenico had to say.

"Do you want to have your baby on a bus? Or, worse, in a camp for internees?"

"I'm still more than six weeks away from having this baby. I'll be fine." It didn't seem the moment to reveal that she'd been feeling stronger and stronger kicks from her baby for a day or two. The movements made Edith's pregnancy — the baby — seem more real to her than ever.

"I don't know when you became so stubborn," said Mrs. Maguire, throwing up her hands in exasperation. "You were so much nicer before the war." She turned to Anna for support.

"Don't look at me," said Anna. "She's strong as a horse. And so what if she has her baby on a bus? There are worse places." Edith hoped Anna's reaction was a glimmer of the spark that had enlivened her before the terrible shock of recent events and not just more of the apathy she'd displayed ever since. "And it's nice for me if she comes," added Anna. Edith coloured slightly; she was always pleasantly surprised when Anna expressed an obvious liking for her.

* * *

Edith was right about the extent of their journey. No more than half an hour after they'd clambered aboard the bus in Shrimpley village, the conductor called out, "Arrow Park, next stop."

The bus dropped them at the gates to the park just as a steady drizzle abated, but there were no signs of a camp. Edith wondered if Bob MacDonald had been given the wrong information and asked a youth who was digging in a nearby flower bed for directions to the place where internees were being held.

"It'll be where the Frenchies were billeted after Dunkirk," said the young man, cigarette dangling precariously from his lips. A column of ash fell off the end of the cigarette and he brushed it from the front of his navy blue overalls. "Right inside the park, missus. Just keep going up the driveway and you'll see the tents when you get to the end." Edith found herself wondering why he wasn't in the army. She was immediately dismayed to think she'd had been swayed by some kind of pervasive war mentality. People were suspicious of every healthy male over eighteen years of age, calling into question their mettle because they weren't away somewhere risking their lives in the armed forces.

Edith and Anna made their way up the paved path. Rhododendron boughs heavy with rainwater pushed in at them from both sides. Dead flower heads covered each tall rhododendron bush, some as high as twenty feet. Edith thought how imposing they must have looked when they'd been in full flower earlier in the year. Where the rhododendrons eventually thinned, Edith thought she saw patches of blue sky on the horizon. She hoped so; she couldn't remember the last time she'd seen clear skies. It seemed to have been dark and dismal for weeks. At a distance, across an expanse of grass, were a dozen or so rows of identical, khaki-coloured tents, laid out like streets. There were ten or more to a row, each one about six feet tall at its peak, more than a hundred canvas shelters.

As they approached, Edith could see that the fabric walls of the tents were spattered with mud. The ridges were supported, but the rain-soaked sides sagged in flaccid folds of damp material. There was nobody to be seen, no sign of any guards. No voices could be heard. It wasn't until Anna and Edith reached the first two facing tents that they saw any inhabitants. In the gloom of the tents, each large enough to accommodate a couple of folding camp beds, Edith could make out the shapes of men sprawled on cots of wood and canvas. An army blanket covered one figure loosely, and the light that fell across the legs of another revealed dark pants that were wrinkled and frayed. A hole in the sole of the man's black sock revealed a pale circle of skin.

None of the men made any sign of having seen them, although Edith thought at least some of them must be aware of their presence. She felt awkward and intrusive, as though she and Anna had come upon the bedroom of a complete stranger. Edith was unsure what to do. She looked at the sodden ground, not wanting to invade these men's privacy any more than they already had. Anna, however, strode over to the opening of one of the tents and spoke gently but firmly in Italian. Edith heard her say the names Carlo and Domenico. But from the murmuring and shaking of heads Edith deduced that none of the men seemed to know their whereabouts. Anna moved on to the next two tents and asked again.

"You there," a voice called. A head had appeared from the opening to a tent at the far end of the avenue of tents. "What's your game, then?" The head disappeared, and a second or two later a British soldier emerged, rifle hanging from his shoulder.

"I look my sons," said Anna. Edith noticed the change in Anna's English. She wondered if Anna was genuinely flustered or if she was under the impression that a lack of English might elicit some kind of sympathy. If it was the latter, thought Edith, Anna was misguided. These days, a foreign accent would be cause for hostile suspicion, at best.

"What's their name?" asked the soldier.

"Baccanello. Carlo and Domenico," replied Anna, the fluent articulation of the Italian names a distinct contrast to her halting English.

"And who are you two?" asked the soldier, glancing at Edith's pregnant midriff.

"*Famiglia*," said Anna. "Mama and . . ." Her voice trailed off and she looked in Edith's direction, leaving the distinct impression that she was a family member.

"I'm not sure about visitors," said the soldier hesitantly. Then he shrugged as if dismissing any doubts he may have had. "What the hell. You look harmless enough, and even if you wanted to help them escape, this lot couldn't get far. Staggering to the latrines and back is about as much as they manage," he said. "I think your sons are two rows over. I'd better take you."

As they walked between the tents, Edith couldn't resist glancing into some of them. The most animated of any of the occupants were two men who were sitting on a camp bed playing a game of cards. "Baccanello brothers?' asked the soldier at the entrance to a tent. *"La porta successiva,"* said a trembling voice, obviously belonging to an older man. "Next door, next door," another, younger voice insisted. But Anna had heard the first voice and rushed ahead to the neighbouring tent. "Carlo, Domenico," she cried. Edith arrived in time to see Domenico start up from his camp bed and Anna throw her arms around his neck. She dropped her head to his chest. She hardly made a sound, not a sob or a cry, but the knuckles of each hand were white as she gripped Domenico's shoulders. Beyond them, there was no mistaking the shape of Carlo, who was lying on the other camp bed. His huge frame was too small for the narrow cot, and elbows, knees, and feet jutted over its sides. When he saw them, he struggled to a sitting position.

"Edith," said Carlo, managing a wan smile. He shifted up the bed and then patted the space next to him. "You look like you need to sit down."

Despite the wooden edge pressing into her thighs, Edith was glad to take the weight off her feet. Carlo reached over and took her hand. Edith was immensely reassured by the dry heat of his palm. She realized that until that moment, she'd harboured a fear that he hadn't actually survived the sinking, that there'd been some terrible mistake and he was in fact dead. At the sight of Carlo's tear-filled eyes, Edith's own vision blurred and she closed her eyelids tight shut.

Deciding that Anna and Edith posed no threat, the guard turned on his heel and pulled the tent flap over the entrance as he left.

When Edith opened her eyes again, Domenico was staring at her. The only sound was Anna's uneven breathing, the sole indication that she was weeping. In the subdued light that filtered through the khaki-coloured canvas, the whites of Domenico's eyes stood out luridly. They reminded Edith of a horse she'd once seen that had been frightened by a backfiring car. Like the horse's, Domenico's eyelids were open abnormally wide, lending him an air of terror bordering on panic.

"Hello, Domenico," said Edith as gently and as normally as she could. "It's good to see you."

Her voice seemed to break some kind of spell. Domenico closed his eyes and lowered his head. When he looked up again, his eyes, apart from dark circles that girdled them, were closer to normal. His tousled hair and the clear skin of his forehead, unlined and unblemished except for a green-tinged bruise the size of a half-crown coin on one temple, made him look as youthful as ever.

"Mama," he said in a low voice, "you're suffocating me." Anna relaxed her grip and lifted her head from his chest. She fished a handkerchief out of the handbag she'd been carrying and blew her nose. "*Non so che cosa dire*" she said, and quickly added, "I'm so happy you're both alive." She extended trembling fingers to Carlo, who grasped them with his free hand, keeping his grip on Edith's with the other. Domenico nodded his head and stared at the trodden grass floor of the tent. Edith looked down and was appalled to see a huge welt, five or six inches of angry, red skin, on top of one of his bare feet.

"What happened to your foot?" she exclaimed.

"I don't know," replied Domenico, looking genuinely puzzled.

Why did I ask such a stupid question, Edith wondered. He must have hurt it when the ship went down. There was a brief silence and then Anna asked in a timorous voice, "Can you tell us about it?" And suddenly there it was, the ghastly fact of the catastrophe, hanging in the air in front of them.

Domenico turned and looked at his mother for a few seconds, then stared at the ground again as though what he was being asked to describe was there at his feet. Carlo stared at Domenico expectantly. Edith was about to suggest — despite an uncontrollable craving to know — that he need not try to tell what would doubtless be a horrifying account. But before she could intervene, Domenico began to speak.

"We were put in a cabin on one of the lower decks, deep in the bottom of the ship. It was probably a cabin intended for crew, because there were four bunks," said Domenico in a low voice. Edith leaned forward a little so she could hear. "Someone said that passenger cabins were on the higher decks and had only two berths. We were glad, though, to be in a crew cabin, because even if we had to climb lots of stairs to get up on deck, it meant we could all be together. We didn't know the other man."

"The other man?" questioned Edith. "Wouldn't that make five of you?"

Domenico looked at her, uncomprehending.

"You said there were four bunks."

"Domenico, being the youngest, was put on the floor on a mattress," explained Carlo. "That's how we happened to be up on deck when the torpedo hit." Edith looked at him uncomprehendingly. "It was stuffy in the cabin," he explained. "I heard Domenico tossing and turning — he had trouble sleeping on the floor. Then Papa began to snore. You know how loudly he snored?" Carlo looked at Anna, who closed her eyes as though the memory was too heartbreaking to bear, but she nodded. "I could tell Domenico was awake. So I whispered to him to come up on deck to try and sleep. When we got there, we realized quite a few men had the same idea, so there wasn't much space, but we found a spot to lie down." Carlo nodded at Domenico, as if to encourage him to continue telling the story. Edith noticed that Domenico's voice grew stronger and his words came faster as he talked. He appeared almost feverish.

"I must have fallen asleep on deck, because next thing I knew, I was woken suddenly. I think I remember a loud bang and maybe a jolt. The man next to us said we must have hit an iceberg, but I didn't believe we could be so far north. I didn't know the ship was on its way to Canada. We knew we must have passed the Isle of Man, but Papa thought perhaps we were being taken to Ireland. Anyway, the ship began to lean to one side. I could hear shouts and there was a hubbub coming from the deck below us."

"Were people panicking?" asked Edith, recalling the newspaper account.

"We were more confused than panicked," said Domenico. "Nobody was telling us what to do. People were struggling into life jackets and somebody handed us a couple, so we put them on. Then I thought of Papa and Paolo. I told Carlo we should go down and tell them to come up to the deck, but everywhere we tried to go, men were pushing their way out and we couldn't get past them. Most of the men were in pyjamas or underwear. All I was wearing were these." Domenico looked down at his dirty singlet and heavily wrinkled trousers. "Up until then, I couldn't believe the ship would sink, but we saw some men throwing rafts over the side and jumping after them. The ship was beginning to lean more. I began to realize that it was going down."

"Slow down, Domenico," said Edith. "You don't have to tell us if it's too upsetting." Carlo squeezed her hand, almost as if to say, leave him be, let him tell it. Domenico looked at Edith unseeingly, his eyes wide again. Anna reached up and stroked his hair. "A man yelled at us that we were going the wrong way," continued Domenico, the words spilling out. "He said we'd been torpedoed and we should turn around and try to get into a lifeboat. I told Carlo we had to find Papa and Paolo, but he grabbed my arm and pulled me toward the side of the ship. I remember hearing three blasts of the ship's siren. Someone yelled out, 'Abandon ship!' The deck was at such an angle that I could see right down into the sea; I remember thinking how odd that the horizon was so high up in the sky. I slipped. I remember putting my hand out, but I don't remember falling." Domenico paused, almost visibly gulping for air. "The next thing I knew, I was surrounded by water. I was under the surface, sinking. It was like a dream. I wasn't scared, but I knew I was going to drown." His voice faltered, as though imitating his slow but inescapable descent into the Atlantic's frigid water. "I thought of Papa and Paolo, and Carlo, and then of you, Mama." Anna let out a brief sob. Domenico closed his eyes. He opened his mouth, but no sound came, so he closed it again.

"Go on, Domenico," said Carlo softly. "Tell them what happened next."

Domenico's eyes opened and he found his voice. "There were explosions, two of them, one after the other, muffled through the water. A man told me afterwards it was the boilers blowing up. The force of it pushed me up through the water." Agitated again, he appeared even younger than his sixteen years, like a young boy so excited he could hardly get the words out fast enough. "When I reached the surface and finally got air into my lungs, it was like exploding. I coughed and spluttered, trying to keep my head up, until I felt something nudge my arm. I grabbed it before I saw what it was, but when I steadied myself . . ." Domenico's breathing was ragged with emotion, but he kept going. "God, it was awful! His head was inches away from me. I could see a gaping hole in his face, a horrible ragged rip, mouth to ear. The whole inside of his mouth was exposed. His tongue . . . Christ, it was huge." Domenico turned to his mother, "I close my eyes, Mama, and I can still see every one of the man's teeth, right back to his ear. One of them had a gold filling."

Anna stroked Domenico's cheek with the knuckle of one finger. His skin appeared pallid and glaucous in the muted light filtering through the khaki-coloured fabric of the tent. Then, as if encouraged by his mother's touch, Domenico continued.

"The water around me was moving as if it was boiling. It was all bodies and floating clothes, pieces of wood, even a couple of life jackets. I couldn't see Carlo, but I saw a man with a great hole in his skull, his face covered in blood, clinging to a piece of wood. He was shouting, 'Aiuto! Aiuto!' But how could I help him? I could barely help myself. I tried to swim, and eventually I got clear. By then the water was calmer."

Edith was relieved when Domenico paused, but when Anna told him that was enough, that he didn't have to tell them any more, he shook his head.

"There were some mailbags that looked as if they were full of letters floating nearby," continued the boy. Edith had the feeling that he was anxious now to tell every detail of his story. She sensed an element of relief in his telling of it. "I managed to hook a mailbag under each arm. I hung there and rested. The sea was calm, and I just bobbed around for a while. I thought of Papa and Paolo and hoped they'd managed to find their way up to the top deck and been able to get clear of the ship before she went down. I have no idea how long I hung there. After a while, I could feel the mailbags sinking lower. Eventually, they were completely waterlogged and they sank.

But those mailbags definitely saved my life. I looked around for something else to hang on to and saw two men about thirty yards away sitting on a raft. I shouted, and one of the men shouted back, 'Come, there is space.' I tried to swim in their direction, but my legs were so numb I couldn't even tell if I was kicking or not. The men pulled some pieces of wood out of the water and paddled their way toward me until I managed to grab the side. The raft was actually a wooden table. I held on to it, trying to gather enough strength to heave myself up. It wasn't so easy. One of the men was terrified I'd tip them up — he said he couldn't swim. But I managed to get on and I didn't sink it. But then the sea began to get a bit rougher. The table started rocking."

Anna shook her head slowly from side to side. Edith shifted around on the camp bed to find a more comfortable position. Carlo kept a tight grip on her hand.

"Can you believe, after everything that had happened, that was my first moment of fear?" said Domenico.

"What do you mean?" said Anna.

"There was no time until then. All I could think of was saving myself. But now I had time to think. I was fine when we were at the top of a wave because I could see other people in lifeboats, on rafts, and things floating around all over the place. There were shouts of encouragement from one boat to the next. But when our table floated down to the bottom of the swell, into the trough, it was so far down it felt as though we couldn't possibly ever come up again. We were completely alone down there. All I could see was an endless wall of green water, no horizon, and no sky unless you looked straight up. I wanted to scream as loud as I could and jump up, but I had to stay absolutely still not to tip us over. It was enough to drive you mad."

"But eventually, help did come," Carlo gently prompted his brother.

Domenico shook his head from side to side, like someone trying to clear his ears of water. "Yes, a plane came over and dropped a package near one of the lifeboats. They got it out of the water and found a message in it. People shouted from one boat to another that a ship, a Canadian destroyer, was on its way."

"You must have been relieved when it arrived," said Edith.

"I suppose so. We were six hours in the water, but it felt like days to me," said Domenico, looking exhausted now that he was nearing the end. Yet there was obviously more that he wanted to tell; he took a deep breath as though summoning all his remaining strength.

"The Canadians lowered some smaller boats that went around picking up men like us who were clinging to objects," Domenico continued. "The destroyer itself cruised from lifeboat to lifeboat. I had awful cramp in my legs and I could hardly climb the rope ladder up to the deck of the ship. If a sailor hadn't reached over and grabbed me, I'd have ended up back in the water." Domenico paused. "The crewmen were very kind," his voice faltered. He took a deep breath. "They gave us hot broth. I never tasted anything so wonderful." Then he glanced at his mother and said, "Sorry, Mama."

Edith couldn't help smiling. Despite everything, Domenico remained the good Italian son, repentant for having praised someone else's food as much or more than his mother's. Anna stroked his hair and shook her head as if to reassure him that she wasn't offended.

"It was nighttime by then and I couldn't see any of the others. I thought I'd see them the next day. When we reached Greenock, I made sure I was one of the first off. We had to give our name to a man at the bottom of the gangplank. He tried to move me along, but I stood my ground.

"I was never so happy to see Carlo in my life as when I saw him coming down that gangplank." Domenico managed to summon up a smile as he looked across at his big brother. "But we didn't see Papa and Paolo come off the boat. So then we thought maybe they'd somehow managed to get ahead of us. I asked the man if their names were on his list, but he just kept telling me we'd be told soon enough who was there and who wasn't.

"They took us to an old factory or warehouse. I'm not sure what it was. The first thing they did was to show us a room with sinks in it. They gave us some soap and told us to clean ourselves up — Carlo and me were covered in yellow oil. Somebody said the oil might have helped keep us warm when we were in the water, but the smell of it was sickening. A lady came and took away our clothes to wash, but she couldn't get all the grease out. She gave me an old pair of shoes and a coat to wear. The shoes are too big and the coat's a little short, but it just about covered me until my clothes were dry." He pointed to a worn pair of shoes sitting on the grass below him. A navy blue pea jacket was draped across the end of the camp bed. Edith could make out a large circle of red fabric that had been roughly sewn to the back of the coat. She supposed it was a way of identifying the internees should they escape, but to Edith it looked disturbingly like a target.

Domenico frowned, shook his head again, and closed his eyes. "After we cleaned up, they gave us corned beef sandwiches and tea. As we started to eat, they began to call out the list of the missing, presumed dead, to check that none of them was among us. They read them in alphabetical order." He continued in a strangled voice, almost as if he couldn't breathe. His eyes were so tightly shut his face was a grimace. "I was so hungry I kept on eating even after they read out Papa and Paolo's names. I knew if I looked at Carlo I'd cry, so I just kept on chewing, taking a bite and chewing some more."

Domenico took a deep breath and opened his eyes, which were brimming with tears. He looked at Anna. "They were still reading out names long after we finished eating," he sobbed, finally breaking down. It was as though he collapsed in on himself; his thorax seemed to cave, his head came down, his chin hit his chest. He sank back on to the camp bed so heavily that the canvas groaned. Then he covered his face with his forearm.

Edith suddenly felt like an intruder. Wanting to give them some privacy, she struggled to stand.

"I need to walk around a bit," she made her excuse.

Carlo stood too, although he had to stoop to accommodate his height, even at the tent's highest point.

"I'll join you," he said quietly.

"There should have been more lifeboats," said Carlo as soon as they'd walked a few yards down the avenue of tents. "That floating pleasure palace for the rich had five hundred more men on board than it was equipped for. There were no safety drills. Is it any wonder there was confusion? And I mean confusion, not panic. One of the soldiers on the train from Greenock loaned me a newspaper. I couldn't believe the slander they wrote about us. 'Rushing the boats . . . Beating each other . . .'" Carlo quoted. "Those stories were riddled with lies."

Edith was at a loss for words. All she could come up with was, "Mrs. Maguire thought as much."

"At least me and Domenico were thrown clear," said Carlo, obviously making an effort to be positive. "The speed and the force of the ship keeling over threw us a long way. I didn't know what had happened to Domenico, but I hoped he'd been hurled far enough to avoid the suction when she went down. I found a piece of wood that another man was clinging to. It looked like part of a broken lifeboat — I'd seen one that smashed against the side of the ship as it was being launched. That was the other thing — it's plain as day that the evacuation of the ship was completely mishandled by the soldiers in charge."

Carlo took a deep breath, obviously trying to control his anger. "The other man holding onto the floating wood had silver hair like my father. I hoped against hope it was him, but it wasn't. The poor old chap's hands kept slipping from the wood. I tried to hold him up, but eventually he said, *'Non ne posso più,'* and let go. His head sank so slowly — I could see his white hair wafting like seaweed in the water underneath me until he disappeared. I told myself I'd die before I let go.

"Eventually, a lifeboat floated close by and I managed to swim to it. After they hauled me up, I must have passed out. The next thing I heard was someone saying, 'He's dead — we'll have to throw him back.' I perked up pretty quick when I heard that, I can tell you. When I made it obvious I was very much alive, they asked me if I'd help row the boat. The chap who'd taken charge, one of the crew from the *Arandora Star*, thought it would be better if we could get clear of the wreckage — not to mention the bodies. There must have been more than a hundred corpses, side by side, head to foot, nudging each other and bobbing all around us. They were packed together — you know the way rubbish seems to cluster on the river down by the ferry dock, like floating islands of refuse? It was impossible to find a space to put our oars in the water without hitting them. Not that it really mattered to the corpses; most of them were horribly mangled anyway."

Edith groaned, her stomach churning at the image.

"I'm sorry, I didn't meant to upset you," said Carlo. "It's just such a relief to talk to someone about it. Most of the men don't want to talk. Domenico hadn't said a word until you two arrived. Seeing you and Mama has been good for him."

It began to rain again. Carlo suggested they go back to the tent. But when they pushed their way through the flap, they saw that Anna was preparing to leave.

"*Ti amo, Domenico,*" she said as she bent to kiss his cheek.

"Goodbye, Mama," said Domenico, lying on his cot and staring up at them. From Edith's perspective, he appeared diminished, like a small boy who has just been tucked into bed by his mother. But despite Domenico's childlike appearance, Edith could discern a maturity in his eyes, a knowing expression that was clearly a result of his having witnessed the terrible unpredictability of life — and death.

Carlo circled Edith with his arms in a careful hug goodbye. The difference in their heights meant that her swollen abdomen pushed against his groin and her head rested on his chest. The rain had increased in intensity, and Edith could feel a fine spray of moisture emanating from the roof of the tent. She wondered how much longer the men could be held at Arrow Park before becoming sick from cold and damp.

Carlo released her and she stepped outside the tent into a drizzling rain falling steadily from a leaden sky. Edith was surprised when an open umbrella was thrust above her head. Her eyes followed a khaki-clad arm past a brass-studded epaulette and up to the fresh face of a young man wearing the peaked hat of an officer.

"Lieutenant Somerville, at your service," said the officer, who didn't appear old enough to have finished school, let alone to have graduated from a military college. "Heard we had guests. Thought I'd wander over and say hello."

"Pleased to meet you," said Edith. The officer was such a stark contrast to Carlo and Domenico — crisp shirt collar and tightly knotted tie beneath clean-shaven, fair-skinned jaw and ingenuous blue eyes — that Edith was taken aback. At that moment, Anna emerged from the tent, dabbing her eyes with her handkerchief.

"Lieutenant Somerville, at your service," repeated the officer to Anna.

"At my service," said Anna. "Then do me the service of returning my sons, now, today." Edith couldn't believe the imperious tone with which Anna had made her demand. She stifled her inclination to be embarrassed.

Clearly taken aback, Lieutenant Somerville nevertheless forced a smile. "I'm afraid I can't hand them over just yet. But I can tell you that, in response to requests by several internees, I've asked my superiors for an assurance that all survivors of the *Arandora Star* will remain in England," he said. "And I'm happy to report that I've been given permission to tell them, and you, that they won't be sent out of the country again. All surviving internees will be kept in Britain, and I'm sure arrangements will be made for regular visits by family and friends."

"Is the Isle of Man in Britain?" asked Anna. "I don't want my sons so far away."

"I can't tell you where they'll be housed, but housed they will be. Housed in England's green and pleasant land, I can assure you of that. As an officer and a gentleman, I give you my word that not a single man will be sent beyond these shores."

Edith looked into the pale, shining eyes of the officer and thought how entirely different they were to the eyes she'd seen just minutes before. Compared to the unfathomable depths of Domenico's world-wise eyes, the officer's appeared as naïve as a newborn baby's.

Anna didn't hesitate to accept Lieutenant Somerville's offer to make them a gift of his umbrella.

"My son Carlo has a very sick wife," said Anna clutching the umbrella with both hands. "He should be at home to look after her."

"Really," said the officer. "I'm sorry to hear that." He pulled a small pad of notepaper from his pocket. "Carlo Baccanello, is that right?"

"Right," snapped Anna.

"I'll see what can be done for him and his wife," he promised.

"You better," said Anna, turning to leave.

"Cheerio, then," called the officer. He stood watching as Anna and Edith moved away, dodging puddles as best they could. Edith suppressed the slight guilt she felt for taking the young man's umbrella by telling herself that he could doubtless afford another one.

As they reached the edge of the open grass and were about to head down the avenue of rhododendrons, Anna stopped and turned to look back. "I feel like I lost Domenico as well as Gianni and Paolo," she said.

"He'll be home before you know it," said Edith in a limp effort to comfort Anna.

"Carlo's a grown man. He's always been strong, since he was little and we were so poor. But Domenico is just a boy. He's only sixteen and he doesn't know hard times. Even if he comes home, he'll be changed. No more youngness," Anna said.

"You can't know that," said Edith gently.

"Like it was wiped out, like he'll never be able to find a happy time to look back on. And nothing to look forward to but bad memories."

As they walked between dripping rhododendrons, Edith regarded the soggy brown petals of dead flower heads and wondered whether Domenico's experience on the *Arandora Star* could have been traumatic enough to obliterate his past and future happiness, as Anna seemed to suggest. She hoped not, but a part of her — another bleak corner of her mind that she hadn't known existed — believed it was true.

Having paid for their cappuccinos at the canal-side café on Le Zattere, Will suggested they retrace their steps through Dorsoduro and walk over to Campo Santa Margherita for some lunch. "It's just one oral gratification after another with you, isn't it?" said Shamus. "Well empty sacks won't stand up, you know," Will mimicked their grandmother's voice.

Shamus couldn't help laughing; the familiar maxim was one that Granny Maguire had often used to coax him and Will to eat when they were children.

As they picked their way through a maze of *fondamente* and narrow streets that they hoped would lead them in the right direction, Shamus thought about the family's Sunday jaunts to Granny Maguire's house in Shrimpley. The outings consisted of a bus journey from their house in Liverpool to the dock at the Pierhead, then a ferry crossing, followed by another bus ride to Shrimpley village, and finally a walk across the heath to Sandy Lane and Granny Maguire's house. Given the time it took to travel there and back it, was a wonder they ever went.

Shamus remembered that it had always seemed odd to him that it was Joe who objected to visiting his own mother, whereas Edith seemed to brighten up visibly at the prospect of a trip to her mother-in-law's. They went at least once a month. And during the school summer holidays, Shamus, Will, and Edith moved lock, stock, and barrel to Shrimpley, leaving Joe to fend for himself in their council house in Huyton, the area of Liverpool where Joe, Edith, and Will had lived since before Shamus was born. Their seasonal desertion was viewed by neighbours as unconventional, but it was one of the few occasions when Edith didn't seem to give a hoot what anybody thought. They left, loaded with suitcases, buckets and spades, and other beach paraphernalia, the day after school finished for the summer and only returned the day before it resumed.

"Here we are," said Will as they rounded a corner and were confronted with the long, rectangular open space that made up Campo Santa Margherita. A babble of voices emanated from vendors and shoppers at a cluster of market stalls that were set up in the centre of the square, not far from where the two brothers were standing. To one side of the stalls was a small building sporting a sign that read "Scuola dei Varoteri" across the top. Shamus could make out the words "School of the Tanners" immediately underneath, in badly lettered English.

"Let's go further up, where it's a bit quieter," said Will, pointing to some outside tables at the far end of the campo, beyond the bustling market.

"Do you remember the Sunday excursions to Granny Maguire's?" asked Shamus once they'd found a table.

"Of course I do," said Will. "I may not have the knack for early recall that you boast of, but I haven't got dementia either."

"I'm just asking," said Shamus. "You're the one who claims to have a bad memory."

"Only of my early years," insisted Will. "And what about the pilgrimages to Shrimpley anyway?"

Shamus explained that it had never occurred to him how long it must have taken them to travel to their grandmother's house. There'd hardly been time for them to throw back lunch before they had to rush home again. He reminded Will how unhappy he'd always been to leave, how he pouted and dragged behind and generally made the journey back to Liverpool miserable for everyone.

"I suppose I felt more at home in Shrimpley than at our house," said Will. "You have to admit it was pretty idyllic there."

"You did live there for the first five years of your life," said Shamus. "I can imagine it *was* idyllic, even with a war on and everything. And with Joe away in the army, you must have been spoiled rotten."

"I think I probably was," said Will pensively. "But when I try to remember, I can never recall actual people or events; I just feel a kind of rosy glow. My first really clear memory is of Joe giving me hell for something or other. No rosy glow there, I can assure you."

Will's uncharacteristic frankness and the heartfelt tone of his voice precipitated a wave of sympathy in Shamus, similar to the one he'd felt for Will earlier that day when the waiter had treated his brother so disdainfully. It was pitiful that a rebuke from their father was Will's first clear recollection.

"At least you have the rosy glow to hang on to," said Shamus, thinking how woefully unhelpful he sounded.

A waitress brought them some menus. *"Ecco qui,"* she drawled lazily and floated back toward the door of the restaurant.

"Nice legs," Will muttered under his breath as she wandered away. Some of the empathy Shamus had been feeling melted away. He shot Will a disapproving glance as he reached for the menu.

Shamus was trying to decide whether to have pasta or a panino when a voice boomed close by, *"Amici Inglesi! Come state?* What a nice surprise to see you again."

He felt the weight of a heavy hand on his shoulder and looked up to see the young Italian they'd bumped into — literally — at the bridge that morning. He towered between Will and Shamus, a huge mitt grasping each brother's shoulder.

"Hello," beamed Will. "Sit down. Join us."

"I can sit for a minute or two, but no longer," said the man, pulling up a chair. "I'm off to a meeting. And this time I haven't forgotten my briefcase." He smiled and held up a black leather case with a gleaming gold clasp.

"I'm Will and this is my younger brother, Shamus."

"You are the younger?" asked the Italian, staring at Shamus and sounding surprised. "But you are the big brother too, yes?" He laughed loudly at what he obviously considered a brilliantly witty observation. Will laughed as uproariously as the Italian. Shamus smiled weakly.

"My name is Armando," the young man informed the two brothers, extending his hand. "Armando Belli."

The surname sounded odd the way Armando pronounced it, with emphasis on the two l's. Shamus immediately thought of belly, as in a big gut, but then realized the root was probably from the Latin word for war. Will grasped Armando's hand and shook it energetically. When it came to Shamus's turn, he had the sensation he was shaking a hot boxing glove, Armando's hand was so warm and enveloping. The sensation unnerved him. He pulled his hand away before their handshake was finished, then worried that Armando may have thought him rude.

"This is quite a coincidence, running into you again," said Will.

"Venice is a small town," Armando asserted. "And each of the *sestieri* is like a small village."

"*Sestieri?*" questioned Shamus.

"Neighbourhoods," Will answered. "There are six of them."

"*Si,* neighbourhoods. Like Chelsea or Kensington, but much smaller. If you live in one of the *sestieri,* like I do here in Dorsoduro, it's not unusual to see the same people every day of your life. And like a small village, we all know each other's business," he concluded with a grin.

Then Armando reached into his jacket pocket and pulled out the cigarette case that had preoccupied Will ever since it fell to the pavement earlier that day.

"Cigarette?" asked Armando as he snapped open the case to offer up a neat row of cigarettes to Will and Shamus.

"We don't smoke," said Will, eyeing the silver case.

"You are very wise," said Armando. He slid one of the cigarettes out from under the narrow elastic strap holding them in place. The case closed with a click of the miniature mechanism that secured it.

"May I?" asked Will and held out his hand.

"Of course," replied Armando and handed over the cigarette case. "It's handsome, isn't it?"

"You don't see many like that these days," commented Shamus, glancing at the case as his brother turned it over and over. Will scrutinized it inside and out, like someone who'd never seen anything remotely like it in his life. "To be honest, it's a bit of trouble," admitted Armando.

"Trouble?" asked Shamus.

"The cigarettes they make today are too long to fit. They must have been shorter when the case was made. It took me a long time to find some small enough. And they have no filter. Very bad for my health," he laughed. "But the thing has been in my *famiglia,* so I like to use it."

"What are these initials?" demanded Will, peering at the bottom right corner of the front of the case. "Do they say C.B.?"

"Yes," said Armando. "They're the initials of *zio*, my uncle. The thing belonged to him."

"Cee-o," said Will. "I never heard that name before. Is it some kind of nickname?"

Before Shamus could show off his knowledge of Italian vocabulary, Armando hastened to explain.

"*Zio* isn't a name. It's the Italian word for uncle," the young Italian pointed out. "You see . . ."

"I see, I see," interrupted Will, clearly sheepish about not having known the word. Shamus wondered what Armando was about to say before Will cut him off so brusquely. Armando had frowned after Will's interruption like someone who's lost the thread of a story. After a second or two, he seemed to have recovered.

"I loved my uncle very much," the young Italian revealed. It crossed Shamus's mind that nobody in his and Will's family would ever claim to love any of their relatives. Not to a couple of perfect strangers, anyway. Or even to the object of their affection, come to that. "He died a year and a half ago, and this was in his belongings. My mother offered it to me to remember him by."

Will stared at the front of the case for so long that Shamus was embarrassed.

"Better give it back, Will. Before Armando thinks you're stealing it." Will handed it over, but with obvious reluctance.

The bored waitress arrived to take their order, but at the sight of Armando, she brightened. They exchanged a few words in Italian and then Armando said, "The *ravioli con zucca* is very good here."

"Then I'll have that, please," ordered Shamus, trying a smile on the waitress. She smiled back and took his menu, then stood staring at Will expectantly.

"Will?" prompted Shamus after a few seconds of silence.

"Same for me, please," Will managed to say, but his thoughts were obviously miles away.

The waitress took Will's menu and grinned at Armando, who winked broadly in return.

Shamus's eye was suddenly caught by a rainbow flag fluttering from the ledge of a window above the restaurant. He could see that four letters were picked out in white in the centre of the spectrum of colours. P-A-C-E. Italian for peace.

"Probably students," said Armando, following Shamus's gaze. "In *Venezia,* they seem united in their opposition to the war in Iraq." He gestured toward the rainbow flag with his head, "Their decision is simple. They're not for him, they're against him."

"Him?" asked Shamus.

"George W. Bush," interjected Will, who still seemed somewhat pre-occupied. "'You're either with us or against us in the fight against terror.'"

"Of course," said Shamus, cursing his slow-wittedness.

"It's not just here that people are making their opinions known. There are plans for a demonstration in *Roma* tomorrow to protest Bush's proposal to invade Iraq," said Armando. "And a massive turnout is expected in London."

"It's not yet a proposal, is it?" asked Shamus.

"Bush is making it pretty clear that if the United Nations won't support an invasion, America will go ahead anyway," said Armando.

Will, who seemed to have pulled himself together, picked up the discussion with Armando. Will maintained it was as much a feud between Saddam Hussein and the Bush father and son as anything else. Armando argued it was all about oil. They both agreed it had little to do with the war on terror or the so-called axis of evil.

"I must go," said Armando, looking at his watch. He stood and ground out his cigarette butt under one heel. "But tell me, where are you staying?"

Will told him the name of the hotel that Edith had booked, which was just around the corner, in the street that linked the square where they were sitting, Campo Santa Margherita, with Campo San Barnaba, where they'd had breakfast after bumping into Armando earlier in the day. Armando became excited at the news.

"*Perfetto,*" he exclaimed, explaining that his family's restaurant was directly opposite their hotel. He urged them to go there for dinner.

"You can't miss it," he explained. "It's the only one on the street. My mother will be there, and maybe my grandfather too. We make very good food — the best in *Venezia.*" He said he'd be sure to drop by the restaurant that evening to see if they were there.

"Arrivederci. Maybe see you later, then," he called as he left.

"Do you think we're being conned?" asked Will once Armando had disappeared.

"You mean young Armando Belli trying to get us to eat at the family restaurant?"

"Yes. Are we the gullible tourists or what?" asked Will.

At that moment, the waitress appeared with their lunch.

"Zucca is squash, right?" said Will after he'd taken a mouthful. "There's a restaurant of the same name in London near where I live. They serve this very dish."

"Remember when food used to be exotic?" asked Shamus.

"What do you mean?" said Will.

"Squash-filled ravioli around every corner in London. And I bet there isn't a cuisine in the world that one can't find at some restaurant or other in Toronto. It's all a bit sad."

"Sad?" scoffed Will. "Why sad?"

"I remember the first time I was in France when I was fifteen, staying with that family I met on a caravan site in Wales."

"Yet another time you left me on my own with Joe and Edith," complained Will.

"It's not like you didn't have friends, and you never seemed to want me around."

"That's not true," insisted Will. "You could be quite amusing when you were young."

"Well anyway," continued Shamus, "I'll never forget the first meal I had at the French family's house when I arrived. Nothing fancy, just a baguette, some Normandy butter, and ham. But I'd never tasted anything so delicious. The bread was fresh, crusty. And so flavourful. All we ever ate at home was pulpy sliced loaves from grease-paper packets. And the butter in France was incredible. English butter was so salty you couldn't actually taste the butter. The ham was amazing too, much more flavourful than the stuff Edith used to boil for hours on end. For me, that meal was the most intense cultural experience — quintessentially French. But now everything is so universal. Young people have all kinds of culinary experiences and don't think twice about them or associate them with anywhere in particular."

"Watch it, Shamus," said Will. "There's a high old fart factor there."

Will adopted a querulous old man's voice. "Things just aren't the same as when I was young." Then he continued in his normal tone, "And it's not like importing food from other countries is anything new. Didn't spaghetti come from China? It was probably the Venetians who shipped it in. I know they had a thriving spice trade. But then the Portuguese threatened to cut them out by sailing to India to buy raw materials direct from the growers. Apparently, the Venetians appealed to the Egyptians to put pressure on the head honcho in Calcutta not to deal with the Portuguese. I seem to remember the Venetians also promised to reward the Egyptians if they attacked Portuguese ships."

"That's not playing fair," said Shamus.

"The Venetians were pretty ruthless when it came to trade," said Will. "And indiscriminate when choosing their allies. They developed a motto when other European states criticized them for conniving with Muslims and not supporting the Crusades: Venetians first, then Christians. It wasn't until Saracen pirates started attacking Venetian merchant ships that they entered the Holy War. And even then it was only because they could see a way of profiting from it."

"How do you know all this stuff?" asked Shamus.

"I read the guidebook. I thought I'd better be well-informed when I knew I'd be here with Mr. I've-got-a-university-degree Smarty Pants," said Will.

"Well at least the Venetians were up front about it," said Shamus, ignoring Will's taunt. "Which is more than can be said for today's lot. The Americans, for example. Why don't they just admit it's all about the oil?"

The waitress arrived to take away their empty plates.

"Dolci? Caffè?" she asked.

"No, grazie," said Shamus.

"Do you have espresso?" asked Will.

"Certo," replied the waitress. She managed a smile and turned away.

"Delicious," said Will before she was out of earshot.

Shamus pretended he hadn't heard.

"Remember Granny Maguire's cooking?" he asked Will.

"And you accused me of being all about oral gratification," said Will. "What is this obsession with food?"

"Remember her mashed potatoes?" continued Shamus. "They were so light, when the gravy hit them they kind of collapsed in on themselves."

"They were riced," said Will.

"Riced?" queried Shamus.

"Yes," said Will. "Granny Maguire forced the cooked potatoes through a thing with little holes. It was called a ricer. Strands of potato shot out like long worms."

"When would you have seen that? We were always sitting at the table, hands washed, well before any food was served."

"Well I remember the potato mush spurting out, as clear as a movie in my head. Even though I probably haven't thought about it since I was little."

At that point, the waitress arrived with Will's espresso.

"Wonderful. Marvellous," said Will and grinned at her.

"Prego," she said and gave Will a winning smile, obviously won over by his effusiveness.

"Hey!" exclaimed Shamus, startling Will. "You must remember that potato ricer business from when you lived at Granny Maguire's when you were a toddler. Which means you had an early memory. Good for you!"

"Don't be so bloody condescending," said Will. But he was smiling, obviously pleased with himself. "Now if I could only remember what that sodding cigarette case reminds me of. I'm sure it has something to do with learning the alphabet."

ENGLAND

Tuesday, August 13, 1940

As Edith, Mrs. Maguire, and Liam were eating breakfast, the BBC announced on the wireless that "man-less" German parachutes had descended on Scotland. Nobody at the breakfast table reacted to the news. Liam scraped a meagre layer of butter onto a piece of toast and helped himself to a teaspoon-sized dollop of marmalade. Mrs. Maguire scooped the last sliver of egg white from inside a hard-boiled egg, her first in a week, and left the spoon in her mouth, savouring the egg until the last morsel had dissolved. Edith shifted in her chair in a futile attempt to escape the backache and leg cramps that plagued her in her final month of pregnancy.

The visit to the tent camp to see Carlo and Domenico had exhausted Edith. She slept for twelve hours that night, only interrupted once or twice by stumbling to the lavatory. It was her last sleep of any considerable length; her bulk and frequent kicks from her baby meant that catnaps were soon about all she could manage, despite her fatigue.

Regardless of her recounting of Domenico's story to Liam and Mrs. Maguire, Liam had still insisted that the deportation was necessary. When Edith and Liam had started to argue, Mrs. Maguire had made it quite clear she wouldn't tolerate any more discussion on the subject. When Liam had been stupid enough to make a remark similar to the one he'd made to Edith about the men being "just a bunch of Italian peasants," Mrs. Maguire smacked him around the head and sent him to his bedroom, where she made him remain for the rest of the day. Liam had been uncharacteristically quiet ever since; barely a word had passed between him and Edith for more than a month. Mrs. Maguire seemed resignedly content with the lack of interaction between them, making no attempt to mend fences between her son and daughter-in-law.

Edith found a relatively comfortable position at the breakfast table and sipped her cup of hot milk and honey, Mrs. Maguire's home remedy for heartburn. Edith couldn't wait to have the birth of her baby behind her — with no more aches or indigestion, maybe she'd be able to sleep. And she'd be eligible for free milk, part of a scheme recently initiated by the government. Edith couldn't imagine herself suffering from malnutrition, but the authorities obviously considered young mothers and children at risk. She had to admit that rationing, especially meat rationing, was now so extreme that it hardly seemed worth the bother to queue, given the measly amounts to which people were restricted. A week ago, Mrs. Maguire had taken the desperate measure of killing one of the hens. It had fed them for several days, and there was still a small bowl of watery chicken broth left in the pantry.

Edith thought how different their lack of reaction to the morning newscast was to the way they would have behaved a few months before. They would have expressed shock and concern at the report of German parachutes, man-less or otherwise. But the day's news was merely the latest in a constant barrage of information and misinformation. Every day brought fresh figures, often followed by corrections to previous numbers. Recently, the Royal Air Force claimed to have shot down sixty German planes; a few days later, it came to light that the number had actually been thirty-one. Edith had become inured to such bald disclosures. She was more affected by thoughts of what she wasn't being told. Since hearing Carlo's and Domenico's accounts, Edith suspected that every single day of the war, people were being subjected to unspeakable horrors that were either not widely known or never reported.

As far as Edith was concerned, the only thing worth listening to on the wireless was a Sunday night programme called *Postscripts,* which had begun in June. It was simply a man talking, but the opinions he expressed made sense to Edith. With his simple, down-to-earth observations on life on the home front during the war, he transformed Edith's rather hazy thoughts and feelings into distinct ideas. She remembered a recent sentence that struck her as obvious once he'd said it: "In the last few months, it has been hard to find, even among women, many who do not unconsciously regard this war as in some way revolutionary or radical." She was a bit piqued by the "even among women" bit — there must be thousands of women whose lives had been utterly transformed. They were more independent than ever before — liberated, in a sense — and probably much more conscious of the revolutionary nature of the war than most men. But the gist of it struck a chord that reverberated in Edith's head for days.

Edith thought of Carlo constantly, but the lassitude that had set in during these final weeks of her pregnancy ruled out any attempts to visit him again. Nevertheless, she was ravenous for news of him. Edith was immensely grateful to Isobel when she let her read a letter from Carlo that had astonished them all.

He expressed deep disappointment at being separated from Domenico. He'd been sent alone to an internment camp at Woolfall Heath in Huyton, on the fringes of Liverpool. He said the camp housed only Austrians and Germans. Carlo had no idea why Domenico and the other Italians hadn't been sent with him, but he reassured Isobel about conditions. He described the unoccupied council houses that made up the camp as being palatial compared to Warth Mills. He begged Isobel to look after herself and not to worry. And finally, he asked her to give his love to Anna and to say hello to Edith and Mrs. Maguire.

The thought flitted briefly across Edith's mind to try to visit him, but the inertia that gripped her stifled the idea before it was fully formed. Whatever energy she had she knew she must invest in herself and the imminent birth of her baby. Carlo seemed safe enough for now. And he obviously didn't have a clue that Domenico had been loaded onto another ship.

Bob MacDonald had brought the news in person. He phoned Isobel on the Wednesday evening after Edith and Anna's visit to Arrow Park to announce he was coming to visit the next day. Bob told Isobel he was bringing some cans of fruit he'd acquired at the docks, but this sounded to Edith like a flimsy excuse. It was a Thursday — Bob should surely be working. Edith was convinced he must have an ulterior motive for this hasty visit, so she made a point of being at the bungalow next door around the time he was due to arrive.

Bob broke the news as soon as he crossed the threshold. After he'd said his piece, he stood, head bowed, in the narrow hallway, cradling a bulging paper bag in one arm. Edith watched Anna's face as she tried to comprehend how her son could have been shipped out of the country yet again.

Since then, Anna seemed to have found a reason to carry on in caring for Isobel. She washed and dressed her daughter-in-law each day and did all she could to keep the spirits of both of them up. Anna and Mrs. Maguire set forth on forays to Shrimpley village to glean what they could in the way of food. Despite what had befallen her husband and sons, Anna seemed not to harbour any grudge toward the British. She saw no connection whatsoever between her neighbours and the policymakers in Whitehall who were responsible for her troubles. She became even more of a friend to Mrs. Maguire. Edith realized that despite their cultural differences, the two women had much in common. They'd both experienced hard times before the war, struggling to feed and clothe their families, and now they shared widowhood as well as motherhood. It became clear to Edith that their differences had become insignificant compared to the experiences they had in common.

Mrs. Maguire helped Anna dig up part of the lawn in front of the Baccanellos' bungalow. Together, they planted some tomato and Brussels sprout seedlings that Anna had coaxed from the farmer down the lane. It was too late in the year for seeds, but Anna put in potatoes, which were already sprouting vigorously thanks to her diligence with the watering can. Occasionally, Anna would succumb to a bout of grief and start crying unexpectedly. Mrs. Maguire, knowing from first-hand experience how it felt, did her best to comfort her friend. It occurred to Edith that there was something rather unfair about being widowed by a war. With so many dying at the same time, a widow's experience wasn't given the same consideration or value. And there seemed to be an unspoken belief that when someone in the prime of life died fighting a war, the loss was less wasteful, which seemed laughable to Edith.

"But the young officer at the tents, he promised," insisted Anna when she heard the news from Bob of Domenico's forced departure from England. "He swore, the word of an officer and a gentleman."

Edith noticed dark rings around Anna's eyes. In less than a month, lines had formed on her forehead and around her mouth. Edith could clearly see the ravages of grief and wondered how many more layers of distress Anna could withstand.

"That must have been the young officer at the dock," said Bob. "He didn't seem to know where to put himself. He came up to me and asked if I was family — I suppose he'd seen me talking to Domenico. I told him I was just a friend, but he kept telling me how sorry he was. He was really cut up, pale as a sheet and close to tears."

"Yes, an officer and a gentleman," repeated Anna, clinging to this straw of a memory of the young lieutenant's promise at the camp in Arrow Park. Edith could see in her mind's eye his pink face and pale blue eyes. The lieutenant's naïve countenance had been a blank canvas, and Edith couldn't help hoping that a few wounds of disillusionment had marked him. "He was just a foolish boy who didn't know any better," she murmured to Anna. But then the thought occurred to her that he might have had something to do with Carlo's staying behind in England. Edith wondered if she was underestimating the young lieutenant.

When Bob stood up to leave, he asked if Edith could walk a little way with him along Sandy Lane toward the bus stop.

"We'll have to take it slowly, I'm afraid," she said. "I feel as if my legs aren't joined to my hips any more. And my balance is a little off; I feel like I'm tipsy most of the time. I can only walk at a snail's pace."

"That's all right," said Bob, "There's half an hour or more before the bus is due."

They walked in silence for a while, dodging puddles that littered the lane until they were out of earshot from the house.

"I had to come and tell Anna face to face," said Bob. "It didn't seem right to tell her over the phone."

"It was very good of you," said Edith.

"The devil of it is, I can't help feeling guilty about what's happened to Johnny and his boys," Bob said. "As though it was my fault the government did what they did." They entered the shadow of a copse of dripping conifers. Underfoot, Edith could feel the softness of soggy pine needles and she smelled the sharp scent of pine resin.

"I know what you mean," Edith said. "It doesn't seem right that we're getting off scot-free when they've had to suffer so much."

"It's those ministry bastards in London who ought to be feeling guilty, not us. Excuse my French," said Bob. They reached a break in the hedge through which Edith could see the estuary, grey and hazy. They stopped there for a minute for Edith to rest.

"At least I spared Anna the worst of it," Bob announced. Edith looked at him anxiously. What on earth could be worse than the news of Domenico being deported? Bob took in a breath and began to describe how he was working in the docks when a friend, who knew of his connection to Gianni and his family, told Bob that he'd seen Jewish refugees and prisoners of war waiting to be loaded into a transport ship, the *Dunera*. The man thought he'd also seen Italian internees. Bob had hurried over to the ship hoping against hope that the man was mistaken. But sure enough, almost two hundred Italian internees, all of them survivors from the *Arandora Star,* were waiting in a customs shed to be loaded onto the *Dunera*. It hadn't taken Bob long to find Domenico.

"Domenico didn't say much, but he seemed almost insane with worry," said Bob. Edith remembered the terrified expression in Domenico's eyes when he'd been describing the sinking of the *Arandora Star*. "I fear he's in for a rough voyage," said Bob. "I could see the sentries were a bad lot."

"What do you mean, a bad lot?"

"Before the Italian men were allowed up the gangplank, the sentries made them hand over watches, crucifixes, and chains, anything of value. Some of the older men were forced to hand over their wedding rings. The soldiers were prodding everybody with their rifles, not just the Italians but German internees as well. Real pigs they were.

"One of the men threw a ha'penny coin, which he said was all he had, onto the dock and told the guards they could have it. They told him to pick it up. When he refused, one ugly brute hit him in the kidneys with the butt of his rifle. He still wouldn't do it, so he got another hit. I think the poor chap must have decided enough was enough, because after the second wallop, he picked up the coin."

"I tried to protest. I yelled at them and asked a sergeant who was standing nearby where he'd found these hooligans. Honestly, Edith, they behaved more like criminals than soldiers. Definitely not what you'd expect from the British Army. I swear they'd been pulled out of some prison somewhere. But the sergeant was just as bad — he told me to mind my own business.

"I watched until all the Italians were loaded. Fortunately, they didn't give Domenico too much of a hard time, but he was limping badly. His foot was bandaged."

Edith remembered the wound on Domenico's foot and hoped it hadn't become infected. He'd be in real trouble if that were the case, on a voyage of God knows how long on a ship with little likelihood of proper medical attention.

"Then the Jewish refugees started boarding," continued Bob. "Compared to the Italians, they were well-dressed, and many carried expensive leather suitcases. They were treated with a bit more respect, but I just knew from the way the soldiers were eyeing their suitcases that those poor refugees weren't going to be able to hang onto them once the ship left port."

As Bob and Edith reached the end of Sandy Lane, a bus hove into view, labouring its way up the hill from the beach.

"I'd hug you goodbye, but I'm afraid of crushing the baby," said Bob. Edith felt a mixture of relief and disappointment. Only a couple of months ago, she'd have been mortified if Bob — or anyone else — had tried to hug her in public. Such displays were frowned on in her family. But Edith liked to think she'd overcome such inhibitions. She kissed Bob fondly on the cheek before he stepped onto the bus. Nevertheless, Edith found it difficult to ignore a lady in a straw hat who stared at them disapprovingly from the front seat.

As Edith slowly made her way home along the lane, the sky darkened and the wind picked up. Edith hoped Domenico's ship hadn't encountered any storms, or torpedoes. She hoped, too, that Bob was mistaken about the sentries and that his journey would be fast and uneventful, and that his foot would heal without incident. It felt odd not to have the faintest idea where he was bound, or for how long. He wasn't dead, but it felt as though he was irretrievably lost nonetheless.

As Will sipped his espresso, Shamus admired the expansive Campo Santa Margherita. The large, open area was more rectangular than square and two to three hundred metres long. The two brothers were sitting at the north end, which was defined by the pink stucco walls of an old church. Shamus had his back to a niche that held a pale statue of a slender woman standing on a dragon's corpse. To his right were a collection of busy shops, bustling bakeries, and small cafés on the street level of ancient three- and four-storey buildings with shutters of various colours at every window. To his left was a stretch of more substantial stone edifices that housed restaurants or hotels. Some boasted gracefully arched windows on their upper floors. They looked rather grand to Shamus, and he wondered if they had once been palazzi. It seemed one couldn't move in Venice without stumbling across some palace or another. A handful of trees were scattered about their end of the campo, leaves drooping languorously as a consequence of a long hot summer. The golden brilliance of late September afternoon sun rendered the whole square monochromatic in a blazing tone of egg yolk yellow.

"I hesitate to bring this up, but do you remember my problem with the alphabet?" Will asked.

"Now that you mention it, I do seem to remember something about your having trouble with reading or something. Didn't Joe used to tease you about it?"

"Yes he did, the prick. The thing was that when I recited the alphabet, I always got the C and the B reversed. I swear Joe used to ask me straight-faced to say the alphabet just so he could make fun of me. And I fell for it every time."

"A-C-B-D?" queried Shamus. "Instead of A-B-C-D?"

"Exactly. To this day, I have to think about it. And that cigarette case of Armando's reminded me of it."

"The initials, you mean?"

"Yes," said Will, forehead creased.

"Well they would, wouldn't they? C.B. Why were you hesitant to bring up your reading problems?"

"Oh," said Will, shaking his head and unfurrowing his brow as though yanking his attention away from another thought to concentrate on Shamus's question. "My childhood dyslexia serves as another reminder of your superior intellect. Four A-levels, all A's. First-class honours, blah, blah, blah." Then Will swivelled swiftly in his seat, peering about for the waitress.

Shamus was dumbfounded by his brother actually voicing any envy about his academic achievements. Shamus remembered how uncomfortable he'd felt when Joe used to hold him up as a shining example to Will — as their father often did — of completed homework, high marks, or exams passed. "Brown-noser," Will would snarl in Shamus's ear, spit flying. Shamus didn't blame Will for harbouring some resentment, but he was surprised that his brother would ever admit to being envious.

"You're easily as clever as I am," Shamus contended hotly — because he meant it.

"Don't humour me," snapped Will. Having attracted the waitress's attention, he signalled her for the bill.

"I'm not humouring you," Shamus insisted. "Nobody makes the kind of money you've made unless they're bloody sharp. What did first-class honours in English lit. get me? I'll be lucky if I don't go blind soon from years of twelve-hour days proofing books. And I've always earned a pittance, with no prospect of a pension. How clever is that?"

"You don't have a pension plan?" questioned Will. "That *is* stupid of you."

They settled the bill and waved goodbye to the waitress, who cheerily called out "*Arrivederci*" as though they were her new best friends. Amazing the difference in her attitude, once she'd realized they were pals of Armando's, thought Shamus.

The brothers decided to wander over to the Peggy Guggenheim Collection, which was housed in a building on the Dorsoduro side of the Grand Canal.

As they manoeuvred the twists and turns, looking for signs to the Accademia, which was en route to the Guggenheim, Shamus thought again about Will's lack of early memory. It struck him as odd that Will had no memory whatsoever of his infant years — in particular about living at Granny Maguire's as a small child. Will had only just reached school age when he left, but most people had some memory of early childhood. Shamus recalled a number of events from his infancy perfectly clearly. For instance, he remembered going with the local Labour Club to see a display of ornamental lights in Blackpool when he was three, and how fascinated he was by all the colours.

Once they entered the palazzo, Will and Shamus lost each other in the series of small rooms that succeeded one another throughout the length of the building. Shamus was overwhelmed by the succession of works that plastered every surface, which seemed to him to constitute a whirlwind tour of every modern art movement known. He pushed his way through the crowd to the doors that led to the front of the palazzo. Once outside, he descended the few steps down to the small terrace that jutted into the Grand Canal and leaned against its cream-coloured stone balustrade.

"*Ciao, caro,*" Will's voice floated from behind him, thinly disguised by an effeminate lisp. He rested his hand on Shamus's shoulder. "Did you think I was a handsome gondolier come to carry you off to his casa on some distant island?" asked Will.

"Yeah, sure," said Shamus.

"I don't think I've ever been out here before," said Will, looking around. "This stone is amazing. Look at the way the light reflects off the water onto the walls." The surface of the building, the colour of ivory, was alive with fluttering ellipses of reflected sunlight bouncing off ripples that lapped at the base of the façade.

"The building looks a bit incongruous — too modern," said Shamus.

"You know, it's a half-built 18th-century palazzo," said Will. "The original owners ran out of money or something. That's why it's only one floor; it was never finished. Peggy probably picked it up for a song."

"I had no idea," said Shamus. "I don't know if it's the association with an American, but I think the place looks like it would be more at home in California, or Texas. Maybe that's why Peggy liked it." "You think?" said Will, looking sceptical. "She wanted a little bit of the good old U.S. of A. on the Grand Canal?"

He leaned over the stone balustrade and looked up and down the busy waterway. Crowded vaporettos plied their way back and forth, surrounded by a host of smaller craft from spiffy, chrome-laden launches to battered tin tubs with tiny outboard engines. A gondola drifted sedately past packed with a cargo of five or six camera-toting tourists, crammed into the cushioned interior like anchovies in a plush-lined can.

"Without giving it much thought, what book first comes to mind?" Shamus suddenly asked Will.

"Has this got anything to do with our previous conversation about your *Coronation Street* addiction?" asked Will. "Some kind of pop culture quiz, perhaps?"

"Come on," urged Shamus. "Just answer the question."

"I don't know," muttered Will. Then, with a note of desperation, "*The Odyssey.*"

"Close, but no cigar," said Shamus.

"Well what book should I have thought of?" asked Will.

"*Wind in the Willows,* of course," crowed Shamus.

"Oh of course," groaned Will, slapping his forehead in a sarcastic gesture. "It's so obvious — furry animals running around the English countryside. What could be more relevant?"

Shamus defended the relevance of the book by reminding Will of Ratty's favourite occupation, "messing about in boats." Will groaned.

"*Wind in the Willows* is the first book I remember," continued Shamus. "Edith read it to me at Granny Maguire's one summer."

"Actually, I remember it being read to me at Granny Maguire's too," said Will. "I think there was a copy lying around her house. I don't think it was Edith or Granny Maguire, though. I think it was a man."

"Uncle Liam?" asked Shamus, willing his brother to remember.

"God no. I doubt if he was interested in me. He was no more than a kid himself at the time."

"It couldn't have been Joe!" said Shamus, sceptically. "He'd have been away at war still."

"No," said Will, shaking his head thoughtfully.

"Who, then?" asked Shamus.

"I don't know, maybe a neighbour. I seem to remember somebody or other being in and out of Granny Maguire's when I was little," said Will, with a sigh of exasperation. "But I have to admit I'm very fond of Ratty, Toad, and the gang. Have you ever read it since?"

Shamus told Will that he'd studied it for a whole term at school. "It's allegorical, of course. You know the interpretation, don't you?" questioned Shamus.

"No, but I'm sure you're going to tell me," said Will.

"The story is symbolic of the social struggle that was beginning at the time when Grahame wrote it," Shamus explained. "He was wistful for the genteel country life he'd known as a child and concerned that a noisy, common way of life, as embodied by the stoats and weasels, was overwhelming a more reflective and considerate society, represented by Badger, Mole, and Ratty."

"You're such a poser," said Will scathingly. "You even talk like a literary journal. It's just a stupid kid's book, for God's sake."

Shamus swallowed as anger mounted in his throat, as scalding as heartburn. His abdomen was as tight as a drum. Sometimes Will infuriated him to the point where he couldn't think straight. But Shamus had long ago resolved not to let it bother him, just as he'd decided there was no point in reacting to their father's narrow-minded attitudes and parochial opinions all the years he was growing up. He'd witnessed too many rancorous battles between Will and Joe to want to fight. Still, a part of him longed to rage at Will now — as he'd sometimes itched to express his fury to his father. He'd love to tell Will how much he sometimes resembled Joe, even though he was well aware it would be the ultimate insult; there'd be no going back if Shamus crossed that particular line.

"Sorry," he muttered instead.

"Canadian!" exclaimed Will in an exasperated tone.

Would he rather I yelled at him, wondered Shamus, absently rubbing his rigid abdominal muscles.

"Look," said Will, "I know I'm sometimes . . . complicated, and you can't help being an uptight, pretentious little prick."

Shamus stared at Will, panic-stricken. The last thing he wanted was a row in public, or anywhere, come to that.

"Just joking," said Will and turned away, leaving Shamus nauseous, but relieved.

Once they'd exited the confines of the palazzo and left the dizzying collection of modern art behind them, the brothers walked aimlessly without uttering a word until they found themselves on a canal-side walk that ran the length of the Rio di San Trovaso, not far from the gondola builders at the boatyard they'd seen earlier that day. Will sat himself down on a low wall. Though still shaken by Will's outburst — despite his brother's claim that he hadn't been serious — Shamus sat down next to him. Small boats were moored up and down the narrow Rio di San Trovaso. Directly across from the brothers, an old man sat on a wooden dining chair in the sun outside his front door. An older woman, a neighbour perhaps, stopped to chat.

"It's just that you sometimes bring out the worst in me," said Will eventually, in that particular low register that Shamus recognized as an indication of sincerity. "To be honest, there are moments when I suspect myself of inheriting some of Joe's less attractive characteristics."

Shamus's initial reaction was to blurt out to Will what a coincidence it was that he'd been thinking the exact same thing. But his usual reticence, combined with the gravity of Will's confession, restrained him.

"Mary tried to make me feel guilty, telling me I was behaving like her father. And I suppose at times I was overbearing and selfish. But it takes two to tango," Will finished in a fierce voice. "Anyway," he added in a more even tone, "the effect was that I began to wonder if I wasn't turning into *our* father — not hers."

"Couldn't you stop yourself," suggested Shamus, "if you were aware of it?"

"Easier said than done. And even if I had, Mary wouldn't have seen it," said Will. "By then, she was off on her radical feminist rant. It was the '80s, and everybody in England was screwed up or screwed over. You wouldn't know — you were off in cotton wool Canada."

Shamus decided not to defend his home of thirty years.

"You've no idea how polarized everybody became in Britain," continued Will. "Everything was politicized. When Mary lost her job at the museum, she believed it was a right-wing male conspiracy, when as far as I could see it was just a cost-cutting measure. Admittedly, the whole affair was badly handled — people weren't very considerate in those days — but it really was simply a question of economics. Then, when I wasn't as sympathetic as she thought I should be, she began to believe I was part of the conspiracy. I sometimes think it was too bad that Thatcher escaped Brighton."

"Brighton?" questioned Shamus.

"The bombing at the Tory conference," explained Will.

"I don't think Margaret Thatcher's demise would have saved your marriage," said Shamus.

"I'm not so sure," muttered Will.

"I've often wondered what happened with you and Mary," said Shamus. "You two were all over each other during the early years. I find it hard to believe that all that affection just evaporated."

"It didn't happen overnight. The four or five years you witnessed before you fled to the colonies were the best of it," said Will. "A dozen or more hellish years later, those early years were obliterated. And once they were, there was no going back. Too much history, as they say."

Shamus was touched by Will's heartfelt description of the failure of his marriage. Will hadn't been so forthcoming for years — not since he and Will had lived together in London.

"Maybe Joe and Edith had the right idea," said Will.

"Now you're going too far," said Shamus, astonished by any acknowledgement from Will, no matter how tentative, that their parents' marriage might have had a positive slant.

"Seriously," asserted Will. "Remember Edith's rule, 'No politics or religion at the table'? I'm sure that was the way they operated all the time. Not just in the dining room but the living room, the bedroom, every nook and cranny of their marriage."

"It never worked with you when we were growing up, did it?" said Shamus.

"Well they got up my nose," said Will. "But in retrospect, maybe it would have been better if I hadn't been so argumentative. And I have to admit that, a lot of the time, I was being dogmatic just to shake things up. And what good did it do me?"

Shamus glanced at Will. The scuffed-suede quality had reappeared in his brother's blue irises. He thought about their father's rampages — the acrimony and physicality of Joe's rages always seemed out of proportion to any provocation that Will had supplied.

"I think you do yourself a disservice by explaining Joe's tantrums away as reactions to your adolescent rebellion. There was more going on than that," said Shamus.

"What?" asked Will.

"I'm not entirely sure, but you know what they say." Shamus risked a bit of teasing, nudging Will gently with his elbow. "We become more like our parents the older we get."

"Don't start that or I'll have to throw you in the canal," said Will. He took a deep breath and grinned at Shamus. Shamus smiled. His stomach felt less tight.

"Ci vediamo," called the woman to the old man as she disappeared into the house next door. Shamus admired its sun-drenched yellow wall, as luminous as buttercups. He remembered a touchy-feely friend of his in Toronto, Oscar, who was always into the latest therapy. Rolfing, Reike, reflexology: Oscar had tried them all.

Oscar had once told Shamus that true intimacy was only possible through conflict and ensuing resolution. Shamus wasn't usually in the habit of remembering Oscar's pearls of philosophical wisdom. But this nugget of nonsense suddenly popped into his head.

Conflict had certainly been a missing element between him and Luke. Shamus remembered occasions when Luke would push him, challenge him with some kind of controversial statement or mild criticism — not as aggressively as Will but, not unlike his brother, a dig designed to provoke Shamus into reacting. Shamus would instantly clam up rather than respond to Luke's goading. Ironically, the closest they'd ever come to a fight was when Luke once accused him of being the most unsatisfying person to argue with.

Suddenly, staring at the contrast between the variety of golds in the pocked stone of canal walls and the impenetrable shades of green in the placid water below, Shamus realized that the missing element in his and Luke's relationship had been something he'd previously felt quite proud of: disagreement of any kind. Shamus suddenly understood that he'd done everything in his power to avoid any open and obvious dispute between them. A sudden flush of guilt overwhelmed him. Since Luke had died, Shamus had felt regret for sentiments not strongly enough expressed while Luke was alive, but he'd never felt such extreme remorse as was seeping into him now. The revelation that, by never having countenanced any discord, he'd robbed Luke — and himself — of something that might have brought them closer was heartbreaking to contemplate. The knowledge that he could never make amends to Luke pained Shamus so much his eyes smarted.

Shamus tried to shake it off, cursing his friend Oscar for his half-baked theories. But something in his and Will's exchange had led him to this realization — he couldn't dismiss his phobia of conflict as delusional or inconsequential. He was alarmed by a sudden catch in his throat and his inability to stop the tears flooding his eyes. What the hell was wrong with him?

ENGLAND

Saturday, August 17, 1940

Edith was sitting in her usual after-supper spot on the porch. The day had begun sunny and clear, as it had been all month. But around noon, a threadbare blanket of cloud crept in from the west. Edith looked across the estuary. In the subdued light of the cloud-covered evening, everything — the choppy surface of the river, fields, hedges, lawn — was rendered in shades of gunmetal grey with only a hint of their actual hue. The sun had feebly surrendered the sky to a full moon, which Edith glimpsed when it crept from behind patches of mottled cloud.

During the past few weeks, since Carlo's move to Huyton and Domenico's forced departure on the *Dunera*, the four women had lapsed into an uneventful existence of queuing, shopping, watering their precious vegetable garden, cooking, and cleaning, all followed by yet more queuing. Edith was filled with admiration for Isobel's resolve to keep active as she wheeled herself up to the kitchen table to help in the canning of fruit and vegetables, part of the quartet's cooperative efforts at stocking up for winter. Each of the women knew that the others were preoccupied to some extent with grief for Gianni and Paolo, or with worry about Carlo and Domenico. But there seemed little point in mentioning the men.

Liam had kept up his sulky behaviour. Edith couldn't excuse him for the things he'd said, but she did believe that he'd been unwittingly swept along in the hawkishly patriotic hysteria that had gripped the country, especially in the weeks after Dunkirk. The boy appeared only at mealtimes, when he hardly talked. Afterwards, he helped with the dishes without saying a word, then he disappeared either into his room at night or outside during the day.

Edith wondered if Carlo, in his council-house camp on the other side of the River Mersey, was gazing at the moon as it wavered above the horizon, sometimes disappearing altogether as ragged cloud cover wafted in front of it. Edith wondered too if her husband was watching the same disc of a moon.

Joe was on her mind because a letter had arrived from him that morning. She was relieved to hear that he was in one piece, but she was disquieted by her reaction to receiving the letter. It was disturbing enough to realize she could hardly remember what Joe looked like, but even worse, the letter had prompted her to recall the unpleasant smell of him in their bed the morning after they were married — a stew of sweat, Brylcreem, and stale smoke, accompanied by the slightly putrid scent of unwashed genitalia that wafted from under the sheet when he reached for a packet of cigarettes he'd left on the bedside table. In an effort to remind herself of his features, Edith had studied the silver-framed photograph of Joe that sat on Mrs. Maguire's Welsh dresser. Despite the artificiality of the studio setting — artfully rippled cloth draped the background — the photo was a good likeness. Yet it failed to fix Joe's image in Edith's brain. The nakedness of his freshly shaved cheeks seemed like an untruth when what was more vivid to Edith was the rasp of his sandpaper stubble against her neck.

There were no stamps or return address on the envelope to provide a clue to Joe's whereabouts; all military letters were delivered free, simply marked "On His Majesty's Service." And it was a miracle it had arrived at all. Joe had spelled the name of the house incorrectly — he'd lived there almost all his life; you'd think he'd know how to spell it — but Edith supposed Shambla was near enough and the postman was familiar with the family name. The heavy black lines of the censor obscured much of the letter. Edith was irritated with Joe for writing anything that the censor might find inappropriate; the hidden sentences were so tantalizing. By comparison to what she imagined they might divulge, the rest of the letter seemed boring. Joe complained a lot about bad food — "foreign muck" — and the fact that there was a shortage of water for a bath. Edith tried, but she found it difficult to worry about her husband, far away from home in some distant and unknown corner of the world, perhaps in danger. Guilty about her lack of concern for her husband, she tried to persuade herself that she was only being sensible — it was pointless to worry over a situation she could do nothing about. The thought that Joe might be staring at the very same moon that she could see hovering above the estuary discomfited Edith. Then it dawned on her that the moon might be in different phases in different places. Edith didn't have a clue whether Joe was on the other side of the world or the other side of the Channel, but her unease was absurdly assuaged by the dubious theory that the moon Joe was looking at probably looked completely different from the one she could see.

Mrs. Maguire's porch wasn't exactly sheltered, and now that night had fallen, Edith was chilly despite the protection of a woollen cardigan belonging to her powder blue twin set. Edith supposed it would be wise to go inside. The last thing she wanted was to catch a cold before the birth of her baby.

Just as she was about to pull herself out of the wicker chair, the air raid siren began its low moan. For a split second, Edith thought it was wind in the firs, but as the wail built toward its climax, howling across the heath from Shrimpley village like a hundred over-amplified harmonicas, she realized its source. There had been quite a few trials over the past few weeks, but they'd always been notified when the air raid siren was to be tested. She didn't remember any warning of a dry run for that evening. Less than a week had gone by since the news that sixty-two people had been killed during an air raid in Croydon, but despite warnings and precautions, it didn't occur to Edith that bombers might be striking as far north and west as Liverpool. Edith assumed that tonight's sounding of the siren was another rehearsal, that she'd simply missed the announcement.

As though to confirm her assumption, the siren's wail diminished, slowly winding down to a faint whine before trailing off completely to reveal normal night sounds of leaves ruffled by the wind and the yelp of a fox up on the heath. She heaved herself out of her chair, but as she turned toward the front door, she heard an unfamiliar noise, a faint drone that seemed to emanate from across the river in Wales. The noise grew louder, sounding like a fleet of not-so-distant tramcars turning in unison, iron wheels grinding against metal rails and approaching fast. By the time Liam dashed out of the house, there was no doubt that the sound was coming from the night sky. Liam stood beside her at the edge of the porch staring intently upwards, obviously straining to see something beyond the scraps of clouds.

"Bombers," he shouted, his voice quivering with excitement at the prospect of a squadron of German aircraft above their heads. Edith turned to find Mrs. Maguire at the open front door. She sensed as much as saw the tautness of her mother-in-law's dim silhouette.

The implication of Liam's word — "bomber" — suddenly became clear. Edith could now discern a laboured, heart-like throbbing of engines that seemed to imply life in the machines above. Later, Edith thought how stupid they'd been to stand on the porch stock still, staring skywards like paralysed rabbits as the bombers passed over.

As quickly as it had grown, the sound diminished as the aircraft moved east beyond the heath and past Shrimpley village. It was obvious they were headed for the River Mersey, whose moonlit surface would guide them to Liverpool. The pulsing grind became a drone, which eventually faded into a silence so complete that it seemed to Edith that her ears were stuffed with cotton wool. The wind had dropped, so even the sound of blowing leaves had subsided, and the engine noise had quieted the foxes, sending them to earth.

"Bugger me," whispered Liam.

The sound of Liam's words broke Edith's illusion of deafness. He was staring at the sky, toward Liverpool. The faint light from the moon made dark sockets of his eyes, and what Edith could see of his cheeks appeared pale and bloodless. He looked, thought Edith, prematurely aged.

"God help them," whispered Mrs. Maguire. Edith, unaware that her mother-in-law had moved from the doorway to stand at her other side, turned to look at her. Like Liam, Mrs. Maguire gazed toward Liverpool, motionless as marble. The three of them stood frozen in the realization that this, finally, was the real thing.

A month before war was declared — difficult for Edith to believe it was only a year ago — she'd watched workmen building an Anderson air raid shelter in her parents' neighbours' back garden on Durning Road in Liverpool. While the neighbours, Mr. and Mrs. Higgins, looked on, the men removed straggling rose bushes and a patch of uneven lawn to dig a square hole about six feet deep — Edith had thought that it looked like two graves shoved together. Several curved sheets of corrugated iron were placed over the hole, and where the iron arcs met at the ridge, they were bolted together with the help of a sturdy metal rail to form a protective roof. The displaced soil, studded with torn sod and uprooted rose bushes, was thrown over the metal covering. Although Mr. and Mrs. Higgins viewed the completed shelter with an expression of smug satisfaction on their plump faces, it seemed to Edith that it offered only damp discomfort with not nearly enough protection. She'd prefer to take her chances in the dryness and warmth of the cupboard under the stairs, despite government warnings that it would offer little help.

Now, standing in the darkness between Liam and Mrs. Maguire, Edith remembered the neighbours' Anderson shelter and its apparent impotence against the onslaught that was surely unfolding less than ten miles away. The shelter might save Mr. and Mrs. Higgins from flying debris, but what if it suffered a direct hit? Edith imagined the corrugated iron roof, twisted and bent, crushing if not piercing the mangled bodies of her old neighbours, their skin and clothes slick with blood and wet clay in their ready-made grave. And what of her parents in the house next door?

At that moment, Edith's baby gave a kick. She mistook the first soft thud deep in her belly as an adrenalin-driven contraction of repulsion at the gory pictures in her mind. But there was no mistaking the urgent thumps that followed — any previous flailing Edith had felt had been nowhere near as persistent. She gasped, all thoughts overrun for a moment by the reality of her baby, suddenly and clearly imagined as a human being with limbs that lashed out. But as the kicking eased a little, thoughts of life and death, the yet-to-be born and the newly dead, crowded Edith's imagination in equal measure and were so dizzyingly vivid that she thought she might faint. She clutched Liam's arm with such intensity that he eventually said, "Ease up, old girl, you're cutting off the circulation." The most he'd spoken to her in almost six weeks. When she didn't respond, he gently uncurled her fingers and slowly guided her, his hand in hers, across the porch and into the house.

The kicks subsided once Edith was settled into Mrs. Maguire's armchair and wrapped in a blanket by Liam, who, of all people, seemed anxious to help. Perhaps he'd mistaken her involuntary gripping of his arm as a sign of reconciliation.

"What we need is a nice hot cup of Horlicks," announced Mrs. Maguire.

"Horlicks, for a deep healing sleep," said Liam, emphasizing in a mock-hypnotic voice the slogan that had appeared in advertisements for Horlicks since the beginning of the blackout.

The sweetness of the malty milk drink usually calmed Edith, and she supposed the manufacturers couldn't be blamed for trying to cash in on the epidemic of insomnia that had resulted from the fear of air raids and general nervousness about the war. Edith would be content if the milky concoction could dispel her fears for Mr. and Mrs. Higgins, not to mention apprehension about her parents' well-being.

Surprisingly, she tumbled into a deep sleep as soon as her head hit her pillow. Her last conscious thought was of the free milk the government was handing out to mothers and children. It wouldn't be long before she could have Horlicks made with the real thing instead of the watery powdered milk they were now forced to use.

* * *

The next morning, Edith awoke feeling different, though everything seemed the same on the surface, Mrs. Maguire cajoling the hens as usual, telling them they'd better not let a few German planes interfere with their laying. In the light of day, the bombers seemed hardly more real than a bad dream, but the imagined repercussions of the raid left a residue of unease in Edith. She felt more alert than usual; her lips tingled slightly; a butterfly or two fluttered in her abdomen. Yet accompanying this amorphous disquiet was a not unpleasant awareness of heightened senses. The sunlight piercing the narrow gap between her curtains seemed more intense than it had the day before. The sliver of sunlit colours glowing on the oriental mat by her bed seemed richer, and the murmuring of the hens outside her open window sounded clearer, their range of notes more interesting. She had to admit to feeling slightly exuberant. She felt, inexplicably, more alive than she had for months, perhaps years.

Edith pushed aside the bedclothes. When she swung her legs over the side of the bed, she remembered that she was pregnant with a baby who was obviously destined for a career in a chorus line, or as a footballer if it was a boy. As she dressed, she smiled at the memory of the baby's furious kicks the night before.

The news from Liverpool about the air raid was disjointed and sketchy, but it seemed bombs had been sprinkled the length and breadth of the city without any apparent logic or plan. A house had been hit here and a warehouse destroyed there, but not in the concentrated onslaught that Edith had envisioned. No deaths were mentioned, but Edith couldn't see how fatalities could have been avoided. She couldn't help but think that the BBC was probably playing it down. When she heard that the RAF had been bombing Berlin at the same time as the Luftwaffe attacked Liverpool, she found it impossible to generate any anger toward the Nazis. Apparently, Churchill had ordered the shelling of the German capital after some bombs had fallen in central London. It seemed to Edith like a senseless game of tit for tat.

Edith tried not to think about Mr. and Mrs. Higgins and their Anderson shelter. She prayed that Huyton, where Carlo was interned, was far enough from the centre of the city not to have been affected. And having hardly thought about her mother and father since she moved to Sandy Lane, she could now think of little else. Despite her father's harshness towards her, Edith was full of concern for her parents' well-being.

Liam had a chum, Alec Simpson, who'd left school at fourteen and travelled to Liverpool every day to work as an office boy at the Cunard Line. Edith decided to ask Liam if he could find out from Alec if there were any accounts of bomb damage in the neighbourhood where her parents lived. Edith could tell Liam was pleased she'd asked — he obviously took it as another sign of the détente between them. The next evening, Liam gave Edith a pretend salute and said, "No bombing to report around Durning Road, Ma'am." Then he smiled sheepishly and said, "Your mum and dad are likely safe and sound — you'll probably hear from them any day now."

ITALY

"Are you crying?" inquired Will.

"No," said Shamus. "Not really."

Will shook his head, frowned, and peered at Shamus, who swatted at a tear trickling down his cheek as if it were nothing more than a bothersome mosquito.

"It's just that I seem to get a bit overemotional lately," Shamus muttered. "For no reason."

"For no reason?" repeated Will.

"No, not really," said Shamus.

"Well you're too old for it to be male menopause," said Will. Shamus sniffed. He pulled out a pocket-size packet of paper handkerchiefs; in the past couple of months, he'd made sure he always had one on hand.

"So what do you think it is?" asked Will.

"I don't know," said Shamus. "It's nothing." He blew his nose loudly.

"Nothing?" Will asked, looking searchingly at Shamus. "Nothing whatsoever to do with having lost your partner of thirty-odd years?"

Shamus knew he'd start sobbing if he breathed. He swallowed hard, held his breath, stood up, and walked away. He let out a gust of air, gulped in more, and held his breath again.

Perhaps he should have listened when his boss suggested at Luke's funeral that Shamus might need "some time."

"I've been mourning ever since we were told it was terminal," Shamus had told his boss, convinced that he needed to keep busy. "And anyway," he added, knowing it would settle any dispute about coming back to the publishing company where he worked, "we're way behind schedule." The six months of solid work that followed — long days of reading manuscripts, reviewing budgets, and checking proofs — had provided Shamus with an ideal excuse not to sort out Luke's belongings. Then he'd found himself in Verona to supervise the printing of a book of photos portraying the Canadian wilderness. In truth, Shamus had literally been in a daze for half a year, almost as if he were running a fever. And now here he was, stumbling around Venice with his brother.

Will caught up with Shamus.

"You okay?" he asked, encircling Shamus's shoulder with one arm.

"Hiccups," Shamus managed to say.

"Right," said Will, letting his arm drop.

They continued along the bank of the canal until they reached a bridge, where they turned to cross Rio di San Trovaso. They stopped in the middle and leaned on the parapet to admire the view along the water towards Giudecca Canal, where they'd had coffee that morning.

"It's hard to believe that all this is built on wooden pilings," said Shamus, eager to draw attention away from himself.

"It isn't," said Will.

"I thought Venice was built on bits of wood hammered into the mud. That's why it's sinking," insisted Shamus.

"Most of it is," allowed Will. "But this bit is said to have a rock foundation, hence its name, Dorsoduro, which literally means 'hard back.'"

"You *have* been swotting, haven't you?" said Shamus. "But all the rest, San Marco and everything else, is built on top of mud, right?"

"So they say," confirmed Will.

"It's weird, isn't it, how people end up in places," said Shamus. "What would possess anyone to start hammering stakes into the middle of a God-forsaken lagoon to build a house?"

"If a horde of marauding Huns was about to sweep into your village to murder you, rape your wife, and set fire to your house, you might be inclined to relocate to an out-of-the-way and inaccessible address, even if it meant putting up with a bit of subsidence and a wet cellar now and again."

"I guess so," acceded Shamus, looking at the cityscape with appreciative eyes. "Still, the building of it must have been a hell of a lot of work, not to mention the upkeep."

"If you're going to escape, you want to make sure that it's to a place where you and your descendants can't be hounded ever again," said Will. "Short of a massive armada, this place would have been pretty much invincible. It was worth the effort."

"I suppose it was easier to be invincible before airplanes," commented Shamus. "There's nowhere to hide now, is there? What with bombers, rocket launchers, and missiles, there's no escape if some power or other wants to obliterate you."

"What a cheery thought," said Will. "Let's check out the church." He nodded toward the San Trovaso church that stood a few yards further along the canal.

The air inside the church felt chilly, and Shamus pulled his jacket around him. Will took the right side and Shamus wandered to the left. He sauntered past some large paintings, stopping to examine a dramatic painting of a horseback rider, and eventually came to where Will stood gazing into a side chapel.

"Check these out — they're incredible," whispered Will.

Shamus looked up at some marble reliefs of angels holding instruments. Each one was beautifully rendered, every face detailed and serene, yet each had its own idiosyncratic features. Eventually, the two brothers turned in unison and walked slowly to the door on the south side of the church.

Once outside, Shamus sat on the low parapet of a nearby wall and lifted his head toward the sun. Will stood next to him and yanked his guidebook out of his jacket pocket.

"Shit, there were a couple of Tintorettos in that church that we missed," exclaimed Will. "Oh well, I'm sure we'll see more; Venice seems to be littered with them."

"Mmmm," murmured Shamus, enjoying the heat of sunlight on his face.

"Hey, listen to this," said Will, studying his book. "Venetian folklore has it that San Trovaso church was the only neutral ground between the Nicolotti and the Castellani." He read aloud: "'The two factions into which the working-class citizens of the city were divided — the former, coming from the west and north of the city, were named after the church of San Nicolò dei Mendicoli, the latter, from the *sestieri* of Dorsoduro, San Marco and Castello, took their name from

San Pietro di Castello. The rivals celebrated intermarriages and other services in this church but are said to have entered and departed by separate doors: the Nicolotti by the door at the traditional west end, the Castellani by the door on the south side.'"

"Seems surprisingly civilized. It doesn't sound like the lines were that clearly drawn after all," said Shamus. "At least when we were growing up, everybody knew who was who."

"What are you talking about?" asked Will, closing his guidebook and settling on the wall next to Shamus.

"Catholics and Protestants," replied Shamus. "Everybody knew who was which."

"Well they never went to the same church like this lot, did they?" said Will. "Not that we made a habit of following people to find out which church they went to. Maybe we should have — I always had trouble telling who was which."

"It wasn't that difficult," said Shamus. "Even if they didn't wear a crucifix, you knew by a person's name or where they lived whether they were Catholic. Sometimes even the most innocuous things were interpreted as a sign of somebody's religious bent. Don't you remember being with Joe that time when he whipped his tie off in the middle of Liverpool on Orangeman's Day?"

"No," said Will. "Is this another of your manufactured memories? False recall, or whatever it's called?"

"I remember because the whole thing was so bizarre. Joe suddenly dodged into a shop doorway, ripped off his tie, and stuffed it into his jacket pocket. It seemed like such an odd thing to do. It wasn't hot or anything."

"I wasn't there," said Will.

"Yes you were; I remember," said Shamus. "Edith asked Joe what he was doing, why he'd taken off his tie. Joe pointed to a parade of Orangemen coming toward us down the street. Bowler hats, orange sashes, the lot. It seems Joe had been wearing a purple tie. He was terrified they'd see it and realize he was Catholic because he was wearing popish colours."

"Popish colours?" repeated Will.

"Purple. It's always associated with the pope and Catholicism," insisted Shamus.

"I know, but a tie, for Christ's sake," sneered Will. "Who'd notice?"

"It's probably just as well he did take it off," said Shamus. "A whole gang of them were playing fifes and drums; they were known as 'kick the pope' bands. They looked pretty rough, and all the worse for a few drinks. I bet a purple tie would have set them off. I remember the loathing on Joe's face as they passed."

"But he wasn't Catholic, not really," said Will. "He never went to church."

"But don't you remember? In his own mind, he was as Catholic as the pope. In those days, I think you had to be one or the other," said Shamus. "Even now, most people assume I'm Catholic. I mean, Shamus Maguire. It's not exactly Hindu, is it?"

"But the Maguire's were originally from Fermanagh in Northern Ireland. We could just as easily be Protestant," said Will.

"You and I know that," said Shamus. "But not many others do."

"This is giving me a headache," said Will, plonking himself down on the parapet next to Shamus.

"What was Luke?" asked Will, stretching his legs out to find a more comfortable sitting position on the stone parapet.

"I presume you're asking about religious denomination," said Shamus.

"Well I wasn't referring to his sexual preference," muttered Will. "That was no secret, was it? Although he didn't look like a fairy, but as cousin Susan once said, you don't look like a homosexual either."

"What does a homosexual look like?" challenged Shamus.

"Politically charged questions like that are very boring," sighed Will, feigning exasperation. "I thought you were over your militant Gay Liberation Front phase."

"Luke's family are good old Scottish Presbyterian," said Shamus. "His great-grandfather came from Aberdeen. And just for the record, I was never in the Gay Liberation Front."

"You went to meetings when you lived in London," Will argued. "When you used to be fun."

Shamus decided to ignore Will's jibe. "I only went once or twice. When I was seeing that older fellow from Glasgow. He was a member."

"Jock the Marxist pederast, I remember him well," said Will. "I liked him. He gave a whole new dimension to the term 'pinko commie.'

You should have stuck with Jock instead of finding a Canadian to whisk you away to God knows where."

"Now that I think about it, Jock couldn't have been more than forty at the time. Everybody seemed ancient when we were in our twenties, didn't they? He and I spent a lot of time in Highgate Cemetery," said Shamus wistfully. "We'd put flowers on Marx's grave every Sunday and then we'd go over to the older section, which was all overgrown, for a bit of slap and tickle in one of the Victorian tombs."

He thought about Will's comment about him being fun when they'd lived together in London. He'd be the first to acknowledge that he'd been more adventurous in those days. But he'd been a lot younger then. And you couldn't be irresponsible forever, could you?

"Did you ever tell Luke about your necrophilic role-playing with a communist in the cemeteries of North London?" asked Will.

"No," said Shamus defensively. "Why would I?" But then he asked himself, why wouldn't I? He daren't answer for fear of following the identical train of thought about conflict and intimacy that had led him to such a guilt-ridden conclusion just half an hour earlier. The last thing he wanted was for Will to catch him crying again.

"Was there a church service when Luke died?" asked Will.

"Yes," said Shamus. "His mother wanted one, and I went along with it."

"I'm sorry I wasn't there," murmured Will, looking down at his feet.

"Don't be," said Shamus. "It was a dour affair. Luke would have hated it."

"I suppose such occasions are important for the living," said Will, turning his head to look at Shamus. "Cathartic ritual and all that, but the only funerals I've ever been to were depressing affairs."

"Well they're not supposed to be a laugh a minute, are they?" said Shamus.

"Why not?" asked Will in a belligerent tone of voice that reminded Shamus of their adolescence.

Shamus raised his hands instinctively in a pacifying gesture. "I guess they can be therapeutic," he conceded. "Now I think about it, Luke's funeral did serve as a kind of punctuation mark — a comma of farewell in a long paragraph of separation."

"Do you work in publishing, by any chance?" asked Will. "That's quite the metaphor."

"That's what it feels like," said Shamus. "An ever-widening black hole of a separation. And some days, I feel like there's a little more distance than the previous day and I panic and desperately pull things out of my memory — a detail of Luke's face, his laugh, the way he would perfectly mimic a barking dog — as painful as it is to remember. But I'll grasp at anything to stop becoming distanced. And the irony is that then, of course, I feel the loss, the separation, even more acutely." Shamus leaned back and studied the blank blue Venetian sky. "The prune of a minister at Luke's funeral kept repeating that 'the price we pay for love is grief.' It sounded a bit New Age for the Presbyterians, and it irritated the hell out of me at the time. But afterwards I had to concede that it had an element of truth."

"It sounds suitably gloomy and self-flagellative, if there is such a word," said Will. "The piss-off is that it takes so incredibly long to recover from the pain of it all," he added, so emphatically that Shamus turned to look at him. "But as time goes by, you're bound to feel less anguished, don't you think?" urged Will. "I'm not saying you need to forget Luke altogether. How could you? But like it or not, you'll feel less dire in time. Won't you?"

Will's probing questions represented his brother's first sincere acknowledgment of Shamus's grief. Will's tone was genuinely sympathetic — so much so that Shamus could almost believe Will had experienced something like it himself. His questions were so pointed it was almost as though he were asking as much for his own sake as for Shamus's. A trickle of tenderness for his brother threatened Shamus's composure. He shifted slightly, and in the process his arm brushed Will's shoulder. "I'm sure you're right," Shamus agreed. "It's just hard to believe you can ever be the same again. Even though I knew, after his diagnosis, that Luke would die sooner rather than later . . ." He stopped for a second to breathe away the compulsion to cry. "Death is such an abrupt loss nevertheless."

Shamus took a deep breath and shifted from one buttock to the other. He was glad he'd been able to articulate some of what he felt without sobbing uncontrollably. He glanced at Will, who was gazing along the small canal, looking toward the next bridge. Shamus wondered what wrenching loss his brother might have experienced to render him so empathetic. It couldn't have been the breakdown of his marriage, which must surely have been a slow if inexorable separation — more like continental drift than an abrupt earthquake. Will's brow was furrowed, probably against the sunlight, but he had the appearance of someone deep in concentration. The normal periwinkle blue of his pupils appeared purple within the shade of each eye socket.

"That damned cigarette case has something to do with all this," Will said.

"All what?" asked Shamus.

"All we've talked about. Loss. Happiness. The price for having loved being grief." Will continued vehemently, "I wish I'd never met that bastard, Armando Belli, or seen his stupid uncle's cigarette case."

"Steady on," cautioned Shamus. "No need to get so worked up about it."

"Why not?" demanded Will. "The thing I find so bloody perplexing is that Granny Maguire seems to figure in it all too."

"In all what?"

"This," said Will, furiously tapping one of his temples as if it were a locked door to a vault of memories. "Let's move on, shall we? My bum is as numb as a nun's nasty."

"Yes, you should get out of the sun," said Shamus, pulling himself up from the low parapet of the bridge where they'd been resting. "You're face is looking a little pink. We don't want melanoma, do we?"

"And yours has gone a few shades toward a dago tan, as usual" said Will. "How come you don't burn?"

"Maybe it's the gay gene," said Shamus. "It won't countenance any disfiguring ugliness."

"You wish," said Will, reaching for his guidebook. "Since we missed the Tintorettos in the last church, let's go over to a place near here that has a Tiepolo ceiling. It's not far, see." He showed Shamus the map.

"Okay. Lead on, Macduff," said Shamus. "Although that's a misquote from *Macbeth*, you know. Shakespeare actually wrote, 'Lay on Macduff.'"

"You're such a nerd," said Will. "I bet you still own an anorak don't you?" He gave Shamus a gentle shove to push him in the direction they were headed.

"Yes I do, actually," said Shamus. "But I don't see what's that got to do with a knowledge of Shakespeare."

"Definitely lived too long in Canada," muttered Will to a non-existent third party.

It was still dark when Edith was woken by a cramp in her lower abdomen. Her first drowsy thought was that her period was starting. Then she remembered that she was pregnant, and this was far too severe to be a menstrual cramp. Edith was instantly wide awake. She grabbed the bedside clock. Its luminous face stared back at her. It was almost half past five in the morning.

As Edith padded along the shadowy hall, she wondered if perhaps she was jumping the gun to arouse Mrs. Maguire. But she was so at sea, not knowing the first thing about what was supposed to happen. Dr. Parry had given her a booklet called *What Expectant Mothers Can Expect*, which gave hints about maternity wear and warned about varicose veins but told her precious little about actually giving birth. She felt a little wave of panic at this first suggestion of the menacing pain of childbirth as she raised her hand to knock gently on her mother-in-law's door.

"You go back to bed, love," said Mrs. Maguire as she slid her feet into her slippers. "It'll be a while yet, and you need to save your strength. I'll make us a nice cup of tea."

As Edith slid between the sheets, still pleasantly warm, she was filled with gratitude toward her mother-in-law. She felt tearful. She thought of her own mother and wondered how she'd coped when Edith was born. Edith's parents had been much on her mind since the nightly air raids on Liverpool had begun two weeks earlier.

The Maguires' initial disbelief at the sound of German planes overhead had been replaced on subsequent evenings by a sense of dread, despite the fact that the bombers were unlikely to target Shrimpley, let alone Sandy Lane, on their way to Liverpool. There seemed little reason for the inhabitants of Shambhala to take shelter. Anyway, it would have been impossible for Edith to fit into the cupboard in the hallway, which was so small it would have been a tight fit for all three of them even if Edith hadn't been pregnant.

The previous evening, they'd been sitting in the living room when the siren moaned into life, Mrs. Maguire installed in her favourite armchair, Liam and Edith at opposite ends of Mrs. Maguire's mammoth couch. Edith was practically immobilized by her bulk — she felt like a whale she'd once seen beached on the sands at Ainsdale when she was seven years old. Despite knowing that the bombers' target was Liverpool and not Shrimpley, they all grew uneasy at the sound of bombers approaching, the now familiar drone of heavy aircraft above the estuary, grinding in their direction. Their bodies were stiff, like bad actors in a stilted play. Mrs. Maguire seemed engrossed in her knitting, needles flying, but her shoulders and neck were rigid with tension. Liam leaned a little too far forward, straining to study the latest *Picture Post* magazine in the dim light, but it was obvious he wasn't taking anything in. Edith found herself staring, eyes unmoving and unblinking, at a smoke-stained firebrick at the back of the empty grate. As the noise of the planes increased, she concentrated on swirls of soot, trying to decide if their shape made the form of a cat or a rabbit.

Once the noise of aircraft engines could no longer be heard and the all-clear siren had ended with a whimper, Liam leaned back in the sofa and Mrs. Maguire's shoulders drooped. Edith tried to find a more comfortable position, but still sought refuge in trying to find shapes in the soot rather than think about what might be happening to her mother and father in Liverpool. And what if the factories in and around Huyton made the area attractive as a target for German bombers? Perhaps Carlo wasn't as safe as she'd believed.

As if in fearful reaction to remembering her misgivings of the previous evening, Edith experienced a second stab of discomfort. When Mrs. Maguire appeared in Edith's bedroom doorway with a cup of tea, Edith was clutching her clock, anticipating another contraction.

"How much longer do you think it'll be?" asked Edith, wondering if the second contraction had been stronger or if she was just imagining it.

"It's hard to tell, love. But I'm sure it'll be a while yet. There's no point in rushing off to the hospital until we're sure," said Mrs. Maguire, gently taking the clock from Edith's hands. Her soothing voice was practically a whisper. "You just rest now, and give me a shout if you need me." Something about Mrs. Maguire's demeanour reminded Edith of sick beds and invalids. The mention of the hospital bed in Birkenhead that Dr. Parry had arranged made her feel even more apprehensive. Rather than heartening Edith, Mrs. Maguire's attempts at reassurance were having the reverse effect. Eager for the comfort of daylight, Edith turned off her bedside lamp and climbed gingerly out of bed to open the blackout curtains. She clambered back into bed and lay through another two contractions, watching through her window as the sun inched its way above some trees at the edge of the heath. Edith's anxiety grew, and by the time Mrs. Maguire appeared with toast and a boiled egg, it was all Edith could do not to express her panic. A walk to the lavatory helped — being upright and ambulatory made her feel more normal. Perhaps she wasn't on death's doorstep after all. But when she noticed specks of blood and mucus in the toilet bowl, her lips tingled with fear. Mrs. Maguire seemed a little vague but was inclined to think a few drops of blood and mucus were normal. Edith tried not to think about it, focusing instead on the glowing tones of morning sunlight that suffused the rooms of the bungalow. Mrs. Maguire insisted that Edith return to bed to eat her egg and toast. When she finished her breakfast, Edith felt slightly nauseated. She lay back, trying to relax.

It wasn't until she heard Anna's voice that Edith realized she'd fallen asleep.

"What you do lying in bed?" demanded Anna from the doorway. "Better you get up, do things."

"Oh I don't know about that," said Mrs. Maguire, peering anxiously at Edith from behind Anna's resolute silhouette.

"Better to move; the baby will come faster. And better!" pronounced Anna. For the rest of the morning, Edith was more active than she'd been for weeks. She was comforted by the warmth of Anna's arm in hers as, at Anna's insistence, they walked up and down the lane. There hadn't been a drop of rain for at least two and a half weeks, not since they'd heard about Domenico's deportation. Puffs of dust settled on their shoes at every step. Anna expounded in lurid detail on the vagaries of childbirth.

"This, what you feel now, is very, very small to what will come. But nothing — not even a man — is as strong as a woman in labour. And God willing, the terrible agony won't continue for too many hours, and then you have not only your child but the most wonderful experience; nobody can take this miracle away from you. I've seen many, many childbirths, and this divine mystery makes me weep with joy every time."

Remarkably, Edith laughed. Despite the graphic picture of pain Anna painted and the fact she was sure her contractions were stronger, Edith was exhilarated. Gulps of cool sea breeze had taken away her nausea and the warmth of the sun on her face invigorated her.

When they returned to the house, Mrs. Maguire was standing on the porch wringing her hands. She'd used the phone next door to call the hospital in Birkenhead and been told that every bed was occupied; doctors and nurses, including Dr. Parry, were overwhelmed with a flood of critically injured people from bombs that had fallen on their side of the Mersey the night before.

"They promised to send a midwife, but heaven knows when," she moaned.

Edith was determined to stay outside for as long as possible. She sat on the porch for the rest of the afternoon as the baby writhed around inside her. As if practising to swim the English Channel, she thought. The twinges grew into pains, and by teatime, each contraction was only five minutes apart and more painful than the worst cramps she'd ever had. It was becoming uncomfortable to sit — Edith felt a burning, stretching sensation in her rectum.

"I think you'd better come inside," said Mrs. Maguire, hovering around the front door. With Anna's help, Edith struggled to her feet. It was then she felt a snap, like a button popping inside her, and a trickle of liquid quickly became a deluge, soaking the wooden porch they were standing on.

"*Brava,*" shouted Anna, grinning broadly. "*Brava.*"

"Oh dear," exclaimed Mrs. Maguire.

Mrs. Maguire looked aghast when Anna jokingly suggested Edith should come and stand over her drought-stricken potato plants.

Mrs. Maguire stoked the fire to heat the boiler and prepared watercress sandwiches for their tea while Anna ran a warm bath for Edith. Liam wandered in from a day spent puttering around down on the beach. He'd left early that morning after Edith had been ordered back to bed by Mrs. Maguire.

"What's all the fuss about?" he asked.

"Baby coming," said Anna.

"Crikey!" said Liam.

The discomfort of Edith's nether parts was somewhat alleviated by soaking in warm water. After her bath, she crawled, pink and perspiring, onto her bed. Anna pooh-poohed Edith's modest objections and insisted on massaging every inch of the young woman's body, stroking and gently coaxing tight muscles into submission, not relenting, for an hour. By then, Edith's pain dispelled any thoughts she may have had about modesty or embarrassment. She screamed so loudly and with such force that the sound seemed to propel her down a steep, rasping slope of pain. When she hit the bottom, she let out a lusty, porcine grunt that horrified and astonished her. It came unbidden from deep in her abdomen.

"Brava," yelled Anna. "Going quick now. You're doing a good job. *Brava."*

It was only then that Edith noticed Mrs. Maguire's firm grip on one of her hands. She must have come into the bedroom during the last giant contraction.

"Liam, Liam," shouted Anna. The door opened an inch or so and Liam's quavering voice answered from the other side.

"Quickly. Bring honey, teaspoon, and a glass of cold water with just a pinch of salt in it," she demanded. "Maybe not long now," she told Edith. "You have to keep strong and drink a little."

"Why didn't you tell me you knew so much about all of this?" Mrs. Maguire admonished Anna. "And there was I, frantic with worry in case the midwife didn't turn up."

Sensing the two women, both mothers and widows, steadfast on either side of her made Edith's throat tighten. She fought back tears. The next contraction pounced. At first, Edith didn't know if she was crying out with affection for Anna and Mrs. Maguire or from pain.

There was a timid knock on the door and Liam's hands appeared bearing a honey jar and a glass of water. For the next hour or so, as dusk fell outside, Mrs. Maguire fed Edith drops of honey between contractions and Anna gave her sips of water.

But then, when Edith thought it couldn't get any worse, another colossal contraction flung her into such a prolonged scream that she thought she'd faint from lack of air. Edith could have sworn she left her body and looked down at herself, a writhing, screeching mass of flesh, shuddering in pain. Then she was swept back into her body, more aware than ever of each spasmodic muscle and stretched nerve. But this time, after Edith stopped howling, the noise continued, like a high-pitched echo bouncing around the house.

"Air raid!" exclaimed Mrs. Maguire.

"I think I see something," Anna shouted over the sound of the siren. "Come, feel your baby," she said. She took Edith's hand and placed it directly onto the crown of the baby's head. Edith could feel the sticky hardness of a tiny, slimy-haired skull. As she geared up to another contraction, the siren moaned to a halt and the ominous sound of aircraft engines came from the southwest. Within the time it took for her to emerge from another searing shortening of her uterine muscles, the grinding drone of German bombers overhead overpowered all other sounds.

"There must be hundreds of them," cried Mrs. Maguire, looking, terrified, up at the ceiling.

"Now Edith," shouted Anna, "keep breathing. We almost there. Push!"

In her mind, as if from afar, Edith watched the contraction intensify to the accompaniment of the incredible din of the bombers above, like observing the tide race toward her up the estuary. Every fibre of her being wanted to tense up and resist, but on a far shore she could hear Anna urging her on. She took one breath, managing with gargantuan effort to curtail a push and take another breath before bearing down again, another breath, another push, until with a triumphant shriek of sheer ecstasy and supreme relief, she made the final push that sent her baby's warm body slithering out of her into a world of absolute mayhem.

Edith couldn't have said with certainty whether it was the thump of the explosion, the screams of her baby, or the fracturing of glass that she heard first. They inundated the convulsing house in concert, a cacophonous chorus of ear-splitting dimensions. She could have sworn the shaking of the house came some time after the great thud and the shattering, but how could that be? The explosion of the bomb in the lane outside must have rocked the house at the same time as the noise reverberated in her ears. If there had been any time lapse at all, it would have been a fraction of a second between the explosion and the eardrum-piercing sound of glass splintering in every window of the bungalow. They'd never considered taping their windowpanes. Who could have predicted a bomb dropping so far from Liverpool? Edith remembered, like a snippet of slow-motion newsreel, the sight of the black material of the blackout curtains in her bedroom window billowing like a satanic spinnaker as they captured the glass shards that then cascaded to the floor below.

"*Brava, brava,*" Anna shouted triumphantly as the explosion subsided. Occasional fragments of glass still dropped like echoes throughout the house. The baby's cries seemed to grow louder in the gathering quiet of the explosion's aftermath. Anna held up the baby for Edith to see. The red and white, blood-streaked bundle with a gaping mouth, attached to a pulsing, purple snake, was the most extraordinary thing Edith had ever seen.

"*Figlio!* You have a son, Edith. You — you have a grandson," Anna crowed, nodding her head in jubilation at Mrs. Maguire. Both the women's faces glistened, cheeks wet with sweat and tears. Underneath the baby's cries, they could hear dull thumps of more bombs exploding up on the heath. Suddenly, Edith heard Liam bellow from the living room.

"Trigger-happy Hun!" he bawled in an obvious attempt at bravado, but Edith could detect a tremor in his voice. "Shot his load too soon," Liam declaimed, to nobody in particular.

Sunday, September 1, 1940

"All present and correct," pronounced Dr. Parry. "Ten fingers, ten toes, two ears, two eyes, etcetera, etcetera. And he seems to have a particularly healthy larynx."

Edith's baby objected vociferously when the cold metal of the doctor's stethoscope touched the warm skin of his chest. He wasn't shy about articulating discomfort — after he was born, his screams had almost drowned out the all-clear siren. But who could blame him, thought Edith. He'd left the sanctuary of her womb for a terrifying world of deafening explosions and shattering glass.

"I had no idea the little blighters could make so much noise," commented Liam as he helped Mrs. Maguire brush broken windowpanes into jagged mounds. The newborn was only quiet when he latched onto Edith's breast, which he'd done as soon as Anna had dealt with his umbilical cord and cleaned him of blood and the tarry feces of his first bowel movement. Edith was astonished at the intensity with which her son drank. She could hear him swallowing and see his ears wiggling madly.

"What are you going to call him?" asked Dr. Parry.

"William," said Edith, marvelling at the doctor's solicitous bedside manner. If it hadn't been for his pale face and dark-rimmed eyes, she'd never have guessed he'd spent the last two nights and the intervening day attending to air raid victims in the hospital in Birkenhead. She thought it saintly of him to visit her on his way home for some well-earned sleep.

"William Patrick," interjected Mrs. Maguire.

"It's so uplifting to see a new life beginning," said the doctor so earnestly that both Edith and Mrs. Maguire took their eyes off William to glance at him.

"Being his grandmother, I think this is the sweetest baby ever born," said Mrs. Maguire. "But you must have seen hundreds of newborn babies, doctor."

"That's true. But after the last thirty-six hours, I was beginning to wonder what kind of a world . . ." His voice petered out and for a second or two he gazed, unblinking, through Edith's shard-framed bedroom window. His expression reminded Edith of Domenico as he'd stared at the canvas wall of the tent in the camp at Arrow Park during his account of the sinking of the *Arandora Star*. Suddenly, Dr. Parry ground the heels of his palms into his eye sockets. When he dropped his hands he smiled, red-eyed, at Edith.

"Congratulations, Edith, on a very clean birth," he said softly.

"That little tear should heal of its own accord. Keep it clean, and I'll be back to check on you both in a couple of days. In the meantime, I'll make sure the district nurse looks in — although it sounds like you've got your own personal midwife next door. She did a good job with his umbilical cord."

"Yes, I don't know what we'd have done without Mrs. Baccanello. She really saved the day," said Mrs. Maguire.

After cleaning Edith and the baby, Anna and Mrs. Maguire had changed Edith's bed; soiled sheets and towels had lain in a crimson-streaked heap on her bedroom floor like recently flayed animal pelts. "I'll bury this in the garden," Anna had announced, brandishing the afterbirth, which she'd swaddled in a pillowcase. "Then we'll soak laundry with hydrogen peroxide — it takes all the blood away." Edith and Mrs. Maguire had exchanged glances, amazed not only at Anna's encyclopedic knowledge of housekeeping but at the way "hydrogen peroxide" had tripped so easily off her lips.

"Baccanello," commented Dr. Parry. "Is she Italian?"

Edith and Mrs. Maguire tried not to look at each other, and neither of them replied.

"It's just that I had a pregnant Italian patient once. I was very wet behind the ears at the time — turned out she knew more about childbirth than I did," he smiled. "Well, cheerio."

Edith was relieved Dr. Parry hadn't been harbouring anti-Italian sentiments. It wouldn't have surprised her, though. The level of discrimination had increased recently after the press vilified Gracie Fields and her Italian-born husband, Monty Banks, who had fled England for America, taking her fortune with them. Edith didn't blame the popular singer, a northern girl like herself. Who wouldn't escape if they had the resources to do so? But resentment was rife, even among the performer's fans.

As Dr. Parry walked out of her bedroom, Edith noticed a copious spattering of dark blotches on the legs of his trousers where the fabric had been transformed from pale grey to dull maroon. She supposed his doctor's white coat must have protected the rest of his clothing from the worst of the blood as he worked through the night. She tried not to think about the amount of hydrogen peroxide the Birkenhead hospital laundry must be consuming.

The dry weather of August persisted and the first morning of the new month was turning out to be as warm as the hottest days of summer. But September was always unpredictable, and the windows needed mending as soon as possible. Mrs. Maguire sent Liam along the lane to see if one of the farmhands would replace their windowpanes for them. There was no point in asking in Shrimpley village. The doctor had told them that a dozen or so buildings had been damaged by the previous night's batch of prematurely released bombs. Anyone with a glazier's skills would be busy for days.

Having sat down in her armchair for a minute or two while she drank a cup of tea before feeding the hens, Mrs. Maguire's head drooped. She dozed, chin on her chest. William also slept, swaddled on the bed next to Edith. Balmy breezes wafted through empty window frames. The only sound Edith could hear was the cooing of a wood pigeon. What a difference twelve hours made, she thought. The torture of her labour and the impact of the bomb seemed unreal, whereas the new life lying peacefully next to her was so evident and present that she was in danger of being overwhelmed by the fact of it. Perhaps it was true that pain couldn't be accommodated by memory. If pain could be remembered, surely there'd be less of it inflicted, Edith reasoned.

The grumbling of hungry hens could be heard outside her window as they clucked in complaint. Edith thought of Joe. She seemed to recall cursing him once or twice during the worst of her labour pains, laying the blame at his door for the agony she had had to endure. She thought of Carlo. She remembered her alarm at the dry warmth of his palms when he shook her hand on the day they met. It seemed decades instead of months that had passed since then. As she dozed, she imagined showing William to Carlo. She dreamt they were in a barn, hens foraging on the floor. Warm air caressed her face, and she and the baby lay on a nest of straw. Carlo bent over them — a nativity scene.

"Edith, are you decent?" Liam's voice sounded so distant Edith wasn't sure she'd heard correctly until she opened her eyes to see him peering around her bedroom door.

"I didn't want to wake the little monster," he whispered. "I've been instructed by the signora next door to give you this soup and bread."

Liam held out a tray with a bowl covered with a plate to keep its contents warm, a spoon, and two sturdy slices of bread slathered with margarine. Edith hadn't realized she was ravenous.

Liam hovered by the side of the bed, obviously keen to examine the new addition to the family.

"Get a chair and sit down, for heaven's sake," said Edith.

"He's certainly got the Maguire hair, black as coal," said Liam. The baby stirred and was suddenly awake.

"The Maguire eyes too," said Liam.

"Don't get too carried away, Uncle Liam," said Edith. "Most babies have blue eyes to start off with. They often change after a while."

"I'm too young to be an uncle," said Liam.

Too immature, more like, thought Edith. But she saw no point in starting an argument. "Do you want to hold him?" she asked.

"I don't know," said Liam, looking dubious.

"Just make sure you support his head."

"Gosh," said Liam. "He's so warm."

"What did you expect?" asked Edith. "He's not an amphibian, even though he might look a bit like one."

"I think that Anna woman might figure into whatever it is I'm trying to remember," Will announced. "She pops into my head every time I think about Armando."

"Who the hell was Anna?" asked Shamus.

"You may remember her from summer holidays in Shrimpley. She was a friend of Granny Maguire's from during the war, and she always wore black," said Will. "I can't remember her last name. Anna Tobacco or something like that."

Will's obsession with cigarettes and the paraphernalia around smoking was beginning to alarm Shamus.

"Are you sure this is the right way?" he asked, changing the subject as he walked behind Will, trying to moderate his normally long stride to avoid stepping on his brother's heels.

Will and Shamus had left the soothing atmosphere of the canalside *fondamenta* for the shadowy twists and turns of a canyon-like streets so narrow that they were forced to walk in single file. Shamus could have stood with his long arms outstretched and touched the walls on either side of the narrow walkway. The four- or five-storey brick façades that lined the slender street were punctuated every so often by an ancient but sturdy door or a metal-barred window.

"We're heading in more or less the right direction," replied Will, glancing over his shoulder at Shamus. "If we bear right at the next bridge, we should come out roughly where we want to be."

"So we're lost," said Shamus.

"Everybody gets lost in Venice," claimed Will. "But not for long. Just relax — we're on holiday."

"I wouldn't call it a holiday by any stretch of the imagination," said Shamus to the back of Will's head.

The brothers slowed slightly as they passed an open door. Framed at the end of a shadowy corridor was a courtyard suffused with citrus light; Shamus glimpsed lemon-coloured sunshine slanting through lime green leaves. They turned into a street that was wider than the last, and lighter as a consequence. Shamus was able to walk alongside Will. Some of the buildings boasted handkerchief-size front gardens with unruly shrubbery constrained by wrought-iron fences.

"Anna Tobacco was never around for the two weeks Joe came to stay," mused Will.

"Why not?" asked Shamus.

"I don't know. But she only ever visited when we were there without Joe," said Will. "I remember that if she was there, we would eat foreign food."

"Why?" asked Shamus.

"She wasn't English, and she always brought unusual food with her. I quite liked it, but I seem to remember you wouldn't eat it. You were a fussy little bugger."

"I don't remember any of that," said Shamus.

"So where's your perfect recall now, eh?" asked Will, looking smug. "Don't you remember them sitting around talking for hours on end? We'd go out to play all afternoon, on the heath or down at the beach, and when we came back, the three of them would still be yakking away."

"I don't remember any Anna. Edith and Joe never mentioned her," said Shamus, brow furrowed.

"Maybe you don't remember because Edith always drilled into us never to mention Anna to Joe. You were always such a goody two-shoes, you probably erased all memory of her."

"I used to wonder what Edith and Granny Maguire found to talk about for hours on end," commented Shamus, ignoring Will's name-calling. "It was odd how well they got along — they seemed so different. Not to mention the daughter-in-law, mother-in-law thing."

"They had their moments," said Will. "There were some subjects they didn't see eye to eye on."

"Like what?" asked Shamus.

"I remember there was always an atmosphere after Anna Tobacco left. They all got on well enough when they were all together, but after she'd left, Edith and Granny Maguire never talked much. I remember a kind of awkwardness between them."

"Why do you think that was?" demanded Shamus.

"I don't know," said Will, suddenly appearing exasperated. "I can't believe I'm talking about this childhood crap."

At that moment, the street widened into a wide area to the south of Campo Santa Margherita, the opposite end from where the two brothers had eaten lunch.

"Here we are, Santa Maria dei Carmini. Exactly where we want to be," crowed Will, obviously delighted that he'd found their way through labyrinthine streets and alleys to eventually reach the large church that lay to their left. He turned and pointed accusingly at Shamus's broad chest. "Oh ye of little faith," he intoned in a booming voice.

Shamus glanced at a rusty street sign high on a nearby wall. "This is called Rio Terrà something-or-other. I thought *rio* meant river."

"It does," said Will moving into the shade of a nearby building. "But sometimes rivers or canals were filled in and made into streets like this one. I suppose they kept the name."

"I must say, you're a good tour guide," said Shamus.

"I knew I was going to have to keep you distracted. Like I said earlier, I spent the last couple of evenings in Dresden studying a travel guide I bought," said Will.

Shamus had to admit that, as children, when Will was playing the solicitous older brother to Shamus, nobody could have been more supportive or stimulating to a younger sibling. On his good days, Will was often more nurturing than Edith or Joe.

"And Edith's bound to ask loads of difficult questions," continued Will. "Although, knowing her, she's probably spent the last few days terrorizing the local library for every book they have on Venice. She'll probably know more about the place than most Venetians."

Will and Shamus wandered over to a side street on the far side of Rio Terrà Sant'Aponal in search of the entrance to the Scuola Grande dei Carmini. Will pulled his guidebook out of his pocket to check the reference to frescos.

"'On the upper floor is one of the most impressive of Tiepolo's Venetian ceilingscapes,'" he quoted.

"Look," said Shamus, pointing at the awkward English on a sign attached to the door. "This place is 'an 18th-century confraternity HQ.'"

"What the hell's a confraternity?" asked Will.

"It says the Scuola was the meeting place for a group of persons united in common purpose," said Shamus.

"Confraternity is a bit of a misnomer, then, isn't it?" said Will. "They obviously didn't know much about brothers."

Apart from the bored signora who took their entrance fee, the place was deserted.

"We should lie on the floor," urged Will, dropping to his knees. "We'll hurt our necks walking around with our heads bent back."

"What if somebody comes?" asked Shamus.

Nevertheless, he stretched out on his back next to Will. The frisson he felt had more to do with childish excitement at their behaviour than from the chill of marble seeping through the nylon fabric of his jacket. A vast expanse of lofty ceiling paintings filled Shamus's field of vision.

"The angel, or Virgin or whatever she is, looks a bit dour, don't you think?" said Will, his voice echoing around the walls of the airy upper room where they lay.

Shamus barely suppressed an urge to laugh out loud. "She looks as miserable as Edith when you and Joe were going at it hammer and tongs," he said. Something about the feel of the floor under his back, proof of discarded inhibitions, allowed Shamus to succumb to the compulsion to laugh. He didn't hear footsteps on the stairs, nor did he see two women enter the room, both with snowy white hair and clad in black dresses. It wasn't until Will abruptly stood that Shamus turned to see two pairs of sturdy black shoes a few feet from his head. The two signore watched as he too clambered to his feet.

"*Buonasera*," he muttered, blushing.

The two women said nothing. One continued to stare at him while the other turned to a solid wooden table immediately behind her.

"*Ecco qui,*" she said to her companion and reached toward half a dozen hand mirrors with plastic handles, which Shamus and Will had failed to notice, lying on a nearby polished tabletop. "*Prendi lo specchio.*" She handed her friend a mirror and then took one herself.

She looked at the two brothers, took a few steps, stopped, and ostentatiously held the mirror in such a way that it was obvious to them that she could comfortably see the reflection of the decorated ceiling in the mirror's surface. She turned toward Shamus and Will, held their gaze for a second, raked their bodies from head to toe with her eyes, and then, after a disapproving lift of her bushy eyebrows, looked away with a dismissive toss of her head.

Will and Shamus bounded down the interior stairs of the Scuola two at a time, leaving the disapproving signore and their mirrors in the upper hall. The brothers burst out of the building, their pent-up laughter erupting in the fresh air. Shamus clutched Will's arm in gleeful exuberance as they were suddenly surrounded by noisy throngs of students pouring out of classes in neighbouring university buildings. They let themselves be swept along by a crowd of young people, reminding each other between bouts of laughter of their stupidity for not noticing the mirrors and of the expression of utter disdain on the women's faces. It wasn't until Shamus caught a glimpse of himself and his brother in the window of a gelateria — a reflection of two middle-aged men grinning idiotically among gleaming chrome containers of ice cream ranging from mouthwash green pistachio to bright-as-fresh-blood *fragola* — that he realized with a jolt the disparity in age between them and the surrounding students. For five or ten minutes, he'd been in his twenties again — the past thirty years might never have happened.

A tide of chattering youths with the humps of backpacks on their shoulder blades propelled the brothers into Campo Santa Margherita. But the crush of students soon dispersed down side streets and alleys that would take them to the bus and train stations of Piazzale Roma or La Stazione Ferroviaria, leaving Will and Shamus marooned at the edge of the spacious square. A nearby fish vendor packing up his stall threw a bucket of ice onto the grate of a drain, frightening a seagull and a crowd of pigeons that had been loitering, hopeful that a discarded morsel might come their way.

"That was fun," exclaimed Will, flopping down on a nearby bench. "Just like the old days. I don't think I've laughed like that since we lived in Notting Hill."

Dribs and drabs of dawdling students trickled from the direction of the university buildings. A girl and boy walked slowly by, the boy's arm draped around the girl's shoulders while she clasped him around the waist. They looked into each other's eyes, seemingly unaware of where they were walking or the world around them.

"Young love," sighed Will, staring at the couple. But then he added in a relieved tone of voice, "Thank God I'll never go through that again."

"Was it that bad?" asked Shamus, settling on to the bench beside him.

"I'd take the sex any day," said Will. "But you can keep the consequences."

"The consequences being . . .?" questioned Shamus.

"Oh, you know. All the compromises of a relationship — watching movies you don't want to see, feeding people you couldn't care less about, taking your holidays in places you loathe. The list goes on."

"I can't believe it was as bad as all that," said Shamus. "You looked like you were having a fine old time when we all lived in London in the seventies."

"I've told you before, that was just the honeymoon," said Will.

Shamus watched the backs of the young lovers as they wandered away. The girl's head rested on the boy's shoulder, hanks of her thick ebony hair flowing over his back. The fishmonger had finished packing up his stall and he took off towards Campo San Barnaba, whistling loudly and trundling a two-wheeled cart loaded with wooden boxes. The seagull pecked aside fluttering pigeons to probe the melting ice mound for possible remains.

Shamus considered Will's insistence that his relationship with Mary had gone sour so soon. He remembered something Mary had said to him the last time they spoke, not long after she and Will had separated. "All I ever wanted was Will." He hadn't understood her at the time and wasn't sure he did now. But he could believe that a relationship might be chipped away by diverging tastes in things like choice of friends, preference in movies, pick of holiday destinations. He could see how easy it would be to become separated by all that you no longer shared, to one day wake up and wonder what had happened to the person you'd once had so much in common with.

"I'm sorry," said Shamus.

"So am I," sighed Will. "But at least we didn't save the marriage but lose our lives in the process."

"I know you don't mean a double suicide," said Shamus. "So what the hell are you talking about?"

"Oh, you know. Stay together despite everything. Compromise to the point where you both become so diluted you're more like zombies than fully functioning people with normal impulses and fulfilled lives."

"Jesus! How many couples do you know like that?" asked Shamus.

"Edith and Joe, for one," said Will. "At least Mary and I didn't have any children to fuck up, thank God."

"You're a bit hard on Edith and Joe, you know," said Shamus. "They probably considered their lives perfectly fulfilled, no thanks to you."

"You're joking! When did they ever go out? Did you ever know them to even see a movie together? Nobody ever ate with us, not counting the waifs and strays. And Joe and Edith never went on holiday; there were just the two weeks that Joe spent in Shrimpley with us every summer. And they never went away anywhere at all after Granny Maguire sold the house on Sandy Lane. Pathetic!" Will concluded.

"After he bought a car, Joe sometimes went for a drive on a Sunday afternoon," reasoned Shamus.

"Yes, but alone, for Christ's sake," exclaimed Will. "He drove to some park or other and sat and read the newspaper, and then he came home. How sad is that?"

"Edith often got out. It was her pushing Joe that brought them down to see us in London that time, even if it was the visit from hell."

"True," said Will. "I admit she had her moments, but they only serve to show what she might have been if she'd had the guts to dump Joe."

"I don't think women 'dumped' their husbands in those days," said Shamus. "They couldn't afford to, for one thing.

"Stop making excuses for them," said Will.

"I'm not," protested Shamus. He remembered that siding with their parents had always been unthinkable when they were growing up.

Even though he and Will may have been fighting, there was an un-spoken agreement to always show a united front against their mother and father.

"In fact I once complained to Edith about she and Joe not being the ideal parents," said Shamus, eager to illustrate his solidarity by relating one of the rare times he'd challenged their parents.

"What did you say?" asked Will.

"I told her that neither one of them had ever offered any encouragement or support when I wanted to go to university — she'd been totally indifferent and Joe was downright disparaging. She got really huffy and told me to stop whining. She said I'd been well fed and fully clothed, and what more did I want. She went on about our generation blaming their parents for everything, said it was about time we took some responsibility for our own lives. She was so worked up about it I thought I'd better drop the subject altogether."

Will said nothing but stared at the seagull as it foraged among the ice cubes.

"I'm surprised you never said anything to Joe about the way he treated you," said Shamus.

There was an uncomfortable silence. Shamus knew he was pushing the limits, venturing across the border into unacceptable subjects. The silence lengthened until it was broken by the seagull, which, giving up on the pile of rapidly melting ice, took off in a flap of wings. The brothers watched as the bird rose gracefully and wheeled through ninety degrees before disappearing in the direction of the Giudecca Canal. "Sod Joe," said Will eventually, looking back in the direction they'd come from. "What do I care?" he exclaimed and jumped to his feet. "Let's have an ice cream," he suggested and strode off toward the gelateria.

ENGLAND

"It's only a day trip. I'll be back before dark," said Edith. "There's absolutely no danger."

Mrs. Maguire looked askance. "But why do *you* have to go?" she asked.

"Isobel can hardly go, can she?" replied Edith. "And according to Carlo's last letter, a note from her doctor will make all the difference."

"Why can't it be posted to the camp? The Royal Mail is still operating, as far as I know," said Mrs. Maguire.

"The camp commander's letter said that Carlo's release could come sooner if Isobel's inability to care for herself can be substantiated in person by an impartial, non-family member," she repeated carefully.

"You're not exactly impartial, are you?" muttered Mrs. Maguire.

Edith reddened slightly but persevered. "William's milk is in the pantry and I'll be back for the evening feed," she said. She thought it best not to mention that if anything should delay her, there was a tin of baby formula in the kitchen cupboard. Edith had been guiltily considering weaning William when Dr. Parry coincidentally suggested it, explaining that, despite the free milk she now received, her nutrition was poor, given rationing and shortages, and her milk may run out.

"Best to get him on formula as soon as possible, just in case," Dr. Parry had said.

"Nothing can beat mother's milk," retorted Anna.

As a compromise, Anna had taught Edith how to express her milk so the baby would be accustomed to feeding from a bottle if formula should become necessary. William hadn't taken to the idea of a rubber nipple on a glass breast without resistance, but hunger eventually overcame reluctance and Edith was relieved she'd been freed from the constraints of breastfeeding without appearing selfish.

Edith was thankful for a temporary halt in the relentless downpour as she crossed the heath to the bus station in Shrimpley village. After the heat and drought of early autumn, November had brought much-needed rain. According to the *Liverpool Echo,* it was proving to be the second-wettest month of the century.

Her umbrella was tucked into the shopping basket Anna had thrust upon her, though Edith couldn't imagine what foodstuffs Anna could possibly spare to send Carlo in the care package the basket contained. She carried the box containing her gas mask securely strapped across her chest.

Although it wasn't actually raining, the air was so saturated that beads of moisture formed on the shoulders of Edith's mackintosh and cascaded down her arms like tiny ball bearings. The ground was covered with fallen birch leaves, slick and startlingly yellow against the sombre background of wet earth. Dripping fronds of frizzled bracken brushed her ankles. Apart from a couple of trips to Shrimpley village, Edith hadn't left Mrs. Maguire's house since she and Anna had gone to the Arrow Park internment camp in July. Now she felt a mixture of exhilaration, guilt, and exhaustion. After weeks of disturbed nights and busy days — she'd had no idea a baby could be so much work — Edith was determined to make the most of her day of liberation, telling herself that William would be fine. He was almost three months old, and Mrs. Maguire and Anna were perfectly capable of coping with his ear-splitting screams when he was hungry or needed changing. With a doting grandmother and a spirited Italian mama dancing attendance, he wouldn't even notice her absence.

As Edith made her way across the heath, she thought about her parents and sister, who seemed more and more like distant strangers as time went on. Edith's concern for her mother's safety after the massive bombardment on the night of William's birth had only been slightly relieved when she heard that the 161 fires reported had all been in the docks and commercial areas. It seemed the bombers had finally found their mark.

There'd been no response to the telegram Edith had sent from the post office in Shrimpley village telling her parents about the birth of their grandson. So a couple of weeks later, she sent another telegram urging them to telephone Isobel next door and leave a message to say they were safe. Edith's mother and father didn't own a telephone, but there was a public phone box a few yards along Durning Road from their house. After several nights of further bombing and still no word, Edith, in desperation, used Isobel's phone to track down her sister, Agnes, at the farm in Lancashire where she worked for the Land Army. When Edith eventually managed to speak to her, Agnes told her that their parents had left Liverpool in July to stay with their great-aunt Bronwyn in the safety of rural Wales. "Well what was the point of telling you?" asked Edith's sister. "You were safe and sound at the seaside."

"Typical," Edith muttered as she returned the receiver to its cradle a little more forcefully than necessary.

So far, so good, thought Edith as she climbed the stairs of the bus just before it pulled out of Shrimpley bus station. The windows were so fogged up on the inside it was impossible to see out. She remembered again that the last time she caught this particular bus, it was with Anna on the day they went to the tent camp at Arrow Park to visit Carlo and Domenico.

They'd heard from Domenico. A crumpled envelope with a muddy partial footprint on it had fallen through Anna's letterbox. The handwriting that covered three flimsy sheets betrayed Domenico's age — the laborious loops and occasional scratching out reminded Edith of a school exercise book. Isobel, Anna, and Edith took turns anxiously yet eagerly reading the account of his nightmarish voyage aboard the *Dunera*.

Domenico wrote about dysentery, bad food, and ill treatment by British Army guards. He also mentioned his constant fear of a naval attack after a near disaster when the *Dunera* had been fired on and a torpedo glanced its hull. Edith could only imagine how terrifying it must have been for him and the other men who'd experienced the torpedo attack on the *Arandora Star*. But they'd survived the voyage to Australia, and the camp near Melbourne was comfortable and the food plentiful. Domenico's letter continued:

> *There are almost too many rations. And the advantage*
> *of living with a bunch of Italian internees is that some*
> *of the best chefs in England are here. We're eating like*

*kings. And there's hardly been a cloud in the sky since
we arrived. Now that my foot is better, I'm working
in the fields and look more like a sunburnt farm hand
every day. The doctor here tells me I will always have
a bit of a limp, but I suppose I'm lucky not to have lost
my leg.*

Ti amo, Mama. I pray you're safe and well.
Your son, Domenico. "

Edith watched as Anna nodded and smiled at the conclusion of Domenico's letter, and noted how easy it seemed for Anna to put his past suffering out of her mind. If even she could forget so quickly, how much easier would it be for other people to forget, or to sweep all the injustice under the rug once the war was over. Edith was well aware that she was censoring Domenico's account when she chose to tell Liam about his horrific journey with no details about his relatively comfortable life in the Australian camp. She worried that the fact of Domenico's survival, not to mention his apparent recovery, might somehow override the horror of all the Italian men's experiences in Liam's eyes.

Edith wiped away the condensation on the bus window with her sleeve and gazed out at partly flooded fields of fawn-coloured stubble. The abbreviated stalks were barely visible above the rain-spattered surfaces of muddy pools. She thought about the fact that she seemed to have become Bob MacDonald's repository for information too dire for Anna's ears. He'd confided to Edith that when he went to check, he discovered that two of the three Baccanello chip shops had been badly damaged. At first, Edith couldn't imagine why Bob didn't tell Anna. It might come as a bit of a shock, but it would hardly be surprising.

"No, you don't understand," Bob had said. "It wasn't bomb damage. They've been vandalized."

He went on to describe broken windows and a smashed front door. Fittings that hadn't been stolen were damaged, chairs broken. Both tills had been smashed to pieces.

"But the worst of it was the shit, excuse my French, everywhere," he said angrily. "I'd like to get my hands on the hooligan who used it to write on the wall," he growled.

"Write on the wall?" repeated Edith, flabbergasted.

"They took a stick or a spoon or something and wrote 'Nazi Wops,' as plain as if it was paint on a brush," said Bob, eyes glinting with fury. Edith realized that Bob needed to tell someone but wished he hadn't described the disgusting details.

"Did you go to the police?" asked Edith.

"They've got their hands full. What with the blackout and the bombing, there's so much burglary and looting they don't know where to start," he said. "I nailed boards over the windows and doors, but it felt like locking the stable door after the horse had fled."

By the time Edith reached the ferry dock, wavering sheets of torrential rain obscured Liverpool from view like great, grimy net curtains strung across the river. Edith made a beeline for the convivial fug of the ferry's saloon. As the boat eased away from the dock, engines labouring, Edith's leather and wooden seat juddered beneath her. She untied her new headscarf, an old one of Mrs. Maguire's, but good-quality silk nevertheless. Her mother-in-law had given it to Edith more than a month before for her twenty-first birthday. Edith patted her hair and searched in her handbag for her cigarettes and matches.

The day before her birthday, September 15, a lone German bomber had been foiled in his attempt to bomb Buckingham Palace in London. Liam couldn't hide his delight when they heard on the wireless during Edith's birthday tea that the intercepting pilot, Sergeant Ray Holmes, hailed from a village about five miles distant from Shrimpley.

"A local lad," he had crowed. "Rammed the Dornier bomber with his Hurricane and knocked it for six, by the sound of it. Then bailed out and lived to tell the tale."

"You make it sound like something out of a Biggles book," said Edith. She'd never actually read any of the popular series about Major James Bigglesworth, the dashing pilot known as Biggles — they were boys' books — but she was sure they must be idiotically unrealistic.

"How many people were killed when the planes hit the ground, I wonder," mused Mrs. Maguire. It came to light a few days later that there'd been no casualties; all the wreckage had miraculously landed in open areas without anyone being hurt.

Isobel had wondered aloud if Sergeant Holmes's stunt might be a good omen for the outcome of the battle for the air above England, which they were told was raging in the south. According to reports, London had been suffering nightly bombings since early September, and daylight dogfights between Luftwaffe planes and the RAF continued in the skies above the city's roofs. Even before the stirring speech Churchill had given that August — "Never in the field of human conflict was so much owed by so many to so few" — people were only too aware of the likelihood of a German invasion if the British air force were to falter. When Edith had heard the news earlier in November that Neville Chamberlain had succumbed to cancer, she wondered what his thoughts had been as a furious war rampaged in the heavens above his deathbed.

Despite Liam's bellicose outburst about the attempted bombing of Buckingham Palace, the birthday tea that Mrs. Maguire and Anna prepared had been more enjoyable than any Edith had experienced in peacetime. All five of them squeezed around Anna's table and ate toast and sardines with the last of the lettuce and some celery from Mrs. Maguire's garden. William lay swaddled on a nearby couch. Edith was a little dubious about the birthday cake Anna had prepared — it was made with stale bread, of all things. Anna had soaked the crusty bread in some rum she'd found in a cupboard. A week or so earlier, she'd discovered rennet at the grocery shop in Shrimpley village and had been using it to make a kind of runny cream cheese, which she added to the rum-soaked bread together with some of their precious sugar ration and a few tablespoons of undiluted Camp Coffee straight out of the bottle. She topped it off with a modest layer of thick cream she'd wheedled out of the farmer down the lane and a generous sprinkling of cocoa powder.

"This is a much better use of that Camp chicory-syrup rubbish than trying to pretend it's real coffee," said Liam, holding out his plate for a second helping. Edith noticed that any lingering qualms he may have had about consorting with the "enemy" were obviously set aside when it came to dessert.

"Not as good as with Italian coffee," said Anna, shaking her head modestly. "When this war is over, I make you proper."

"But it's delicious," asserted Isobel. "As good as my mother's." Anna couldn't have asked for a higher compliment. The air raid siren had moaned into life halfway through the proceedings. They were silent for its duration. Edith noticed Isobel's hands trembling more than usual. And as the familiar drone of aircraft wafted across the river, Isobel developed a tic in her eyelid. But it wasn't long until the planes passed over, the all-clear siren sounded, and the five of them carried on where they'd left off. "This is by far the best birthday I have ever had," pronounced Edith when they were finished. She hadn't minded at all that there was none of the usual palaver surrounding a twenty-first birthday. She felt far too mature for the traditional custom of being given the "key of the door."

In bed that night, Edith had experienced the same irrational elation she'd felt the morning after they'd first heard bombers overhead. She told herself it must be because of the congeniality of the evening. Or perhaps the news, in the form of the camp commander's letter, that Carlo was safe and well. She definitely felt more relieved knowing her parents were out of harm's way, although she couldn't forgive them for not letting her know that they'd moved out of Liverpool. Or maybe it was merely from the fulfilment she felt as she tucked William into bed beside her. But she wasn't convinced by any of her justifications. Edith was well aware that her euphoria was irrational, even inappropriate.

Edith was jolted from her ruminations by the bump of the ferry as it nudged the floating dock on its arrival in Liverpool. She stubbed out her cigarette with the toe of her shoe, gathered up her basket and gas mask, and made for the door.

When Edith emerged from the enclosed ferry gangway onto the pavement of the Pier Head, she stopped and stared in horror. The face of the city had been hideously transformed. A fifty-yard section of the arched overhead railway that ran the length of the docklands — under which people often sheltered from the rain, hence its nickname, the "dockers' umbrella" — was down, the sturdy iron supports lying higgledy-piggledy on the road below. Tangles of abbreviated rails protruded from the severed ends of sections left standing. The whole mess looked more like a demented roller coaster than a railway. Nearby, she could see a ten-storey building with a multitude of cavernous black holes where windowpanes had once reflected daylight. The dock buildings to her right were transformed into a vast builder's yard littered with heaps of bricks and spiky piles of splintered wood. Several towering cranes that had once neatly lined the dock were reduced to a twisted cat's cradle of steel girders.

Yet the city seemed defiant in the face of such disfiguring adversity. Pedestrians and traffic moved in and around the devastation with a determined air of normalcy. Trams crowded with people arrived and left; a car deftly manoeuvred between debris.

Edith tried her best to match the surrounding stoicism. She scanned the Pier Head for her tram and, having spied it, walked briskly over and climbed aboard. The windows had some kind of fabric, muslin or cheesecloth, stuck to them. Edith supposed it was a precaution against flying glass in case a bomb blew out the tram's windows. A small area of each window, not much larger than a peephole, had been left clear so that travellers could see where they were.

But Edith's bravado soon withered as the tram trundled through bomb-scarred streets and she peered, sick with consternation, through the round section of clear window. She saw yawning gaps where the faces of buildings had been blown away. Her eyes couldn't resist the zigzag imprint of a lost staircase that wound its way up a sheer exposed wall, four storeys high. Each ghostly landing was defined by a different pattern of wallpaper. Edith wondered about the fate of the residents who'd once made their considered choice of wall covering. She thought about their eager anticipation of newly decorated walls, not knowing what was to befall them. The tram picked up speed and rattled past a block of flats. Edith glimpsed gunmetal grey sky through empty window frames where only a sturdy stone façade was left standing. Beyond the smoke-streaked edifice, she could see the remains of the rest of the building: a carnage of flesh-coloured bricks and mangled pipes. Thin strips of wooden lath poked up here and there, reminding her of crooked crosses. For forty minutes, as the tram travelled through Liverpool, evidence of bombing was never out of Edith's sight. As she watched the citizens of the city go about their daily business, seemingly oblivious to the destruction surrounding them, Edith wondered if she could ever achieve their equilibrium.

Eventually, the tram halted at the terminus where Edith must change for the bus that would take her to Huyton and Carlo's internment camp in Woolfall Heath. The city's appearance was so altered that it wasn't until she stepped off the tram that it dawned on her that she was a ten-minute walk from her parents' house on Durning Road, where she'd grown up. She resolved that, if she had time on her return journey, she would take a side trip to see if the house was still standing. But for the moment, she was preoccupied with trying to decide how a disinterested party might behave with the commander of an internment camp.

* * *

When Edith arrived at the double barbed-wire fence that encircled Woolfall Heath housing estate, a guard opened a gate just wide enough for Edith and her basket to squeeze through. Another soldier inspected the few things Anna had sent: a jar of applesauce, a piece of cheese no larger than a packet of cigarettes and a couple of sausages, hard as rock but that Anna maintained were good to chew. The soldier wrinkled his nose at the sausages but eyed the cheese and applesauce hungrily. Edith remembered Bob's description of the guards on the *Dunera* who'd stolen internees' belongings as they embarked, but the soldier handed everything back to Edith without a word.

A brisk young woman in army uniform ushered her into the stuffy interior of an ill-lit wooden hut. A white-haired officer indicated a chair next to an electric heater, with a single bar glowing bright orange, and told Edith to sit and warm herself.

"Baccanello, Carlo. Here we are," said the white-haired officer, leaning across a desk thick with file folders. "His tribunal date is scheduled for December 15," he read from Carlo's file. "Almost certain to be designated a class B," he said, looking up from a sheaf of paper.

"Class B?" questioned Edith.

"Free to go, but restricted in his movements," said the officer. "He'll probably have to report to a police station every so often, that sort of thing."

"It seems too good to be true," said Edith.

"You knew his father and brothers, I presume?" asked the officer.

"Yes," said Edith. "Why weren't they given a tribunal, I wonder."

The officer sighed. "You're not the first to have asked that question," he said. "I'm afraid the answer has been rather swept under the carpet."

"I don't understand," said Edith.

"There was a bit of an inquiry, you know. Chap called Snell, Lord Snell, issued a report."

"About the sinking of the *Arandora Star?*" asked Edith, eager for it to be true.

"Er, not exactly," said the officer awkwardly. "I mean, the sinking prompted the investigation, but Lord Snell has been more concerned with the selection process for Italians. Apparently, he concluded there'd been a bit too much enthusiasm on the part of security forces." He cleared his throat before continuing. "Unfortunately, that's all that was said. And that'll be the end of it, probably. The man in the street doesn't care; he has his own skin to worry about. And Snell's report has been rather overshadowed in Whitehall by the latest wrangle over the rights of internees. I don't mind telling you that conditions in this camp wouldn't meet Geneva Convention standards. I've been hounding HQ for more resources ever since I came here."

Edith said nothing, surprised at how forthcoming he was being. He was obviously frustrated by the situation.

"You know, if you applied the rules they dreamt up for selection of the chaps in this camp, by rights the royal family should have been interned too. They're more German than some internees, actually," he smirked.

Edith felt her cheeks grow hot. "This isn't a joke. It's supposed to be up to people like you to do something! This whole internment thing has been a national disgrace . . . actually." She mimicked the officer's voice when she spoke the last word. Her fingers were trembling; she'd never felt so angry.

"Steady on. I'm not unsympathetic, you know," said the officer, giving her a penetrating look.

Edith took in a calming breath. "Sorry," she said, making an effort to control her emotions. After all, she was supposed to be an impartial witness.

"Here's the letter from Carlo Baccanello's wife's doctor that confirms the diagnosis of multiple sclerosis," Edith said, trying her best to sound efficient and helpful. "And I can attest, as a neighbour, that Mrs. Baccanello desperately needs him to take care of her. Sometimes it's all she can do to struggle from her bed to her wheelchair."

"I'll relay your report to the tribunal and I'm sure Mrs. Baccanello will have her husband back at home to take care of her in no time," said the officer. He stood and extended his hand. Edith was taken aback but accepted the gesture, appreciating that he'd at least made an effort. The officer looked her in the eye and smiled, then peered out of a window. "I think you'll find Baccanello just outside — he was told to expect a visitor."

A few yards from the hut stood Carlo, grinning at the sight of her. He sported a heavy black beard, his hair was tousled, and he wore a ragged khaki jacket. He reminded Edith of gypsies who used to come to her parents' door selling clothespins or "lucky" sprigs of heather. Without hesitation, Carlo strode toward Edith and embraced her, hugging her in such a way that her arms were pinned to her sides. Then he released her and bent to kiss her on both cheeks in quick succession, his beard brushing her face. Edith's cheeks blazed and she wondered if the officer was still looking out of the window, but there was no hint of awkwardness or embarrassment on Carlo's part as he stepped back to gaze at her.

"What a treat," he said. "I was hoping the mystery guest would be you."

"Are we going to stand here all afternoon?" said Edith, glancing toward the officer's hut.

Carlo didn't move. "I can't tell you how happy I am to see you," he beamed. "And so slim. It's hard to believe you were ever pregnant."

"Carlo, I'm pleased to see you too," she said primly, hoping she didn't appear quite as elated as he did, even if she might feel it. "But isn't there somewhere we can go?"

"They told me I could take you to the food hut," he replied. He turned and with a flourish of his arm proclaimed, "Welcome to my estate." They were standing in the centre of a street lined with newly built houses. Had it not been for the double barbed-wire barricade and the towers from which armed soldiers watched, Edith could have believed they were visitors to a spanking new council estate peopled by fortunate Liverpool families who'd managed to escape the slums.

As they made their way to a large hut situated in the middle of one of the side streets, they passed knots of men talking in a language Edith took to be German. "Many of the men are German Jews," explained Carlo. "They managed to get out of Germany in 1938. They tell stories of their shop windows being smashed by soldiers and their stock stolen. German firemen stood by idle while their properties burned. It's ludicrous to think that they'd ever be loyal to any German army. Hugo — he's one of seventeen men in my house — jokes that if Hitler does invade, he'll be delighted to find a barbed-wire pen full of Jews like him ready and waiting to be slaughtered."

Edith winced. She'd read of Jews being killed in Germany for no other reason than that they were Jewish. She might not have believed any nation capable of such a thing were it not for the internment policies she'd seen enforced in England. After all, she reckoned, it wasn't such a huge leap from unwarranted imprisonment to unjustifiable execution.

"Seventeen men in one house?" she questioned.

"Yes, it's a bit of a tight squeeze, but the straw mattresses we sleep on don't take up much room," explained Carlo. "The worst of it is that they commandeered this part of the estate before the builder had installed the boilers. When we want a proper wash, we have to use sinks outside, with water heated by a portable stove."

Carlo ushered Edith into the narrow dining hut, where rows of bare wooden tables crowded each side. Several men sat talking in low voices. Some were reading. One man, head bent and hair falling across his face, was drawing on a page from a newspaper. Edith coughed in the fug of cigarette smoke and coal fumes but welcomed the warmth supplied by a black iron stove that was squeezed between the rows of tables.

After they found a seat, Edith reassured Carlo of Isobel's well-being, describing Anna's expert care. He nodded, and for the first time since she'd arrived, his face was serious. "Poor Isobel. Why is it that the most gentle souls seem to be dealt the worst hands?" he said. Edith, at a loss as to how to respond, reached for Anna's care package.

"You don't know how marvellous this tastes," said Carlo, chewing on one of the sausages Anna had included. "I can't remember the last time I had real food. We rarely get anything better than a piece of salt cod and a slice of bread."

But when Carlo saw the jar of applesauce, his eyes watered and he blinked back tears. "Paolo loved my mother's applesauce," he said in a hoarse whisper. "Remember when we were all in the garden looking at the blossoms and anticipating a bumper harvest of apples? Was it really only a few months ago?" Edith was suddenly thrust back to that sunny spring day, warm air heavy with the scent of blossom. She pictured Paolo and Domenico sprawled on the lawn, giggling.

The last thing Edith wanted to do was to cry, so she was glad of the distraction when the door of the hut opened and a man in his late twenties or early thirties carrying a sheaf of rumpled papers stepped into the room.

"Hugo," cried Carlo. "Come and meet my good friend Edith."

"A sight for sore eyes," said the man in an accented voice as he settled onto the bench next to Carlo.

"You should see his drawings," said Carlo to Edith. *"Bellissimo."*

"Here," said Hugo, pushing his pile of frayed paper across the table in Edith's direction. "It's not often I get the chance to show my masterpieces to a member of the fairer sex."

"Can anyone exhibit their work here?" asked the man who'd been sketching nearby.

"Certainly, Walter," said Hugo. "Come, show our guest what you have."

Walter added a few sheets of newspaper next to Hugo's collection. Some were rippled, the paper distorted by wet paint that was now dry.

The first work that Edith gingerly picked up was a watercolour that depicted the interior of the hut they were sitting in. It was a mealtime and men crowded the tables. Muted colours accurately portrayed the dullness of the tones and the dimness of the light. But what Edith noticed most was the attitude of the men. Shoulders were rounded and slumped. Most supported themselves with an elbow while they ate, head down. It was clear that none of them were talking. Here and there, newsprint showed through the painting, and Edith could make out a headline that proclaimed, "Vitamins Enlisted To Win The War." She wondered if the message had been kept clear of paint as a comment on the internees' poor diet. Another drawing, on a ragged piece of wallpaper obviously torn from a wall, showed a crowd of men standing outdoors, with the barbed-wire barricade and council houses sketched into the background. The men wore hats and coats, hands thrust deep into pockets. The scene was imbued with a sense of apathy, perhaps because it was obvious the men were mute, staring speechless into space. The incomplete figures of some of the men struck Edith as eerie. A pencil line that depicted a leg petered out before it reached a foot, or a wash of colour that filled a body ended raggedly halfway down a man's back. It was as though the men had been purposely rendered as half-people.

"Look, here we are getting clean," said Carlo, pulling out another tattered piece of paper. Men, naked from the waist up, were pictured outdoors at a line of sinks next to a smoking stove. At one side, Edith could make out some pitched tents. The words "Manchester Guardian" could be seen through the paint.

When Carlo moved the drawing aside, Edith could see that a portrait of a man's head lay underneath, painted by Hugo onto a page from a newspaper. The man wore a blue shirt and a red tie. Behind him, a window was roughly sketched, but the man's face and neck were bursting with detail. He was gaunt, with a receding hairline. Tendons and muscles had been rendered so effectively that Edith could feel the tension in his neck and face. The set of his mouth suggested resolute perseverance under duress, but the price paid was revealed in large pouches that hung beneath cynically sorrowful eyes. Edith could hardly look at the face. She could only hold the man's desolate, uncomprehending gaze for a second or two before having to shift her focus to the unpainted newsprint around the portrait itself. An advertisement urging people to buy National War Bonds sat at the top of the page.

Edith had never been so affected by a work of art in her life. "It's very good," she said, without making any effort to look at more of the sketches. She knew her comment was a woeful understatement, but she couldn't begin to describe how the painting made her feel.

"Now you've gone and scared her," said Walter, wagging a finger at Hugo. "It couldn't be a truer representation, though, I'll give you that," he whispered admiringly.

The three men stared at the portrait for a full minute, saying nothing.

"Who is he?" asked Edith.

"Nobody, and everybody," said Hugo.

* * *

It was only half past one when Edith left the camp in Woolfall Heath. If a bus came quickly, there'd be plenty of time to dash over and take a look at her parents' house on Durning Road before catching a tram to the ferry. The thought had no sooner crossed Edith's mind than one of Liverpool's familiar green buses rattled around a bend in the road.

Once settled in her favourite seat upstairs in the front, Edith pulled out the Spam sandwich she'd brought from Shrimpley. She thought of Carlo and his daily portion of salt cod and tried not to think about how weary she'd become of canned luncheon meat. Because Spam wasn't rationed, Mrs. Maguire bought at least three tins a week. Even though there were precious few alternatives, Edith wished the stuff wasn't so readily available.

Edith had told Carlo the good news about the likely outcome of his tribunal.

"With luck, you'll be home before Christmas," she concluded.

"Luck, and all the help you've given me," said Carlo.

"Rubbish," said Edith.

"I don't mind telling you, it's hard to keep our spirits up," Carlo said in a low voice. "So many of us are sick. And there's been a couple of suicides."

Edith glanced at him in alarm.

"Don't worry. As long as I keep thinking about Isobel and Mama — and you — I'll get through."

At the gate, he hugged Edith as he'd done when she arrived. She'd anticipated the moment and was resolved this time to ignore her inhibitions. She'd purposefully positioned the box containing her gas mask so it wouldn't come between them. And now, with free arms and a basket empty save for her umbrella and her sandwich, she stood on tiptoe to reciprocate Carlo's embrace.

The coarse fabric of Carlo's jacket chafed her cheek as she pressed her forehead into the heat of his neck. His clothes smelt of smoke, and there was more than a hint of perspiration emanating from under his shirt collar, but she inhaled as much of Carlo's scent as she could before finally relaxing her grip on his waist.

When they pulled apart, she smiled and walked toward the gate. Edith said goodbye to the guard with hardly a thought about whether he'd witnessed their farewell embrace. Once outside the barbed wire, she turned to wave to Carlo. He stood where she'd left him, one hand upraised. Even at this distance, she could see his eyes were sparkling. She liked to think that their usual luminescence was exaggerated by the pleasure of having seen her.

* * *

As Edith walked down Durning Road, she could see that there was a commotion a little farther up the street from her parents' house. Two fire engines, an ambulance, and a couple of army vehicles were parked haphazardly in front of a smouldering mountain of debris where the old Edge Hill Training College used to stand. As she drew closer, she could see that forty or so men were atop the pile, tearing away at blackened wood, chunks of concrete, and twisted metal pipes. Ants on an anthill, thought Edith as dust-covered men staggered off the vast heap laden with massive chunks of masonry and burned rafters. They threw their burdens to one side and turned back for more. The air was full of the smell of burned paint and wood, and Edith thought she could also detect a disturbing whiff of coal gas. She stopped near a huddle of four women, two arm in arm, another with an arm around a friend's shivering shoulders.

"When?" was all Edith could say.

"Early this morning," said one of the women. "Direct hit with a landmine. But it's taken them all day to put the blaze out. The gas pipes blew."

"Landmine?" questioned Edith.

The woman turned her head, pale-faced and hollow-eyed, in Edith's direction.

"Where have you been?" she asked sarcastically. "Landmines are what they call the bombs with parachutes. Float down lookin' as harmless as dandelion seeds."

What next, Edith thought, aghast.

"But what are they digging for? Surely nobody was in the building at that time of night," said Edith.

"They told people to use the cellars as an air raid shelter. They reckon there were three hundred of them down there. The terrible thing is, the heating pipes burst. My husband said the bodies they've found so far look more like boiled hams than people."

The woman with the quivering shoulders let out a wrench of a sob.

"Keep it to yourself, can't you," exclaimed her companion. "Her sister and four little ones are under that lot."

Edith turned abruptly on her heel and hurried toward her parents' gate. The house looked dusty but undamaged. Apart from the criss-cross pattern of tape on all the windows, it appeared exactly as it had when she'd lived there. Standing with her back to the horror, she could almost persuade herself that everything was normal, and more so at the back of the house, where Edith was almost out of earshot of the hubbub across the street. An occasional male shout was all she could discern. Edith welcomed the air of damp serenity that hung over the small square of unkempt lawn.

"Edith. Edith, love, is that you? Are you all right?"

Edith turned to find Mrs. Higgins standing on her back steps, peering over the fence that divided the two properties.

"What on earth are you doing there?" she asked. "You look like you've seen a ghost. Come on round and have a cuppa."

A hot cup of tea would certainly be welcome, and if Edith hesitated, it was because she was astonished by Mrs. Higgins's offer. In the past, neither of the Higgins had given her the time of day, and had certainly never invited any of Edith's family into their house. The Higginses always considered themselves a cut above everyone else.

"Come on, love," urged Mrs. Higgins. "Kettle's just boiled."

"All right then," said Edith. "Thank you."

"We were in the Anderson, of course," said Mrs. Higgins, referring to her back-garden shelter. Edith could make out the grass-and-weed-covered hump through steamy kitchen windows. "If we hadn't had the Anderson, we'd have been under the school with the rest of them," continued Mrs. Higgins. In the past, Edith would have expected more than a hint of smugness from her former neighbour. But, on the contrary, Mrs. Higgins sounded profoundly shaken, her voice weighed down with the apologetic humility of a survivor. She moved closer to Edith and lowered her voice to a whisper.

"We'll go in the front parlour. Mrs. Reeves is in there. They managed to get her out early on. Apparently she was in the section where the roof held, so she wasn't hurt. But she's in a bad way nonetheless."

Edith was amazed. The Reeves family lived across the street in one of the terraced houses and were definitely not Mrs. Higgins's kind of people. The father, uncle, and three grown sons had somehow avoided the army. Before the war, they'd been regularly in and out of prison for petty pilfering or breaking and entering, as a consequence of which they were referred to by one and all as "the Reeves thieves."

"You mean Mrs. Reeves from over the road?" asked Edith doubtfully.

"Is there another?" retorted Mrs. Higgins, looking askance at Edith.

Mrs. Reeves sat on the edge of a blue velvet easy chair, arms crossed, rocking backwards and forwards. A pink blanket was draped over her shoulders; it appeared startlingly clean in comparison to Mrs. Reeves. In the past, she'd often appeared unkempt, but now she was downright dishevelled. Her hair was encrusted with a thick layer of dust and her forehead bore smudges of soot. Edith could clearly see evidence of dried blood around the ragged fingernails of her grimy hands. She didn't look up when Edith and Mrs. Higgins appeared.

"Try and take a few sips, dear," said Mrs. Higgins, putting a cup of tea on the table beside her. She gave Edith a knowing look, as if to confirm the diagnosis she'd given in the kitchen. Edith and Mrs. Higgins finished their tea in silence. Mrs. Reeves didn't even glance at hers but continued to rock.

After what Edith considered to be a polite interval, she said, "I really should run or it'll be dark before I get home," and stood up to leave. "They should never have put us down there," blurted Mrs. Reeves and stopped moving backward and forward to stare, wild-eyed, at Edith. "A death trap, that's what it was. A bloody death trap!" Now that she'd lifted her head, Edith could see distinct rivers of white skin on her dusty cheeks where tears had washed away the dirt. Edith was grateful to Mrs. Higgins for ushering her out of the room into the hallway, leaving Mrs. Reeves to her rocking. At the front door, Edith was taken aback when Mrs. Higgins embraced her, pulling her to her ample bosom.

"You and your parents are better off out of it," she said. "I wish to God we had somewhere to go."

"Will she be all right?" asked Edith, tipping her head in the direction of the front room.

"I doubt it," whispered Mrs. Higgins. "They pulled more than a hundred people out, but there must be almost two hundred still under there, including her husband, brother, and all the sons. There's little hope for any of them at this point."

Neither woman moved or looked at each other. After a few seconds, Mrs. Higgins said, "She can stay with us for now, poor thing."

Edith had the habit of always sitting on the same side of a tram or a bus if there was a seat vacant. On her journey back to the ferry dock, she was appalled all over again at the acres of blasted buildings on the other side of the tram route, stretching as far as she could see, even more extensive than she'd seen on her outward journey.

It was raining by the time she arrived at the bus station in Shrimpley. The sight of Fred Saunders, waiting optimistically in his taxi, was too tempting. As she settled onto the cold leather seat, she told herself she didn't care if anybody thought her extravagant, she deserved the ride home to Sandy Lane. And now that she was receiving five shillings weekly in child allowance for William, she could just about afford it.

As the taxi wound its way down the hill from Shrimpley village, Edith tried not to think about the people who'd been sheltering under the bombed school. She peered out of the car window at a landscape that was darkening as the daylight dwindled.

ITALY

"Prego, signori?" asked the fine-featured young man behind the counter of the gelateria. He looked young enough to be a first-year university student with his long, lustrous hair but a smooth, beardless jaw.

"What flavour do you want?" Shamus asked Will.

"*Bacio* means 'kiss,' right?" questioned Will.

"Yes," said Shamus. "Probably after sweets with the same name, which are made of chocolate and hazelnut. But if you want that particular flavour, you'll have to ask for it yourself." He smiled apologetically at the boy, who was paying careful attention to the two brothers, patiently waiting for them to make up their minds.

"*Per me, un cono con cioccolato e stracciatella, per favore.*"

"*Certo, signore,*" said the boy. Then he turned to Will, a wide smile crinkling the corners of his eyes, and asked in perfect English, "And a *bacio* for you, sir?"

Will had the good grace to blush. He laughed and said to the boy, "I don't know why I assumed you couldn't speak English! But you'll be relieved to hear that I don't actually want a *bacio*. I'd like one scoop of pistachio and one of vanilla, please."

"You're right," said the boy, grinning and nodding his head vigorously. "I *am* relieved."

Once served, Shamus bid a sheepish goodbye to the young man, who waved good-naturedly over the till, and the brothers returned to the bench where they'd been sitting, fingers wet and sticky from swiftly melting ice cream.

"You're lucky the poor boy didn't have you up for sexual harassment," said Shamus. "God only knows what he was thinking."

"Oh shut up. You sound like Edith talking about the neighbours," said Will. "He wasn't thinking anything. In fact, he obviously enjoyed having one over on us. The Shamus who lived with me in Notting Hill would never have missed an opportunity to ask a lovely lad like that for a kiss."

Shamus licked his ice cream cone and considered whether Will's question was warranted. It was true that when he and Will were both living in London — Shamus at university and Will in his first job after technical college — an occurrence like the one at the gelateria would only have been cause for merriment.

"It's a different time," said Shamus.

"What is?" asked Will.

"Now," replied Shamus. "Exchanges like that were okay in the '70s. People take things more seriously these days."

"I don't," said Will. "Although Mary was fond of telling me I should."

Shamus resisted the compulsion to suggest that perhaps Mary had been right. Tired of merely licking, he took a bite of his ice cream cone, then immediately regretted it when the jolt to his teeth set his temples throbbing.

"You're more like Edith the older you get," Will proclaimed. "You worry too much about what everybody thinks."

"I thought we'd agreed that Edith has her moments of devil-may-care," muttered Shamus, slurping the last of the ice cream before it melted completely. Then he tried in vain to clean his fingers with the diminutive, now sodden napkin in which the cone had been wrapped.

"She may have had, but any remnants disappeared around 1982, or whenever it was she went to Greenham Common," said Will. "Yours disappeared when lukewarm Luke carried you off to Canada."

Shamus was immediately flooded with resentment and indignation. It was one thing for Will to pick on Shamus, but quite another for his brother to criticize Luke.

"Is that what you were getting at earlier when you said Luke had his faults?" Shamus demanded. "Why don't you just spell it out instead of making smart remarks, for Christ's sake."

"Even you have to admit Luke was a bit . . ." Will seemed at a loss for words. He seemed to know he was treading on thin ice.

"A bit what?"

"Quiet," said Will.

"Quiet? Is that the best you can do?" snorted Shamus.

"All right then, he was boring. And he brought your boring side out too. When you were with Luke, you reverted to the silent-but-clever routine you always pulled off at home when we were kids."

Shamus was astounded. He'd had no idea that Will had such a low opinion of Luke. But — oddly — he wasn't angry at Will for his admission. Maybe because his own views about Luke were unshakeable. Yes, Luke had been quiet; that was why Shamus had been so attracted to him. He was such a welcome relief. But Luke had certainly not been boring.

"And what's more, he lured you away," added Will when Shamus didn't react.

Shamus couldn't help laughing.

"How old are you? Six? Seven?" he asked. "Do you realize how ridiculous you sound?"

Will said nothing and wiped his fingers with his sopping paper napkin, stained here and there with green pistachio ice cream.

Shamus stared at his brother as though trying to see inside his head. Was the reason for Will's hostility in the last thirty years because he hadn't liked Luke? Shamus didn't know what to make of the obvious resentment Will harboured about his leaving England.

"I've got to find somewhere to wash my hands," said Will, looking around. He appeared embarrassed and avoided Shamus's glare. "Even though the sun isn't quite over the yardarm, let's sit at one of these cafés and order an aperitif. I think we need it. Then we can use the facilities without being yelled at for not being a customer. And who knows," he added, in an obvious attempt at bravado and to change the subject. "Maybe Armando will show up with his damn cigarette case."

But his plan was thwarted by the fact that all the café tables were occupied. A bevy of young mothers sipping drinks of various hues monopolized several tables, talking animatedly while their children chased each other around a nearby tree. The sun was sinking toward the horizon and the buttery light of day had deepened to copper. It seemed to Shamus that the façades of the buildings lining the square resembled painted theatre scenery. The early evening light that bathed the east side could easily have come from orange-tinted floodlights instead of the dying rays of the sun. The stage seemed set for an opera.

"If it wasn't for all these bloody Italians, we'd be able to find a place to sit," said Will out of the side of his mouth. Shamus was about to tell Will to shut up when a voice behind them said, "You're welcome to sit at this table."

Will and Shamus turned to find a white-haired man looking up at them, legs crossed. His swarthy face, high cheekbones, and long nose gave him an aquiline appearance. Dark eyes, topped by abundant black eyebrows, added to his hawkish looks. Shamus put him in his eighties. A crimson bow tie drew Shamus's gaze to the man's throat. Suddenly aware that his glance had impolitely extended into a stare, Shamus stuttered, "We wouldn't want to bother you."

"No bother," the man said. "I promise not to talk to you if you don't want. Sit, sit." He motioned toward two empty chairs, one on each side of the small table. Shamus noticed that the man's English bore only a trace of an Italian accent.

"Very kind of you," said Shamus, pulling back one of the chairs to sit down. Will sat on the other.

"Yes, very hospitable, thank you," Will said. "I'm Will Maguire, and this is my brother, Shamus."

Shamus thought how appropriate the phrase "turn on the charm" was when it came to Will's ability to do just that.

"Umberto Benecasa," said the old man and held out his hand. His fingers were punctuated by shiny knobs of arthritic knuckles, a chunky gold ring nudged up against one of them.

"This square is particularly picturesque, isn't it?" said Will, looking around with an earnest expression of appreciation.

"Some of these buildings are old palazzi," said Umberto. "The one next to the hotel, for instance. You can tell by the shape of its arched windows."

Shamus felt a glow of self-satisfaction that his theory about the palazzi had been correct. The brothers ordered drinks, and as they waited, Shamus listened to Will and Umberto trade questions and answers about the history of the square. It turned out that Umberto, as well as being a native of Venice, was also a retired university professor.

"And I take it that the statue up there is of Santa Margherita," said Will, sounding to Shamus like an eager student currying favour from a teacher.

"*Si, bravo,*" said Umberto. "She's standing atop the dragon from which she was miraculously delivered. I'm not sure why that qualified her to be the patron saint of pregnant women, but there it is."

"Please excuse me," said Will, smiling at Umberto. He looked secure in the knowledge, thought Shamus, that he'd scored points with the old professor. "I have to avail myself of the facilities." Will stood and disappeared into the café in search of a bathroom.

"You are the older brother, no?" asked Umberto.

"Will would love you for saying so," replied Shamus, "but no, I'm the younger." Ever since he'd overtaken Will in height at sixteen years old, Shamus had been accustomed to being mistaken for the elder.

"He's an interesting fellow," said Umberto.

"Interesting?" asked Shamus, pride and envy jostling for position at what he took to be Umberto's approval of his brother's curiosity about Venice's architectural history.

"All us 'bloody Italians,'" Umberto quoted, and laughed.

Shamus felt the blood rush to his face. He'd been stupid not to realize that Umberto must have heard Will's comment.

"He didn't mean it," stuttered Shamus. "It sounds racist, but he's really not."

"Why do you feel you must defend him?" asked Umberto.

"He's my brother," said Shamus before he could stop himself. "It's what I've always done. Our father was pretty hard on him growing up," he said, cursing himself for spouting what sounded like cliché-ridden excuses. His intestines tightened, and resentment of Umberto rose in his throat like reflux.

"You look quite agitated," said Will, glancing at Shamus and Umberto as he returned to the table. "I hope you boys aren't talking politics."

"Something of that nature," said Umberto, smiling.

Shamus said nothing. He looked up at the statue of Santa Margherita staring innocently back from her niche high on the dirty-pink stucco wall, feet resting on the prone figure of the dragon.

"How many times do I have to tell you?" piped Will, imitating their mother's voice. "No politics or religion at the table."

"Excuse me," said Shamus, wondering what on earth Umberto must be thinking of Will's performance. "I'm going to wash my hands."

Shamus had to bend to examine his face in the mirror of the cramped restaurant washroom. He'd caught some sun; he bared his teeth and was gratified to see how white they appeared in comparison to his tawny skin. Hardly a filling among them, either, not bad for fifty-six, he thought. He looked into his eyes. Did his brother ever discern in them echoes of the past as Shamus did in Will's? Those days when they were under Joe's thrall seemed like eons ago. Shamus let out an exasperated puff of air. Why couldn't he just let it all go?

Shamus was suddenly taken by surprise with an intense yearning for Luke. As he made his way back to the table, it crossed his mind that perhaps Luke had fulfilled a need for the intimacy of family but without the burden of childhood associations with family conflicts. Along with everything else that Luke had meant to Shamus, had he also been a welcome and uncomplicated substitute for his brother and his parents? Whatever the reason for missing him at that moment, Shamus heartily wished it was Luke he was rejoining at the café table and not the mismatched duo of his brother and the elderly Italian.

As Shamus approached, he caught the tail end of a story Umberto was telling.

"—so in a spirit of friendly competition, many Venetians flocked to Treviso for a mock battle between two armies of children, each armed with scent and flowers, for possession of a so-called Castle of Love. But the occasion was completely spoiled when a fight broke out in earnest between Paduan and Venetian spectators."

Will laughed and Umberto's eyes twinkled.

"We're talking about how wars begin," said Will.

"Which means you're discussing religion or politics — or both," replied Shamus, sitting in his place opposite Will. "Naughty boys."

"I was telling Umberto that I'd recently been in Dresden," said Will, taking a large mouthful of Campari and soda.

"And I told Will that I was in Dresden during the war," said Umberto. "I was a communications officer and was taking training there in a new radio system. This was a few years before Dresden was utterly destroyed by Allied bombers, of course. "

Shamus deduced that Umberto must have been in Mussolini's fascist army. It seemed odd to be having drinks with someone who'd fought for the other side, even if it had been more than half a century ago.

"They're still restoring the old buildings in Dresden, nearly sixty years later," interjected Will. "The repercussions of World War II seem to go on and on. I read somewhere recently that the money Britain borrowed from America to pay for the war won't be fully paid back until 2006. With interest, it'll have totalled more than $49 billion."

"I think they began reconstruction of Dresden fairly recently. Since the reunification of Germany," said Umberto. He turned toward Shamus. "I was telling your brother how happy I sometimes felt during the war. I suspect it's a product of survival. Having come safely through particularly intense and dangerous experiences, chemicals are released in the brain that give one a sense of euphoria. Later, however, it wasn't unusual to feel some survivor guilt. Especially if one had closely avoided a situation where people died in such profusion."

Shamus nodded his head. He was much more able to relate to a guilt theory than to Umberto's supposition of a survivor's ecstatic high.

"There are certainly a lot of English people who consider the war years the best time of their lives," said Will.

"You know, I just realized why Santa Margherita was made the patron saint of pregnant women," announced Umberto. The old man's statement took Shamus and Will by surprise and they stared at Umberto expectantly.

"The story goes that, after the dragon swallowed her, she lay in its stomach. But then she made the sign of the cross, at which point the dragon exploded, freeing her. How stupid of me not to have made the connection for all these years."

"I can see how you might not," said Will. "I wouldn't have thought an exploding stomach was something pregnant women would want to be associated with."

"We Venetians don't seem to mind a bit of gore," said Umberto with a chuckle. "After all, we stole St. Mark's body and smuggled it here from Alexandria under a cargo of cabbages and pork. I'm willing to bet the vegetables and meat in question were eagerly consumed nonetheless. Later, after the sack of Constantinople, we collected the head of St. Philip, the arm of St. Stephen, some bits of St. Paul, and one of John the Baptist's teeth and brought them all here."

"Amazing," said Will, smiling at Umberto with boyish delight. He knocked back his Campari. The last of the fuchsia-coloured liquid hovered in the glass for a second before disappearing down his throat. "Let's have another drink," he said, signalling to a nearby waiter who was clearing the glasses left behind by the departing group of mothers. As twilight deepened, street lamps flickered into life, shedding pools of pallid light on the footworn paving stones of Campo Santa Margherita. The women were bidding one another effusive farewells and calling their children to their sides.

"It's time I was heading home too," said Umberto. "My housekeeper will have left dinner for me."

"Well there's no reason to rush off then, if she's left it. Is there?" questioned Will. "Time for one more, surely."

But Umberto wasn't to be persuaded. Before he turned to leave, he looked from Will to Shamus and back. "Take care of each other," he said, and winked.

"Why does everybody have to rush off all the time?" muttered Will when Umberto was barely out of earshot.

"He wasn't that interesting, was he?" asked Shamus, surprised by the hurt tone in Will's voice.

Will ignored the question. "I think old Umberto had a bit of a crush on you, though," he commented.

"Don't be ridiculous," said Shamus. "You were the one who seemed smitten, trying to cajole him into staying."

"I hate it when people leave before I want them to," said Will with such vehemence Shamus was startled. Did his brother realize he was harking back to his earlier comment about Luke "luring" Shamus away? Rather than feeling irritated by Will's admission of his low opinion of Luke or his childish outburst, Shamus felt strangely sympathetic toward his brother. He experienced the same concern he'd always had when he thought about how Joe had treated Will.

When they'd each finished their second Campari, Will suggested they find Armando's family restaurant.

"It's a bit early." Will glanced at his watch. "But I wouldn't want to miss young Armando Belli. I'd like another gander at that cigarette case of his."

Shamus was about to suggest that Will's obsession with the silver case had reached proportions worthy of any fetish. But he thought better of it.

ENGLAND

"It's colder than a witch's whatsit in here," said Liam, blowing on the fingertips of one hand. "Can't we shove another piece of coal on the fire?"

"Don't be so crude, my lad," admonished Mrs. Maguire. "If you're cold, put on another pullover. And while you're up, switch on the wireless. It's nearly time for the ten o'clock news."

Even in the daylight-filled evenings of summer, Edith had found Mrs. Maguire's cluttered living room claustrophobic. Now, on the shortest day of the year, with windows swathed by blackout curtains and doors tightly shut in the ongoing battle against freezing drafts, the room was decidedly tomblike. The only light came from the dim bulb in a wrought-iron floor lamp, positioned behind Mrs. Maguire's chair to illuminate her knitting.

"At this rate, we're more likely to die of exposure than any air raid," muttered Liam as he kicked aside the draft excluder — a fabric sausage made from one of Mrs. Maguire's old stockings stuffed with rags — from the foot of the door, where it was meant to block the icy air that seeped into the living room from the unheated hallway beyond.

In the three weeks since Edith's visit to Woolfall Heath, there'd been no word about the result of Carlo's tribunal. Edith cursed herself for passing along to Anna and Isobel the camp commander's suggestion that Carlo might be home in time for Christmas. Hadn't she learnt from bitter experience not to take people at their word?

Since then, sporadic air raids had hit Liverpool almost every night. Just when it seemed to Edith that the bombers might be giving them a break, the air raid siren would howl and the grinding drone of enemy aircraft could be heard above their heads. A school pal of Liam's was visiting his grandmother in Birkenhead when a bomb hit her house; the friend and his granny were both killed. Edith worried that the tragedy might spark more warmongering from Liam, but although the news certainly shook him up, he didn't seem vengeful.

He merely took to muttering gloomily about "people playing football one minute and being dead the next." After a week or so, he seemed to have reverted to his old self, but once or twice Edith came across him staring into space, a woebegone expression clouding his features. And when Edith had told him the news about Carlo's impending release, he seemed genuinely pleased.

Edith didn't believe there was any excuse for the authorities that had imprisoned harmless waiters and tailors, but she decided to give Liam the benefit of the doubt on his mindless prejudice against Italians. She put Liam's period of ardent jingoism down to the fact that most of the general population had been rendered temporarily insane by propaganda and the paranoia that ensued. She couldn't really point a finger. After all, she'd gone to the extreme of getting married partly because she'd been made to think it was the patriotic thing to do. It seemed to Edith that the latest madness had reached its zenith when parents and teachers began urging children to contribute their pocket money toward the cost of manufacturing Spitfires and Lancaster bombers. They were told that rivets cost sixpence a piece, a guinea covered the price of a Spitfire's thermometer, and twenty-two pounds of their savings would pay for a small bomb.

After the air raids began, Edith had expected even more extremes of resentment and bitterness, but people were strangely less vindictive than before. The idea of reprisal was generally thought to be repugnant. She heard several residents of Shrimpley say that nobody — friend or foe, English or German — should have to experience what the people of Liverpool were being forced to endure.

Edith was engrossed in pondering exactly why the population's eye-for-an-eye attitude had softened when she was startled by the sound of her mother-in-law pulling aside the wire-mesh guard that sat in front of the fireplace. Mrs. Maguire prodded the coals with a metal poker until a few plucky flames reluctantly flickered to life.

"This is the BBC Home and Forces Programme." Edith could barely make out the words above the crackle of interference on the radio. "Here is the news; this is Wilfred Pickles reading it.

"Over the last twenty-four hours, there has been some penetration of our defences by enemy aircraft, causing some damage and a few casualties."

"I don't know why you bother listening to the radio — they never tell you what's really going on," said Liam from the doorway. "Alec Simpson was in Liverpool this morning, and he said part of the Cunard Building burned, half the Adelphi Hotel's in ruins, and forty people were killed in a direct hit on the railway in Bentinck Street. There was a crowd of them sheltering under the railway arches, poor beggars."

"Shut that door, you. This lamp'll be showing through the front door glass," said Mrs. Maguire. "The last thing we want is Mick McGirty hammering on the door again."

Edith, who'd felt vaguely guilty about her unpatriotic thoughts concerning Mick McGirty, was relieved to hear that Mrs. Maguire obviously shared her opinion that the air raid warden for Sandy Lane was taking his duties a little too seriously. Mick McGirty was thin as a rake, with protruding cheekbones and small, unnaturally bright eyes. He wore a helmet too large for him, emblazoned with a large black letter W for warden. He'd called on them three times in the last month to complain, rather officiously, that a glimmer of light could be seen at their window. Liam maintained that the W on Mick's helmet stood for weasel.

"Do you know that before the Great War, when I was in service, Mick McGirty started work as a stable boy at the big house? He was such a filthy child we called him Dirty McGirty," said Mrs. Maguire. "His dad was a rag and bone man. There were ten kids, wild as a band of gypsies, the whole tribe of them." Then, remembering the time and place, she said, "But I suppose he's only doing his duty." And then, to dispel any doubt of her commitment to the war effort, she invoked the often-quoted democratic maxim, always uttered in a suitably stoic tone of voice, "We're all in this together, after all."

Liam, who'd returned wearing so many layers of clothes he appeared twice his size, muttered, "If I hear anyone say that again, I think I'll throw up." Legs made stiff by two pairs of pants and arms constrained by several pullovers, his attempt to sit down on the couch became a free fall that concluded with a crash landing. As the cushions compressed and old springs creaked, the reverberations reached Edith at the other end of the sofa.

"Steady on," said Edith, glancing at William, now almost four months old, who was lying, encased in various woollen garments and a pair of corduroy rompers, between her and Liam. But William seemed to enjoy the disturbance; he gurgled and kicked his legs. Encouraged by the baby's obvious delight, Liam bounced up and down to repeat the commotion.

Mrs. Maguire was so intent on her knitting she didn't notice the fracas on the sofa. She'd returned from Shrimpley village with a three-penny leaflet of patterns for three dolls — a sailor, a soldier, and an airman. Announcing that she was sick of knitting plain squares to be made into blankets for refugees, she'd embarked on the complicated project of making dolls for displaced children. They weren't very big, ten or twelve inches tall, but it'd taken her a full week to put together half a sailor. She'd started with him because she had lots of navy blue wool from an old cardigan she'd unravelled. She'd knitted plenty of socks in the past and was used to manipulating four needles at once, but the dolls were fussier than any socks. She was beginning to think perhaps she should have stuck with the blanket squares. Mrs. Maguire was counting stitches under her breath when the air raid siren began its unearthly warbling. They all groaned in unison.

"Darn it, now I've gone and lost count," said Mrs. Maguire.

As the thrum of airplane engines increased in volume, Edith reached out to place a protective hand on William's tummy, Liam stared at the ceiling, and Mrs. Maguire's thumb and forefinger stalked ponderously along her knitting needle, counting off stitches. At the sound of a distant thud, not unlike a large apple falling from a tree, Edith started. The next thirty seconds brought more thuds, some closer than others. Edith picked William up and held him to her.

"Maybe we'd best squeeze into the cupboard under the stairs," said Mrs. Maguire.

The sound of a loud thwack at the back of the house almost drowned out her last words. The thump, like the blow of a heavy sledgehammer, was followed by a loud hissing noise.

"Gas masks," shouted Mrs. Maguire, jumping to her feet. "Where are the darned gas masks?"

"Wait," shouted Liam. "Turn the light off."

There was such authority in his voice that Mrs. Maguire instantly reached out and turned off the lamp behind her chair. Liam struggled to his feet, rushed to the side window, and pulled aside the blackout curtain. The room was flooded with white light. Edith's first thought was that it must be moonlight, but she dismissed the notion in a split second; the illumination was too strong, more like that of searchlights, coming from somewhere behind the house.

"It's an incendiary bomb," yelled Liam. "I read about them just the other day." He ran toward the kitchen. "We'd better see to it or the whole house'll go up in flames."

Mrs. Maguire ran after him. Edith, without thinking, followed, with William clasped tightly to her chest. For a brief second, she saw Liam's bulky silhouette against the brightness of the open back door, then he was gone, into the light. Mrs. Maguire was at the sink filling a zinc bucket with water. Edith hovered indecisively. As soon as the bucket was full, Mrs. Maguire grabbed the handle and made for the door. Edith followed.

When she reached the threshold, Edith saw Liam, shovel in hand, frantically digging at the ground. A few yards beyond him was the source of the light, a white fireball of dazzling intensity and much too close for comfort to the wood-framed henhouse. It hurt Edith's eyes to look at it. She turned so that her body protected William from the harmful glare. Edith could hear the panicked squawks of chickens above the hiss of the conflagration.

"Liam, get out of the way," shouted Mrs. Maguire, bearing down on him with a bucket of water.

Liam turned his head and saw her approaching.

"Noooo," he shouted, stretching himself to his full height and raising his arms like a goalie at a football match. The pail of water, which must have been icy cold, hit him squarely in the face and chest.

"Nnnot wwwaaater," he gasped. "It'll mmmaake it wwworse."

Mrs. Maguire stood there, bucket dangling, mouth open in shock, but Liam immediately returned to his digging and soon began to frantically thrust shovelfuls of earth onto the blaze. After much hissing and crackling, the white-hot fire slowly diminished until one last heaping spade of sandy soil finally killed it.

Liam threw the shovel to the ground and turned around. Even in the dim light, and with afterimages of the heart of the fireball dancing ghostlike in her pupils, Edith could see that he was completely soaked. The topmost pullover hung off him like loose skin; wet hair was plastered to his forehead.

"Isn't it bad enough that the Hun is out to get us without my own mother trying to drown me?" he protested indignantly.

Mrs. Maguire and Edith clung to each other, legs trembling, laughing uncontrollably, with the baby sandwiched between them. William seemed to sense the extent of their relief, and he cooed and hiccupped in Edith's arms.

When Edith's hysteria subsided, she looked up and saw points of white light dotted around the surrounding fields. Up on the heath, a few small fires burned where the bracken had caught. The bombs didn't seem to have hit any buildings, but she could imagine the havoc they could wreak in more densely populated areas.

As she wiped the tears from her eyes, the banshee wail of the all-clear siren could be heard moaning its way down the hill from Shrimpley village. The smell of charred bracken hung in the air.

Tuesday, December 24, 1940

Anna seemed intent on celebrating Christmas in as normal a fashion as possible. She'd been squirrelling away provisions for weeks and was planning a special meal for that evening. Liam had helped her chop down a small conifer up on the heath and they'd dragged it home and set it up as a Christmas tree in Anna's living room. Cotton wool snow and a few strands of tousled tinsel was all Anna could muster, so Mrs. Maguire contributed a box of decorations, which comprised a bedraggled fairy with a bent wand and various mismatched shiny metal balls.

"She's being so brave. The first Christmas is bloody hard," confided Mrs. Maguire. "There's something about annual occasions that gets you every time. I was crying inside the whole year after Mr. Maguire died. But I put on a brave face for Joe; Liam was just a baby and didn't know any better."

Liam seemed not to have suffered any ill effects from his soaking on the night of the firebombs. Once they were back in the house, Mrs. Maguire had peeled off layers of dripping wool and vigorously towelled his wet hair. Afterwards, sipping on a cup of hot milk in front of the fire, Liam had outlined to Edith in triumphant but tedious detail his knowledge of phosphorus. Somehow, Liam knew, in the mysterious way that men and boys seemed to be acquainted with such things, that phosphorus was the main ingredient in incendiary bombs. He'd learned about its adverse reaction to water in a chemistry class at school; he claimed that Mrs. Maguire's bucket of water would have made the blazing bomb burn all the more fiercely. The things people learn during a war, marvelled Edith.

Anna and Isobel hadn't let the rain of firebombs frighten them. "Maybe we hear something," shrugged Anna. "But we just turn up the wireless so they don't bother us." Her cavalier demeanour wasn't unusual — many people coped with the mortal dangers of air raids by adopting a fatalistic attitude. Bombs seemed to be falling in the Shrimpley area more frequently. Perhaps the German Luftwaffe was running out of trained airmen. Edith imagined fuzz-jawed German bombardiers experiencing their first air raids, bowels loose with fear. They were obviously pushing the button, pulling the lever, or deploying whatever device released their lethal load, before the pilots reached the intended target of the Liverpool docklands.

It had taken the hens a while to settle down after the bomb that landed so close to them — it was days before they laid after their night of excitement. And that afternoon, Mrs. Maguire had given the hens another scare when she dragged one of their number out of the henhouse and lopped off its head. The unfortunate chicken was to serve as the Christmas bird on their table the next day.

Along with a Christmas card from a cousin of Mrs. Maguire's, the postman delivered another letter from Joe. It was sure to be a response to the note Edith had sent just after William was born. It seemed to take at least six or eight weeks for her letters to reach him and the same for his response to reach her, and the lapse of time made Joe seem extremely distant.

Edith was eager to read his reaction to becoming a father. An image had occasionally come to her mind since William was born, rather like a portrait photograph of their family unit: Mum, Dad, and William. It was an unrealistic, rose-tinted representation, not unlike the one in which she'd imagined herself, before she married Joe, as the stoic and patriotic wife of a serviceman fighting in foreign parts.

"Dear Edith," wrote Joe. "Well what a surprise! I'd forgot exactly when you were due, but I was pleased as Punch when I read the news. The first name will have to go, though. I want my son to be called by his second name, Patrick."

Joe continued in much the same vein as in previous letters. The same complaints about foreign food. A long paragraph about the lack of a bathtub; communal showers were apparently available, but they were "unsanitary." Joe maintained there was "nothing like a good soak in your own bathwater to make you feel really clean."

He wouldn't like the newly instituted six-inch rule, thought Edith. It had been decreed that baths were only to be filled to a level of six inches, to cut down on coal consumption for heating water. Edith had no idea how the rule could possibly be enforced. Liam joked that they should be sure not to tell air warden Mick McGirty when their bath nights were or he'd show up with a tape measure.

Many of Joe's sentences had again been obscured by the censor, which always irritated Edith. As far as she could tell, there was no other mention of their son.

"What on earth is wrong with William?" demanded Edith of Mrs. Maguire.

"I don't know," replied Mrs. Maguire, her look of alarm betraying that she misunderstood Edith's question.

Once Edith explained that she meant William the name, not her actual baby, Mrs. Maguire appeared relieved. "I always thought you were treading on thin ice there," she admitted.

"Why?" Edith asked. "It's a perfectly good name."

"A bit too Protestant for some, though, love," said Mrs. Maguire. "William of Orange? King Billy?" she added with a frown.

Edith looked at her, incredulous.

"Is that why you suggested Patrick as his middle name?" she asked.

"Well I thought it might keep some people happy." Mrs. Maguire sighed. "But obviously not," she concluded.

* * *

"If you ask me, it's uncivilized having Christmas dinner on Christmas Eve," muttered Liam as he, Edith, and Mrs. Maguire trooped in the dark across the lawn and through the conifers to the bungalow next door. "Well nobody did ask you, did they?" said Edith. She was reluctant to mention that Anna had told her the Christmas Eve meal was a peculiarly Italian tradition. "We look like the three kings," she laughed. They each carried an offering: Liam cradled half a dozen bottles of pale ale in his arms like shiny brown sextuplets, Edith lugged a bucket half full of coal, and Mrs. Maguire held on with both hands to a large dish of baked apples. Edith was looking forward to Anna's cooking. When she'd brought William over half an hour earlier and delivered him to the safety of Isobel's arms, Anna had been crashing around in the kitchen, talking to herself.

"Just think of it as a Christmas Eve party, Liam. We'll have proper Christmas dinner tomorrow," said Mrs. Maguire, who'd spent all afternoon plucking and dressing the chicken.

Edith noticed that any reservations Liam might have had about the evening seemed to disappear when it came to eating. Anna had managed to conjure up a veritable banquet. The extravagance of half a dozen candles illuminated dishes of fish: sardines and mackerel, several cans' worth. Anna bemoaned the scarcity of spaghetti in Shrimpley but had made her own version with flour, eggs, and water. Throughout autumn, tomatoes in various stages of ripeness had populated Anna's window ledges. As soon as a batch reached the desired shade of crimson, Anna would cook up a few more jars of sauce.

They were soon all tucking in to her homemade pasta, chins glistening with tomato juice. It had taken Edith a while to be able to negotiate the long strands with a fork, but after a few meals at Anna's house, she'd become quite adept. Anna cut up Isobel's portion so she could eat it with a spoon. Edith had noticed her tremors become steadily more acute in the last few months.

As Anna and Edith were clearing away dishes to make way for the next course, Isobel surmised, "Maybe Hitler's decided to give it a rest for Christmas. If there's going to be a raid, we would usually have heard the siren by now."

On the wireless, a carol service was being broadcast live from Westminster Abbey. They'd heard that the capital had been attacked for seventy-six nights straight in September, October, and November and almost continuously ever since. Nevertheless, the choir sang "Ding Dong Merrily on High" with gusto and there was no sound of sirens or bombs in the background. Maybe London was enjoying a reprieve too, thought Edith.

The next course Anna served was delicious. Edith marvelled at how she'd managed to find so much good meat.

"The secret is to make it tender," said Anna. "It looks like a lot because I beat it until it's nice and soft. Spreads it out and makes it flat." Along with the thin pieces of juicy meat coated in breadcrumbs Anna served wedges of roasted potato and Brussels sprouts from her garden. There was so much meat that there were three of four pieces left once they'd all had their fill.

Replete, they sat listening to the honeyed voices of the Westminster Boys' Choir on the wireless. Firelight flickered on the hearth mat and candlelight softened their features. Edith's thoughts wandered to Mrs. Reeves and the women she'd seen huddled opposite the bombed school on Durning Road. What kind of a Christmas Eve might they be having, she wondered. She wasn't sorry when a loud knocking on the front door interrupted her thoughts.

"It'll be that weasel, Dirty McGirty," said Liam.

"I'll tell him what to do with his warden's hat," said Anna, heading for the door.

A few seconds later, they heard Anna's voice raised in exclamation. Edith, Liam, and Mrs. Maguire stood up in alarm at the sound of her shouting in Italian. Edith made for the door. As soon as she reached the dim hallway, she recognized the figure of Carlo silhouetted against the front doorway; there was no mistaking his tall outline. Anna was clinging to him, weeping in great, chest-heaving sobs.

Carlo's arrival sparked such a strong flood of emotion in Anna that Edith was afraid for her. Carlo led his convulsing mother into the living room and gently steered her to a chair.

"*Gianni,*" Anna bellowed. "*Dove sei, Gianni?*"

Carlo's arrival seemed to have released a tide of intense grief in Anna; his presence obviously highlighted the absence of her dead husband. Mrs. Maguire sat beside her and grasped her around her shoulders. Carlo knelt on the floor in front of Isobel's wheelchair and put his head on her knee. She stroked his hair, fingers trembling. After a minute or two, Carlo sprang up and gave Liam a bear hug, topping it off with a generous kiss on each cheek. Once released, Liam sat down abruptly and took a long swig from his unfinished bottle of beer.

"*Gianni. Paolo. Gianni, dove sei?*" Anna repeated again and again — an impotent incantation, a futile, grief-driven attempt to resurrect her dead husband and son. As though encouraged by Anna's complete lack of inhibition, Edith couldn't help but let go herself. Once encircled by Carlo's arms, she gladly ditched all restraint and bawled unashamedly. Edith's relief at Carlo's return seemed to throw into sharp relief the accumulated anguish of the last few months: the horrific news of Gianni's and Paolo's drowning; the pain of Domenico's story of the sinking of the *Arandora Star;* the suffering in the face of the man in the internment camp portrait; smouldering bomb sites and imagined boiled-ham bodies; Mrs. Reeves's raving — all vividly fought for space in her mind's eye. Edith sobbed with more abandon than she'd ever experienced, even as a small child.

As her breathing returned to normal, each harrowing experience seemed to diminish, leaving Edith weak as a newborn yet indescribably lightened. The sound of William howling in Isobel's bedroom, where she'd put him down before they sat down to eat, brought Edith to her senses. God knows how long he's been crying, she thought, blowing her nose and mopping her eyes. Then she calmed him down and brought him into the living room.

Carlo grasped Edith's blanket-bundled baby in both hands and held him up in front of his face to examine him. Carlo's features softened in the unique, almost idiotic manner that only babies are able to effect. Edith couldn't believe how small William seemed in Carlo's hands. Carlo kissed him gently on the forehead, and his beard must have tickled. William couldn't have been more winning as he gurgled and smiled, fists opening and closing with pleasure.

"Carlo, *caro,* you must be starving," sniffled Anna, having recovered from her outburst. She hurried into the kitchen.

"Is *cavallo,*" replied Anna to Carlo's question about the meat. He'd wolfed the remainders down in seconds.

"*Cavallo,*" repeated Liam. "Doesn't that mean horse?"

"*Si,* horse," confirmed Anna. "I tell that butcher over and over to find some horse. It's not rationed, and there must be many people round here only too glad to sell their animals. Finally he took my advice. It's good, yes?"

Anna was obviously perplexed by Liam's reaction. A look of horror and repulsion had appeared on his face, which sent Edith into paroxysms of giggles. Anna looked to Mrs. Maguire for an explanation, but Mrs. Maguire just shook her head and smiled.

"Baked apple, anyone?" she asked.

Thursday, March 13, 1941

"For why he has to go over there?" demanded Anna. "Isn't it enough they killed his father and brother and sent another brother to the other side of the world?"

Edith was stooped over Mrs. Maguire's living room table changing William's soiled diaper. She knew Carlo had explained to Anna about the condition of his release, which was that he must work part-time in the Civil Defence Corps in Liverpool. Edith was glad she had a safety pin in her mouth so her lack of response to Anna's questions wouldn't put her in an unsympathetic light. Edith was in fact relieved to hear Anna rail against the injustices meted out to Gianni and the boys. Although aware that it was presumptuous of her and more than a little demeaning toward Anna, Edith retained a nagging concern that Anna's outrage at what had happened to Gianni and the boys might fade with the passage of time. She wasn't sure why she was so disturbed about this. Perhaps because the whole affair was so patently unjust. It'd be insufferable if the facts were swept under the carpet and forgotten.

Carlo's role in civil defence required him to spend three nights each week in the stricken city, helping out wherever he was needed. He always phoned Isobel in the morning after a night of work to tell her he was safe and let her know whether he was returning to Shrimpley or grabbing a few hours of sleep at Bob MacDonald's before his next spell of duty. And Carlo seemed to have been more fortunate than most — because of Isobel's illness, he'd been allowed to remain a civilian. Many other internees had been forced to join the Auxiliary Military Pioneer Corps, which was reputed to be the dumping ground for criminals and all types of unsavoury characters. But Carlo had claimed that men in the Pioneer Corps shouldn't be sneered at, that they were the workhorses of the army, labouring at the front to dig roads, repair bridges, and haul supplies in support of fighting units. "Wars are won as much from hard labour behind the lines as from the result of actual fighting at the front," Carlo had said.

Edith had already come to that conclusion. She thought a term that had recently entered the lexicon, "browned off," perfectly expressed a general exasperation with all the shortages and deprivations, and she had to admit she fully shared the sentiment. Edith didn't know exactly where the expression originated, but she could come up with a few possibilities. Was it from the flavourless, overcooked food that people had to eat? Or perhaps it was a reflection of the ubiquitous brown army uniform. Whatever its source, the expression was taken up by almost everybody. People were browned off with lining up and with rationing, browned off with air raids and with seeking shelter, browned off with the blackout, browned off with coal and petrol shortages. Liam, always one for the latest lingo, peppered his speech with the expression. Mrs. Maguire had told Liam recently that she was "browned off with him saying he was browned off with every little thing."

Another word that tripped off their lips as though they'd been saying it all their lives was Blitz. Edith couldn't recall when she first heard the word. Liam told her it was an abbreviation of the German *Blitzkrieg*. "Speed and surprise," said Liam. "Speed and surprise." The Blitz quickly became the name everybody used for the ferocious German air raids on British cities. Even Anna employed it as readily as if it were a word she'd been familiar with since she'd first arrived from Italy, more than twenty years earlier.

Although keen that the discrimination suffered by Anna's husband and sons not be forgotten, Edith was sorry to see that Carlo's release and return from the internment camp in Woolfall Heath, rather than heartening Anna, seemed to have dispirited her. Given Anna's reaction the night Carlo came home, Edith guessed that the sight of him was a constant reminder of the absence of the others. Anna still helped care for Isobel, but she was less likely to offer encouragement when Isobel became dejected by her declining mobility. Anna and Mrs. Maguire continued to work together on one project or another, but there was less of the amiable jollity that had marked their first cooperative efforts.

Anna's ingenuity in finding food, however, had increased. Many people were malnourished and shelves were scarcely stocked in most shops, but Anna devised ways to put provisions not only on her own table but on that of the Maguires as well. She was furious when her plan for abundant meat was foiled after the increasing use of horses for food came to the government's attention and they imposed rationing on horsemeat as well as beef, lamb, and pork. Not to be outfoxed, Anna started setting snares up on the heath. Rabbit became a regular item in both kitchens on Sandy Lane. Anna was often up before dawn to pick mushrooms or gather dandelion leaves, which even Liam had been enticed into eating.

Then Anna discovered that ducks and geese weren't rationed and cajoled a local farmer into selling her six goslings that now patrolled her garden. The young geese were showing signs of maturing into the fierce sentries that their species were reputed to be. To Edith's delight, they pecked at Mick McGirty's trouser legs and cackled furiously to warn of the intrusion of the air raid warden in their territory. He hadn't returned since. The goslings trailed behind Anna, doting on her as if she was their mother. But Anna seemed only to view them in the cold light of an investment. She was anticipating income from their sale once they were grown, as well as looking forward to a few roast goose dinners.

"They may as well shoot Carlo in the head as send him into those air raids," said Anna, plonking a dead rabbit on the table next to the baby. The rabbit's head fell to one side, making it look as if it was peeping at William from under its floppy ears. "He's sure to be killed some night soon." William gurgled, and clearly attracted by the softness of the rabbit's fur, stretched one arm in the direction of the animal's ears.

"Not last night, thank God. When I called on Isobel earlier, she said he'd phoned to let her know he's on his way home for four whole days," said Edith, making no attempt to hide her delight. "You must have been up on the heath murdering rabbits when he called."

Anna grunted and headed for the back door.

The early morning had been so foggy that Edith hadn't been able to make out the hedge on the other side of the lane, but now the sun was breaking through and the estuary, glistening with high tide water, could be seen through the retreating mist. Edith decided to bundle William up and take a walk on the heath. Perhaps she'd run into Carlo returning from Liverpool.

Many people had been browned off with the winter weather in January and February; there'd been more snow than Edith had ever seen in her life. Liam had unearthed an old sled, and they'd all — except Isobel, of course — taken turns whizzing down the meadow on the other side of Sandy Lane, careening toward the beach, cheeks smarting and lips tingling. Seeing Anna and Mrs. Maguire take a turn reminded Edith how comparatively young they were — neither was yet fifty years old. Still, Edith thought it unlikely that either of them would have allowed themselves to be seen climbing aboard a sled had it not been for the unconstrained atmosphere of wartime. Edith had clung to Carlo from the back of the sled until they veered wildly to one side and overturned in a tangle of arms and legs.

During some particularly heavy snowfalls, Carlo hadn't been able to travel to Liverpool. Edith, Carlo, and Isobel had spent snowy days curled up under blankets in front of the fire, reading or just gazing at a few flickering flames while Anna busied herself in the kitchen. Carlo took delight in playing with William, keeping him amused for hours. And when he tired, Carlo cradled the sleeping baby in the crook of his arm while he held a book with his other hand.

Physical contact with Carlo had become as natural and uncomplicated to Edith as scratching an itch. They often hugged in greeting or as a farewell. She didn't think twice about resting her feet in his lap while stretched out on the sofa. Anna didn't seem to notice, and Edith suspected she considered it perfectly normal behaviour. Isobel just smiled and nodded benignly. If Mrs. Maguire had any thoughts on the subject, she kept them to herself.

Edith now rarely thought much beyond a day, two at the most. Uncertainty was so rife that there seemed little point. As a result, consequences weren't given the same weight as they once had been. It occurred to Edith that her behaviour was singularly different than it had been before war began. It was clear that peace would be a long time coming — if it came at all. She'd written to the chemist in Liverpool to tell him she'd have to give up the flat above his shop. He'd written back to say he'd store their few belongings until she could retrieve them. The loss of the flat caused her marriage to seem less real, and Joe also seemed farther away.

Once up on the heath, Edith could see signs of spring. Tightly wound shoots of bright green bracken had begun to unfurl. Gorse bushes, which were always dotted with one or two blooms, were now thick with bulging yellow flower buds sprouting from every bough. The air was cool but clear, now that the fog had dissipated.

Edith climbed to the crest of the hill that peaked behind Mrs. Maguire's house on Sandy Lane so she could take in the panorama of the estuary and the Welsh hills beyond. People maintained that you could glimpse the summit of Mount Snowden, the highest point in Wales, on a clear day, but Edith had no idea where to look. She could definitely see a jagged hilltop far to the south but was at a loss as to its name.

"What a sight for sore eyes," Carlo's voice called out from behind her. Edith turned but could see nobody. She was flummoxed — Carlo wasn't exactly small.

"Over here," Carlo called.

Edith veered from the path that followed the crest of the hill and walked a few feet through a thick carpet of heather in the direction the voice had come from. She peered through the branches of a dense thicket of gorse bushes. In the heart of the thicket, Edith could just make out Carlo, who was lying on his stomach in a perfectly round bowl, ten or twelve feet at its widest, about three or four feet deep at the centre, and generously lined with grass. It was obvious he'd been able to spy on Edith, spotting her feet through a few sparse lower branches of gorse. But thick upper branches, eight feet tall, hid him from her, or anybody else who might be passing.

"It's a bomb crater," called Carlo. "I discovered it a couple of weeks ago. I like to lie here for an hour or so to wind down on the way home. I stare at the sky and try to drive all the sights and sounds of the job out of my head. The grass is as sweet and comfortable as clean sheets. Come and give it a try." He turned on his back and lay, hands under his head, gazing at the sky. Careful to protect William from the plant's sharp spines Edith pushed her way through the thick screen of gorse. She placed William on Carlo's chest and lay down next to them. The generous growth of springy grass felt cool and pleasant.

"It must have happened during the air raid the night William was born. When our windows shattered," said Edith. She imagined the bomb landing in the middle of the gorse thicket, where the carpet of lush grass had taken root in the soil loosened by the blast. It seemed like a miracle that something designed to obliterate could ultimately engender such lusty and vigorous growth.

They lay silently. Edith glanced over at William, who slept peacefully, perhaps lulled by the gentle rise and fall of Carlo's chest as he inhaled and exhaled. One of Carlo's burly hands, the one farthest from Edith, held her baby securely in place like a protective paw. Edith could hear the breeze in the gorse, but lying at the deepest point of the depression, she, Carlo, and William were sheltered from any chilliness. Edith could feel the warmth of the spring sunshine on her face.

"I need to tell you something," Carlo suddenly said in a voice husky with emotion.

"All right," replied Edith, wondering what on earth he'd say.

"Something — I think you say bittersweet — happened when we first arrived on the job last night," Carlo said in a low voice. "Before the air raid began."

"Oh?" said Edith.

"Someone reported a noise coming from under the rubble at a house that took a direct hit four nights ago. A couple of us were sent to take a look. Sure enough, we could hear a faint tapping. We sent for help. It took about an hour, but eventually we dug down to a space no bigger than an airing cupboard. It must have been part of a cellar. A beam had fallen, and under it was a space, and in the space was a young woman around your age."

"She was still alive?" asked Edith.

"Still alive, and completely unhurt. It was amazing."

"That must have been gratifying," said Edith.

"We were happy for that, but the bitter part was, she was clutching a baby around the same size as William. But he was dead."

Edith gasped and instinctively reached a hand toward William's inert body.

"The mother wouldn't talk but clutched the baby to her. We couldn't coax her to let go. She clung to him with what little strength she had, which was a lot, considering how long she'd been trapped. Eventually, someone came and took them both away."

Carlo and Edith lay still for a minute or two.

"I'm so afraid, Edith," he said, turning his head to look at her.

"You have every right," exclaimed Edith, swivelling her head to meet his gaze. "It's very dangerous, working while bombs are falling. Exposed, in unsafe buildings."

"No, you don't understand. I'm not afraid for my life. I'm frightened that I'm losing a sense of the value of . . . my brain is . . ." Carlo stopped, obviously struggling to find the right words. "You can't imagine the work I'm doing."

"Try to explain," urged Edith, recognizing his need to talk. "Take your time."

Carlo hesitated, then spoke slowly but clearly.

"Some nights — most nights, actually — we come across parts of bodies torn apart by shrapnel or glass, or by the actual impact of a bomb. We collect whatever we can find in large baskets or on stretchers to transport to the mortuary. The first few nights, when I started, I didn't think I could take it. But you'd be surprised how the urgency of the job at hand quickly makes you forget the churning in your stomach."

Carlo stopped for thirty seconds or so. Edith could hear his breath sough through the hairs in his nostrils.

"Sometimes, if there's more than one person, it's difficult to know what parts of which body the pieces belong to," he continued. "Once we arrive at the mortuary, we help the attendants try to form whole corpses, racking our brains to remember which bits we found close to each other. We make out it's for the relatives, but that's only partly true. Of course, some semblance of a person with a torso, arms, and legs has to be put together so that families can imagine their loved one under the sheet when it's inched back to reveal a face — if that's even possible. But regardless of other people's concerns, we feel a compulsion to piece together a complete body, a person. We seem to need to do it, for ourselves."

Carlo hesitated and turned his head away to gaze up at the sky. Edith sensed that for whatever else he had to say, he couldn't look at her when he spoke. She too swivelled her head and saw a few specks, seagulls, slowly circling so high above that as they spiralled, they disappeared from sight and reappeared, like tea leaves rising and falling in a recently stirred cup of tea.

"What scares me is that after a while, you get so hardhearted," said Carlo, lowering his voice. "You forget what exactly you're dealing with. Last night, we were at a bombed house, completely destroyed, where we were told two sisters had been. Apparently, they were in their early twenties. Their mother was on the night shift at the Kirkby munitions factory and their father was away with the army. We found them — in bits and pieces — around where the cupboard under the stairs had been.

"Later, at the mortuary, I was feeling pleased with myself because we'd made a good attempt at one corpse. But then I was irritated when I realized we'd somehow overdone it. We didn't have enough parts left over to make another whole body for the other sister. We had to start again and take from the first girl to try and make it appear there were two.

"It was getting late, after dawn. The girls' mother had probably been told; perhaps she was on her way to the morgue. I was tired of the stench and of having my hands covered in dried blood — the whole damn thing was making me sick. I felt resentful and angry for being put in such a situation.

"Then one of the men I work with said something."

Edith kept staring straight ahead, up at the sky. It didn't seem right to look at Carlo at that moment. Not being Catholic, she'd never been in a confessional, but Edith could understand how the divulgence and witness of guilt-ridden secrets must be easier when confessor and priest are each invisible to the other. "What did he say?" Edith asked, hesitantly.

"He said, 'Just like a jigsaw puzzle, isn't it?'"

Edith reached out and grasped Carlo's free hand. He clutched hers.

"Reduced to seeing someone as a bloody jigsaw," Carlo murmured. "*Madonna!* It's terrifying."

They lay for a long time hand in hand. Edith could hear the plaintive screams of seagulls above the sound of the wind riffling the gorse.

"I'm sorry," said Carlo, at last. "I should have kept this to myself."

"No, no," said Edith. "It's all right. I'm glad you told me." She wasn't sure she was telling the truth. She felt pitifully inadequate. William stirred and murmured. Carlo moved as if to sit up. Edith turned to him and tugged at his hand to stop him. Carlo looked at her expectantly. His brown eyes looked darker than usual, stained with distress. Edith felt her old inhibitions attempting to muzzle her. She had to make a concerted effort to overcome them.

"I know and you know," began Edith, "that if you had met those young women when they were alive, you probably would have liked them. Perhaps you might have even flirted with them."

"Edith," Carlo protested.

"No, listen," she said. "They may have lowered their eyes modestly or thrown back their heads and laughed, or they might have taken offence. But either way, it would have been a human exchange. Afterwards, each of you goes on your way, both feeling a little more alive, one way or another."

"I don't know what you're getting at," said Carlo.

Edith had to admit she wasn't sure herself. She was feeling her way across unfamiliar territory. A part of her bridled at such frank talk. She heard her mother's voice: "Some things are best left unsaid, my girl," followed by a disapproving sniff.

"I'm just saying that, as grisly and unpleasant as what you're being asked to do is, I don't think there's any harm in thinking of it as a jigsaw puzzle. It doesn't mean that you think any less of the person that the pieces may once have been."

A flicker of self-doubt must have shown on her face, because Carlo squeezed her hand reassuringly. "You're right, but what worries me is that I begin to see everybody — you, me, everybody — as just pieces of flesh," he said. "I'm frightened that life is looking more and more worthless. Here one minute, gone the next."

Edith looked at the gorse, its buds bursting. She turned her head. Seagulls continued to whirl far above.

"You know, you could just as easily come to the conclusion that life is more valuable — precious," Edith argued.

"You make it sound like I have a choice," said Carlo.

The bitterness in his voice shook Edith. She felt a pang of intense misery borne out of a sudden awareness that not only did they have no control over the events that were overtaking them, but little or no choice about how they reacted to such life-altering times.

Edith thought about the insanity of the incident Carlo had described. She imagined the girls' mother, exhausted after a twelve-hour shift at a munitions factory — likely making bombs — rushing to the mortuary after hearing that her daughters had been killed in an air raid.

The breeze seemed to have picked up. Despite the shelter afforded them by the gorse bushes and the slope of the bomb crater, Edith was suddenly chilled.

"We'd better head for home," said Carlo, letting Edith's hand drop so that he could lift William carefully from his chest.

"At least it looks like the Americans will begin to help more," said Carlo. His and Edith's hands were reunited as he helped her to her feet. "The newspapers are saying Roosevelt has the power to give us anything we need now that this Lend-Lease Act has passed. Perhaps there'll be more food in the shops soon."

"But then your mother will be out of a job," said Edith.

"You think my mother will ever let herself be out of a job?" Carlo said, walking ahead with William in his arms.

ITALY

27-09-2002   **18:50**

The brothers strolled past brightly lit shop fronts on the street that wound its way from Campo Santa Margherita in the direction of their hotel and, they presumed, Armando's family's restaurant. Shamus felt slightly drunk. Surely there wasn't that much alcohol in a couple of glasses of Campari and soda, he thought.

"Hey, I tell you what," said Will. "I do have one distinct memory from when I was little."

"What?" asked Shamus.

"I remember eating rabbit," said Will proudly.

"How did you know it was rabbit?" asked Shamus.

"I remember seeing them lying around more than once when I was little, before they were cooked. Their ears didn't move, and their fur was very soft," said Will. "I seem to remember one of the neighbours catching them up on the heath above Granny Maguire's place."

"Then, when I was older," added Will. "I remember Edith dragging me to that bombed-out church at the corner of Renshaw Street whenever she took us into Liverpool. Do you remember?"

"I think so," said Shamus. "The old church with no roof."

"Yes, the roof was never replaced after the Blitz," said Will. "They kept it that way as a memorial to all those killed in the air raids during the war."

"Do you really think the Yanks will start rounding up Muslims?" Shamus asked.

"What?" said Will, thrown by the abrupt change in topic.

"You told Umberto it wouldn't be long until they were rounding up Muslims."

"Where've you been?" Will questioned. "They began to nab so-called suspects the day after 9/11. There are reports that they're expanding their naval base in Cuba to accommodate the poor bastards. I suppose they're not subject to the regular rule of law if they keep them outside the United States."

"I missed a lot of news when Luke was ill. I knew they'd apprehended Afghans, Taliban and the like, but maybe I've lost track of things."

Shamus's attention was caught by a particularly handsome jacket on a mannequin in a shop window. He stopped to examine it, thinking how he'd lost interest in fashion and buying clothes. Everyday life had ground to a halt for him during Luke's long illness.

"You may be surprised to hear this, but I've taken to telling people if I like them," announced Will, standing next to Shamus in front of the shop.

"What do you mean?" Shamus asked.

"You know, if there's something about somebody I find particularly attractive, I make a point of telling them," said Will. "I'm trying to be more overt about my feelings."

"I don't think a comment like 'beautiful breasts' qualifies as baring your soul," said Shamus.

"And you wonder why I don't make a serious contribution to our discussions," snapped Will.

"Sorry, sorry," said Shamus. "Please tell me what you mean and I promise not to mess around."

"Okay, we'll try again," said Will in a long-suffering tone. "One day, I was leaving a business lunch with a group of underlings, and one of them said something to me. He said that he really liked the way I always included everybody in the conversation. He said he just wanted me to know that he admired the way I gave everyone a chance to express themselves."

He was probably hoping for a raise, thought Shamus.

"Anyway," continued Will. "I was really chuffed, because I always think I run roughshod over everyone and never give anyone a chance to say anything."

Shamus was sorely tempted to point out to Will that he'd described himself to a tee. But then he realized his brother was in fact quite considerate. He really only wanted the best for people — people he liked, at least. It was surprising to Shamus that his brother hadn't turned out more like Joe. Somehow, Will seemed to have bucked the old tenet that dictated, like father, like son.

"So I decided to learn by my staff member's example and make a conscious effort to tell people if there was something about them I liked."

"Should I be worried that you haven't complimented me once in the last twelve hours?" said Shamus.

"Haven't I?' asked Will. "I probably meant to. I have to admit I find it a bit of a challenge with you." He grinned. "Just joking! But seriously, for instance, I wish now that I'd told Umberto how well he speaks English."

Once they reached the front door of their hotel, they saw that the restaurant lay directly opposite, as Armando had said. And just as he'd said, it was the only one in the street between Campo Santa Margherita and Campo San Barnaba. A few yards further ahead lay the bridge where they'd met Armando that morning. Rio San Barnaba gleamed under the light of a lamp on the far bank. The surface of the river moved slightly — it had a viscous quality, more like oil than water.

The windows of the restaurant glowed, but the sign above the door wasn't illuminated. Had they been looking for the restaurant by name, they might easily have missed it. The words "Da Baccanello" were virtually invisible in the shadows above the doorway. Neither brother noticed them as they walked toward the restaurant entrance.

When they pushed open the door, they were confronted by a large, low-ceilinged room, tightly packed with empty tables covered in scarlet tablecloths and adorned with startlingly white napkins folded into glistening wine glasses. The walls of the restaurant were lined with wood-framed photographs. As far as Shamus could tell without looking more closely, they made up a who's who of the world's celebrities. Some were simple headshots with a scrawled message. Others, obviously snapped in the restaurant, seemed to be of showbiz stars and other personalities flanked by one or sometimes two Italian men. Probably the owners, thought Shamus — they were too far away for him to see them in any detail.

"*Buona sera,*" said a tall woman as she walked toward them from the back of the restaurant. She appeared to be in her early fifties. Shamus noticed what perfect posture she had. Tall, with wide shoulders and a long neck, she held herself magnificently.

"Forgive us for being so early," said Will. "I hope you'll take pity on a pair of hungry tourists. It's just that Armando recommended you to us. Armando Belli?"

"*Si, è mio figlio,*" said the woman. "My son, yes. Please sit wherever you'd like."

Once Will and Shamus had seated themselves at a table next to the window, she asked them how they knew Armando.

"We met him this morning on the bridge just down the street. We literally bumped into each other," smiled Will.

"He probably collided with you on purpose, any excuse to talk to a tourist," she smiled. "He likes to show off his English, so he's often a little too sociable."

Shamus was impressed that Signora Belli seemed to have understood Will's double entendre about bumping into her son. Why was it, he wondered, that so many English speakers didn't learn foreign languages in the way that others learned English? Armando's mother placed a pair of menus on the table and asked if they'd like a bottle of mineral water to start.

"Yes, please," said Shamus. "*Frizzante, per favore.*" He guessed that Signora Belli's hair was doubtless as luxuriant as her son's, had it not been pulled back tight to her scalp and held in place just above the nape of her neck with a tortoiseshell clip.

"Is Armando here?" asked Will.

Armando's mother explained that it was much too early for her son but that he'd doubtless appear later in the evening. She left them to examine the menu as she went to fetch their bottled water.

"So to continue where I left off, I don't think we were given many pats on the back," said Will.

"Mmmm," murmured Shamus, having forgotten what Will was talking about outside the restaurant but not wanting to admit it. He'd opened his menu and was poring over the two-page list of dishes on offer.

"Not a lot of positive reinforcement, or whatever it's called these days," continued Will.

"You mean as kids?" asked Shamus, absently.

"Yes," said Will. "Although I have to admit it just wasn't done when we were growing up, was it? And some parents do go over the top these days: 'Very good, Tristan. Excellent. Well done for putting one foot in front of the other. Clever boy!'"

"I suppose Edith and Joe's diffidence didn't make for much of an example. 'You were well fed and fully clothed. What more do you want?'" parroted Shamus, mimicking their mother's Liverpool accent. He thought of his own reticence toward Luke. "I know you thought he was boring, but I worry I didn't tell Luke enough good stuff," he said, glancing at his brother.

Will looked embarrassed. "I'm sorry about what I said earlier, not the best timing in the world," he muttered. But then, in typical Will style, he insisted, "I'm not sorry I said it, though."

"Which means you meant it?" asked Shamus.

Will appeared confused. "I don't know quite what I meant. But I do believe you were more alive somehow when we were living in London. I used to envy your lust for life, for Christ's sake. I really missed you when you left."

"That lust for life, as you call it, might have killed me if I hadn't met Luke," said Shamus, trying not to show how moved he was by Will's revelation about missing him. Then, when Will frowned, Shamus explained. "AIDS. If I hadn't met Luke, who knows what might have happened."

"It wasn't just the multiple boyfriends," said Will. "You were a laugh a minute."

Shamus reflected on Will's words. He looked down at the leather-bound menus with gold-embossed lettering. Perhaps he had paid a price for opting to follow Luke to Canada. He had no doubt that he'd loved Luke, but was the move an unconscious attempt to put himself out of harm's way? That rationale would hardly have been fair to Luke. He thought about the missing element he'd pondered earlier that day. The spark that hadn't been present at the heart of his relationship with Luke. Shamus didn't like to think that perhaps he'd unknowingly sacrificed some kind of *joie de vivre* for the security of a steady relationship.

"Whatever I was or wasn't, I still think I could have been more demonstrative with Luke."

"You are joking, aren't you?" said Will, his voice laced with disbelief.

"What do you mean?" asked Shamus.

"You and Luke. My God, you were forever telling each other how wonderful you were. It was downright embarrassing."

"Really?" asked Shamus.

"God yes," insisted Will. "You went on and on telling Luke how much you fancied him and why. I seem to remember Mary asking me why I never told her the kind of things you told Luke. Pain in the arse, you were."

Shamus was amazed.

"And don't you remember the time I yelled at you two to keep your hands off each other at the dinner table at our place in Notting Hill?" asked Will. "I remember feeling guilty at the time — you jumped apart as if I'd caught you sodomizing each other, and you were only holding hands."

"That was the year we met, though," said Shamus. "In the first flush of love and all that. And we never quarrelled. You implied earlier today that the fact that Edith and Joe never quarrelled indicated a lack of affection."

"For Christ's sake," said Will in exasperation. "They never quarrelled because they never said anything to each other! For instance, I remember precisely the constipated conversation when Joe came home from his first day after he'd been given that promotion to head foreman, or manager-in-chief of the warehouse or whatever it was." Will parodied exactly Edith's accent and disinterested tone. "'How did it go then, Joe?'"

Shamus couldn't help giggling.

"'All right, yeah,'" Will mimicked Joe's offhand response. "And that was it for the rest of the evening," concluded Will, barely able to get the words out for laughing.

"Mind you, sometimes they could be quite expressive, despite their economy of words. I was there when Edith got back from her ill-fated trip to Greenham Common. All Joe said was, 'Caught a cold, then, have you?' He couldn't have exhibited more disdain if he'd made a half-hour speech."

Armando's mother arrived at that moment with their water. She smiled at the two laughing men and asked them if they were ready to order. "Oh, sorry," said Will sheepishly. "I haven't even looked at the menu yet." She assured them there was no hurry and told them to call her once they'd decided. Then she made her stately way behind a small bar at the back of the restaurant and disappeared through a swinging door that Shamus assumed led to the kitchen.

"It's odd how fact can so quickly become fiction and vice versa," said Will. "We're so bad at remembering."

"What do you mean we?" asked Shamus.

"I bet you misremember situations," said Will. "Like not recalling how expressive you were to Luke, for instance."

Shamus's mood changed instantly, and he felt ridiculous as he fought back the sudden threat of tears. He still wasn't convinced he'd been demonstrative enough, particularly in the couple of years before Luke died.

"I came across an old letter recently that Mary had written to me after we were first married," Will continued, oblivious to his brother's internal struggle. "If anyone had told me how loving she'd once been, I wouldn't have believed it. Too much shit in between."

"I'm not sure we can ever express enough love," managed Shamus.

"Okay, now we're wandering into Hallmark greeting card country," said Will, hastily opening his menu. "Let's order so we can change the subject."

"To hear some people talk, you'd think this Bevin chap was the second Messiah," said Liam from behind his newspaper. Edith could read the headline on the front page that hid Liam's head from view. "Bevin Wants 100,000 Women." Then, in smaller type, "State to Keep the Children."

"Bob MacDonald certainly idolizes him," said Edith. "Apparently, he came up with a scheme that gives dock workers permanent employment."

"He seems too good to be true. Says here he opposed Regulation 18B in the House of Commons when it was introduced," Liam's disembodied voice continued from behind the newspaper. "That's the one that gave the government the power to lock people up without a trial."

Liam's statement hung in the air. Edith was instantly aware of a new atmosphere in the room. The newspaper quivered slightly in Liam's hands. Edith wondered whether, in mentioning the regulation in this way, Liam was making a tacit apology for his past attitude toward the Baccanello family. She remembered Bob MacDonald saying that if it hadn't been for Regulation 18B, Gianni and the boys would never have been interned, at least not without a tribunal. She could have sworn that Liam's allusion to the rule was his idea of an excuse, an awkward attempt to explain his behaviour at the time.

Their silence continued. Birds chirped outside the open window, but no further sound, not even a whisper of a breath, came from behind Liam's newspaper.

"So it is," she finally muttered, trying to sound as noncommittal as possible. Was that an acknowledgment, she asked herself. By not saying anything specific, had she accepted Liam's apology — if that's what it was? Whatever had occurred, the uncomfortable atmosphere dissipated instantly.

"Bevin also believes we should open a second front to help the Soviet Union," continued Liam in as normal a voice as ever, as if absolutely nothing had passed between them. "Hah! Churchill calls him the Minister of Disease." Liam lowered the paper. "Dis-ease. Get it?"

"I get it, Liam," sighed Edith. She dismissed their exchange. Whatever it had been, she was too tired to think about it.

"I see they've stopped publishing the Atlantic shipping losses," commented Liam. "I'm not surprised. The lists were getting so long that if Gerry got his hands on the newspapers, he'd feel pretty proud of himself. Doesn't look like we'll be munching on American chocolate any time soon after all."

Edith wouldn't mind the lack of chocolate if she could only get some sleep. She could hardly remember when she hadn't had dark rings under her eyes. Everybody was exhausted. The Germans seemed to be targeting the west side of the Mersey more than ever. For hours on end, they heard explosions farther up the peninsula. After six consecutive nights of heavy air raids, fatigue was endemic.

The worst of it was that more bombs were falling in their vicinity. One of the bungalows on Sandy Lane — Shangri-La — had suffered a direct hit. Fortunately, the house was empty. The owners, Mr. and Mrs. Aitken, had moved to Scotland after the first batch of bombing, the night William was born. "We've had our fill of this nonsense," Mr. Aitken had told Mrs. Maguire the next day. "We're away up to my mother's house in Drumnadrochit."

During the raids, Edith was loath to shelter in the cramped hall cupboard. It was too claustrophobic. Mrs. Maguire debated if she should apply for a Morrison shelter. She was eligible for a free one since her income was less than £350 a year. Edith had seen a photograph in the newspaper of the odd-looking Morrison shelter, which was meant to sit inside people's houses. It was the height of a table, with a steel surface on top of a metal frame and wire mesh stretched over all four open sides.

"Looks more like a cage than a shelter," said Liam.

The accompanying text explained that a person was required to crawl into the "cage" during an air raid. If the house came down, the steel top and frame were designed to shield the inhabitant from falling beams and masonry.

"But what if the place goes up in flames and you're trapped in the darned thing?" ventured Liam.

"I don't think we'll bother," concluded Mrs. Maguire. "There must be hundreds of people who need them more than us."

So they huddled in the living room during raids.

Liam had taken to jiggling his right knee rapidly up and down. He started as soon as the air raid siren sounded and didn't let up until the welcome relief of the all-clear signal. Liam's new habit probably helped him, but it drove Edith up the wall. Nevertheless, she didn't have the heart to tell him to stop. Instead, she would do her best to comfort William, who cried inconsolably at the sound of the larger explosions. Edith wondered if he associated them with the trauma of his birth. The pace of Liam's quivering leg would accelerate when William started to cry. Mrs. Maguire knitted stolidly throughout, only halting when the house shook or if a bomb dropped close enough that they could hear a whistle as it fell. Edith tried to tell herself that, even at their worst, the raids couldn't be as bad as in Liverpool. The thought didn't give her much solace — especially on nights that Carlo was over there on duty.

It had, of course, been Liam who'd found out about the decoy fires. He had burst through the kitchen door as Edith and Mrs. Maguire were preparing their tea. Despite the cool weather, Liam was perspiring heavily.

"There had to be a reason we've been hit so hard lately," exclaimed Liam. "You'd think someone would have let us know."

"For heaven's sake," said Mrs. Maguire. "Calm yourself, lad."

It turned out that Liam and a friend had been looking for birds' eggs in the countryside to the northwest of Sandy Lane. They'd walked further than they realized and found themselves four or five miles up the peninsula, so they decided to cut through some fields to the Dee shore and make their way back to Shrimpley by the way of the beach. Suddenly, out of nowhere, they were accosted by two soldiers in full battle dress with guns at the ready. They were told to clear out of the area and make their way home by the inland road.

Birds' eggs were promptly forgotten. Liam, being Liam, persuaded his pal that they should climb a nearby hill so they could take a look at the area the soldiers were patrolling. From their vantage point above the cliff-top, they could clearly see the fields that bordered the coastline. Liam could make out what looked like a series of huge metal troughs. There were so many, he reported, that they covered at least three or four sizable fields. It had been hard for Liam to see clearly, but he described a network of pipes running parallel to the troughs. There were also several brick buildings around the perimeter, which Liam described as bunkers.

"We were stumped," said Liam, eyes shining. He was clearly relishing his role in reconnaissance. "Couldn't think for the life of us what on earth was going on."

"I don't know about stumped," said Mrs. Maguire. "You should be spanked. You could have been shot for a spy, for heaven's sake."

"Then, on the way down the hill, we met Raymond Clitheroe and his brother," continued Liam, so anxious to conclude his story that he completely ignored his mother. "Raymond reckons the troughs are filled with oil or paraffin or some such. Then, when the Gerry bombers are almost overhead, our lads set light to the whole works. Apparently the flames are massive. Raymond was up in the woods last night and saw everything."

"Well he's very stupid, whoever he is," said Mrs. Maguire distractedly. It was clear to Edith she was troubled by Liam's account.

"Raymond Clitheroe's in the sixth form at school," said Liam indignantly, as though this fact automatically bestowed absolute authority on the boy.

"Aren't you a bit old for bird-nesting?" asked Edith. She was trying to buy time to sort out her thoughts. But she'd also never understood boys' predilection for collecting things. The first thing Liam had done the day after William was born was to comb the garden for pieces of shrapnel from the bomb that had fallen in the lane. He couldn't have been happier when the men who came to fill in the bomb crater and replenish the grit on the road's surface had handed him an eight-inch-long piece of jagged metal they'd found embedded in a nearby tree trunk. Its sharp point and glinting surfaces reminded Edith of surgical instruments she'd once seen in a veterinarian's office.

"I've never found a robin's egg. It's a huge gap in my collection," Liam said. Then, realizing he'd been distracted, he blurted, "But don't you see? They're using the fires to fool the bombers. To make it look like the river is the Mersey, not the Dee. And to trick Gerry into thinking our shore is actually Liverpool and the docks. That's why we're getting hit so much lately. I ran all the way home to tell you," he said, appearing hurt that he hadn't been greeted with more gratitude.

Mrs. Maguire glanced at Edith.

"Why on earth didn't they warn us?" Liam asked, looking to his mother and then to Edith for an answer.

Edith noted the clarity of Liam's blue irises, as pristine as cornflowers.

"If it's true . . ." began Mrs. Maguire.

"Of course it's true," contended Liam.

"If it's true," she continued, "they could hardly tell everybody, could they? That would be letting the cat out of the bag."

Liam seemed to reflect on Mrs. Maguire's words.

"They didn't have to broadcast it on the wireless," he muttered. "But they could have alerted a few people."

"Well they wouldn't share the secret with just us, would they?" said Edith. "Think how many people would have to be told. They might as well write Hitler a letter."

Liam glanced around the room as though searching for someone who could offer an alternative explanation. Then, gradually, credence arrived. The muscles on Liam's face slackened, and Edith could see innocence drain away from his eyes, like cornflowers wilting.

"So we're nothing more than a bunch of sacrificial lambs," he said. "And to add insult to injury, we're not supposed to know it."

Again Edith and Mrs. Maguire glanced at each other.

"It's not exactly cricket, is it?" said Liam.

Edith couldn't help but wonder what game Liam thought was being played when Gianni and the boys were arrested.

* * *

"I'm darned if I'm staying here," Liam declared later that evening, jumping abruptly to his feet. The air raid siren had sounded as usual, and explosions could be heard to the northwest. "If I'm going to be a sitting duck . . ." he spluttered, so indignant he could hardly get out his next thought, ". . . well then, I may as well take a gander at the lure," he eventually finished. His mixture of waterfowl and fishing metaphors completely stumped Edith. She had no idea what he was getting so worked up about until he proclaimed, "I'm going up on the heath to see if I can see those decoy fires."

"Don't be such a ninny," cried Mrs. Maguire, but Liam had already disappeared through the door to the kitchen. "That boy's enough to make a saint swear," exclaimed Mrs. Maguire, rushing out after him. Edith could hear her calling from the back door. William, disturbed by Liam's ruckus, made a valiant attempt to cry, although Edith suspected he was too tired to put his heart into it. She rocked him back and forth until he fell back to sleep, then laid him carefully in one corner of the sofa, next to her.

Mrs. Maguire returned and sat heavily in her chair.

"That stupid boy will be the death of me," she muttered. "But I'm darned if I'm running all over the heath looking for him." It was obvious to Edith, however, as the sound of aircraft and the thud of explosions continued, that Mrs. Maguire was desperate with worry. "Jesus wept!" she exclaimed when she dropped some stitches from her knitting.

"Look," said Edith. "I know exactly where he'll be — on the path at the top. I'll go and drag him home. It won't take me more than ten minutes."

"Don't be silly," said Mrs. Maguire. "We don't want you both blown to bits."

"It sounds like the bombing is all up around Birkenhead. It'll be safe enough," she insisted. "Keep an eye on William." As Edith made for the door, Mrs. Maguire reluctantly transferred to the sofa to sit next to her slumbering grandson. "Take the torch" she yelled.

On her way past the kitchen cupboard, Edith grabbed the detachable bicycle headlight that they used for a light. Once outside, Edith stood for a few seconds while her eyes became accustomed to the dark. Then she headed up the track that led to the brow of the hill, where she often stood to admire the Welsh peaks on the other side of the estuary. Wartime frugality prevented her from using the headlight to light her way — it was powered by two precious batteries that had become almost impossible to replace if they ran down. She could just about make out the path, but in her haste she stumbled on a tussock of grass and slid a few feet down the hill. She could hear the drone of aircraft engines and the rumbling of bombs in the distance. She cursed Liam and thought, too late, that perhaps she should have recruited Carlo, who was at home next door enjoying a night off duty, to help her.

As soon as she crested the hill, she realized that Liam had been right about the decoy fires. She could see several massive conflagrations lining the coast that stretched toward the tip of the peninsula. Edith was astounded by the transformation of the landscape to the northwest, toward Birkenhead. The usual bucolic daytime scene had mutated into a seething panorama of light and sound. Clusters of searchlights picked out bulging contours of white clouds and billowing lobes of dark grey smoke that lent form and dimension to the night sky. A constant flashing and flickering, like an accelerated lightning storm, threw the silhouettes of distant buildings into sharp relief for brief seconds. Sometimes a shard of light would endure and burgeon into a bright yellow and orange inferno that spewed fountains of sparks into an indigo void. It was all Edith could do to not stand and gaze in awe. A few minutes later, she almost fell over Liam, who was lying on the ground next to the path at the highest point of the hill.

"Edith," he shouted to make himself heard above the constant rumbling of explosions, droning of bombers, and distant staccato crackling of anti-aircraft guns. He reached up, grabbed one of her hands, and pulled her down beside him. Edith could feel the chill of damp grass through her tweed skirt.

"Isn't it marvellous?" he yelled. Edith glimpsed the reflection of lights in his shining eyes. She had to admit the scene was mesmerizing. From her new perspective, she could clearly see the nearest decoy fire, which couldn't have been more than three or four miles away. A deep red glow emanated from an area the size of several football pitches. Every thirty seconds or so, some kind of flammable material must have been released in several locations over the furnace-hot expanse. Geysers of white flame erupted forty or fifty feet into the air. Sometimes only one or two were active, which was spectacular enough, but then ten, fifteen, as many as twenty spouts of dazzling light leapt into the atmosphere. Their rippling reflections could be seen in the nearby waters of the estuary.

"This is a sight better than Guy Fawkes night," shouted Liam. "Have you ever seen such fireworks?"

Farther up the coast, Edith could see what she presumed was another vast decoy fire, an arrangement of blazing rectangles shoved together in smaller or greater numbers, all flaming furiously. Edith supposed that from the air, the grid of fires would resemble a neighbourhood of burning buildings. She gazed at the landscape — firestorms, besieged communities, demonically illuminated night sky. The sheer magnitude of it was breathtaking. She'd never been confronted by anything so terrible yet so beautiful. She felt a kind of reverence for the scale of the creativity, the audacious ingenuity of the manmade hell that lay before her. But it was only a fleeting moment of misplaced admiration before, along with a growing awareness of the dampness of frigid earth beneath her, she began to feel disgust at the sheer waste that the scene represented. She thought of the cost of war in manpower and resources, let alone the number of human lives. And for what? To defend against — or wreak more — havoc and destruction than had ever been wrought before.

"Liam," she yelled. "You're bloody well coming home with me now. Your poor mother's worried sick."

Perhaps it was the power of the rarely invoked swear word or the fury in Edith's voice, but the effect on Liam was instantaneous. He clambered to his feet and dutifully followed as Edith picked her way along the hilltop path toward the track leading down to Mrs. Maguire's house.

As they descended the track, Edith noticed that she could still hear the drone of aircraft engines. She thought the brow of the hill would have muffled their sound. The din of explosions was certainly lessened on this side of the rise; she couldn't hear the stutter of anti-aircraft guns at all. Perhaps it was just that the bombers were so much higher, thought Edith. She could hear Liam stumbling down the incline behind her.

At the sound of the first explosion, down near the beach, Edith realized that the airplane noise was coming from the estuary immediately ahead of them and not from the north, as she'd thought.

In her panicked haste to reach the comparative safety of the house, her feet slipped out from under her and she saved herself from falling with a hand outstretched behind her, scrabbling upright despite the pain of grit embedded in her palm. An explosion reverberated from the direction of the meadows above the beach.

After that, Edith wasn't sure what she heard first — Liam's warning shout or the sound of a bomb hurtling through the air above them, the sickening whistle of a high explosive that they'd all learned to recognize. Whichever it was, she flung herself to the ground. But in the urgency of the moment, she forgot to allow for the steep gradient of the hillside. She pitched forward into space and tumbled sideways, rolling over and over down the hill until she came to an abrupt halt in a particularly dense patch of heather.

The moment she came to a stop, Edith felt the ground shudder. An abrupt change in air pressure, along with the thundering of an eardrum-ripping blast, rendered her momentarily deaf. Moments later, she felt a hail of earth and pebbles hit her clothes and hair and instinctively covered her head to protect herself. Before the next explosion, Edith could have sworn she heard, despite the water-filled quality of her blocked ears, the scream of an animal in the throes of being killed by a fox. Ridiculous, she thought, pressing herself harder into the ground. Five or six further explosions reverberated around the heath. Edith kept her arms over her head even though it was clear that the bombs were falling farther and farther away as the airplane flew toward Shrimpley village. Despite the wool of her pullover and the flesh of her bicep covering her uppermost ear, Edith definitely heard more screams between the din of each bomb blast.

By the time the remnants of the final explosion had echoed across the heath and Edith tentatively removed her arm from her head, the screams had become a series of whimpers interspersed with the sound of gasping. She heard Mrs. Maguire's nearby shouts — "Liam, Liam" — and finally realized it was Liam who'd been screaming.

"Edith, bring the light," yelled Mrs. Maguire. Edith could see her dim silhouette several yards up the hill, hurrying toward the sound of Liam's whimpering. Miraculously, Edith was still clutching the bicycle headlight. As she struggled to reach Liam, she could see Mrs. Maguire hunched over her son's body. Edith thought she could see one of Liam's feet moving, as if he were trying to grind the heel of his boot into the earth to give him traction to stand. Mrs. Maguire snatched the bicycle headlight from Edith and directed the narrow beam onto Liam's face. His skin was so pale that it glowed, like phosphorescence on a clock face. His forehead shone with perspiration. His lips were pulled back in a grimace, teeth glinting in the lamplight. Liam's eyes were so tightly shut that sharp shadows of wrinkles radiated across his cheeks and brow. Mrs. Maguire examined his head, running her fingers through his hair and feeling behind his neck. She raked his body with torchlight, passing the beam up and down each arm. The fingers of one of his hands formed a tight fist while his other hand opened and closed as though grasping for something. The lamplight travelled down his right thigh. Four or five inches below his knee, the beam illuminated a mass of glistening, bloody flesh. Out from under it, Edith could see a strand of mother-of-pearl-coloured sinew snaking its way into the beam of the torch.

"Holy Mary, Mother of God," gasped Mrs. Maguire. Yet she had the presence of mind to direct the beam all the way down Liam's calf to examine the extent of the damage. At first, Edith thought Liam must have lost his shoe. His leg ended in ragged, blood-soaked trouser fabric draped against the emerald freshness of a young frond of bracken. Then she realized that the bottom part of his leg and his foot were not there.

"We've got to stop the bleeding," said Mrs. Maguire. "Here, hold the light." She stood and lifted her skirt. She yanked at the waistband of her nylon slip, and Edith could make out the underskirt's pale shape in the darkness as it fell gracefully to Mrs. Maguire's feet. Edith heard the sound of ripping fabric.

"You'll have to lift his thigh while I loop this underneath," said Mrs. Maguire, putting the lamp on the ground with the beam aimed at Liam's upper leg. Edith hesitated, imagining the pain she was about to inflict.

"Quickly," urged Mrs. Maguire.

Somehow they managed to apply a makeshift tourniquet, while as heartwrenching as Liam's screams and bellowed schoolboy curses were, what moved Edith to tears was their mildness. Not a single obscenity or blasphemous expression crossed his lips. He howled what sounded like "Crikey" a few times and once shrieked "Lummey," sounding more astonished than pained. Then he suddenly became silent.

As soon as Mrs. Maguire finished tying a knot, she grabbed the lamp and examined his face. He was unconscious, his eyes closed, but he was breathing, although in snatched, shallow gulps.

What followed was a blur of panic and haste. Edith remembered bursting into Anna's house, so tearful and out of breath that she could barely explain. As soon as Carlo wrested from her exactly what had happened, he rushed into the darkness to fetch the farmer down the lane. The two of them managed to lift Liam onto an old wooden door. They carried him to the rear of the farmer's van and slid him in, door and all. Mrs. Maguire jumped in after him, calling to Edith to fetch her handbag as fast as she could. Anna insisted on accompanying them — she sat in the passenger seat and refused to move. Edith watched, only vaguely aware of Carlo's arm around her shoulders, as the van took off helter-skelter down the lane, bound for the cottage hospital in the next village.

As soon as the van disappeared, the soulful wail of the all-clear siren could be heard. Edith suddenly remembered William. She ducked away from Carlo, shouting a hurried explanation as she dashed up the path to the house.

William was lying fast asleep in the corner of the sofa where she'd left him. Edith sank to her knees on the hand-hooked rug in front of the fireplace, where embers and white ash were all that was left of the fire. She had no idea how long she lay in a heap, but it couldn't have been more than five or ten minutes, because there was enough life remaining in the grate for a shovelful of coal to slowly ignite. When she picked up Mrs. Maguire's copper coalscuttle, the pain of grit embedded in her palm surprised her.

Having revived the fire, Edith went to the kitchen and held her hand under the cold-water tap. She laboriously picked at the skin until all the grit had been removed. Clear water dribbled over the surface of her bleeding palm, and she watched as brief swirls of crimson crept across the white stoneware sink. She wrapped her fist in a towel and stood stock still, completely at a loss. For a few seconds, her mind went blank. Then she went to fetch a blanket from her bedroom and settled onto the couch next to William with the idea that she should wait up for Mrs. Maguire.

Edith fell into a trance, gazing mindlessly at the flickering coals, incapable of thought, until eventually she fell into a troubled sleep.

Tuesday, July 29, 1941

"I caught the last bomb of the Blitz," crowed Liam to Fred Saunders as he threw himself onto the back seat of the taxi beside Edith.

Edith smiled when Fred, who was hard of hearing, replied from the front seat, "Nay lad, there's plenty more buses where yours came from. They run till eleven o'clock tonight."

"Not bus. Bomb," yelled Liam. "I caught the last bomb."

"I'd leave it if I were you, Liam," suggested Edith. "You have to realize nobody can tell there's anything wrong with you unless they see you walk. And even then they'd probably just assume you'd had one too many in the pub."

Liam was in fact too young to drink alcohol in a public house. But in the almost three months since he'd lost his leg, Liam had displayed astonishing perseverance and resolve, quickly learning to walk without the aid of a stick. Edith had begun to think of him as older than his years.

Liam's claim of having been hit by the last bomb of the Blitz was not strictly correct, since other cities — Birmingham and London, for instance — suffered a further two or three nights of bombardment. But it could possibly have been the last bomb of the raids on Liverpool; Edith hadn't heard an air raid siren or a single explosion since the evening Liam was hit. For the first few peaceful nights, she'd slept soundly for ten to twelve hours, although once or twice she'd woken abruptly, heart racing, believing that she could hear airplane engines or a siren. When it turned out to be Mrs. Maguire on the way to the toilet or the screech of an owl on the heath, Edith sank back into a heavy slumber. William, who had only ever known nights of air raids and explosions, seemed to enjoy the novelty of uninterrupted sleep.

The general consensus was that Liam had been lucky, although the relative nature of good fortune was illustrated by Mrs. Maguire's account of an exchange between Anna and the doctor who'd attended to Liam.

Part of the so-called luck attributed to Liam was that the medic on duty at the six-bed hospital in the next village had been a field surgeon during World War I. Despite his grandiose manner, the elderly doctor was an expert in the amputation of limbs and had, according to nurses and physiotherapists, performed an excellent job on Liam's leg.

Mrs. Maguire described the arrogance with which the doctor had announced the results of the operation to her and Anna. "It's very good news," he trumpeted. "It appears that shrapnel severed the leg midway between the knee and the ankle. I removed some nasty metal fragments lodged in remaining sections of the tibia and fibula. But the knee was completely unharmed. He should make a perfect recovery."

"Good news?" questioned Anna loudly. "You tell this mother it's good news her son loses a foot!" Mrs. Maguire had tried to quiet Anna, but she wouldn't be silenced. "Perfect recovery!" Anna cried. "Next thing you going to tell us he play football for England."

What Anna and Mrs. Maguire didn't know was that if Liam had lost his whole leg, it would have been much more difficult for him to use a prosthesis. The fact that his knee had been saved meant that he would have little trouble rehabilitating.

"Why didn't the doctor tell us that?" asked Mrs. Maguire of the nursing sister who eventually explained it to them.

Carlo appeared as soon as Fred Saunders's taxi drew up outside Mrs. Maguire's house. He opened the car door for Liam and extended a helping hand.

"I can manage on my own," insisted Liam, a hint of irritation in his voice. When Edith had paid Fred, she looked up to see Carlo watching Liam's progress up the path with an expression of unmitigated admiration.

"It's a miracle," Carlo whispered.

Edith wouldn't have described it as miraculous exactly, but she did find it remarkable that Liam was alive, let alone walking. After she'd seen his appalling injury in the lamplight and imagined the amount of blood he must have lost, she didn't believe he could survive. Liam had been told that another element in his "luck" was that the village hospital had plasma in storage. If he'd gone to Birkenhead, where hundreds of air raid victims were being treated, chances were they'd have run out of plasma and couldn't have done a transfusion.

Liam walked up the garden path with a slight lurch. His right step, the one he took with his artificial leg, was faster than the other. He seemed to hurry through it and to hold his left arm out to balance himself as he put weight on his prosthesis. He wore the shoes he'd been wearing the night he was hit.

When Edith had awakened the morning after Liam was injured, Mrs. Maguire still hadn't returned home. Edith couldn't help but fear the worst. Her muscles were stiff after the evening's exertions, and a night on the sofa hadn't helped. She'd been filling the kettle for tea, trying to protect her sore palm as she did so, when she heard Carlo's knock. Edith gasped when she opened the door and saw Liam's shoe in Carlo's hand.

"Where was it?" she asked.

"On the slope, a yard or so from where he was lying," said Carlo. The shoe was undamaged, and the only evidence of blood was a small stain on the inside. The obvious question of Liam's missing foot hung in the air between them, but Edith didn't ask and Carlo didn't mention it.

Edith offered Carlo a cup of tea. While they sat silently at the kitchen table, she tried to ignore Liam's single shoe, which sat on the floor beside the back door where Carlo had placed it. But before her cup was half empty, Edith took the shoe to Liam's bedroom and deposited it, out of sight, in the bottom of the wardrobe in his bedroom.

She hoped Carlo would give her some sign of empathy or reassurance, but when she returned to the kitchen, he didn't react. He merely sipped his tea and stared out of the window. Edith resented Carlo for causing her to feel embarrassed by her squeamishness. The thought crossed her mind that perhaps Carlo had been right about himself — maybe he was becoming too accustomed to carnage.

When they'd heard that Liam was to be fitted with an artificial lower leg and taught to walk again, Edith plucked up the courage to show the shoe to Mrs. Maguire. She was relieved when, after a moment of silence, Mrs. Maguire displayed her usual pragmatism. "They say they'll start rationing clothes and shoes next month," she said. "It's just as well we haven't thrown the other one out. I only bought those shoes for him last September for school. There's plenty more wear in them yet."

Mrs. Maguire didn't balk when Edith hugged her — the first embrace Edith could remember between them — but she muttered, "Don't be so daft."

Carlo and Edith followed Liam up the garden path and into the house. For half an hour, they talked about everything but Liam's leg. When Mrs. Maguire went into the kitchen to start preparing their tea, Carlo stood up to leave.

"Carlo," said Liam from the sofa. "I hear you found my shoe."

"Yes," said Carlo.

"What happened to my bloody foot?" demanded Liam. Edith couldn't help starting, not only at the abruptness of his question but also at his swearing. There'd been a number of soldiers in the rehabilitation hospital with Liam; he'd doubtless picked up his bluff manner and bad language from them. She supposed it was only natural that his recent experiences had bestowed on Liam some attributes of manhood.

"Bad choice of adjective, sorry," muttered Liam, quickly reverting to his old self. Carlo sat down again, next to Liam on the couch. "I gave your foot a decent burial up on the heath," he said.

Liam looked at the floor and nodded his head. "This might sound peculiar," he said, turning to look at Carlo. "But I'm glad it's accounted for." Edith thought, despite thinking of him as more of an adult since the night he'd lost his foot, that his eyes still had a childlike quality about them, as though he were pleading to be understood.

"I know," said Carlo softly, gently covering Liam's nearest hand with one of his own. "Believe me, I know," he repeated.

Edith felt a pang of guilt for having questioned Carlo's sensitivity. She'd been mistaken in assuming that his more restrained manner had meant that he cared less.

"And now I'd better get this peg leg off and lie down on my bed for a while," said Liam, heaving himself to a standing position. "I'm not supposed to wear it for too long at a stretch until the skin on my stump toughens up."

Carlo stood to leave. Edith followed him out on to the porch. It was a sunny afternoon, and though the weather had been unseasonably hot for most of the month, they'd had some rain in the past couple of days and the vegetation gleamed with springlike freshness.

"It feels such a relief to have some peace since Hitler turned his attention to Russia," said Carlo, leaning on the porch balustrade with two elbows. "And I'm quite enjoying the rebuilding effort. It's so much better than looking for bodies." He turned and smiled at Edith. "You wouldn't believe the amount of reconstruction going on, especially around the docks. There must be two thousand troops working there, as well as a thousand or more of us civvies."

"You were good to Liam," said Edith. "Mrs. Maguire will probably never tell you, but I know she's grateful for what you did to help him the night he was injured, not to mention retrieving his shoe and everything."

"But of course she thanked me," said Carlo. Edith chided herself; she should have known better than to underestimate Mrs. Maguire. "I tried to tell her that it wasn't so difficult for me, but I'm not sure she understood . . ." his voice petered out. "It's wonderful to see Liam up and about," he quickly continued.

"I know what you mean," said Edith, but she found it difficult to take much comfort from Liam's rehabilitation. It seemed too unfair that he'd lost his foot in the first place. Watching his efforts in hospital as he teetered on his new leg, grasping two parallel bars on either side of him for support, had enraged Edith. She felt as if she was watching a deviant version of a nestling learning to fly. But Liam had seemed far from angry or despondent about his loss. He had shouted with glee when he managed his first few steps without the support of the bars. Even William, who she'd taken along for a visit, had crowed with delight at the jubilant cries of congratulation from the physiotherapist.

"It's going to be a beautiful evening," said Carlo, looking out over the meadows toward the beach.

"Yes," Edith agreed, following his gaze to stare at the sunlit panorama below Mrs. Maguire's house.

"Let's take a walk later," suggested Carlo. "We could stroll up to the crater."

"I suppose Mrs. Maguire could keep an eye on William for a couple of hours," said Edith, maintaining her gaze across the estuary, where a network of sandy channels were swiftly becoming engorged with the inexorable waters of the incoming tide.

* * *

Whenever Edith looked back on that evening — as she often did — she never ceased to wonder at the deftness with which she and Carlo made love for the first time.

Yes, it had been a strange and difficult period. And yes, she had yearned for solace after the concentrated horror of the Blitz. The comforts of life had been few. Food was scarcer than it had ever been, and what had once been a day's provisions were now expected to last a week. Obviously, everybody's life was dislocated. There were few who didn't have friends or family members who had moved away, disappeared, or been killed, and many had experienced all three varieties of loss. And in the face of the future's complete unpredictability, almost everybody had become accustomed to thinking ahead only as far as a month, or less. Long-term consequences seemed non-existent. Life hung, not in the balance exactly, but in absolute uncertainty.

But notwithstanding all that, Edith could never understand the ease with which her affair began. The vagaries of war simply didn't seem justification enough. "Even so," Edith always said to herself in subsequent years on the frequent occasions she revisited the memories of her liaison with Carlo, always with a frisson of excitement and only a hint of self-reproach. Sometimes Edith would look at herself in a mirror and say the words aloud: "Even so, even so." Then Edith would silently remonstrate, as though searching for more fuel to add to her fire of incredulity, that she and Carlo had been married to other people. In both their worlds, a wedding vow wasn't something to be taken lightly. Just five years earlier, the monarch's association with a woman who had broken her marriage contract had precipitated the extraordinary act of his abdication.

It was telling that Edith never took into account the fact that she'd been only twenty-one years old and Carlo twenty-eight. Why did she deny herself the irresponsibility of immaturity? Liam would sometimes say, decades later, "At that age, you'd do anything with anybody if you thought you could get away with it." Edith didn't know why she never learned not to roll her eyes and say, "Speak for yourself." Because then, when Liam gave her a knowing look, she was always forced to look away, angry and frustrated that she wasn't able to explain that it hadn't been as simple or as crude as he suggested.

After Edith and Carlo had tentatively pushed through the gorse bushes, Carlo threw himself down in the middle of the bowl of the crater, sprawling luxuriously on the thick grass. Edith lay down next to him and reached for his hand. She experienced not even a hint of the inhibition that she'd sometimes experienced before with Carlo — this time, there were no butterflies in her tummy. It was easy to be sanguine if you weren't thinking further than the present moment. The air in the crater was reassuringly warm. Edith felt the supple mat of vegetation beneath her and could smell the fecund scent of uncultivated earth.

For the next couple of hours, nowhere existed for Edith except the bowl of a grass-lined bomb crater in the gentle heat of a sunlit early July evening. Carlo and she made love as affectionately and considerately as friends but at intervals reverted, with the primeval urgency of animals, to an unalloyed frenzy of pure lust. Edith was amazed at the sensations her body was capable of. Being with Carlo was a more sensual and pleasurable experience than she ever could have imagined. She also believed it was the most communicative she'd ever been. She expressed herself with every caress, every squeeze, every bite, moan, and thrust, every spasm.

Afterwards, Carlo retrieved his silver cigarette case from his corduroy jacket, lit two cigarettes, and handed one to Edith. They lay spent and perspiring, watching drifting smoke as dreamily as if under the influence of opium. Carlo stroked Edith's naked thigh with the knuckle of one finger. She thought no further than the formula for William that she'd need to mix when she got home.

ITALY

"Where are you from?" asked Armando's mother when she arrived at their table to take their order.

"Canada. But originally from Liverpool," replied Shamus.

"Oh Liverpool!" she exclaimed. "My papa was born in Liverpool."

"But you're not English, surely," said Will. "You don't look it. And you have an Italian name."

"No no," she said with a laugh. "My grandparents moved there in 1919, looking for a better life." She went on to describe visiting the city when she was a girl. "I'd discovered the Beatles, and I was crazy about Paul. I was only fifteen years old, you understand," she explained. Then she laughed and described how she'd taken the train all on her own. "I didn't see Paul, but I was glad I went when I did. My grandmother died a year later."

She went on to tell them that although her father was born there, he'd left when he was a boy and always swore he'd never go back.

"It's not the best of cities, but banishing oneself forever seems a bit extreme," Will said.

Armando's mother looked puzzled. Shamus explained that Will was wondering why her father never returned to the city where he was born.

"He had some very bad experiences there during World War II," she explained. "So he came here and opened this restaurant, nearly sixty years ago. Papa will be seventy-eight years old this year."

The two brothers ordered a bottle of Valpolicella *ripasso*, a shared dish of *baccalà* to start, then *spaghetti alle vongole* for Will and *risotto alle seppie* for Shamus. Shamus wondered if they ought to have ordered a white wine with seafood, but Will preferred red. Shamus's concern was put to rest when Armando's mother nodded in approval. *"Perfetto,"* she beamed as she wrote the last item with a flourish. When their food arrived, Will looked with disgust at the black mess on Shamus's plate.

"It looks like one of Edith's treacle tarts gone badly awry."

"It's rice with cuttlefish, cooked in its own ink," said Shamus. "It's delicious."

"If you happen to be a Goth," said Will.

An Italian family of six adults and four children arrived as the two brothers were eating. It took little effort on Signora Belli's part to shove some tables together to make a space large enough for them. A few minutes later, a trio of efficient-looking German women pushed their way hesitantly through the door, clutching guidebooks.

"Ist hier der Bachannalia?" asked one of them, mangling the name. When Armando's mother confirmed they were in the right place, the women looked mightily relieved and took a seat on the other side of the room from the brothers. Shamus was glad they hadn't sat next to him and Will, given his brother's loud comments about the German couple in the café that morning.

Armando materialized as they were finishing their food. *"Buona sera,"* he beamed. "I'm so happy you came."

"We didn't expect to see you so soon," said Shamus. He explained that his mother had said that Armando probably wouldn't appear until later.

"I can't stay for long. I have to see a person about a dog, yes?"

"See a *man* about a dog," corrected Shamus.

"This is what you say in England to be *misterioso,* yes?"

Shamus and Will laughed and agreed that this was the case.

"Actually, it's a girl about a date," smirked Armando.

Unbeknownst to the young Italian, his mother had come up behind him and heard what he'd said. She launched into a tirade in Italian that Shamus understood to mean that Signora Belli hoped his date wasn't another American or Scandinavian tourist. She demanded to know why he couldn't find a Venetian girl, get married, and settle down.

"Basta, Mama!" Armando remonstrated. His mother cuffed him lightly around the head, sending a hank of his thick hair flying. She cleared away the brothers' dirty dishes and told them she'd return soon to see if they'd like any dessert. Armando sat at their table, saying he'd chat with them for a few minutes before it was time for him to leave.

"Your mother told us that your grandfather was born in Liverpool," said Will. "You didn't mention it when we told you we were from there."

Armando explained that there were too many family stories to keep straight. He'd forgotten half of them — especially those about the Second World War.

"I know the feeling," mumbled Will.

"But you're too young to remember," asserted Armando. "You couldn't even have been born."

"On the contrary," said Will smugly. "I was born during an air raid in 1940. Our house was hit by a bomb just as I emerged."

"It explains his bellicose nature," interjected Shamus.

Armando clearly didn't understand, but when Shamus explained, he smiled, nodded, and raised his fists as he'd done that morning on the bridge. He pretended to throw a punch at an imaginary adversary.

"I'm sure I remember the sound of explosions when I was born," said Will, ignoring Shamus's remark and Armando's charade.

Shamus laughed and explained to Armando that as children they'd spent every summer at their grandmother's house, where Will was born. And how every summer they'd had to hear the story of the bombing raid on the night of Will's birth.

"Was this in Liverpool?" asked Armando.

"Just outside. Our grandmother lived in a village in the countryside not far away."

"Why were they bombing the countryside?" asked Armando.

"They were bombing the city, but they dropped a few outside as well. Some kind of mistake on the part of the Germans, I think," explained Shamus. "There were lots of bomb craters in the land around my grandmother's house."

"Hey, remember that one that Edith would take us to, up on the heath?" asked Will excitedly. "She said it was from one of the bombs that fell while I was being born. I loved that place. It was like a magic circle, totally surrounded by gorse. We'd lie in it for hours, making up stories, talking about life. "

Shamus was astonished. For someone with few early memories, Will was having a veritable flood of them.

Armando jumped up and announced it was time for him to leave. Shamus thought he was probably bored stiff with all their old family history.

"Before you go, would you have a cigarette to spare?" asked Will. Shamus couldn't believe his ears. He was too stunned to point out that Will had given up smoking years before.

"I thought you told me you didn't smoke," said Armando.

"I still partake now and again," replied Will.

"You'll have to go outside to smoke it, you know," said Armando as he slid the object of Will's obsession out of his jacket pocket and snapped open the clasp. Once Will had taken a cigarette, he asked Armando if he could examine the cigarette case once more.

"C.B.," recited Will. "Something Belli. What does the C stand for?"

At that moment, Signora Belli came to ask about dessert. "We have some *tiramisù,* freshly made today," she tempted them. By then, Armando had launched into a complicated explanation to Will of the significance of the initials on the cigarette case. Will was staring up at the tall young man, listening attentively. Shamus, not wanting to appear impolite, and not giving a toss about the metal case, ignored Armando and Will. He asked Armando's mother if she'd made the *tiramisù* herself.

"No no," said Signora Belli. "I have to admit I'm not so good at that kind of thing. But it is an old family recipe." She went on to describe in some detail the various steps and ingredients that went into the dessert's making. In the background, Shamus could make out Armando laboriously repeating names and dates.

"What do you think, Will?" Shamus asked his brother once Armando's mother had finished outlining the recipe. "How does *tiramisù* sound?"

Will didn't appear to hear him. He was frowning and staring at Armando intently.

"Will?" Shamus insisted. But Will ignored Shamus and continued to stare at Armando. Receiving no response from the brothers, Armando's mother said something to her son in Italian, obviously a repeat of her earlier comment about the unsuitability of his non-Italian girlfriends.

Armando flew into a rage. He snatched his cigarette case from Will, shouting and gesticulating in his mother's face with his other hand. Signora Belli tried to calm him, but there was no placating the young man and he stormed out of the restaurant without a goodbye or a backward glance.

To Shamus's amazement, his mother appeared completely unruffled by her son's tantrum. *"Signori,"* she declared, as though nothing untoward had occurred. "If not *tiramisù,* perhaps some coffee?"

"Order me whatever you're having," muttered Will to Shamus. He stood, then hurried out of the restaurant holding up the cigarette he'd taken from Armando, leaving Signora Belli with the impression that he was going out for a smoke.

Shamus was amazed by Will's behaviour and totally taken off guard by Signora Belli's equanimity in the face of her son's outburst. He asked for the first thing that popped into his head.

"Do you have any *vin santo?"*

"Certo, we have. Two glasses and some *biscotti?"* Signora Belli inquired with a smile.

The sweet wine and biscotti had been delivered by the time Will returned. He appeared calmer.

"You okay?" asked Shamus. "Did you really smoke that cigarette?"

"I'm fine," insisted Will. "And no, I haven't suddenly taken up smoking again. I threw it away. I just wanted to ask Armando something, but he'd run off by the time I got outside."

Will was obviously unwilling to explain further, so Shamus dropped the subject. The two brothers sat in silence, staring at the other patrons. The Germans mumbled softly to each other, while the Italian family seemed to be conducting several conversations at the same time. Shamus remembered his Italian friend Vince telling him that the demonstrative Italian was a stereotype. But Armando's mercurial personality seemed to prove that stereotypes existed for good reason.

"I guess *La Serenissima* isn't always so serene," said Shamus, referring to the contretemps between Armando and his mother. Will didn't respond. It was only after they'd drunk their *vin santo* and sampled a *biscotto* each — "on the house," declared Armando's mother — that he seemed disposed to talk.

"As far as *La Serenissima* is concerned, Venice's motto might be 'Peace,' but its emblem is a winged lion," Will commented. "Symbol of ferocity in trade and war."

"Well I'm not used to people ranting and raving," declared Shamus.

"You wouldn't be, would you?" said Will distractedly. But then he started talking about how Edith had had a bit of a hysterical collapse a couple of months after Joe's funeral. He said it was too bad that Shamus had run off back to Canada — he might have profited from the experience.

"Why didn't you tell me?" asked Shamus, wondering what the hell Will meant by him "profiting from the experience."

"It was around the time Luke became ill again. I didn't want to bother you," said Will. "In fact, I thought at first that she was upset by your news. She phoned, ostensibly to tell me she'd spoken to you and that you'd told her Luke's cancer had recurred."

"I phoned her the day we got the news. That was February 2001," said Shamus, without having to think for even a second. He wondered if he'd ever forget the dates of each grisly stage of Luke's ordeal. "It was only two months after Joe died," said Shamus thoughtfully. "Maybe it was too much for her, coming so soon after that."

"She started to sob over the phone," said Will. "Which was unusual, you have to admit. Edith can be pathetically affected by things, but she's rarely moved to tears."

Shamus had to agree. On the rare occasions that he'd seen her cry, her tears were born out of compassion for some unknown victim of circumstance. He remembered that during his time at university, Edith had wept openly at the news that more than a hundred children had died in a mudslide that buried a school in Wales.

"She volunteered to come over to Canada and help, you know," Shamus said. "After I told her that Luke would have to go through more chemo and radiation."

"Why am I not surprised?" said Will.

"Luke probably wouldn't have minded, but I was worried she'd show her concern by trashing Canadian health care, or been so apprehensive about the situation and disoriented by Toronto that she'd be more of a liability than an asset."

"You were right," said Will. "It could have gone either way."

His brother's words went some distance toward reassuring Shamus. But he still wondered if his refusal of his mother's offer had been yet another example of his eschewing intimacy for fear of a messy outcome. Edith's proposal had been a rare acknowledgment of the depth of his relationship with Luke; Shamus wasn't convinced he'd made the right decision in rebuffing her. He dipped a *biscotto* into his sweet wine and sucked on it until the sodden crumbs dissolved on his tongue.

"Anyway, she seemed to be in bad shape on the phone, so I suggested I go up to Liverpool to spend the weekend with her," continued Will. "She was a bit mopey when I arrived. I tried my best to cheer her up. but she didn't really snap out of it. Then, as I was leaving, I tried to reassure her by telling her that you were strong and Luke was in good hands and not to worry."

"That was good of you," said Shamus, wondering if it were true.

"The thing is, she looked at me as though she didn't know what I was talking about," said Will. "I remember I was late for my train so I just said, 'Shamus? Luke? Cancer?'"

The implication of the three words hit Shamus like a steam shovel. Oblivious, Will continued.

"She tried to pretend she hadn't forgotten. She overcompensated by going on and on about how awful it was, 'Why do people have to die so soon?' or something along those lines. And then she started sobbing. I gave her a bit of a hug and she seemed to pull herself together. But then she got angry, shouting something about everybody dying at the same time. She looked at me, one of those accusatory glares of hers, as though it was my fault. I said something inane about Luke's prognosis not being great but that he could live for a good few more years yet."

One year, one month, and two weeks, thought Shamus. If you could call it living.

"Then she said, scathingly, as though I was stupid, that she hadn't meant Luke," said Will. "So I assumed she was referring to Joe. I had to run like hell to catch my train. The whole affair was very odd."

"Maybe it was a delayed reaction to Joe's death," said Shamus.

"Maybe," repeated Will. "Although it must have been around then that Armando's Uncle Carlo died," he said, leaning forward and fixing Shamus with a significant look.

"What the hell does that have to do with Edith?" asked Shamus, frowning and examining his brother's face. "You seem a bit off-colour. What's wrong with you?"

"Nothing," muttered Will, appearing uncharacteristically guarded. He merely ran his fingers over the gold-embossed letters on the front of his menu.

ENGLAND

Sunday, October 18, 1942

Carlo gingerly pushed his way between gorse boughs bristling with tiny spines and disappeared, leaving Edith in the hidden bomb crater to fasten her skirt and swivel it around her waist so the zipper sat at the back, where it belonged.

"Jesus, Carlo, you scared the living daylights out of me." Although hidden from view, Edith instinctively ducked down, heart pounding, at the sound of Liam's voice. "What the devil are you playing at, jumping out from behind bushes right in front of people?"

"I was, um, looking for mushrooms," stuttered Carlo.

"Mushrooms?" questioned Liam. "You won't find them up here — it's way too dry and sandy. You'd have better luck down in the meadows. And isn't it a bit late in the day? Everyone knows early morning's the best time for picking mushrooms."

It was a good thing Liam was such a snot, thought Edith. He was so keen to put Carlo down that it didn't seem to occur to him that Carlo might have been behind the gorse bushes doing something else entirely.

"Can you show me a good mushroom place?" asked Carlo.

"Now?" Liam queried.

"No time like the present," replied Carlo cheerily.

"Oh all right," said Liam.

Edith could hear the sound of her brother-in-law's chatter fade as he and Carlo descended the hill. She let out a long exhalation of relief. For more than a year, since she and Carlo had been meeting in the crater, their affair had remained undiscovered. Today was a close call; a few seconds later, and Liam would have seen Edith emerging from the bushes behind Carlo. But it appeared their secret was safe, for now. What had Liam been doing, Edith wondered. He was surprisingly dextrous for a young man with one foot, but she hadn't known that he still made a habit of wandering around the heath.

She and Carlo had managed to meet four or five times a month as long as it wasn't actually raining or freezing. Edith was dismayed at the thought that they might be forced to give up their trysting place for fear of Liam finding out. Edith would feel totally bereft if she were to lose her precious hours of escape and abandon.

When they'd become lovers, Edith and Carlo had entered into an unspoken agreement not to touch each other in public. Up until then, there'd been frequent friendly hugs and Carlo had often put his arm around Edith's shoulders in a neighbourly fashion. What they hadn't realized was that their sudden restraint had given Mrs. Maguire more cause for suspicion than if they'd carried on as before. But Edith's mother-in-law was not unsympathetic. Mrs. Maguire had grown remarkably fond of Edith — she was the daughter she'd never had. And she'd always thought her son's marriage had taken place in too much of a rush and for the wrong reasons. Joe's desperation to have a wife, any wife, to pine for him while he was away was typical of a selfishness she disliked in her sons — Joe and Liam were two of a kind in that respect.

She thought about the trouble between Joe and Carlo when they'd been teenagers. Carlo had matured early into a broad-shouldered, deep-voiced young man, whereas Joe had been boyish and slight and had taken years to grow out of his acne. When Carlo went out with a girl that Joe'd had his eye on, quarrelling and fighting ensued and never really subsided.

Then there was the young man Mrs. Maguire had been enamoured of during her husband's absence in World War I. Who knows what might have happened if she hadn't been in service and under the scrutiny of the housekeeper and Mr. Parkinson, the butler? 'There but for the grace of God,' said Mrs. Maguire to herself as she made a conscious decision not to make her daughter-in-law's attachment to Carlo any of her business.

She wasn't alone. Throughout the length and breadth of Britain, people were turning a blind eye to romantic liaisons that would never have been tolerated during peacetime. Edith had read that in Birmingham the rate of babies conceived to married women while their husbands were overseas had tripled since 1940. She was grateful to Carlo for the care he took. She supposed that a married man buying condoms would be no cause for comment at the chemist's shop.

For Isobel's part, if she suspected anything, she certainly didn't show it. She treated Edith like an old friend. She was sometimes irrationally anxious, but Carlo believed her fearfulness to be a symptom of her disease. She never seemed ill at ease with Edith. And she adored William. Her whole demeanour changed around the little boy. Isobel was clearly delighted when William grabbed onto her wheelchair to clamber up to her lap. It had occurred to Edith that perhaps Carlo was having marital relations with Isobel. After all, she reasoned, just because someone was wheelchair-bound, it didn't mean they'd taken a vow of chastity. When she shyly brought up the matter with Carlo, he explained that Isobel had lost interest years earlier, soon after she'd first become ill.

Edith decided to hang on in the crater for a while to make sure Liam was well out of the way before she made her way home. Mrs. Maguire had promised to keep her eye on William for the afternoon. As far as she was concerned, her daughter-in-law had gone to the village library to exchange a book. Edith had made it to the library and back in less than an hour, lots of time left over to spend with Carlo.

Edith sat down on the grass, which was flattened and bruised from their latest exertions, and lay back, put her hands behind her head, and thought about Liam. She didn't actively dislike her brother-in-law. In fact, having witnessed his loss of innocence over the decoy fires, coupled with the loss of his foot, she had tremendous sympathy for him. And as if adolescence weren't tough enough, coming of age during the war can't have been easy. She remembered how Liam had spent hours lying on his bed during the early Bore War months, listlessly reading his *Picture Show* magazines. He'd made no secret of the fact that he hoped the war would be over before he was old enough for a uniform, despite his ardour over all that fifth column business. His fanaticism back then still made her sick, but she had to acknowledge that, in a way, he wasn't entirely to blame. He'd been just another adolescent, easily swayed by popular belief. Just like later, after Paris fell and the French surrendered, when he'd voiced an opinion often heard in England: "Well now we know where we are! No more unreliable bloody allies!" he'd exclaimed. "Any more of that language and I'll put you over my knee. You're not too old for a good spanking," Mrs. Maguire had admonished. But Liam's sentiments were often heard about the defeat of the French. No less a person than a Royal Navy admiral was quoted as saying that he felt happier now that they had "no allies to be polite to and to pamper."

After the evacuation of Dunkirk, Liam had taken to reciting Shakespearean battle cries, manically proclaiming, "This England never did, nor never shall, lie at the proud foot of a conqueror," or "Once more unto the breach, dear friends, once more . . . for when the blast of war blows in our ears, then imitate the action of the tiger." He'd babbled about the triumphs of Alfred the Great and Lord Nelson. Edith had been alarmed that he might be viewing the war as some sort of game. Or, alternatively, had he instinctively grasped the seriousness of the situation and been excavating history in a desperate search for a reassurance of victory?

And finally, like most of the population of England, once the perils of the Blitz were over and despite victory in the Battle of Britain, Liam sank into a kind of resigned lethargy. Hardships were daily occurrences, but somehow they found enough to eat and clothes to wear. Uncertainty was rife, but if one learnt to overcome anxiety about what might happen, there was a degree of equanimity to be achieved in not thinking beyond the next day. Even the active involvement of the Americans in the past months had failed to whip up the kind of optimism it might have generated earlier. Liam wasn't alone when he expressed his feelings of resentment. "Trust the Yanks to come waltzing in after we've all endured three years of hell," he'd complained. "And you can bet they'll take all the credit if Hitler and the Japs lose in the end."

Edith's thoughts moved on to the letter she'd received that morning from Joe. The only time Edith was forced to think beyond her wartime idyll was when a letter from Joe arrived. At least they didn't come too often.

Each letter was identical in its boring detail of inedible food and bad hygiene. Once or twice, the censor's black pen missed a couple of allusions, details that made Edith suspect that her husband might be somewhere in the Orient. He seemed to consume a lot of rice. He'd once mentioned that he'd been served goat and that, even after he'd been able to overcome his disgust, the dish turned out to be too spicy to swallow. Once or twice he'd grumbled about the relentless sun and how parched everything was, but in subsequent letters he groused about being constantly soggy from continuous rains. He made it clear that he missed English food and weather, but he never expressed any such sentiment about Edith. When she thought about what he'd said in the Grafton on the night he proposed — about wanting "someone" to come home to — she couldn't help wishing she hadn't fallen for all the patriotic nonsense about keeping the home fires burning for a husband overseas. But then, thought Edith, if she hadn't married Joe, she'd never have met Carlo.

She sometimes wondered why she dutifully replied to every one of Joe's letters. Despite what she thought of as her newfound independence, Edith's sense of decency made it impossible to do anything else. And she didn't think it was right to complain to him about the deprivations they were suffering. Especially since, despite them, she was the happiest she'd ever been. At the risk of sounding as boring as he did, Edith told Joe about the weather, their abundant garden, and of course William's "firsts" — first tooth, first faltering steps, and first word, which had been "Ganny," referring to Mrs. Maguire, the grandmother he adored. Edith included the occasional snapshot, taken with an old Kodak Brownie belonging to Liam. She was amassing quite a collection of baby photos. Some were of William in Anna's arms, others of him being given a piggyback ride by Carlo. Edith had gazed in disbelief at a recent one of him sitting on Isobel's knee, gripping both arms of her wheelchair and grinning at the camera. She found it difficult to believe that William was already two years old.

Mrs. Maguire had given Edith an old, leather-bound album to paste her photos in. The first few pages had a couple of prints already stuck to them. One was of Mr. and Mrs. Maguire, taken just after the last war. Edith couldn't believe how much Joe's father resembled the studio photo of Joe that Mrs. Maguire kept on the Welsh dresser.

And judging from a photo of Joe as a baby, disquietingly identical to William, the family likeness would endure.

Carlo's affection for William was perfectly obvious to anyone. He often grabbed the boy and swung him in the air, laughing uproariously while William screamed with delight. The lad had a fascination for Carlo's shiny cigarette case; whenever it appeared, he reached for it and seemed perfectly content to stroke its smooth surface for minutes on end.

Edith stirred herself. Enough time had passed that she could safely make her way home without arousing any suspicion. She dusted off her skirt, picked up her library book, and cautiously pushed her way between two gorse bushes growing closely together. She was relieved to see that the coast was clear.

"I need another," announced Will as he downed the last drop of his *vin santo*.

Shamus decided not to join his brother. After two glasses of Campari, half a bottle of Valpolicella, and a glass of sweet wine, he'd had enough.

"Boring fart," declared Will. They opted for espresso instead. Shamus ordered decaffeinated. By then, the restaurant was packed; every chair was occupied and an energetic young woman who resembled Armando was helping Signora Belli in the dining room. His sister, wondered Shamus, or perhaps a cousin. When she brought them their coffee, Will asked if Armando's grandfather was in the restaurant.

It was obvious the young woman's English was limited. "*Si,* is here," she replied. "*Nella cucina.*"

"Would he come and speak to us?" asked Will.

"Is very busy." Then she assumed an apologetic air and said, "He no like English people. *Scusi mi.*"

"Well that told you, didn't it?" said Shamus. "What are you up to?" he said suspiciously.

Will gave a dismissive wave of his hand. "Let me try something else," he mused. "Do you remember the huge row Joe and Uncle Stumpy had one Christmas?"

Uncle Stumpy was the name the brothers had adopted for Joe's brother, Liam, on account of his missing leg. Will had dreamed it up, but Shamus had soon adopted it too. When Edith had heard their nickname for their uncle, she'd admonished the two brothers for being cruel. "Cruel my arse," Will had said. "The miserable old scumbag deserves it." Rather than reprimand Will for his bad language, Edith had simply dropped her objections and said nothing more on the subject. The two had called Liam Uncle Stumpy ever since. Joe, unlike Edith, hadn't been able to disguise his amusement, smiling to himself every time the name came up.

"I doubt if I'll ever forget that Christmas — it was like World War III," said Shamus.

"But do you remember any of the specifics, like what exactly caused the fight?"

"Not really," admitted Shamus. "All I remember is Uncle Stumpy calling Edith names, and the next thing we knew, Joe had him by the neck and was beating his head against a wall."

Will went on to describe his memory of the altercation. He told Shamus that Liam had been needling Edith all that Christmas day. He claimed that the more Liam drank, the more he laid into Edith, with dark hints and suggestions of some kind of unpatriotic behaviour during the war.

"Until eventually he burst out with actual accusations, calling her a 'treasonous bitch' and a 'Nazi lover,'" said Will. Shamus listened, appalled, as Will described what had happened before Joe beat the living daylights out of his brother. Shamus couldn't believe he'd forgotten the slurs against his mother. All he remembered was vomiting mince pies and cider right after Joe had thrown Liam out onto the street.

"He even called you a little bastard," claimed Will.

"Well he had that wrong," declared Shamus.

When his brother failed to respond, Shamus added, "I'm not so little, am I?"

Will smiled, but Shamus noticed that his eyes didn't exhibit much amusement.

"What can you expect from someone who used to say that the prosperity of the '50s made the war seem worthwhile?" said Shamus, trying to jolly his brother along. "Liam thought wars were a necessary evil, like the plague or the Great Fire of London."

"And you think I'm psychotic," said Will. "I'm sanity itself compared to Uncle Stumpy."

The restaurant was in full swing. Armando's mother and the young woman who resembled her moved swiftly back and forth bringing plates of pasta, fish, or meat balanced skilfully on their hands and arms. The door into the kitchen swung open and closed every few minutes, giving the brothers a tantalizing glimpse of Armando's grandfather's territory but without a sighting of the old man.

"Hmm, it would explain why Joe had such a hold over Edith," mused Will to himself. "It all fits."

"You don't really believe there was any truth to his ravings?" asked Shamus in astonishment.

"Well you must remember how easily Joe was able to put a stop to some of Edith's crazier ideas. Especially if it meant her being away from home."

"He almost didn't get his way about that trip over here around the time we moved to London," said Shamus.

"I'd forgotten about that," exclaimed Will. "The war memorial in Bardi. That tussle went on for at least six months."

Shamus had had no idea why Edith chose to dig her heels in about that particular event. As far as he could remember, it had been an expedition to commemorate the little-known sinking of an obscure refugee boat during the war.

"But they never actively quarrelled about it, did they?" said Will, as though to prove a point rather than asking a question. "It was the usual silent war of wills. Edith would quietly tell someone she was going to a war memorial in Italy, and Joe would equally quietly and determinedly contradict her."

"Well Joe must have had some big guns that we weren't aware of," said Shamus. "She just stopped talking about it one day and never mentioned it again. We really didn't know them very well, did we?"

"That's not our fault," claimed Will.

"I suppose not," said Shamus. But he was left feeling guilty for never having bothered to find out about Edith's and Joe's past or inner lives. The more he thought about it, the more he concluded that he'd been arrogant in respect to his parents, presuming that there was nothing about them of particular interest. He wondered if everybody assumed their parents weren't worth closer scrutiny.

The trio of German women pushed past their table on their way out. Will moved his chair to allow them to pass more easily and nodded and smiled at them. Shamus wondered if his brother realized they were German. But then Will called out, *"Auf Wiedersehen."* The women turned and automatically reciprocated his greeting.

Will's affability prompted a sudden and overwhelming urge in Shamus to confide in him. "God, I miss Luke," Shamus moaned.

Will glanced at his younger brother. He asked in a gruff voice, "Was it very hard?"

Despite the cryptic nature of Will's question, Shamus welcomed it as though it were a long-anticipated visitor. Ignoring the bizarre implications of his and Will's earlier conversation about Luke, Shamus allowed the last few years to unwind in his head. He visualized himself and Luke sitting in the stifling atmosphere of doctors' overheated waiting rooms, then both of them reeling at the shock of an eventual diagnosis, followed by countless hours spent at endless clinics. Luke's terror of radiation treatments; the horrors of chemotherapy; the cruel promise of a remission, swiftly followed by the devastating disappointment of a recurrence; his bearing witness to Luke's terrifying physical decline and the excruciating ache of love for the shadow of a body he'd once lusted for; the unbearable loneliness he'd experienced in the hours between each daily hospital visit. And finally, he heard again Luke's whimpering death rattle, hardly audible above the clamour of plastic meal trays being stacked in the hospital corridor outside his room.

"Yes, it was hard," he muttered, throat constricted and eyes swollen with barely contained tears.

"I knew it must have been," said Will. "But I didn't know how to help."

"There's nothing you could have done," said Shamus, turning to look at Will. He felt overwhelmingly grateful to Will for being so sympathetic.

Will stared at Shamus sceptically.

"You've helped a lot by dragging me to Venice," insisted Shamus.

"Yeah, right," said Will. "Disneyland for adults."

"It's been much more than just a distraction," said Shamus. His next admission surprised even himself. "I've never wanted to bother you."

"You've always been far too unselfish, not to mention conscientious," Will stated.

"Well somebody had to be," said Shamus, fumbling in his pocket for a tissue. "It wasn't easy growing up with a couple of autistic parents and a psychotic brother."

A deep voice interrupted them. "My daughter tells me you gentlemen are from Liverpool."

The two brothers looked up at a tall, thin man with bushy white hair and black, fathomless eyes. Despite his opening line, which addressed both brothers, Armando's grandfather, Signora Belli's father, stared unblinkingly at Shamus. The old man wore a white chef's apron and matching trousers.

"Originally," explained Will, trotting out the line he'd used all day. "But my brother here lives in Canada and I live in London."

"Canada," repeated the old man, eyes still fixed on Shamus. There was an awkward pause, then Will pulled himself up in his chair as though summoning up some kind of nerve.

"I hope you don't mind me asking," he dithered uncharacteristically. "But when you lived in Liverpool, did your family live in the actual city or outside? You didn't live in a place called Shrimpley, did you?"

The old man turned his gaze — reluctantly, it seemed — to Will. If he'd heard Will's question, he chose to ignore it. "Was the food to your liking?" He spoke slowly, as though searching for every word, one after the next, but his English was completely devoid of an Italian accent.

Shamus assured him that their meal had been delicious. Armando's grandfather nodded. Then he stared, wordless, at Shamus for four or five silent seconds. Eventually he limped slowly back to the swing door and disappeared into the kitchen.

"Miserable old coot," cursed Will.

"What in God's name was that all about?" demanded Shamus.

Saturday, May 27, 1944

"Is it true that Liam Maguire has a peg leg?" the girl at the next table asked her friend. Edith turned her head slightly so she could better hear the other young woman's reply above the waltz music that the band — a motley collection of violins, piano, trumpets, and a single saxophone — was inexpertly playing.

"Apparently," said the friend. "He told Betty Simpson he lost a leg in France. But he claims he doesn't want to talk about it; he says his memories of the Normandy beaches are too painful."

"You'd never know there was anything wrong to see him dance, and he's *sooo* handsome," cooed the first girl. "I can think of a few ways I could ease his painful memories, leg or no leg." A second or two later, when the band abruptly ground to a halt, the girls' shrill laughter rose above the din of dancers' voices.

It was a sign of the times that the annual Shrimpley Yacht Club Spring Ball was back in full swing for the first time in five years, the last one having taken place in 1939, just before war was declared. The event always took place in the club's so-called lounge, a barn of a room with open rafters and unpolished floorboards. And despite the exclusive tone of the dance's title, non-members were welcome. Anyone able to afford the price of admission, one shilling and sixpence, could attend. So Edith had cajoled Carlo into taking her. Since Mussolini had been ousted and Italy had joined the Allies, she saw no reason for Carlo to be wary about going out and about more.

Tables had been cleared from the centre of the room to make space for dancing. Red, white, and blue crepe paper streamers were draped to either side of a makeshift bar, behind which wooden beer crates were piled almost to the rafters. A half-dozen frayed Union Jacks that had seen better days on the masts of sailboats hung limply above the dance floor. It would turn out to be the hottest evening of the year, despite the early date. The room was wreathed in cigarette smoke and packed with perspiring people. But in spite of the oppressive heat, most men wore a suit or a uniform with jacket and tie. Edith was glad the blackout was a thing of the past; every window and door was wide open in an attempt to catch any cooling breeze that might waft in from the gathering darkness outside.

Edith wasn't surprised that Liam was lying about the circumstances surrounding the loss of his leg. In her opinion, he'd always had a tenuous grip on reality, as revealed by his infatuation with Hollywood and his blind prejudice against the Italian population during the time of internment.

Edith had to admit that Liam's obsessive nature had doubtless helped him to rehabilitate quickly and successfully. He'd fanatically followed the career of a young pilot named Bader, who had gone on to become a top-performing fighter pilot and the pride of the RAF despite losing both legs after he'd crashed in the execution of a flying stunt before the war. Liam had pinned a photo of the smiling airman to his bedroom wall, next to a piece of paper on which he'd written in large black letters his favourite Bader quotation: "Make up your mind you'll never use crutches or a stick, then have a go at everything." A recent BBC broadcast had claimed unanimous admiration of Wing Commander Douglas Bader, even among the enemy. It seemed obvious to Edith that the British authorities were using the legless man as an example to help bolster public morale. The radio program recounted a story of how the Luftwaffe had allowed a British plane to parachute a prosthetic leg to Bader in a German prisoner of war camp after one of his own peg-legs was lost when he was shot down and captured. Edith wondered if the Nazis had subsequently held their celebrated prisoner in such high esteem. She'd heard that the troublesome pilot had made so many attempts to escape that his captors were threatening to take away his legs altogether.

A maxim attributed to Bader that Edith had to admit struck a chord with her was, "Rules are for the guidance of wise men and the obedience of fools." She was surprised that the quote was reported so widely; it didn't seem appropriate for wartime — too undisciplined by far. But the left-wing newspapers seemed to like trumpeting it, keen as they were to get across their egalitarian ideals in anticipation of an immediate postwar election. Edith supposed that, once a person became popular, their words were fair game for any stripe of manipulative media, government or otherwise.

When had she become so cynical, she asked herself. All she knew was that, despite her contentment during the last two or three years and her freedom from the social constraints of prewar life, she'd also experienced a cumulative world-weariness. Since it had become obvious that Hitler was on the run, there'd been a lot of wild promises from every variety of politician about the creation of a brave new world once peace prevailed, but Edith feared that at war's end things would be no better than they'd been before. Most people waited with high expectations for the anticipated British invasion of France that would presage the end of the war in Europe. But if the freedom Edith currently enjoyed was a feature of wartime life, what could peace possibly offer her? She supposed she'd get her husband back. She wondered if he was still in one piece, and immediately felt guilty when the idea of Joe returning whole and unharmed filled her with trepidation.

Liam was standing on the other side of the dance floor, talking animatedly to his fawning dance partner and grinning at her gushing responses. His black hair gleamed in the electric lights. Even from a distance, Edith could appreciate the vivacity of his startlingly blue eyes and the flash of his white, even teeth. The black hair, eyebrows, and lashes that both Liam and Joe had inherited from their father had once prompted Edith's father to express concern that the Maguire boys surely had a "touch of the tar brush." "Don't be daft," Edith's mother had told him. "With those periwinkle blue eyes, those lads are as Celtic as they come."

On several occasions during the three years since his amputation, Liam's prosthetic leg had been lengthened to match his rocketing height. He'd worked determinedly at developing his muscles, rigorously exercising on the porch no matter what the weather. Liam's bulk, and perhaps the experience of losing his foot, lent him a mature appearance that belied his twenty years, and Edith could see why young women would easily fall for his yarn about being part of the Normandy invasion. She was surprised he hadn't made himself out to be a pilot who'd been forced to ditch his crate after being hit by a Messerschmitt, but that was too incredible a story, even for Liam. Nobody would believe that a lower-middle-class lad from the outskirts of Liverpool could become a pilot in the RAF.

Edith had trouble remembering Joe's exact build — it was nearly four and a half years since she'd last seen him — but she thought her young brother-in-law was less slight and at least three or four inches taller than the husband she found difficult to picture. Thinking about Joe made Edith uneasy. For most of his four-year absence, she'd been successful in not letting her husband invade her thoughts, but with all the recent talk about "bringing our boys back home," he'd encroached more and more.

She nervously lifted her empty glass to her lips and pretended to drink the last drop of Bitter Lemon when in fact she'd already drained it some minutes before. Carlo would be back from the bar with another at any second. Meanwhile, the band had embarked on a cacophonous quickstep. Edith could just about make out the melody of the popular refrain, "If you were the only girl in the world." The music's furious pace didn't seem to faze Liam; as he and his partner swirled past Edith, he gave her a broad wink.

As soon as the quickstep ground to a halt, Carlo pushed his way between panting dancers clutching a bottle of beer for himself and a glass of Bitter Lemon for Edith. Unlike most of the men, he wasn't wearing a suit or a tie. He sported a pair of light grey trousers and a crisp white shirt.

"I don't know why people say the English are reserved," said Carlo, raising his voice above the clamour of laughter and voices. "This is livelier than any Italian dance I've ever been to."

As if on cue, the band burst into a lively foxtrot. Standing nearby were two boys swigging beer from bottles. Edith recognized one of them as a pal of Liam's. They were making catcalls at two young women who were dancing together and then laughing uproariously at the girls' expense. Why they wouldn't just cut in and dance was beyond Edith. She was forced to put her mouth close to Carlo's ear to make herself heard. "It's a combination of war and beer," she said. "I'm sure dances weren't this raucous in peacetime."

"I was only ever at Italian dances, at the Fascio," Carlo yelled back. "Isobel used to love to dance." He regarded the dancers cavorting, a mournful expression on his face. Edith felt a prick of jealousy — she wondered if he'd be as sad for her if she were unwell like Isobel.

Lately, Carlo had begun to express his fears about Isobel's worsening health. When she'd first been diagnosed, after experiencing dizziness and problems walking, there had been periods of remission during which she was relatively normal, but she'd had no relief for a couple of years now. And a few weeks earlier, Carlo had told Edith that Isobel could no longer straighten her legs. She was always exhausted yet had trouble sleeping. Anna did her best, but Carlo was worried that he and his mother weren't able to care for Isobel properly. He'd heard about a discovery, made in America before the war, that had led to a better understanding of multiple sclerosis, and he'd wondered aloud to Edith if he shouldn't take his wife to a hospital in the south of England where they were practising new methods of treatment developed by American doctors. Although Edith thought such a move unlikely, she experienced apprehension bordering on panic at the prospect of Carlo and Isobel leaving.

At that moment, the band changed pace and slid into a different rhythm, another waltz. Their repertoire seemed somewhat limited.

"Shall we dance?" asked Carlo, thick eyebrows raised in query. Edith nodded, stood, and took his proffered arm, which seemed perfectly natural under the circumstances.

No sooner had Carlo placed his hand on the small of Edith's back and pulled her to him than he stumbled, crashing into Edith. They almost lost their balance.

"Look where you're going, you bloody wop," shouted one of the young men who'd been harassing the two girls a few minutes earlier. Edith realized that he'd given Carlo a shove.

"Nobody invited you anyway," yelled the other. "Why don't you go back where you belong?"

It seemed laughable to Edith that these two skinny boys were confronting Carlo, who had the height and build of a heavyweight boxer. He stood, bull-like, and frowned at the two youths. People stopped dancing and stared.

"What are you looking at, you stupid Nazi?" asked the first boy. The band, having noticed that nobody was moving, ground to a ragged halt. One of the trumpet players let slip a couple of tuneless notes before petering out altogether. Carlo narrowed his eyes, lifted his shoulders an inch or two. Edith noticed he'd made fists. She was seething with anger, but she didn't see the point of a fight.

"Come on, Carlo," she said, pulling at his arm. "Let's get a breath of fresh air." But Carlo stood his ground and stared, unblinking, at the boy.

"Yeah, bugger off *Carlo*," said the second boy, mimicking Edith's voice when he spoke Carlo's name. Despite his bravado, the boy edged away slightly. "And take your traitorous tart with you."

Had the boy not anticipated Carlo's reaction, there's no doubt he'd have been throttled. As it was, Carlo only managed to grasp the lapel of the boy's suit jacket, which came off in his hand when the lad jumped out of Carlo's reach. Edith couldn't imagine how Liam managed to insert himself between Carlo and the boy with such speed. He materialized, wavering a little, his good leg supporting his weight, with one hand on Carlo's heaving chest. The boy with the missing lapel stepped behind Liam and was quickly joined by his friend.

"I think it best you make yourself scarce," said Liam to Carlo. "We don't want any rough stuff, do we?'

"So they make the trouble and I have to leave," said Carlo, looking intently at Liam.

Liam shrugged and held Carlo's gaze for a few seconds.

Eventually, Carlo threw down the lapel he'd ripped off and headed for the door. As Edith followed him, Liam gave her a knowing look that infuriated her all the more. Some people turned away when Edith caught their eye as she and Carlo marched out of the yacht club, but many returned her glance with a hostile stare. They'd hardly stepped out of the front door when Edith heard the band start up again.

"I don't know how anyone can dance to that unholy row anyway," said Carlo and emitted a mirthless snort of a laugh. Then he took Edith by the arm and turned her to face him. "Are you all right?" he asked.

"I'm fine," replied Edith, although, truth to tell, she was shivering, despite the oppressive heat. Carlo encircled her shoulders with one of his long arms as they made their way up the shadowy road that wound up the hill to Sandy Lane. Edith thought her shivering must have been the result of shock as much as anger. She was shaken to the core by the rancorous stares of some of the dancers at the yacht club. She'd never experienced such naked malice directed toward her. She couldn't believe how naïve she'd been to think that her relationship with Carlo had gone unnoticed or wasn't remarked on by other people. She could almost hear her mother's voice asking the question that had dogged her all her life, "What will people think?" Edith thought she'd risen above such petty concerns; she was disturbed to discover she hadn't.

By the time they turned in to the lane, they could hardly hear the sound of the band emanating from the yacht club below. All Edith could discern was a tinny vibration like a cheap radio playing in a distant room.

The fracas at the dance and people's reaction to it was a rude awakening for Edith. Life on Sandy Lane had been utterly self-contained for the past three years. Radio broadcasts and the occasional newspapers had been Edith's only contact with the outside world, apart from infrequent forays to Shrimpley to glean groceries from shops depleted by rationing. In the past few months, soap, dried fruit, rice, sago, tapioca, canned fruit, condensed milk, breakfast cereals, syrup, treacle, biscuits, and oats had all been added to the long list of rationed items. Yet it didn't seem to Edith that she lacked for much. The period when they were constantly "browned off" with the inconveniences of war had gradually transformed into an interval of resignation followed by reluctant appreciation. They weren't short of clothes, furniture, and household items, even if their socks were darned, the sofa was shabby, and pans were dented. Liam continued to grumble occasionally, but even he complained in a lighthearted manner. When Mrs. Maguire had only been able to buy whale meat at the butcher for the third or fourth consecutive week, he'd broken into song at the dining room table, using the popular Vera Lynn hit as the melody:

Whale meat again
Don't know where,
Don't know when,
But we'll eat whale meat again
Some sunny day.

"Daft lad," Mrs. Maguire had muttered, smiling to herself.

Edith's sole conversation with anyone other than Carlo, Mrs. Maguire, Liam, Anna, or Isobel was with Bob MacDonald during his occasional visits. Only Liam had friends or acquaintances outside of their two houses. Edith supposed that their isolation was what had made the past three years so idyllic. To most people, Edith's recent life would seem like one long holiday of picnics on the beach and walks on the heath. Even working in the garden or trying some of the war recipes, such as turnip stew with nutmeg, seemed more like fun than a chore.

And of course William had provided a joyful focus. He was a happy, well-loved baby. They all doted on him and spoiled him rotten — he'd received no end of attention. He loved "helping" Mrs. Maguire in the kitchen. She let him rice the potatoes because William took great delight in watching long, thin worms of cooked spud spurt from the network of little holes in the ricer. And Carlo was devoted to the boy. He'd taken to appearing at Mrs. Maguire's door around William's bedtime to read aloud to him before he went to sleep. Before they had left for the dance that night, Carlo had finished reading *Wind in the Willows* to William. Their book sessions always finished with a goodnight hug, and this time, Carlo had added in a teasing tone that if William wasn't a good boy, he'd get Badger and Ratty to come sort him out.

But now Edith's bubble had been well and truly burst. She kicked herself for suggesting that she and Carlo go to the dance in the first place. It had never occurred to her that people would know who they were or anything about them. She wondered if Liam had played a part in spreading whatever gossip was circulating.

These thoughts swirled around Edith's head as she and Carlo made their way along Sandy Lane. They passed the Aitkens' bungalow, Shangri-La, which had been bombed during the Blitz. The roof was blown off, but three of the four walls and a central chimney had been left standing. Since then, the house had been overrun with convolvulus, the ruined shell hidden by the mass of tangled vines. Edith couldn't discern a single straight line of wall or chimney silhouetted against the night sky. Shangri-La appeared to have been completely consumed by the rapacious plant. In the dim light, Edith could make out a couple of trumpet-shaped white flowers that glimmered malevolently in the dark.

The evening had been uncannily still, not a breath of wind or a sound except for the sporadic call of an insomniac blackbird. But now a breeze rustled the leaves on trees and in hedges. Edith caught the flash of distant lightning over the estuary. The evening's events had made her uneasy, anxious. She felt as if tendrils of prewar life were inexorably snaking toward her.

"I was thinking we might take a walk on the heath, but it feels like we're in for a storm," said Carlo.

For almost two years, "a walk on the heath" had been their euphemism for an hour or so of lovemaking in their grass-lined crater. A few hours ago, Edith would have felt a sharp pang of disappointment at not spending time with Carlo up on the heath, but in the light of the evening's revelations, she needed time to think and consider.

"I don't think we want to be found fried to death by lightning in each other's arms after tonight's little scene," muttered Carlo.

Edith's immediate reaction was to claim that nothing would make her happier than to be found dead in Carlo's embrace, but a sharp crack of lightning, immediately followed by an ear-splitting crash of thunder, put paid to her words. As they dashed along the lane, Edith could feel heavy drops of rain on her bare shoulders and arms. When they reached Mrs. Maguire's gate, Carlo lifted Edith off her feet with a hug, kissing her neck at the same time. As he sprinted away down the dark lane, Edith stood, not caring about the torrential downpour, to watch the indistinct blur of his white-shirted figure. As Carlo turned into the gate to his garden, a flash of lightning vividly illuminated him. Caught for an instant, Carlo appeared frozen, one hand reaching for the gate latch. The wet fabric of his shirt was plastered tightly to his body and Edith could make out the muscles in his back and upper arm. But by the time her eyes readjusted to the ensuing gloom, Carlo had disappeared entirely.

Friday, August 18, 1944

"We have a letter this morning from the hospital in the south of England," said Carlo as he lay down next to Edith on the fragrant grass lining of the bomb crater. Edith lay on her back, hands behind her head. A dome of azure sky arched above her. In her peripheral vision, she was aware of gorse bushes encircling them, bristling with flowers as yellow as mustard powder.

Despite the comforting warmth of sunlight and the sweet smell of bruised grass in the air, Edith was unnerved. She knew that Carlo's English grammar deteriorated when he became emotional; the fact that he'd used the wrong tense alarmed her. Also, he'd insisted they take a walk on the heath only minutes after she and William had arrived to have an afternoon cup of tea with Isobel. William was delighted with the prospect of being left with Anna and Isobel, who always spoiled him. But Edith worried the two women might be suspicious about her and Carlo's abrupt decision to take a walk. She'd grown more and more uneasy ever since the evening of the yacht club dance.

"We *had* a letter," said Edith, putting emphasis on the correct form of the verb.

"We had a letter," repeated Carlo, sounding vaguely irritated. Nevertheless, he reached out and enveloped Edith's hand in his. The dry warmth of Carlo's palm did little to reassure her — it felt too much like commiseration.

"The hospital have agree to take Isobel as an out-patient," Carlo said.

Edith didn't bother to correct him. She was overwhelmed with a sense of dread.

"When are you leaving?" she mumbled, barely able to get the words out.

"Tomorrow morning," said Carlo. "We take a train from Lime Street station at a quarter past nine."

Edith gasped, her stomach lurching.

Ever since the dance, followed a week or so later by the successful invasion of France, Edith had known that things were sure to change.

And when Carlo had heard that the Allies had reached Rome, he seemed relieved yet sad. Edith knew he too was well aware that the liberation of Europe would, ironically, signal an end to their freedom. Carlo had told her on a couple of occasions that Isobel's doctor had been in touch with the hospital in southern England where new techniques to treat multiple sclerosis were being used. Despite all this, the news of Carlo's departure affected her more than she'd anticipated. She cursed herself as her eyes filled and her throat constricted.

"Damn," she said, unable to fight off her tears. "Damn, damn, damn."

Carlo rolled onto his side to examine Edith's face, then wiped her wet cheeks with one of his thumbs. Edith wasn't sure when sorrow and consolation transformed into desire and passion. Carlo began by kissing her face, as if he was literally attempting to kiss her tears away. She held his head, weeping, hands cupped gently around his hefty skull. But soon Carlo's mouth was on hers. When she tasted salt, she imagined it must be her teardrops. It was only when she opened her eyes briefly that she realized Carlo was crying too. Edith became aware of saliva, tears, and mucus mingling in their mouths and on their lips and faces, but she was beyond caring. Clothes were roughly undone; in his haste, Carlo ripped a button off his trousers. Edith tugged fiercely at hanks of Carlo's hair and his stifled cries of pain echoed in their mouths. She was astonished at how quickly her orgasm arrived. Thousands of nerve endings urgently signalled a blinding climax that erupted with such force that she let out a series of keening wails — anyone hearing her would have found it difficult to tell if they were sounds of ecstasy or lament. Carlo immediately followed her, groaning with each spasm, *"Ti amo, Edith. Ti amo. Ti amo. Ti amo."*

In the silence that followed, Edith said in a low voice, "I love you too, Carlo." It was the first time she'd ever said it, to anyone. The fact that Edith believed it to be the last lent her words a hollow sound she despised. They lay quietly for several minutes as Carlo indulged his habit of slowly stroking Edith's thigh with his knuckle. Edith watched, miserable beyond tears, as virginal white clouds paraded slowly but steadily in front of the blue infinity beyond. A couple of bickering seagulls passed overhead. One had food in its beak; the other dive-bombed its companion, shrieking with resentment. "Well," said Edith eventually, in as resigned and pragmatic a tone of voice as she could muster, for which she hated herself, "we'd better get on with it."

When they returned to the house, Anna insisted that Edith stay for another cup of tea. Anna and Isobel seem to have assumed that Carlo had told Edith his plan. Now Anna was keen to tell Edith her scheme to regain the businesses lost at the time of internment.

"We own three shops, even if they're a wreck," Anna pronounced. She was resolved to move, lock, stock, and barrel, to Liverpool. "And I'm no afraid of those doodlebugs," she insisted, referring to the occasional rocket the Germans were launching at various targets around Britain. "Compared to what we've seen, they're no worse than a few midges. With or without Gianni and the boys, it's still a good living over there."

Edith did a good job of maintaining her composure as she left. Isobel clung to her shoulders as she bent down to hug her. Even when Carlo cried shamelessly, without embarrassment, Edith managed to hold herself together. William looked bewildered and tried to comfort Carlo by slipping his tiny hand between Carlo's thick thumb and forefinger. And Edith might have got away with it, but William gave the game away. Just as Anna and Carlo were closing the front door behind them, he asked Edith in a loud voice why she was crying. As she hustled him away, dabbing her eyes, the thought occurred to her that she was behaving ridiculously. She should be beating her breast and wailing out loud, not scurrying away like a petrified insect. As she entered the shade of the conifer copse, William's hot hand in hers, she thought about how changed she'd considered herself to be since the war began, almost five years earlier. But could she really be so different if she remained tight-lipped and stoic with Isobel and Anna at the prospect of parting company with them and Carlo? Wouldn't the new Edith have insisted that she and William accompany Carlo and Isobel, regardless of what anybody thought? Why on earth was she putting such a tight lid on things?

When she and William emerged from the shadows of the conifers, Edith looked forlornly around Mrs. Maguire's garden. She could clearly see the regimented stripes of grass made by Liam as he'd passed back and forth with the mower earlier that day. He'd neatened the edges of the lawn with a spade; straight, clean cuts defined the boundary where sod met the soil of flowerbeds. William pulled his hand from hers and ran toward the house, shouting at the top of his lungs, "Granny, Granny, we're home."

Edith felt a surge of panic. She realized she was in danger of losing any ground she might have gained in the past few years by behaving in a fashion that ran contrary to everything she was feeling. Emotions weren't meant to be kept in check and regimented like lawns and flower borders. They were messy and unkempt; they needed space and air. She resolved to return to Carlo and Isobel after she'd helped Mrs. Maguire prepare the tea. Edith would propose that she travel with the Baccanellos to the hospital in the south of England. They'd need help, she reasoned. Carlo couldn't cope alone. But more importantly, she'd tell them how much she loved them both and how she couldn't bear to be parted from them . . . and damn the consequences.

The front door banged shut behind William, and Edith strode across the lawn after him and ran up the steps to the porch. She felt an exuberant sense of liberation combined with a self-congratulatory glow. She'd triumphed over the powerful compulsion to "do the right thing," as her mother would phrase it, which, Edith now understood, often meant the exact opposite.

Later, she would go over the events of that day over and over in her head. How would things have turned out, she asked herself, if she had reacted more quickly, spoken up as soon as she'd made her decision? Why couldn't she have just turned on her heel there and then to rush over to the bungalow next door and pour out her feelings to Carlo and Isobel? Instead, she pulled open Mrs. Maguire's front door to find William standing in the hallway gazing through the open door to the living room, an odd expression of awe and shyness on his face.

"This is your daddy, home from the war," Edith heard her mother-in-law say in a gentle voice.

"Hello, Will," said a male voice, followed by a second or two of silence.

William examined his feet.

"I thought he'd be bigger," said the voice.

"He's only four years old," reasoned Mrs. Maguire.

William turned his head to see Edith framed in the front doorway.

"Mummy," he blurted, and ran to her side. He hugged her thigh, gripping her skirt with both hands.

"Don't be silly," said Edith, as much to herself as to William. Her heart was thudding and she found it difficult to breath.

She took William's hand and hesitantly walked the six or seven steps to the door of the living room, weighed down with trepidation. Joe was sitting in the chair facing the door, where Mrs. Maguire usually sat.

"There's a sight for sore eyes," he said.

At first, Edith took Joe's expression literally. Where Joe's ample right eyebrow used to be was a misshapen, hairless ridge. His right jawline looked as if it had been unsuccessfully rubbed out with an eraser; there was no distinct contour between his face and his neck, just a mess of shiny white skin. The scars were startling in contrast to the darker colour of the rest of his face and neck. His healthy skin was almost the same colour as the khaki army jacket he was wearing. She'd always believed he and Liam shared the same peaches-and-cream complexion. Now Joe's colour seemed alien to her. It must be the result of being in a tropical climate for so long, thought Edith. Joe's straight black hair was greased and combed back, helmet-like, as she recalled it always had been. She remembered with a jolt the piercing blue eyes that gazed unblinkingly at her. It was all Edith could do not to look away. Her stomach fluttered and she felt a looseness in her bowels.

"Hello, Joe," she said.

"Where've you been?" he asked. "I've been here for a while. I caught the bus from Birkenhead and walked across the heath. I'd forgotten how beautiful the gorse blossom is this time of year. I can't tell you what a relief it is to see green grass again." An expression flickered around his lips, not quite a smile and yet not a smirk.

"I've been saying goodbye to our neighbours," said Edith, glancing at Mrs. Maguire. "They're leaving tomorrow. Isobel's going down to that hospital near London."

"Oh," said Mrs. Maguire, unable to disguise her expression of shock. "Are you all right?" she asked Edith.

"Why shouldn't she be?" asked Joe.

"We've all become quite attached to each other, that's all. We're going to miss them, aren't we, Edith?" said Mrs. Maguire. She jumped up from the sofa. "Now sit down, love," she said, almost pushing Edith down onto the couch. "I'll take care of the tea. You and Joe have a lot to talk about. Come on, William, come and sit next to your mummy."

"Hey, Will," said Joe. "I bet you'd rather sit on my knee, wouldn't you?"

"My name's William," muttered William, climbing onto the sofa next to his mother.

Edith passed the next forty minutes in a dazed stupor. Joe talked incessantly, even with his mouth full of Mrs. Maguire's scones. A few crumbs spun out of his mouth and landed on the front of his tunic. Edith wondered if perhaps his injury made it difficult for him to work his jaw.

"You shouldn't eat with your mouth full," said William, who'd been staring at Joe, wide-eyed.

"And children should be seen and not heard," Joe shot back, eyes glinting. Then he seemed to relent. "But you're right, Will," he concurred in a gentler tone. "I've been too long out of polite company, you see. You must keep me on my toes." Then he continued, galloping along as if he was trying to cram an account of the past four years of his life into a couple of hours. He told them he'd been stationed in a massive supply depot in southern India.

"Everything from tanks to toilet rolls," he explained. "Taking deliveries, recording inventory, shipping to theatres."

"Theatres?" questioned Edith.

"Theatres of war," said Joe, looking at Edith as though she was from another planet. "Pacific, Indo-China, all over. I was damn good at it, and all. Made sergeant in the first year." He proudly tapped three stripes on his sleeve.

Is it me, Edith thought, or is he talking double Dutch? She felt like Alice at the mad tea party. Joe was gabbling as incoherently as the mad hatter. William fell asleep, like the dormouse, with his head resting on Edith's knee. Mrs. Maguire took the part of the March hare: she asked an occasional question, but none that made any sense to Edith. The only query that seemed logical was when her mother-in-law tentatively asked her son about his scars.

"Do you want to tell us what happened?" Mrs. Maguire timidly inquired, looking at the right side of Joe's head and nodding slightly.

"Damn silly, really," said Joe, looking sheepish. "Some shelves collapsed in the stores. Got banged in the face by a load of trenching tools. You wouldn't believe how sharp they are, and one of them took out some of my jawbone. I spent a month in hospital. Funny thing was, I contracted malaria while I was there. Delirious as a drunk for days. The fever still hits me now and again."

He studied his boots, appearing apologetic. Edith supposed he thought his story ridiculous. The homecoming warrior bearing battle scars from shovels falling on him in a warehouse — not exactly a tale of bravery and derring-do. She felt a pang of sympathy for him.

"Your left side was always your best anyway." She tried to smile.

Joe glanced at her and smiled back, gratefully.

"I'm entitled to some kind of reconstructive surgery," he muttered. "They tell me I'll look like Errol Flynn when it's finished."

"Couldn't they make it Clark Gable?" asked Edith, making another attempt at a smile.

At that moment, she heard the sound of the back door opening and slamming shut.

"That'll be Liam," said Mrs. Maguire.

Joe sprang to his feet. Edith thought how small her husband seemed. She knew Joe was slight, but he looked skinnier than she remembered. She thought about his letters, full of complaints about the food he'd been given.

"Hello, our kid," said Joe when Liam appeared. Edith thought his smile looked forced — there was an unnatural brightness to his eyes.

"You've certainly shot up," Joe remarked.

Edith could tell that it took Liam a split second to recognize his brother. Then his face cracked into a broad grin.

"The conquering hero returns," Liam exclaimed. In his haste to shake Joe's hand, he stepped forward with his prosthesis, which was contrary to what he'd been taught. Liam had always been told it was better to lead with his good leg. As a result, he lurched more than usual. Joe noticed immediately and reached out to support him. They fell into an awkward embrace. Liam seemed embarrassed; he took a hop to the sofa and plunked himself down on the cushion next to William, who moaned and woke up.

"You look like you've had one too many," said Joe, resuming his seat in Mrs. Maguire's easy chair. She was perched on an upright dining chair she'd dragged from the table.

"No such luck, old boy," said Liam, in a mock upper-class accent. "It's this damned peg leg." He lifted the grey flannel fabric of his trouser leg up to his knee and tapped loudly three times with his knuckle on the shiny pink surface of his bakelite calf. Above an ankle formed of white cotton batting, the chrome core of Liam's prosthesis could be clearly seen, like a shiny exposed bone. Joe stared at it in horror. Why did Liam always have to make such a drama out of everything, wondered Edith. Was he trying to one-up Joe in the injury department? It would have been much better if he'd broken the news gently rather than displaying his false leg ostentatiously, as if it was a trophy.

Joe dropped his chin to his chest and his head fell. He ran a hand though his hair. He let out a sob. Mrs. Maguire and Edith exchanged apprehensive glances.

"I'm sorry," wailed Joe, looking up, his face glistening with tears. "Sorry."

Edith felt it was up to her to do something. She eased William from her lap and went to Joe's side. She sat on the arm of his chair and put an arm tentatively around his shoulders.

"It's really not that bad, Joe," insisted Liam, having the good grace to look remorseful. He hastily pushed his trouser leg down.

Joe sobbed again. "It's not the leg," he managed to mumble. "It's, it's . . ." But he couldn't talk for weeping, his chest heaving.

"There there," said Edith, rubbing Joe's back. "It's all right. It's all right."

Joe seemed to take this as a sign to abandon all inhibition and he bawled, snot streaming from his nose and saliva drooling from his mouth. William stared in disbelief at the wailing, scar-faced stranger whom people maintained was his father. Joe didn't seem able to control himself; he continued to weep unrestrainedly, gasping occasionally when he ran out of breath. Edith gave her mother-in-law a desperate look of appeal. Mrs. Maguire jumped to her feet.

"Off to bed, young man," said Mrs. Maguire, sweeping William up in her arms. "Edith, you take Joe to my room — he's obviously dog-tired. I'll bed down in your room with William tonight. Liam, make yourself useful — make us all a cup of tea."

Joe sobbed unceasingly for more than an hour, clinging to Edith's arm as she lay next to him on Mrs. Maguire's double bed. He reminded Edith of William when he'd been younger and was overtired. Joe appeared powerless to stop weeping, like a little boy incapable of rising above his fatigue. In William's case, it would typically be a reaction to the tensions of a busy day. It seemed to Edith that Joe was overwhelmed by the anxiety of his homecoming — perhaps he was relieved, too. She tried to imagine what it must be like to complete the long journey home to England and return to Shrimpley after spending more than four years in a place as far-flung as India. She couldn't put herself in Joe's place, but she knew it must have been daunting, to say the least.

Eventually, Joe seemed to cry himself to sleep, but every time Edith tried to separate herself from him, he half woke and held tight to her arm. She thought of Carlo and her earlier resolution to visit him and Isobel before they left the next morning. Her head was aching — she'd never felt so conflicted in her life. Joe was the husband who'd asked her to marry him so he'd have someone to come home to — this was the foundation of her marriage contract. And she'd gone along with it, hook, line, and sinker. Even if it hadn't been before God, she'd nevertheless said "I do" out loud in front of witnesses and signed on the dotted line. How could she leave him now?

Around midnight, she murmured to Joe that she had to go to the bathroom. He begged her drowsily to hurry back and released her arm.

After she'd helped him struggle out of his clothes, Joe had slid between the sheets. Edith was glad that he didn't appear to be injured anywhere other than his face, although he was painfully thin. She winced at the sight of his chest, each rib evident under taut white skin. Joe's face, neck, and arms were the only areas discoloured by tropical sun; the rest of his body was as pale as the bed linen.

Having relieved herself, Edith retrieved her cigarettes from the living room and went out onto the porch. As far as she could tell, Carlo and Isobel's bungalow windows were unlit. She sat heavily on the top step of the porch stairs and lit a cigarette. As she inhaled the first lungful, she thought about things she'd recently heard about what was termed "the new woman." For example, women who were paying people to look after their children while they went out to work. And not posh mothers either, but factory workers. She'd heard that some women were hitchhiking places, taking their cue from American soldiers who did it to save their travel allowance. Women were wearing trousers, not only for work, but merely for comfort and convenience, which seemed to Edith to represent a devil-may-care, independent attitude. Why shouldn't she go with Carlo and Isobel? Isn't that exactly the kind of thing the postwar woman would do?

Edith had to admit she sometimes had difficulty thinking of herself as a full-grown woman, but on the other hand, during the past year, she'd often felt sixty-five years old rather than twenty-five. Edith shivered, as much with nervous exhaustion as from the cool evening air.

In the limpid night sky, an infinite number of stars were visible. There were so many in some places that they resembled white dust rather than individual pinpricks of light. Edith gazed at the moon over the estuary. She could clearly see the silhouette of the Welsh hills, as solid and constant as ever.

Edith felt insignificant. A wave of apprehension hit her. She worried that nothing — especially herself — was any different than it had been before the war. She'd heard a lot of chitchat about the social justice that would be created after the war was finished. Even newspapers like *The Times* claimed to support the idea of more equality for all citizens. Edith had read about a report recommending sweeping government programmes to end the injustices of the prewar era. Things like doctors and hospitals would be free, unemployed workers would be given a subsistence income, and old people would be cared for by the government. Edith had wondered at the time if the government-sponsored study wasn't just a ploy to boost the war effort. If people thought there was something worth fighting for, they'd be more easily persuaded to risk their lives, she reasoned.

She remembered something that had struck her when the report's author said it on the radio. He had said, "The purpose of victory is to live in a better world than the old world." Would there be a better world for her? And what about Joe? What about his world? She suddenly felt incredibly weary. She stubbed out her cigarette and stumbled back into the house vowing to get up early to see Carlo and Isobel, to at least say goodbye.

She had to reach across her husband's sleeping form to turn off the bedside lamp. Before her fingers could touch the switch, Joe's eyes snapped open and he gripped Edith's forearm so firmly it hurt.

"I took Latin at school, you know," he hissed. "I'm not stupid."

Edith's first thought was that he'd lost his mind. His missing eyebrow contributed to his deranged appearance. Her heart rate quickened as she wondered how best to deal with a lunatic. Humour him? Call Mrs. Maguire? What if he became violent?

"I know what *tee amo* means, you know," Joe insisted, gripping her tighter.

It only took a split second for Edith to realize that her husband was referring to Carlo's orgasmic protestations of love in the bomb crater earlier that day. Joe had obviously overheard as he made his way home across the heath. She stared, mortified, into Joe's glittering blue eyes for what seemed like hours.

Had he merely eavesdropped on her and Carlo? But what difference did it make whether he'd only listened or actually watched? Edith had once walked in on her parents making love. She'd arrived home one night from a dance. Her parents' light was still on, so she put her head around their bedroom door to let them know she was home. The sight of her father's scrawny buttocks had shocked her, but what she remembered most vividly was the grime and dirt on the soles of her mother's feet. If Joe had seen her and Carlo, thought Edith, she could imagine the tawdry sight in the crater as it must have appeared to him: her pale legs locked around Carlo's bucking hairy haunches, urging him on with her heels like a rider on a stallion. Their animal yelps of lust! Her face turned hot with embarrassment and shame. When her liaison with Carlo had remained unmentioned, it had been easy to fool herself that she didn't care what people thought. But now that her husband — a maimed soldier returning from a four-year term of duty — had obviously heard her, probably seen her, his wife, in the adulterous act . . . the fact of it nauseated Edith with embarrassment and guilt.

But as quickly as she'd become shamefaced, so Edith began to feel indignant. What did a husband expect after being away for such a long time? And didn't she love Carlo? She hoped Joe had overheard her say so. She wished with all her heart that she'd said it louder and with more emotion.

"You're hurting me," Edith protested.

Her voice broke Joe's ferocious glare. He released her, sank into the mattress, and folded in on himself, fetus-like. He began to weep again.

Edith turned out the light. She lay staring at indistinct shadows of leafy branches on the ceiling. Joe continued to sob. Edith's mood swung back and forth from remorseful chagrin to resentful irritation to deep, skin-tingling shame. At one point, Joe let out a heartfelt whine, as if experiencing anew everything that troubled him. Edith automatically reached out a hand. She patted Joe's shoulder, as she would have done with William if it were he who'd cried out in his sleep and not his father. She watched as gloomy silhouettes of leaves, tossed back and forth by a breeze that had sprung up outside, danced in and out of focus on the ceiling above her.

* * *

Edith woke abruptly at the sound of a car door slamming in the lane outside. She knew immediately it was Fred Saunders's taxi. The night's shadowscape of leaves had disappeared from the ceiling, leaving a blank canvas of luminous daylight. Edith could hear the raucous dawn chorus of birdsong. She turned her head and glanced at Joe's slumbering shape to confirm that the events of the previous day had actually occurred and weren't just a bad dream. Once her husband's presence was confirmed, she lay inert. She didn't so much think about the details of Joe's return as let the fact of it sink in, as if she were a dry sponge being slowly permeated by an insidious liquid.

She heard the bang of a second car door being pulled shut. Still she didn't move. At the sound of the taxi's engine attempting to catch, Joe stirred. He flung out an arm. It lay heavily across Edith's abdomen.

In a perverse way, she appreciated the weight of it on her body. She experienced an ambivalence she remembered from childhood — the reassurance of the safety and security in her mother's restraining grasp versus the yearning to explore a world beyond the parental lap. Had she really changed so little that she allowed the heft of a man's arm stop her from leaping out of bed? But it wasn't just any man's arm — it was her husband's. And she felt in its bulk all the restraint and inhibition of her upbringing, which, although abhorrent, was familiar and thus perversely welcome.

After several attempts, the taxi's motor spluttered to life. When Edith heard William's shouts above the sound of the engine, she tensed. The pitch of his voice was unnaturally high, as though he was overexcited or exceptionally upset. She was about to push Joe's arm aside when she heard Mrs. Maguire's voice. It had a stern but reassuring tone and Edith relaxed, secure in the knowledge that William was being cared for by his grandmother.

When the roar of the taxi diminished along the lane, the birds seemed to rouse themselves to new heights. But as Edith lay staring at the bare ceiling, their song gradually subsided until all she could hear was a single plaintive cheep.

"Why in God's name did you ask about Armando's grandfather living in Shrimpley?" demanded Shamus. "You surely can't imagine he was one of the 'maybe' Italians you 'think you remember' living next door to Granny Maguire."

"Edith could have planned all this, you know," said Will. He waved his hand, indicating the dining room around them. Will's obvious dodging of his question left Shamus with the impression that his brother was feeling embarrassed about interrogating the old man.

"All what?" demanded Shamus.

"This restaurant just happening to be right across from the hotel she chose, of all the hotels in Venice," ventured Will, sounding unconvinced. "Do you think it's possible she meant us to come here?"

"I think you've had too much sun," sneered Shamus. "And you don't usually give her so much credit for ingenuity. It has nothing whatsoever to do with Edith. It was all Armando's doing. You heard what his mother said, he simply likes to befriend foreigners — and browbeat them into eating at the family restaurant."

"I admit Edith couldn't have anticipated our banging into Armando, at least I don't think she could," said Will, suddenly looking confounded. "But I bet you any money she arranged to stay right opposite this restaurant because she knew it had something to do with something that happened during the war." He frowned darkly and nodded his head at Shamus.

"That's one something too many," teased Shamus. "You're turning into one of those conspiracy theorists. You'll be telling me next you believe the World Trade Center attack was engineered by the CIA."

"You mean it wasn't?" said Will, faking astonishment.

The restaurant was calmer. Most people had finished eating and were sitting talking, or sipping from glasses or coffee cups. Armando's mother sat behind the small bar making out bills and the young woman sat cross-legged on a barstool, examining her nails. The two brothers sat silent for several minutes.

"Talking of 'somethings' that happened during the war, do you know how Liam lost his leg?"

"Christ, you're like a terrier with a bone. What is it with all this dredging up the past?"

"Well do you?" demanded Shamus.

"No, but that's no surprise. We don't even know the truth about Joe's war wounds," Will replied. "Not that I care."

"Uncle Stumpy once told a drunken story about Joe being ambushed by a platoon of shovels in India," said Shamus. "But I think that was just sibling rivalry about whose injury was more heroic."

Will maintained that the story about Joe sitting it out in a warehouse somewhere in the Punjab, being waited on hand and foot by nubile serving girls, made it sound like his war had been a complete boondoggle.

"I think you're projecting," said Shamus. "Or fantasizing. Or both. I think we were a bit unfair on Joe."

"What?" Will asked, gasping with disbelief. "Why on earth would you say that?"

"His scars," said Shamus. "They made him look so forbidding. Even though the kids on the estate called him Mental Maguire, it was always to his back and at a safe distance. They were all petrified of him. It was the missing eyebrow, I think. It made him look disturbed even when he was perfectly content."

"The old bastard was never content," said Will.

"He must have scared the shit out of you when you first saw him," said Shamus. "How old would you have been — four or five?"

"Do I *have* to try and remember?" asked Will.

"Not on my account," answered Shamus. "Anyway, it couldn't have been that bad if you can't remember."

When Will objected, saying that Joe's homecoming had in all likelihood been a "hellacious nightmare," Shamus pointed out that Will had claimed earlier in the day that Sandy Lane had been idyllic.

"It probably was, before Joe arrived on the scene," speculated Will. Then he seemed to hesitate; Shamus had the impression he was searching for appropriate words. "Shrimpley's still pretty high up on my list," Will admitted.

When Shamus surmised that by now the place was probably crawling with monster homes belonging to millionaire Liverpool footballers Will said, "Sandy Lane has a few more houses than it used to, but it's still a cul-de-sac with a field at the end. And Granny Maguire's place is exactly the same."

"How the hell do you know?" Shamus asked.

Will explained that he'd been back to take a look at the house the last couple of times he'd visited Edith in Liverpool. Then he admitted, appearing slightly bashful, that he'd taken a friend to show off where he'd been born.

"Who?" Shamus asked.

"Her name's Laura," said Will.

"You sly dog," gasped Shamus. "It's taken you all day to tell me you've got a new squeeze."

"She and I are trying to buy it, actually," said Will. "As a kind of weekend, retirement place."

"What, Granny Maguire's place?" Shamus asked, incredulous.

"Yes. It's in pretty bad shape, though. It doesn't look as if anything's been done to it for ages. And the garden's a mess. The old lady who owns it might be the woman whose husband bought it from Granny Maguire — they've lived there for more than forty years. He died a few months ago, and she's scheduled to go into a retirement home in December."

Shamus wasn't sure what astonished him most, the fact that Will had a girlfriend or his revelation about Granny Maguire's house. He felt envious and a little indignant.

"Why didn't you tell me sooner?" he asked.

"It didn't seem appropriate," said Will.

"Appropriate!" exclaimed Shamus. "What does that mean?"

"How do I tell someone whose been going through what you've had to endure for the last few years with Luke that I've found an iota of contentment? Not during an infrequent transatlantic phone call, that's for sure."

Shamus was immediately moved by Will's obvious consideration for him. His eyes watered and he was forced to swallow.

"You'd like Laura; she's terrific," continued Will. "Admittedly, there isn't the frenzied hurly-burly of the early days with Mary. But that proved to have its dark side, didn't it? And I'm not a young stud any more."

"Were you ever?" Shamus couldn't resist asking.

"I think you and Laura will get along well," said Will. "She told me I seemed as content and happy in Shrimpley as in the three minutes after I ejaculate and before I fall asleep, so why not retire there."

Shamus laughed. He remembered the old saw about one of the advantages of being gay — no call for all that after-intercourse conversation that women are reputed to demand. He remembered with a smile how Luke's post-orgasmic breathlessness often shifted to snoring after about thirty seconds. "This Laura sounds like she's got your number," he said. "I suppose she's sixteen years old."

"Give me some credit," said Will. "She's a year older than me, actually. She's a potter, quite a successful one. We plan to build a glassed-in studio for her on the old porch."

Shamus remembered the porch. Granny Maguire had often sat there in a wicker chair and perched Shamus on her lap. She would sometimes hold a heavy pair of binoculars to his eyes so that he could examine the fields and hedges of Wales on the far side of the estuary.

"Surely the heath's gone?" questioned Shamus.

"Miraculously, most of it has been saved from developers, thanks to one of those archaic English laws that holds common land sacred," Will replied. "You wouldn't notice any difference from when we were children. Everything looks much smaller, of course. Funny how that happens," he added, sounding genuinely perplexed.

Shamus asked if the bomb crater was still there.

Will described how the crater had taken a bit of finding but that it was still there. He related how the gorse had encroached somewhat and that heather was growing where the grass had been. "But it makes for a nice springy mattress," he concluded. When Shamus suggested that Will must have tried it out, his brother insisted he hadn't tested it in the way Shamus imagined. "We lay there for a while," explained Will. "But Laura said she found it creepy, lying in a crater made by a bomb. I guess she doesn't have the positive associations we have."

"She can doubtless see it for what it is," insisted Shamus.

"What are you talking about?" demanded Will.

"We don't seem able to fully appreciate the damage that was wrought," said Shamus.

"But I told you, she's only a year older than me," retorted Will. "Why would she be any more or less aware of the war than we are?"

"I'm not talking about the war itself. I'm talking about the aftermath," said Shamus.

"What aftermath?"

"The repercussions," said Shamus. "Craters. Scars. Bomb sites. Life. Whatever."

Will frowned and looked intently at Shamus for a second or two before speaking. "And you could also say that it's all bullshit. That the war is just a big fucking excuse."

"All right. Keep your shirt on," said Shamus. He felt a slight glow of satisfaction, maybe relief, that Will, true to form, was becoming enraged at the idea of the war being used as a scapegoat for their family's dysfunction, if that's what it was. He asked Will if he'd told Edith about his scheme to buy Granny Maguire's house, because he was curious, but also to change the subject.

"Yes," replied Will. "She asked about the crater too. When I told her Laura and I had lain in it, she looked very dewy-eyed. You and Edith are two of a kind."

At that moment, the kitchen door swung open for the umpteenth time, but on this occasion there was a crash as a plate the young girl had been carrying fell from her tray. The two brothers looked toward the commotion. Signora Belli started to berate the girl for her clumsiness as the two women squatted to clear up the mess of spilled dessert and the shards of a plate. Armando's grandfather stood in the kitchen doorway, but he was paying no attention whatsoever to the brouhaha taking place at his feet. Instead, he stared intently at Will and Shamus.

"I swear that old bastard reminds me of something that happened when I was little," Will suddenly announced.

"Christ, maybe it's not just the sun," groaned Shamus. "I think you've really flipped."

Edith's War

"No, really, listen. I'm sure there's something to it," Will pleaded.

"Go on then," said Shamus, intrigued by the sincerity of his brother's appeal.

"I remember a black taxi piled with suitcases. There was a wheelchair sticking out of the taxi's boot. Granny Maguire had to stop me from running after it when it drove away. My arm hurt from her holding me back."

"Maybe the wheelchair belonged to Uncle Liam," Shamus suggested.

"I don't think so," said Will. He shook his head as though trying to clear his mind. "I doubt if Uncle Stumpy would have had any truck with wheelchairs."

"This is ridiculous," exclaimed Shamus, frustrated at not knowing what the hell Will was on about. "Why bother bringing it up if you can't remember the details?"

"You know what I think?" said Will, obviously irritated with Shamus's reaction. "I think that all this probing of the past you've been encouraging all day long has more to do with you than with me." Shamus stared at Will, who nodded with eyes open wide, as if urging Shamus to acknowledge the accuracy of his submission. Shamus was accustomed to thoughts of Luke flying into his head out of nowhere for no apparent reason, but the force with which the next notion hit him took him by surprise. Shamus suddenly realized that Will was probably right: his preoccupation with his and his brother's shared past was patently selfish. It wasn't about Will at all but more about Shamus's suspicion that he'd somehow failed Luke. He'd become convinced that he hadn't been expressive enough, loving enough, caring enough. As a result, he was desperate to understand how his shortcomings — real or imagined — had originated. And Will, by his mere presence, had unwittingly supplied the wherewithal for Shamus to scour his early life for some kind of explanation. But why shouldn't he use Will to figure out the nature of his neurosis, if that's what it was, Shamus asked himself indignantly. Also, Shamus reasoned, if his curiosity about their childhood was truly only all about himself and his frantic desire to better understand his guilt in relation to Luke, why would his brother be such a willing participant? And why did he appear so frustrated whenever Shamus asked a challenging question?

"It's not like you haven't been obsessing about it too," he pointed out. "Look at your fixation on Armando's cigarette case."

Will evaded the accusation. "Would you rather not have known that this little movie popped into my head — of a taxi disappearing down Sandy Lane and Granny Maguire holding my arm to prevent me from running after it?" he asked.

"It would certainly explain your psychosis over being deserted or left behind," mused Shamus.

"I don't have any problems with that," exclaimed Will indignantly.

"Of course you don't," said Shamus in mock reassurance. "Hey! You never said it was Sandy Lane before."

"Didn't I?" asked Will.

"Okay," said Shamus, plunging into the fray despite his inner revelations about his own selfish reasons for getting to the truth. "Whose could it have been if it wasn't Uncle Liam's?"

"The woman next door had a wheelchair," said Will in a casual tone.

Reluctant to ask, but so taken aback by the nonchalance of Will's surprising disclosure he couldn't resist, Shamus demanded to know what woman Will was talking about.

"I don't know who she was," replied Will in an exasperated tone of voice. "She lived next door to Granny Maguire."

"In that funny little bungalow the other side of the fir trees?" questioned Shamus. "How could anybody in a wheelchair live there? Weren't there steps up to both doors?"

Will allowed that he couldn't rightly remember. He scowled with the effort. "There's a lot we have to ask Edith about tomorrow," he concluded, waving at Signora Belli for the bill.

"Why would Armando's grandfather remind you of that, do you think?" asked Shamus.

"Maybe because the memory of that taxi disappearing makes me feel pissed off, like I felt earlier when the old bugger ignored me. I don't know, and maybe I don't care."

With that, Will appeared to completely remove himself from the conversation. Typical, thought Shamus. Will playing his old trick of pulling the rug out from under his brother just as they were getting somewhere.

"Let's leave it to Edith to explain — if there's any explaining to be done," Will muttered. "I'm going to the little boy's room." He threw his credit card down on the table in front of Shamus and walked toward the sign at the back of the restaurant.

Armando's mother arrived with the bill on a small plastic tray decorated with white letters advertising something called Fernet-Branca. Shamus immediately plonked his and Will's credit cards on the tray. *"Mezzo, mezzo?"* asked Signora Belli. When Shamus nodded in agreement, she made her way back to the bar.

Will seemed to take ages in the bathroom. By the time he returned, Shamus had calculated the tip, signed his credit card receipt, and was ready to leave.

"Maybe you'd better make a visit to the toilet too," said Will as he sat down. He appeared exhausted, drained and pale. It had been a long day for both of them, thought Shamus. Then he noticed that strands of hair at Will's forehead were wet. He'd obviously doused his face with water.

"Are you all right?" he asked his brother.

"I'm fine," replied Will, but in a tone of voice that implied he might have reason not to be. "Seriously," he urged. "Go and take a look at the photos on the way to the loo."

Something about the tone of Will's suggestion compelled Shamus. And he did have a slight urge to pee. He stood and walked toward the rear of the restaurant. He hesitated for a second or two at the entrance to a narrow corridor with a door at the end. The walls here were almost as cluttered with framed photos as those of the restaurant. Courtesy of three spotlights spaced at equal distances along the length of the corridor, some of the photographs were brightly lit.

The shots were clearly older than the ones out in the restaurant. Shamus estimated by the suits and dresses that people were wearing that they'd been taken in the 1950s. The first photograph he examined was of a glamorous blonde woman holding a bouquet of flowers, roses maybe. On either side of her were two men who appeared to be in their thirties. Shamus assumed the younger-looking man to be Armando's grandfather. Even in an old black and white photo, there was no mistaking his tall silhouette and intense, black-eyed stare.

When Shamus transferred his scrutiny to the other man, his scalp tightened. He had the unsettling sensation that he was looking at a photo of himself when he'd been in his late thirties, maybe early forties. He quickly moved on to other, better-lit photos. Every single one featured Armando's grandfather standing with Shamus's doppelgänger.

As he passed quickly from one photo to the next, Shamus's skin prickled and the urge to urinate became stronger. He was so reluctant to tear himself away from the photos that he only just made it to the urinal before losing control of his bladder.

ENGLAND

Friday, September 13, 1945

"Such beautiful brown eyes," exclaimed Anna. "He's a giant, too. How heavy you say he was?"

"Nine pounds," Edith replied. "I was expecting the worst, but he came out fairly easily. Even though Will was smaller, his was a much more difficult birth."

"Chaymus," said Anna.

"Shamus," corrected Edith. "Sh — like she or Sheffield."

"Shamus," repeated Anna. "It's a good name. Sounds proper British,"

"It's Irish," said Edith.

"Same thing," Anna retorted.

Edith smiled. If Anna had overheard the conversation surrounding the choice of Shamus's name, she wouldn't have been so quick to dismiss its national distinction.

"We don't want any more Protestant names," Joe had insisted. "William, for Christ's sake." He shook his head in disgust.

"I don't know why you're getting so worked up," Mrs. Maguire suddenly interjected. She'd been unusually quiet since Joe's return. Edith wondered if she was missing Anna, who'd moved to Liverpool a week after Carlo and Isobel left. "What's in a name anyway? William's not so bad," she concluded.

"Not so bad?" questioned Joe. "You couldn't get more Protestant if you tried."

"Why are you so concerned?" demanded Mrs. Maguire "You haven't stepped into a church since your voice broke. And anyway, if that's your worry, why are you so intent on losing the only bit of the poor boy's name that people might think is Catholic?"

"What on earth are you talking about?" Joe asked.

"You want to call the lad Will," said Mrs. Maguire. "Don't you realize you're dropping the Liam part of it?"

Joe was speechless.

"Just goes to show," Mrs. Maguire had muttered angrily. "No wonder we're always at war. Most men can't see further than the ends of their own noses."

Edith smiled to herself at the memory of Mrs. Maguire's indignant expression and Joe's wide-eyed stupefaction at his mother's logic.

"It'd be far too confusing to call Will Liam — as well as Liam," Joe had said in befuddled exasperation, glancing from his son to his brother and back. Mrs. Maguire's parsing of the name had shut Joe up for a day or two, but over the months he'd worn them all down. William had reluctantly begun to answer to Will.

Anna reached over and tickled Shamus under his chin. He gurgled winningly.

"Let's pray that this one never knows any war," said Anna.

"Unlikely that he won't," Edith said in a resigned tone of voice. "But let's hope it was an omen he was born on VE day," she relented. "Coming into the world on the first day of peace has to count for something. I was so exhausted when I heard all the commotion outside the hospital that I thought at first they must be celebrating his birth. The fireworks reminded me of the air raid on the night Will was born. Do you remember?"

"Hah!" exclaimed Anna. "That was what you call a welcome."

Edith stood up and laid Shamus in his carrycot. He clutched one of his feet and drooled happily.

"This is a nice house," said Anna, looking around appreciatively at the combined living room and dining room with extensive windows at front and back.

When Joe had announced that he'd arranged to rent a brand new council house for them in Liverpool, he'd proudly puffed up his chest, which had become a little less bony despite continued rationing. Joe was nothing if not a dutiful husband. Within a month of returning, he'd wangled the council house for his family to rent and he'd found himself a job — a warehouse manager at a motor parts factory on the outskirts of Liverpool. Edith supposed she was lucky to be married to a demobbed soldier who was gainfully employed. Work was hard to find for the flood of returning servicemen, many with no qualifications or experience. On the evening of VE day, while she'd been in hospital with Shamus, a husband had come to visit his wife, who was another new mother on Edith's maternity ward. The man wore a badge that said "Pity the Unemployed." They made a sorry sight, the woman, baby, and out-of-work ex-soldier. Edith's heart went out to them. How were they going to scrape together the hospital charges? What kind of a life would their baby have? At least Shamus had a father who earned a decent wage. Then she caught herself — how easily she'd slipped into thinking of Joe as Shamus's father.

"Whereabouts is this house?" Edith had asked Joe, full of trepidation although she told herself there must be quite a few new housing estates being built apart from the one where Carlo had been interned.

"Woolfall Heath," Joe had said. The illogical idea entered Edith's head that Joe was well aware the house was on the very site where Carlo had been held. She was convinced he'd chosen the location just to taunt her.

"It's a lovely house with three bedrooms. All modern conveniences — an inside bathroom as well as an outside privy. With a coal shed and all." Joe's periwinkle eyes glittered with excitement. He had often become emotional since his return, brimming with hyperactive enthusiasm one minute, deeply despondent the next. Edith put it down to poor sleep; he had frequent nightmares. He often cried out in the night, then sat bolt upright in bed, short of breath and perspiring heavily.

"There's even an electric fire in our bedroom," Joe bragged. "Set right into the wall. No more freezing winter nights for us."

"I don't want to live in Woolfall Heath," said Edith.

"Why not?" Joe demanded, so obviously confounded that Edith felt guilty for believing he'd known about Woolfall Heath's connection to Carlo. Joe clearly had no idea that the estate had been used as an internment camp.

"It's too far out," said Edith limply.

"But it's only half an hour into Liverpool," reasoned Joe. "And it'll take me no more than fifteen minutes to bicycle to work in the other direction."

"Is there a school for Will?" asked Edith, casting around in desperation for an excuse not to live there.

"Of course there's a bloody school!" Joe shouted.

"All right, no need to yell," said Edith. She had no option but to go along with Joe's plans, so she told herself they were lucky to be renting a new house with three bedrooms. And Edith didn't want to risk Joe getting worked up and taking things out on William again.

Unlike Edith and Mrs. Maguire, William hadn't been reticent about mentioning his missing pals Carlo, Isobel, and Anna. For the first few days after they left, he complained bitterly about their absence. To make matters worse, he was openly wary of Joe. Any attempt by his father to ingratiate himself was met with a cool reaction from William. Edith could see what an exasperating effect his son's attitude, combined with William's endless questions concerning the Baccanellos, was having on Joe. She tried her best to distract William from the subject of their ex-neighbours, but there seemed to be more hours in the day since Joe's return from India. She couldn't divert William's attention every single minute.

One afternoon, a week after Joe's homecoming, they were sitting having a cup of tea. Joe had just arrived back at Mrs. Maguire's house, morose from a fruitless day of job-hunting in Liverpool. William looked up from the floor, where he was playing with some toy farm animals, and said, "I wish Carlo was here. He could moo like a real cow. And baa like a sheep, too."

When Joe leapt to his feet, his cup and saucer went flying. The saucer broke in two when it hit the floor, and hot tea splashed on Edith's legs. Joe grabbed William by one arm and yanked him to his feet.

"I never want to hear that wop's name again, you hear?" Joe shouted at the top of his lungs, his mouth mere inches from William's face. His cheeks were crimson and gobs of saliva were hitting William in the eye as he yelled at the boy. William squeezed his eyelids tight shut. Joe shook his son with all his might.

"Do you hear me?" he yelled. Edith could see William's head bounce back and forth, and his body bucked as Joe shook him, like a small animal being viciously worried by a predator. "Do you hear?" Joe shouted again.

Mrs. Maguire jumped to her feet. She managed to pull Joe's hand from William's arm and push him away. She swept William into her arms. William was deathly pale and ominously silent, obviously so shocked he was beyond tears. Edith took him from Mrs. Maguire and rushed him to her old bedroom, where William and his grandmother now slept. As she left the living room, she threw Joe a look of hatred, but he'd sunk into Mrs. Maguire's easy chair, head in his hands.

Edith rocked William in her arms until night fell. "There there," she cooed. "It's all right now. Everything's all right." Before he eventually fell asleep, William stared up at Edith. The cornflower blue irises of his eyes appeared bruised with injured bewilderment. It reminded her of the expression in Liam's eyes on the day he'd discovered the decoy fires and understood that the world wasn't as pleasant as he'd thought.

When Edith lay down next to Joe in bed that night, she said, "I don't care what you do to me, but if you ever lay a hand on William again, I'll leave you and take him with me." Joe didn't respond, but he had nightmares for most of the night.

After that, Joe had been the picture of restraint for a while. He made a monumental effort to befriend Will, but the damage was done. Confronted daily by a hostile son, it wasn't long before Joe lost his fragile resolve. The older Will grew, the more frequent were the skirmishes between him and his father.

"Show me the garden," said Anna to Edith. "He'll be all right for a few minutes." She nodded her head in Shamus's direction. Edith led the way through the kitchen, with its gleaming Parkinson gas stove, to the back door. They trooped past the outside toilet and the coal shed.

"Grass and potatoes?" queried Anna, glancing around. "That's all you grow?"

"Joe says there's too much clay to grow anything else. It's not like the sandy soil in Shrimpley."

"He doesn't know what he's talking about," announced Anna. "He should grow *spezie: basilico, rosmarino.* I could sell in my shop."

Now that fishermen could safely take to sea again, fish were more readily available. Anna had reopened two of the family's fish and chip businesses, quietly hiring local managers to run them both.

To be on the safe side, the name above the shops was changed from Baccanello's to plain Fish and Chips. But against everyone's advice, Anna had insisted on converting the third location, the one nearest the city centre, into a grocery shop. She carried whatever produce she could get her hands on. She paid Italian friends for their *spezie:* fresh herbs like basil, rosemary, sage, and thyme. She stocked garlic, onions, and other garden produce. And she sold her own and other women's homemade tomato sauce, pickles, and preserves. Anna had grand plans to import foodstuffs from Italy — spaghetti, olive oil, cheese, and coffee — once foreign trade resumed.

"You wait and see," Anna insisted. "Once this city gets back on its feet, plenty people going to want more than just fish and chips. Already I got people, posh people too, come to my shop. One is the wife of a *professore* at the university," she boasted.

She hadn't turned a profit yet, but Anna's fish and chip shops were more than enough to support her for a while. Edith couldn't believe the new endeavour would come to much, but she admired Anna for trying.

"Once Domenico gets to Italy, he'll send me lots of good things to sell," she insisted.

"Have you heard from him?" asked Edith.

"Not since he left Australia," said Anna. "But by now he should be in Italy, God willing. And since that *stronzo* Mussolini is dead, things there are going to be better."

News had reached England a week before Shamus was born that Mussolini and his mistress had been killed and their bodies put on public display, hung by their feet with meat hooks, heads dangling. Edith was disgusted by the news; she didn't think anyone deserved such treatment, no matter what they may have done. She recalled Isobel's description of the positive things Mussolini had achieved.

"It's a shame Domenico doesn't come back here to help you with the business," said Edith.

"It's okay," said Anna. "Why would he come back here after what they did to him? I understand when he says he couldn't live here no more. Better he go to Italy with his chef friends than be bitter and unhappy here. He'll make a wonderful restaurant; you'll see."

"Aren't you tempted to join him?" asked Edith.

"No, this is my home now," said Anna. "And it's funny — I don't blame anyone for what happen no more. It was a war. Bad things go on in a war. But the war is over now. You got to put it behind, pick up and carry on. And anyway, Carlo's still here. When he's able, he'll come back to help for a while."

Edith felt a pang of painful emotion not unlike grief at the sound of Carlo's name. It was similar but less intense than her reaction to the news that Gianni and Paolo had been killed. She supposed her time with Carlo was dead and gone forever. Certainly the war years were already beginning to take on an unreal quality, like a cinematic, larger-than-life fantasy. Edith panicked slightly at the thought that the future held merely a disquieting detachment from the worst of those years, like waking from a bad dream, and heartwarming nostalgia for the best of them. It was unthinkable that such intense experience could recede so quickly. She remembered how adamant she'd been that nobody, especially Anna, forget the tragedy that had befallen her husband and sons, not to mention all the other Italian men and their families. But as time passed, it proved difficult to be vigilant.

"How is Isobel?" asked Edith.

"I think she does okay but not too well," Anna said sadly. "They live in a little ground-floor flat and she goes to the hospital almost every day. Carlo never complains, bless him. But I can tell he gets fed up."

"Give them my love when you write," said Edith, gazing at the square of lawn and the host of lush potato plants. Joe grew more excited as the time approached when he could harvest his first crop of spuds.

"*Il mio Dio,* I have terrible news about Isobel's poor brother-in-law, though," Anna suddenly exclaimed. "Let's go inside so I can tell you."

The two women trooped back into the house. Edith was full of apprehension about the news Anna was about to impart.

"Isobel's sister's husband was on his way back here from Australia," explained Anna. "Him and some others from the *Arandora Star.* But their ship was hit by a torpedo and they were all lost."

Edith was suddenly catapulted back to the day when Anna had received the telegram about Gianni and Paolo's deaths. It must be difficult for Anna to relive the experience through the tragedy she was describing. "Can you imagine those poor boys who survived the *Arandora Star?*" Anna asked. "To be torpedoed again. It's horrible."

"No, I can't imagine," said Edith. She reached for Anna's hand to comfort her. She was always taken a little by surprise at her lack of inhibition with Anna. There was no one else with whom she'd display affection in such a physical manner — certainly not Joe. Edith and Anna sat in silence, side by side and hand in hand, on the sofa for several minutes.

Edith glanced around the plainly painted living room. They hadn't been able to afford much furniture. Joe had acquired wartime utility chairs and a sofa, a plain three-piece suite. He'd also bought a basic table and four chairs. Some people said that the war had been an effective social leveller — no matter how rich you were, you could only obtain the same as everybody else. But that was only partially true; a thriving black market had emerged. If you were willing to pay the price, you could buy almost anything. There'd also been hope that the lesson of the war for political parties would mean more united cooperation and endeavour between them. But it seemed to Edith that only a few weeks after the defeat of Germany, they were as polarized as ever.

Edith stroked the top of Anna's hand with her thumb. She thought about the internment of the Italians and how different her war would have been if she'd never met Carlo and his family.

"You know," said Anna. "We all think we're so clever. I know I used to be too proud. I had a good husband, three handsome boys who speak English and get along so good at school. Three fish and chip shops, a nice house — I thought I have it made. And then, bang, suddenly it all disappeared. When a war happens, it shows you we don't know nothing. War or no war, we're all like leaves being blown around. No matter how much we think we're the boss, we're not."

Edith patted Anna's hand. "It's hard to imagine you as anything but the boss," she said.

Anna smiled. Shamus gurgled.

Edith went to the carrier, lifted Shamus out, and held him up for Anna's inspection.

"Say bye-bye to Anna," she said.

"Oh is it time already?" Anna said. "I suppose I won't see William."

"Afraid not," said Edith. "He's usually home from school by now, but it'd be too risky for you to wait. Joe will be home in half an hour or so."

When Edith had written to Anna to invite her to come to meet Shamus, she'd explained that Joe mustn't know about the arrangement. Anna didn't question it. She and Mrs. Maguire were of a piece — neither woman commented on Joe and Edith's marriage, just as they'd never mentioned Edith's relationship with Carlo. Edith was never sure whether either of them knew the full extent of it. But there was a clear understanding between Edith and Anna that Joe wouldn't want to be reminded of Edith's time spent with her and Carlo and Isobel; Anna must visit while Joe was at work. Edith was relieved when Anna didn't seem to mind.

As Anna retreated down the garden path and along the street, bound for the bus stop at the corner, she waved vigorously to Edith and Shamus. Edith felt guilty for not telling Anna about her blood relationship to Shamus, but she'd made a solemn promise to Joe. And Edith, being Edith, would never break her vow.

"So nobody knows this baby isn't mine except you and me?" Joe had queried, his voice quavering slightly in the darkness of the bedroom.

It had taken Edith three days to pluck up the courage to tell Joe she was pregnant, and even then she could only do it in the dark when they were lying in bed, separated by a good inch or two of bedsheet. She'd considered telling Mrs. Maguire first, but she'd seemed a little distant since Joe's return, Edith hadn't had the nerve.

Edith had been tortured with fear and apprehension when Dr. Parry confirmed her worst fears that she was pregnant with Shamus some time after Joe returned from India. Joe had hardly touched her since he'd arrived home. He recoiled if their limbs came into contact within the confines of Mrs. Maguire's double bed. Edith was relieved yet felt oddly put out. It occurred to her that perhaps she disgusted him. If so, she wouldn't necessarily blame him.

All the way home from the doctor's office, she turned the situation over and over in her mind. Edith cursed herself, and then Carlo, for being so hasty and thoughtless the last time they'd seen each other. Their usual caution had evaporated in the heat of the moment.

There'd been all kinds of stories in the newspaper about men returning from war to find newborns or pregnant wives at home. Edith had read an account of a soldier who'd beaten his unfortunate wife almost to death — she was in her eighth month of pregnancy. It seemed so unfair when the general population tacitly accepted that husbands overseas had used prostitutes. Some had even had girlfriends in France or Italy or wherever they'd served. But nobody blinked an eye about it.

As she walked across the heath from the doctor's office, Edith noticed, despite her desperation, a hint of autumn in the air. The bracken had turned brown. As she trod on sagging fronds, crumbling them underfoot, the dead leaves gave off their peculiar acrid scent.

"Yes, it's true," Edith whispered to Joe in the murkiness of their bedroom. "Nobody knows this baby isn't yours."

"Not even the doctor?" questioned Joe.

"Not even the doctor," confirmed Edith.

They lay in silence. Edith could hear Joe's steady inhalations and exhalations. She could almost hear him thinking. Edith was strangely disappointed at his unemotional reaction.

"All right, Edith, here's the bargain," Joe eventually said.

"Bargain?" questioned Edith.

"You never, ever, tell anyone who the real father is and I'll say nothing about it either. To all intents and purposes, it'll be our child."

Joe spoke with such finality that Edith didn't know what to say. A part of her screamed that the truth should out, that Joe's plan was downright dishonest. And what about Carlo? This was his baby too. He was entitled to a say in the child's future.

"And I never want to hear Carlo or his family mentioned ever again," said Joe, as if he'd been reading Edith's mind.

Edith thought about the husband she'd read about who'd beaten his pregnant wife.

"But why?" she said, genuinely baffled as to Joe's motivation, not to mention his phlegmatic reaction.

There was a rustling of bed linen as Joe turned to face her. "I have to admit that when I asked you to marry me, before the war, I was scared. Scared of the army, scared of never coming back. I never made any secret of the fact that I wanted someone to come home to," he said, sounding aggrieved.

"I know," said Edith.

"But I realized when I was away that I was more attached to you than I thought," Joe spoke quickly, as though to get the words out and over with as quickly as possible. "And more than anything, I wanted to have a normal, happy life," he continued at a less frantic pace. "You wouldn't believe the things I saw. I may not have been on the front lines, but in India I saw people living the worst lives you can imagine. I saw sickness and poverty that I can't describe." There was a catch in his voice. Edith thought perhaps he'd start to cry, but he seemed to pull himself together. "Days after I arrived, I saw a mother lying dead in the street from illness and hunger with a baby crying at her shrivelled breast. I asked the man I was with, an Indian worker from the warehouse, what would happen to the child. Do you know what he said?"

"What?" Edith asked.

"He told me the baby would die, that the mother was an untouchable, the lowest caste. Nobody would save the child. It was terrible, Edith, terrible. I saw children maimed by their own parents so they could earn money as beggars. I vowed I'd come back here and live in a nice house and raise our children and have a normal life. And that's what I'm determined to do. I'm willing to put everything else behind us. Aren't you?"

Edith stared at the darkness above her head. She could hear a wind outside; dry leaves rustled in the garden. Did she want what Joe wanted? What about the fantasy of living with Carlo and Isobel? Was Joe's idea for their future life any less of a fiction? She thought about her mother and how much she would have approved of Joe's plan, on the grounds that the neighbours need never know a thing. As far as the world was concerned, she and Joe were having their second child — the fruit of a loving reunion. The thought that the sole rationale for such a life-defining choice might be the approval or disapproval of others was almost enough to make her refuse Joe's offer. But she had to admit she was relieved that no explanations would need to be made. And the intensity and sincerity of Joe's words had impressed her. So instead she said nothing. Seconds ticked by, and she could feel Joe's eyes probing the darkness for her response.

"So what do you say?" asked Joe eventually.

"I don't know," said Edith. "I'm so confused."

"Look, Edith," murmured Joe. "I don't blame you for what happened with Carlo. I was away for four years, for Christ's sake; it's a long time. It's just that I'd been looking forward to coming home for so long — and Carlo, of all people." Edith heard him swallow loudly, choking back his emotion. After a few seconds, he continued, "It wasn't exactly what I'd pictured, that's all." Edith felt a flush of shame when she imagined what he'd witnessed on the heath on the day he returned.

"How can you say you love me?" said Edith.

"You might not believe this, but I think I love you more than ever." Joe gave out a humourless laugh. "After I saw you with Carlo up on the heath, I was ready to kill you, divorce you, beat you. I don't know what. But when I saw you standing in the living room doorway looking so independent and adult with Will holding your hand . . . I almost broke down there and then."

The wind had gathered strength; the bedroom windows rattled. The seconds ticked by.

"All right," said Edith in a low voice.

"Pardon?" Joe asked.

"All right," said Edith a little louder. "It's a deal."

"All right," Joe repeated. "It's a deal."

The bed creaked slightly as he rolled over, away from Edith.

Edith lay and listened to the wind as it roared out of the west. She tried to dissect her emotions, but she found it impossible to separate the interweaving threads — hopelessness, relief, disappointment, a sense of security, sadness, the warm glow of being wanted — that wove in and out of her crowded mind. She certainly couldn't decide which, if any, was most dominant. But as she lay awake, she thought about the soldier who'd beaten his pregnant wife. Such a stark contrast to Joe's astonishing generosity — perhaps fuelled by self-interest, but magnanimous nonetheless.

Edith lingered on the doorstep of her council house after Anna had disappeared. When she'd first come to live in Woolfall Heath with Joe and William, Edith had spent hours trying to work out the layout of the internment camp as it had been when she visited Carlo. She knew without a doubt that the wooden hut in which the German artists showed her their work had been two streets away, in Shepton Road. But she wasn't sure where the boundary of the camp had actually started. She simply couldn't work out where the double barbed-wire fence had stood. The streets looked so different now with lawns and freshly painted window frames on all the houses. After a few weeks, she stopped trying to remember. Although her skin had come out in goose pimples when the thought first occurred to her that their house might have been the very house where Carlo was billeted. And every now and again, she wondered if she was standing on the spot where she and Carlo had hugged as she left the camp.

As Edith gazed up the street, she remembered the reservations she'd had before she returned his embrace for the first time. She remembered the effect of his smell, but she couldn't for the life of her recall what he smelled of. Sweat and damp wool, probably, but she couldn't conjure it up no matter how hard she tried. But smells are never easy to remember unless you experience them again, Edith told herself as she turned to go back in the house, jiggling Shamus up and down to make him crow with delight.

Monday, June 1, 1953

When Edith heard the letterbox snap shut and the flutter of falling envelopes, she wiped her hands on her pinafore, glad of the distraction. She hated Mondays — washing days — although it was easier now that both boys were at school and she didn't have Shamus to worry about as well as the laundry. She left a wet sheet sandwiched between two rubber rollers of the mangle, half of it flattened and limp, the rest of it sodden and dripping into the dolly tub, where it had soaked overnight along with half a dozen other sheets and pillowcases.

As she bent to pick up the letters from the doormat, she smiled at the familiar swoops and curls of Anna's flamboyant writing on the topmost envelope. Underneath was a postcard from Edith's sister, who was holidaying in Wales with her husband and her two girls, Susan and Brenda. The front of the card was divided into four photographs of various bays and beaches. Capital letters in the centre proclaimed GREETINGS FROM THE ISLE OF ANGLESY. On the reverse, Edith's sister had written in her familiar scrawl, "Weather is here. Wish you were beautiful. Love, Agnes." Typical, thought Edith.

The other letter was addressed to Mr. Joseph Maguire, Esq. The words "Liverpool Corporation" were spelled out in black letters in the top left-hand corner of the envelope. It would be either a bill or information concerning the housing estate. It seemed the council was forever resurfacing streets or replacing lampposts. Money certainly wasn't scarce these days. People — government officials and employers — were predicting that the economic boom would continue for some time.

Edith had to admit she and Joe were benefiting from the country's burgeoning prosperity. Joe had worked enough overtime to afford the deposit on a television, and it had been delivered in time for the Cup Final a few weeks before. They were buying the television on hire purchase, but it didn't look as if they'd have any trouble paying the instalments. The football match was a battle between two local teams, Bolton and Blackpool. Since they were the only family on the street to have a television, half a dozen male neighbours had invited themselves over to watch the game, and every one of them arrived clutching bottles of beer. Edith didn't understand how they could all see the screen — it wasn't much bigger than the postcard she'd received from her sister. But Joe had turned up the sound so loud that, even if they couldn't see the action, the men could hear Kenneth Wolstenholme's stirring commentary. Edith thought the windows would crack from the sound of seven grown men screaming hysterically in her living room after Blackpool won with a goal in overtime.

It had been a different scene at Shamus's eighth birthday party a week later. A dozen rambunctious children fuelled by an abundance of jelly and cake had been totally silenced by the wonder of television. They gazed in mute awe as two puppets and a talking flower cavorted around the tiny black and white screen. Edith couldn't believe it. Even though the three figures spouted complete gibberish, every child's attention was completely taken up by the programme. *Bill and Ben, The Flowerpot Men* became Shamus's favourite show despite the fact that he was too old for it.

Edna and Charlie Martin, their next-door neighbours, were coming round the next day to watch the Coronation of Princess Elizabeth. And Mrs. Maguire was arriving that evening from Shrimpley to stay over for the big event. Edith pulled a pack of cigarettes and some matches from her apron pocket and plonked herself down on one of the easy chairs in the living room. She lit a cigarette and tore open the envelope to Anna's letter. She was a little disappointed to find only one sheet of paper but smiled in anticipation of Anna's written English, which was often hilariously bad.

Friday, may 29

Cara Edith,

Sorry, but this to tell you that Isobel has die. She go peacefull last Wednesday. Carlo bring her back here and we have the funerale tomorow, Saturday. He not so sad. Poor Isobel sick so long. She free now. If this reach you in time you must come for funerale. Isobel will lie to rest in Gorsey Lane cimitero. But you come to my house before 11 tomorrow morning. We leave here then come back after. Lots of good things to eat. Carlo will help me in the shop for now but maybe soon he stay with Domenico in Venezia. Hope you well. Come soon visit shop if you no come funerale.

Love, Anna

"Damn," said Edith out loud. "Damn, damn, damn."

She usually always received a letter the day after it was posted. Why hadn't Anna's letter arrived on Saturday? Surely she'd have sent it as soon as she wrote it on Friday. There'd have been time to go to Isobel's funeral if it had come in the morning post. Joe worked on Saturdays, so the coast would have been clear.

"Damn," Edith said again. She took a long drag of her cigarette and slowly exhaled, watching as smoke drifted toward the ceiling. Then she decisively stubbed out her half-smoked cigarette in a nearby ashtray.

For the next two hours, Edith worked like a demon. She wrung out sheets and pillowcases as fast as she could and hung them on the clothesline in the back garden. She washed three of Joe's shirts and some of his underwear, pounding them vigorously on her washboard. Once the washing was all safely pegged up outside, Edith grabbed the chip pan from under the sink and quickly peeled some potatoes. By the time Shamus arrived home from school, his midday meal of chips and two fried eggs was sitting in the oven ready for him. Will wouldn't be home; he ate school dinner at Prescot Grammar, where he was finishing his second year. Shamus looked a bit surprised when Edith sat him down at the table and put his plate in front of him without insisting he wash his hands.

"You get that down you, love," said Edith, gaily. "I'm just nipping upstairs to get changed. We're going into Liverpool for an afternoon out."

Edith agonized in front of the mirror as to which of her three good dresses to wear. She and Edna, her neighbour, had given each other Toni home perms a week before, and Edith was glad to see her hair was still awash with undulating waves. It wasn't until she and Shamus were standing at the bus stop and Shamus asked why they were going into Liverpool that Edith began to have qualms.

"To see my old friend Anna," she answered breezily, as though it was an everyday event. "She's got a little shop. I thought it would be fun to drop in. Do you remember Anna?"

"I think so," muttered Shamus. But Edith doubted him. He hadn't seen her since the summer before last, and he'd been at school during Anna's most recent visits to Woolfall Heath.

Shamus, who had turned eight years old in May, was looking more and more like Carlo as he matured. He had brown eyes as opposed to the periwinkle blue that Will had inherited from his father and grandfather. And Shamus's complexion was less pale than Will's, who had startlingly white skin, typical of the Maguire clan. Shamus was bulkier, a good three inches taller than Will had been at his age.

But apart from these differences, the two boys looked like brothers in many ways. Both had black hair, and their long noses and slight overbite were reminiscent of Edith's. Their voices were similar — they each had an adenoidal Liverpool accent. But lately, Edith had seen distinct flashes of Carlo in some of Shamus's expressions. He had a way of gazing at Edith, as if he was looking right inside her, that thrust her back to Shrimpley Heath. She could almost smell the scent of bruised grass in the bomb crater where she and Carlo had lain.

As soon as Shamus had arrived home from hospital as a newborn, the dynamics of their household had changed for the better. During the nine or ten months after Joe had returned from the war, he and Will had had a stormy relationship. Will argued constantly, which sent Joe into paroxysms of rage. Despite Edith's threat of leaving if he laid a hand on his son, Joe had sometimes smacked the boy across the head. Edith tried to justify his behaviour by telling herself that everybody gave their children an occasional whack. But with Shamus around, Will and Joe's spats became less frequent. His presence had given both Joe and Will a new focus. Will seemed delighted by his little brother. Edith once overheard him praising Shamus's beautiful brown eyes to Mrs. Maguire. And once Shamus could walk and talk, he followed Will around like a devoted puppy. Will was extremely patient, often letting Shamus knock around the estate with him and his friends.

Edith was amazed that Joe showed not an iota of resentment or prejudice toward Shamus. Quite the reverse, he doted on the boy, especially when Shamus was small. Joe rubbed his stubbly cheek against Shamus's baby face, which caused Shamus to shriek with delight. Joe perched Shamus on his knees and recited "Ride a Cock Horse to Banbury Cross," trotting the boy up and down to the rhythm. He'd act out the horse galloping faster and faster until finally he'd open his knees and pretend to let Shamus tumble to the floor. Then he'd swoop the screaming boy up into the air and start all over. Will laughed at Joe's shenanigans with Shamus, but in a cautious way, as though not able to believe this more playful aspect of his father's character. Edith had to admit that Shamus brought out a softer side to Joe. Perhaps relations between Joe and Will would have been less strained if they'd been together from Will's birth. But, she hastened to tell herself, Will hadn't lacked for attention as a baby. He'd been doted on by Carlo, Anna, and Isobel, not to mention Mrs. Maguire.

"Aren't I supposed to be at school?" asked Shamus, once they'd struggled up the bus's winding staircase and found a seat at the front.

"One afternoon won't hurt," Edith said. "I'll write you a note in the morning." She wished Shamus was a little less conscientious. Most children would be delighted to have a half-day off school.

As the bus rattled along, Edith's qualms resurfaced. She began to wonder if she'd been reckless in bringing Shamus along with her. What did she hope to achieve? Wasn't it unfair to both Carlo and Shamus to let them meet? Not to mention Joe. Maybe Carlo wouldn't be at the shop, thought Edith. But even if he were, she reasoned, she wasn't obliged to divulge the facts about his relationship to Shamus.

As the bus rattled past the end of Durning Road, Edith was distracted by memories of the bombed college and wondered what had happened to Mrs. Reeves. After the war, Edith's parents had never returned to their house on Durning Road. They'd stayed in Wales, where rents were cheaper and her father had found a job with the local council. If she'd had to change from the bus to the tram, Edith might have even dropped in on her old neighbour, Mrs. Higgins. But Edith didn't need to break the journey, now that the tram had stopped running; her bus ran right through, all the way to the Pier Head. Only a couple of the city's old tram routes were still operating. Edith craned her neck to glimpse the site of the bombed college, but the bus trundled past the end of the street too fast. She wasn't able to see if anything had been erected on the site of the old Durning Road school.

Their route into the centre of Liverpool was peppered with bomb sites overrun with weeds. Occasionally there were signs of rebuilding, but a surprising number of undisturbed acres remained littered with broken bricks, shattered glass, and splintered window frames. Leafy saplings had sprung up here and there, lending a park-like atmosphere to mounds of assorted rubble. Flocks of marauding starlings migrated from one young tree to the next or settled around the perimeter of a flooded cellar, splashing and preening in water the colour of strong coffee laced with the emerald slime of algae.

"Wow, look at the size of those beams," exclaimed Shamus as they passed the end wall of a four-storey building that had been shored up with a forest of massive wooden girders. Edith was glad that he seemed to have forgotten he was playing truant.

After the bus dropped them off, Edith took a couple of wrong turns in the maze of small streets off London Road. Just when she'd decided she should give up her foolhardy expedition and go home, they turned a corner to find themselves directly opposite a tiny corner shop with Anna's Fine Foods picked out in gold paint on a dark green background. A large basket of golden onions stood outside the front door, which was garlanded on either side by strings of creamy garlic heads.

"Over there!" cried Shamus. Edith could hardly turn tail now that he'd spotted the place.

"Edith!" cried Anna from behind a wooden counter that had obviously been scrubbed so many times it had the patina of old marble. "This my old friend from the war," she explained to the woman she was serving. The woman smiled faintly at Edith. Edith noticed the shine of expensive shoe leather and the fine weave of the woman's woollen tweed suit. She wondered if the woman was the professor's wife Anna sometimes talked about.

"Come back Saturday — I should have the dark-roast coffee you like then," said Anna as the woman turned to leave.

"We'll be in the Lakes this weekend. Put a couple of pounds aside for me and I'll pick them up next week," said the woman imperiously.

"Will do, Mrs. Hornby," sang Anna. "See you next week."

"Who wears pearls to go shopping?" asked Edith, after the woman was safely out of the shop.

"Rich people," replied Anna. "Her husband owns a shipbuilders' yard in Birkenhead. But she comes over here every week. She says my coffee is better even than at the Kardomah." Perhaps Anna's strategy for her shop wasn't so hare-brained after all, thought Edith as she glanced around at shelves crowded with bottles of honey-coloured oil and jars packed with preserves. Chunks of cheese filled a large oval platter covered by a sparkling glass dome. A couple of haunches of smoked ham hung from the ceiling, together with a length of mahogany-coloured sausage the width of Edith's wrist. Armfuls of leafy herbs almost hid the white galvanized jugs that held them at each end of the counter. The whole scene was bathed in diffused daylight filtering through the ancient rippled glass of the shop's front windows. The smells were enough to make Edith ravenous, with the pervasive aroma of roasted coffee beans floating above the scents of cheese, ham, and herbs.

"You get my letter?" asked Anna. Then she went on without waiting for an answer. "Such a lovely *funerale*. Not so many people. The war finish off a lot of them," she said in a matter-of-fact tone of voice. "I got so much food left over I don't know what to do with it. When we close, you must come back to my house and eat."

"We can't stay long," said Edith. "I just wanted to come and pay my respects."

"Carlo is in the back," said Anna, with a tilt of her head in the direction of an open doorway behind her. "Go in and tell him to make a cup of tea. I find something for this young man."

"Not too much, now," warned Edith. She knew she spoke too sharply, but her mouth was dry with nervousness at the prospect of seeing Carlo. "You'll spoil his tea," she murmured.

"Just a little bit of crystallize ginger," protested Anna. "You like that, no, Shamus?"

"I dunno," said Shamus. He was looking around him with wide eyes. Edith could tell he was amazed at the exotic wares and unfamiliar fragrances of the shop. He'd only ever been in the local Co-op with its bare light bulbs and unsavoury whiff of cheap cheddar, cardboard, and detergent.

"Come," said Anna, beckoning Edith to move behind the counter. Edith made her way toward the open doorway, suddenly slightly out of breath with anticipation.

A rectangle of sunlight from the open back door lit up the bare concrete floor of a spacious back room. In the shadows to one side, a stack of wooden cartons had been crammed together to make a low table on which stood a set of scales. Carlo sat on an upturned bucket, hunched over the weights. He seemed to be apportioning some kind of dry beans from a voluminous hessian sack into individual paper bags. He leaned forward to shake a few more of the white-and-red-streaked beans into a brown paper bag, concentrating intently on the scale. His knees almost touched his chest. He looked to Edith like an overgrown child playing at being a shopkeeper. Any nervousness disappeared at the sight of him. Edith felt instead a warm glow of affection.

"Hello, Carlo," she said.

He glanced up, obviously startled by the sound of Edith's voice. *"Madonna!"* he exclaimed, struggling to his feet.

"That's what you said the first time you met me," said Edith, laughing.

"I never claimed to be very original," replied Carlo, beaming down at Edith from his full height. He leaned down and kissed her — rather chastely, thought Edith — on each cheek.

They grinned at each other wordlessly. Then both began to speak.

"I'm so sorry — " said Edith.

"How are — " blurted Carlo.

They laughed.

"Anna told me to tell you to make some tea," said Edith. As Carlo busied himself with lighting a gas ring and filling a kettle from a tiny sink, Edith told him how sorry she was about Isobel.

"It was a blessed release," said Carlo. "But I miss her. She was such a lively soul when she was healthy, and I loved her very much." Edith glanced away as he wiped a tear from his cheek. Odd, she thought, that she was embarrassed by Carlo's show of sentiment. She recalled the naked displays of emotion they'd once shared. But she found them difficult to visualize now. Those distant scenes seemed more like a dream sequence than real life. Even though Carlo had changed little physically — the addition of some lines around his eyes made him more handsome, if anything — there was a distinct lack of attraction on Edith's part. Certainly no desire.

Carlo inquired politely about Joe. When he asked about William, Edith had to think for a second who he meant. She'd become so used to calling her son Will she'd forgotten the name they all called him during the war. It wasn't until they were just about to return to the interior of the shop, Edith bearing a cup of tea for Anna as well as one for herself, that Edith gave any thought to Shamus.

"Anna tells me you have another son," said Carlo.

"Yes," said Edith, trying to sound casual. "Shamus. I brought him with me — he's in the shop here with Anna."

"Hello, young man," said Carlo, reaching to shake Shamus's hand. "Very pleased to meet you."

"Hello," muttered Shamus, an expression of awe flooding his face as he gazed at the huge hand that completely enveloped his own.

"He's a handsome lad," said Carlo, smiling at Edith.

"Yes," said Edith. She wasn't sure what she'd expected of her visit, but she was experiencing an anticlimactic sensation. She felt oddly detached.

As they sipped their tea, Anna chattered about her customers. Carlo smiled occasionally at Edith. Shamus examined Carlo carefully, staring at his face. The irrational thought occurred to Edith that perhaps he suspected. Maybe he recognized a familiar characteristic in Carlo's features. When Carlo winked at Shamus, the boy blushed and drifted off to a nearby shelf to examine some jars of preserves.

Just as Edith was about to suggest that she and Shamus take their leave, the door opened and a large, florid-faced woman strode into the shop. Anna hastened to serve her.

"We really should be going," said Edith to Carlo. She took Shamus by the hand and waved goodbye to Anna.

"Let me walk you to the bus stop," replied Carlo.

As the threesome walked down the street, Edith and Carlo exchanged pleasantries. Carlo mentioned he might join Domenico in Venice.

"He wants help to expand his restaurant. Business is good," explained Carlo. "Quite a few rich Americans are discovering the charms of Venice — Domenico's restaurant included." Edith felt no regret that Carlo might soon leave Liverpool. Nevertheless, she gripped Shamus's hand a little tighter at the news. At that moment, they turned the corner into London Road. Later, whenever Edith thought about what happened next, she saw the series of events like a film or a newsreel.

A black cat bolted out of an alley a few feet in front of them, obviously frightened by something between two houses, straight into the path of an oncoming truck that was barrelling along the road beside them. Edith let out a startled scream and quickly turned away, burying her face in Carlo's chest. When she lifted her head a few seconds later, she was aware of Carlo's hands on her shoulders. The truck hadn't stopped; she could hear its engine receding in the distance. Perhaps the cat had escaped. She stared into Carlo's eyes, mere inches from her face. There was a glimmer in the depths of his eyes, something she thought she recognized. Compassion, shock, pain? She knew immediately that the cat had been hit. It was the first real connection to Carlo she'd felt that day.

Then she remembered Shamus. She whipped around to see him, still clutching her hand, staring at the dismembered remains of the black cat, which was lying in a widening pool of scarlet blood. She squatted down, and grabbing her son by his shoulders, turned him away from the gory scene. Eyes level with his, she searched his face for signs of distress.

Shamus's face reminded her of Domenico in the internment camp tent in Arrow Park after he'd survived the sinking of the *Arandora Star*. Witnessing the death of a cat, gruesome as it was, might seem minor in comparison to the experience of the *Arandora Star* disaster, but Shamus seemed almost as shaken as Domenico had been. His face was ashen, and not only was the colour of his irises identical to Domenico's, but they held the same damaged quality. She recognized the frightening insight they revealed, the unbearable awareness of mortality. She gathered her son to her bosom and he buried his face in her chest.

"Come," said Carlo, easing Edith to her feet by her elbow. He scooped Shamus up in his arms. The trio hurried past the cat's bloody remains towards the bus stop on the corner. Edith was relieved when a bus arrived almost immediately.

"Goodbye, Edith," said Carlo as the bus drew near. He gently eased Shamus down to the paving stones and pulled Edith to him, hugging her tightly. She clutched his shoulder blades.

"Write to me. Let me know how you're doing," Edith called as she grasped Shamus's hand and boarded the bus. "Anna has my address."

"Yes, certainly," called Carlo. "I'll write and tell you all about Venice."

On the way home, Edith tried her best to distract Shamus, to keep his mind off the gory scene he'd witnessed, but she soon ran out of things to say. Before long, both mother and son were silently staring, each deep in their own thoughts, out of the bus window.

There were signs of the forthcoming Coronation everywhere they looked. Shop windows were decorated in red, white, and blue streamers and bunting was strung from one lamppost to the next. Two huge golden letters — E and R — had been hoisted up the side of a block of flats, which seemed a bit premature to Edith. Elizabeth wouldn't actually be reigning until the next day, after the Coronation ceremony was over.

28-09-2002   **04:53**

Shamus cursed the young woman at Da Baccanello, who, he was sure, had given him proper espresso instead of the decaf he'd ordered. He hadn't been sleeping well, that was certain. He was never sure if the dead cat was a dream or if he merely thought about it in the night when he was half asleep. Whichever, the vivid scene regularly appeared to Shamus whenever he was upset about something or other. He couldn't shake the sight of the cat, body grotesquely squashed and ripped, with guts poking out like pink rubber inner tubes bursting from a short, furry tire. A pool of glistening blood grew steadily wider, shockingly crimson against the black tarmacadam surface of a road. That, and a hazy memory of being on a bus with Edith. He thought he remembered red, white, and blue bunting fluttering. He was a child, perhaps seven or eight. It was a weekday, and he was feeling guilty because he was supposed to be at school.

As he tossed and turned, Shamus imagined he smelled Da Baccanello, right there in his hotel room. But the aromas were far stronger than in the restaurant. A powerful mélange of cheese, herbs, and smoked meat, but most dominant was the smell of roasted coffee. As usual in Shamus's recurring dream-memory, a large man peered down at him. Shamus couldn't make out the man's features. All he saw was a fog of black stubble that darkened the man's jaw. The massive man took Shamus's little-boy hand in his. Shamus was never sure whether to feel alarmed or comforted when his fingers disappeared into the man's warm mitt of a fist.

That was usually it — the end. But tonight, where Shamus's customary version normally left off, there was a continuation. This time, the man's face swung into focus — it was Shamus's thirty-year-old face. The man with his adult face was smiling back at child Shamus from a black and white photograph, smiling and winking, even though the shot was a still photo. An animated still photograph in a dark wooden frame.

Shamus jerked awake again. He stumbled to the bathroom to urinate.

Earlier, outside Da Baccanello, the two brothers had stood and inhaled the cool, salty Venetian air. Rectangles of illuminated windows glowed in stucco walls; here and there delicate threads of light traced the outline of closed wooden shutters. Shamus and Will strolled somewhat uncertainly to the bridge where they'd met Armando that morning. Both appeared the worse for wear. Perhaps from a long day of walking or maybe too much sun. Possibly as a result of the alcohol they'd consumed. Deep in their individual thoughts, neither one spoke. The handsome edifices that Will had admired earlier in the day appeared mellower, their edges softened by the luminescence of yellow-tinged lanterns. The clattering sound of a woman's heels hitting cobblestones echoed from a nearby street, underscoring the absence of any other noise. Shamus could clearly make out the pitted surface of a bright full moon that floated above the floodlit façade of San Barnaba church.

The two men stood on the bridge for a good ten minutes in contemplative silence until eventually Will spoke. He recited a line that had always concluded a television show they'd watched when they were living in London. *The Magic Roundabout* was a kid's show, but it had become something of a cult classic for the brothers' generation. Shamus and Will had never missed an episode. In those days, one or the other of them would sometimes bid goodnight before retiring to bed by parroting the phrase spoken by the narrator at the end of every show. The brothers always injected a large dose of irony, indicating that the day's events had been particularly harrowing or overwhelming.

"'That's enough excitement for one day. Time for bed, said Zebedee,'" quoted Will, staring unseeingly along the shining ebony surface of the canal, lit sparingly by a few wan lamps.

Despite it being forty years later and halfway across Europe, the words persisted as a clear indication to both brothers that they'd had more than enough — it was time to turn in. They made their way up the short stretch of street to their hotel, parted in the lobby without a word, and retired to their separate rooms.

As Shamus staggered from the hotel bathroom to his bed, images returned to him — the trip on a bus with Edith, bomb sites flashing by, a grocery shop, a shadowy-jawed man. But what he recalled most vividly — as always — was the incredibly strange tenor of the whole trip. There was a disturbingly distinctive quality to it. The day had had a taste and a colour all of its own.

He'd sometimes considered grilling Edith about the likely cause of his recurring recollections, but something, some nebulous logic, always prevented Shamus from bringing them up. He had the distinct impression he wasn't supposed to probe.

Shamus doubted if he'd go back to sleep; there was too much to think about. He tossed in his bed. At one point, a foot smashed against the bed's wooden baseboard, stubbing his big toe. He moaned in pain.

During the night, a dense cloud cover had seeped westward across the Adriatic Sea. Daylight was steadily strengthening, but with the sun obscured, the shadows of Venetian towers and palazzi were indistinct. Close to the walls of buildings, the light was murky, but at the shadows' blurred edges, the gloom grew pale, as soft a grey as the plumage on the breasts of pigeons that fluttered in and out of St. Mark's airy square. It was fortunate that fog, which often shrouds and obscures Venice's skyline, hadn't accompanied the clouds. Edith's plane was due to arrive in six hours.

ENGLAND

"Come on, Edith," yelled Joe from the living room. "You're going to miss the best bit."

"All right, all right," shouted Edith as she lifted the last of the hot sausage rolls out of the oven and onto a plate.

She was fed up with all the fuss surrounding the Coronation. The excitement had been mounting for weeks, with special articles in newspapers and magazines. Mechanical propelling pencils and mugs adorned with portraits of the young princess had been handed out as souvenirs to all the children at school. Will and Shamus each had their own. The Co-op shop was piled high with tins of a special mix of chocolate biscuits, with photos of Princess Elizabeth and the Duke of Edinburgh printed on the lid in garish colours. Everything was Coronation this and Coronation that — Coronation blend tea, Coronation fruitcake. Edith had had just about enough. Then to cap it all off, there was to be a street party later that day and everyone was expected to decorate the front of their house for the occasion. Joe had worked almost until dark the evening before, labouring up and down a ladder to hang red, white, and blue bunting and crepe paper streamers from the gutters and window ledges.

And now here they were, a full hour into the television programme, and the princess had only just arrived at Westminster Abbey. For sixty minutes, Edith had endured the sight of an endless stream of royalty and dignitaries, described by announcer Richard Dimbleby in his breathless, overly respectful tone of voice as they dashed from their cars and into the Abbey to avoid the incessant rain that dripped from the canopy that was supposed to protect them. Shamus had soon grown bored and disappeared upstairs to read his latest *Beano* comic. Will, on the other hand, seemed quite content to sit next to Mrs. Maguire on the sofa and gaze mindlessly at the screen. "Look, Mum, you can see the rain in London," he called.

Edith's interest was finally piqued by the sight of the ample figure of the Queen of Tonga, who rode in an open carriage despite the drizzle. She appeared genuinely delighted to be there. Her white teeth were clearly visible against her dark skin as she grinned from beneath her umbrella at the thousands of sodden onlookers who thronged the route to the Abbey.

Charlie Martin had finished off the bowl of Twiglets that Edith put out. The end of the savoury straws seemed like a good excuse for Edith to decamp to the kitchen on the pretext of fetching more snacks.

Edith supposed she was still a little rattled by the previous day's outing to visit Anna and Carlo. On the way home, she'd tried her best to divert Shamus from thinking about the death of the cat, but she knew she'd failed miserably. That evening, while she handed flags and streamers up to Joe on his ladder, she'd puzzled over her lack of any reaction at seeing Carlo again. She tried to rationalize it by telling herself that it had been a long time, almost nine years. She'd been twenty-five years old the last time they were together, and now she was thirty-four.

As Edith put the plate of sausage rolls on a tray, together with some cucumber sandwiches, she thought about the flood of affection for Carlo that was so unexpectedly released after the cat's horrible accident and Shamus's traumatic witnessing of its death. It had been oddly reassuring to feel something for Carlo — she was afraid that she might have become incapable of caring. But she found it disturbing that it had taken the drama of the cat's violent death to spark any emotion in her.

"Edith, come on." Joe's shout echoed from the living room. "They're getting ready to crown her." Then, in a louder bellow, he yelled, "Shamus, get down here. This is history in the making, this is. You'll never see the like again."

Edith bustled into the living room and set the plates on the coffee table. Charlie Martin was reaching for a sausage roll before she had a chance to sit down. Shamus appeared and perched himself on the arm of Edith's chair. She reached up and brushed his hair out of his eyes. "Get off," he complained, and jerked his head away.

"Shh," hissed Joe.

Edith stared at the flickering screen. The young princess appeared tiny compared to the grandiose figure of the archbishop looming over her. Edith became transfixed by the pomp and ceremony as the princess was helped into heavy robes and loaded down with numerous bejewelled objects: an orb, sceptre, and ensign. Then she was topped off with such a massive crown that Edith wondered how she didn't buckle under the weight. Commentator Richard Dimbleby explained with his usual gravitas that the throne symbolized the mound of earth the early kings of England had sat on at the conclusion of their coronations. The tradition had been that they were lifted there on the shoulders of their nobles so that the surrounding throngs of citizens could see them.

Edith thought about her history lessons at school, which, when she looked back on them, seemed to consist only of accounts of rebellions and descriptions of battles. She wondered what wars would take place during Elizabeth's reign. She supposed it was cynical of her, but she couldn't believe all the talk of the last war having brought everlasting peace. After all, people had touted World War I as the "war to end all wars" just twenty-five years before the outbreak of World War II. Perhaps for a while, after Hiroshima and Nagasaki, she might have hoped there'd be peace for a while. After all, she reasoned, nothing would be left if every bomb killed seventy thousand people. But then the Korean War had started a mere five years later. Edna and Charlie's son, Bill, had been one of the first of eight hundred soldiers killed so far. And who knew where this so-called Cold War with Russia would lead?

The new queen moved out of the Abbey, her long, fur-trimmed train held by six maids-in-waiting.

Edith remembered how adamant she'd been that nobody forget what had happened to Gianni, Paolo, and the rest of the Italians on the *Arandora Star*. How naïve she'd been to think that remembering would be enough.

"Bloody marvellous," gloated Joe at the images of the queen's gleaming coach trundling through the wet streets of London toward Buckingham Palace. When Joe was happy, his disfigurement made him look grotesque rather than joyful. Whenever she urged him to take up the army's offer of reconstructive surgery for his jaw and eyebrow, he always muttered, "Maybe. Maybe." Edith was convinced that Joe had Liam's artificial leg in mind when he avoided having the surgery, that he was engaged in a kind of perverse fraternal rivalry about which one displayed the worst war wounds. Which was ridiculous to Edith, knowing that neither injury was inflicted during battle or combat.

"Makes you proud to be British, doesn't it?" Joe crowed.

"Waste of money, if you ask me," muttered Will.

"Anybody like a drink?" asked Edith quickly, to forestall any rejoinder from Joe.

"Mine's a small sherry," said Edna.

"I could murder another cup of tea," said Charlie.

Edith put the kettle on and poured Edna her glass of sherry. By the time she carried the tea and sherry into the living room, the queen was installed on the balcony at Buckingham Palace with the Duke of Edinburgh, Prince Charles, and Princess Anne at her side. Richard Dimbleby was still droning on, this time about the dawning of a new Elizabethan era, brighter and more robust than the last. Although not believing a word of it, Edith was suddenly hit with a feeling of exuberance.

"I think I'll have a sherry too," she said gaily.

"Get me a beer while you're at it," Joe called out as Edith made her way back to the kitchen.

"Is there any pop left?" shouted Shamus.

"I'll have a glass too," yelled Will.

How is it possible to have sons who are old men? This was Edith's immediate thought when she spotted them less than forty feet away. It was hard to miss Shamus, his head plainly visible above a crowd of waiting Venetians. Next to him she picked out Will, peering over the shoulders of the people in front of him. Then her two sons disappeared, obscured by a crowd of a dozen teenage English schoolchildren and their teachers who pushed in front of Edith. The uniformed kids were clearly excited to be on a school trip to Italy, and they jostled each other at the bottleneck of a gate that led out of the customs hall and into the gleaming, marble-clad airport lounge.

When Edith came within hailing distance of her sons, it was obvious that neither of them had spied her. They were staring beyond her, faces inanimate. Edith realized they'd missed her at the gate and were still searching there for her familiar figure to emerge.

She hadn't seen Shamus for almost four years, and his face was puffier than she remembered, the hair at his temples startlingly white in contrast to his tanned skin and the inkiness of the rest of his head. He appeared worn, slightly slumped, like beige fabric whose weave and weft has lost its tension. Will, on the other hand, seemed frayed, as though wound too tight for too long. Deep furrows at his brow and either side of his mouth betrayed taut facial muscles. Startled wisps of grey hair sprang from behind each ear. Edith recognized the familiar expression that had flickered around his eyes for almost his entire lifetime. His wariness made her ache for a way to reassure him that nothing bad was about to happen.

"I'm here, you dopes," Edith called out when she was just a step away from them.

The two old men were instantly transformed into her children. Will beamed, periwinkle blue eyes shining exactly as they had when he was a toddler. They were Joe's eyes when he was at his best.

"Nice to see you too," Will said as he put one arm around her shoulders and kissed her cheek. Shamus pulled his shoulders back and grinned, delighted to witness such amiable relations between his mother and brother. He wondered if Edith had shrunk; she seemed astonishingly small. But full of beans, Shamus marvelled.

"Hello, Edith," he said.

"You'll have to bend down so I can give you a kiss," said his mother. Now that Shamus's tanned face was animated, his teeth gleaming, she was struck by a memory of Carlo. Not that the resemblance was as strong as it had been. The Carlo she envisioned was much younger and, she had to admit, somewhat indistinct.

"So how do you like the glamorous life of a jet-setter?" Will asked. He took her bag, surprisingly compact for one who wasn't a seasoned traveller.

"It's lovely once you get off the ground," said Edith. "But all that fuss beforehand. You know, they made me take off my shoes so they could X-ray them. Did they used to do that before that dreadful business in New York?"

"Not so much," Shamus replied.

"Even during the war, nobody asked to examine my shoes," said Edith. For the first time in sixty years, she'd remembered the guard at Carlo's internment camp, who'd examined every item of food she was carrying. Could you really hide a bomb in your shoe, Edith wondered.

Will and Shamus guided their mother toward the exit. Outside a pair of sliding glass doors, the smell of cigarette smoke hung in the air. A man and a woman stood next to an ashtray on top of a gleaming chrome pedestal, furtively smoking.

"It's quite a walk to the vaporetto dock," Shamus told Edith. "Should we look for a wheelchair?"

"I may be old, but I'm not crippled," she exclaimed.

Luke would have needed one, thought Shamus.

"How far is it exactly?" asked Edith, feeling slightly repentant for her ungracious response.

"No farther than your daily walk to the shops," said Will. "We'll take it slowly; there's no hurry."

They set off along the walkway that led to the vaporetto, Will and Shamus instinctively taking up positions on either side of their mother. Shamus held her arm and Will carried her bag.

"Are you tired?" Will asked. "Do you want to go straight to the hotel?"

"Do I look tired?" Edith asked disdainfully. But then she relented, agreeing that it would be a good idea to drop off her bag. Then they'd be free to enjoy the rest of the day.

Once they boarded a vaporetto, along with the group of chattering English kids who'd been on her plane, Edith sat between the two brothers. As the boat picked up speed, she stared with a bemused expression of wonder at the waterscape of wooden pilings, churning boats with turbulent wakes, wheeling seagulls, and the hovering horizontal outlines of distant islands. The lagoon mirrored the gunmetal grey of the cloud cover and it was impossible for Edith to tell where water ended and sky began.

When the driver announced that they were approaching San Michele, Edith asked, "This is the island with a cemetery, isn't it?"

Will looked at Edith curiously before confirming that it was. "Why do you ask?" He spoke loudly to make himself heard over the noise of the boat's motor.

"No need to shout, dear," said Edith, patting his hand. She resisted the impulse to point out that she wasn't yet deaf. "Somebody I knew during the war is buried there, that's all."

"Is it Anna?" Will asked.

"Do you remember Anna?" she asked, in obvious amazement.

"We were talking about her yesterday," said Will.

Edith noted he hadn't specifically replied to her question, although the answer was obvious.

"No, it's not her," Edith said. "Anna stayed in Liverpool after the war. She was buried at Gorsey Lane."

"Who is it then?" Shamus asked.

Edith looked at him, pondering the array of different answers that presented themselves. Shamus noticed Edith's eyes grow narrower. She appeared perplexed. She gazed along the expanse of jade-coloured water that met the boat just a few feet below the window.

"He was Anna's son," Edith eventually said. "He came to Venice after the war to join his brother. He never went back to England." Shamus nodded and watched as the ochre-walled, cypress-studded shore of San Michele drew closer.

"But you knew where he was buried," he said abruptly. "You kept in touch?" The boat's engine slowed as it approached a wooden dock. Edith nodded vaguely and turned her attention to the glass and metal structure that sat on the old timbers of the quay. It was almost identical to a Liverpool bus shelter.

"I couldn't remember Anna's last name," said Will.

The English schoolchildren were making a racket. Full of hyperactive excitement, they yelled to each other, pointing out one thing or another that struck them as "weird" or "naff." Edith didn't appear to have heard Will's comment about Anna's last name.

"Is this really an island?" she asked. She peered out of the window. It was obvious the graveyard stretched over several acres, as far as the eye could see, along avenues branching off in all directions. "How stupid of me. When I envisioned a cemetery on an island, I thought of something a bit smaller than Hilbre."

The island that Edith had mentioned lay in the Dee estuary near Granny Maguire's old house. Shamus had a vague memory of going there for a picnic on one of their holidays to Shrimpley. When the tide was out, it was possible to walk to the island. He seemed to remember taking a local train a few miles along the coast and then trudging across an expanse of wet sand to a windswept rise of rock and tufted grass. The whole outcrop couldn't have been more than half a mile long and a hundred yards wide. The place could be thoroughly explored in less than an hour.

"Were you thinking of visiting Anna's son's grave?" asked Will.

Edith looked out at the rows of hundreds of gravestones interspersed with flowers, many of them plastic in garish colours. In the far distance, she could see the stone walls of what appeared to be tombs. The cemetery at San Michele turned out to be very different from how she'd imagined, and Edith felt oddly detached. The place held no significance for her.

"It doesn't seem important to actually see his grave — not any more," said Edith. "And I'm sure it's the last place Shamus would want to visit."

"It wouldn't particularly bother me," said Shamus. "I think of Luke all the time anyway."

"You know, I think every single one of the cards and letters I was sent after Joe died said silly things along the lines of time being the ultimate healer. Well I long ago came to the conclusion that time doesn't so much heal as anaesthetize. And given enough time, the pain might even be dulled to the point where you don't think much about it — which isn't necessarily a good thing. But it never actually goes away."

Raising his eyebrows, Will exchanged glances with Shamus. "If you have your friend's name, they'll probably have some kind of record. They could tell us where he's buried," he suggested. "How long ago did he die?"

"A year and a half ago, a couple of months after Joe died," said Edith.

She smiled reassuringly and took one of each son's arms. "It's enough to just be here with you two. I don't need to go chasing after dead people."

As the vaporetto moved away from San Michele to continue its journey to Venice proper, Edith considered the differences between her two sons. Not just the physical disparity, but the enormous variation in their personalities. She remembered how Joe and Will had battled tooth and nail. It seemed as though Will would do anything, even fight if necessary, to hold Joe's attention. She could never work out why he'd bothered. It was as if Will couldn't stand the thought of Joe ignoring him, even though Will obviously despised his father. And the more Joe and Will fought, the more distant Shamus became. He'd grown less communicative and completely undemonstrative. Edith felt guilty for thinking of her younger son as a bit of a cold fish. She couldn't help wondering if it was her fault he was so reserved. She'd always hoped he was a bit more outgoing when he was out of the house, away from her and Joe.

"They showed us today's BBC news on the plane," Edith remarked. "How do they do that when you're up in the air?" Will and Shamus looked at each other. Will shrugged. "Anyway," Edith continued. "You should have seen the crowds in London, thousands and thousands of people gathering to protest Bush's sabre-rattling. A much bigger turnout than was predicted, apparently."

"It won't make a blind bit of difference," pronounced Will emphatically. Shamus wondered why his brother still played the provocative adolescent. Joe wasn't there to bait. And their father would probably have agreed with Will anyway.

"Do you wish you'd gone to London to demonstrate instead of coming to Venice?" asked Shamus.

Edith glanced at Shamus. "I feel awful for saying this," she said. "But I'm afraid I agree with Will."

"I'm surprised, Edith," said Shamus. "Letting the side down a bit, aren't you? What happened to 'Lest we forget' and all that."

"Don't criticize your mother," Edith snapped.

"I was only joking," muttered Shamus.

"Well it's no joking matter," Edith retorted. Edith thought about how insistent she'd once been that her war not be forgotten — graves always reminded her of why she'd felt so strongly, but they didn't help her feel one iota of the determination she used to have.

"You hit a nerve, that's all," she relented, and rested her hand on Shamus's knee. She felt suddenly very small and within whispering distance of the host of souls that they'd left behind on San Michele, Carlo included.

Edith looked across to the silhouette of Venice, a couple of bell towers bristling, and imagined Carlo living there every day for some fifty years. Carlo had been an infrequent but constant letter writer from the day he'd left England until a few months before his death. He'd described to Edith days spent at the restaurant with Domenico, the birth and growth of nephews and nieces, and the city he obviously loved. But Edith had never fully comprehended the reality of his everyday life. She'd always viewed his return to Italy as a kind of exile from England, lived in a limbo-like state. The fact that he'd never remarried strengthened her belief.

Now she realized that she was mistaken. She suddenly understood that Carlo's quotidian life had been played out for many years among the unfamiliar buildings she could see across the expanse of choppy water before her, just as her existence had been spent with Joe in Liverpool. Ordinary people leading ordinary lives. She supposed war had made them all — herself, Carlo, Anna, even Liam — extraordinary for a while, but it seemed a dubious distinction.

The threesome watched as the boat drew closer to the Fondamenta Nuove. It struck Shamus that the unremarkable waterfront didn't make for a particularly imposing introduction to Venice.

"It looks more impressive when we get over on the other side," he assured her.

"It's fascinating," replied Edith. Shamus glanced at her. She did seem enthralled by the sight of people passing to and fro in front of the unexceptional stone façades of Fondamenta Nuove. Edith was wondering if Carlo had walked by there often in all the years since she'd last seen him. Time that was considerable in comparison to the short period they'd known each other. Yet the intervening decades were only significant to Edith in their ability to fade memory.

"What do you make of Will buying Granny Maguire's old place?" Shamus asked her.

"I forgot to tell you," interrupted Will before Edith had a chance to answer. "I phoned Laura last night from the hotel. It looks like the old lady is going to accept our offer."

"So Shambhala will be yours," said Edith. "That's wonderful."

"What?" Shamus asked. "Where?"

Edith reminded him that Shambhala was the original name of Mrs. Maguire's house. She told Shamus it wasn't surprising he'd forgotten; nobody mentioned it much, knowing that Mrs. Maguire considered naming bungalows too pretentious for words.

"Well it is a bit much, isn't it?" said Shamus. "Shambhala means a place of peace, tranquillity, and happiness. It's a nice house, but it's not exactly Shangri-La."

"That was the name of another bungalow farther down the lane," said Edith in a matter-of-fact tone. "It was bombed during the war."

Will laughed. "What were they thinking with the hippy names?"

"Well it was the days of the Raj and all that," retorted Edith. "Indian influence was everywhere. You could buy curry powder in the Co-op even then. My own mother made kedgeree."

Will explained that the houses on Sandy Lane still didn't have numbers. He told them how the solicitor had taken ages to figure out the deeds and the legal stuff without a proper address.

"I seem to remember that one of the Buddhist texts prophesies that when the world declines into war and greed and all is lost, some king or other will emerge from Shambhala with a huge army to vanquish the dark forces and usher in a worldwide Golden Age," said Shamus.

"Well that'll never happen," said Will.

"Never say never, dear," admonished Edith weakly. She sounded like an inept actress, insincerely mouthing a line she didn't believe.

The vaporetto had entered the first of the narrow canals and waterways that would take it through the Arsenale and out into the Canale di San Marco. The boat's route took them past forbidding marine buildings belonging to the old shipyard. The dirty bricks and brine-rotten wooden pilings reminded Edith of Liverpool docks.

The manner in which Edith had spoken — every word tinged with defeatism — grated on Shamus, irrational as it seemed. He could feel bile rising in his gullet. He couldn't contain himself. He didn't care what he and Will had planned, he couldn't wait a minute longer.

"Edith, there's something I need to know — to ask," he stuttered.

"What's that, dear?" asked Edith, taken aback by the quiver of emotion in Shamus's voice.

"Was Carlo Baccanello my father?" Shamus asked.

Edith's mind went blank and her lips smarted with alarm. All she could take in was Shamus's face. His normally olive skin had paled. She looked into her younger son's eyes and his brown irises stared back, pupils enlarged and impenetrably black, eyelids blue-black with fatigue.

The night before, when he'd reeled back from the urinal in Da Baccanello having seen himself at every stage of his life in the photos that adorned the restaurant walls, Shamus had found Armando's mother, who Will had discovered was called Anna-Maria, sitting at the table with Will. All the other customers had left.

"You certainly took your time," Will had said. "I knew you'd find those photos engrossing."

Then, without hesitation, Will had put forward his theory about Carlo's paternity of his brother. Or should he start referring to Shamus as his half-brother, quipped Will in an attempt to lighten the moment.

While Shamus had been staggering from one photo to the next, Will had pushed his way into the kitchen to confront Armando's grandfather — Domenico Baccanello. Every one of Will's questions had been answered in the affirmative. The clincher came when Domenico admitted that his brother, Carlo, and Edith had corresponded regularly for years. So when Carlo died, Domenico had felt obliged to write to Edith. He'd told her about the funeral on San Michele. But he insisted that Carlo had never mentioned fathering any children. Nevertheless, Will had insisted, trying unsuccessfully to hide his excitement, "You've got to be his son. You always were too big to be a Maguire. Just think, you're not a freak after all!"

"Not Edith. She couldn't have," Shamus had repeated time and again. But after an hour of going over the evidence several times, and after Anna-Maria Belli had brought two large glasses of Fernet-Branca, the dark, bitter *digestivo* advertised on the small tray the bill had arrived in, Shamus had been ninety-nine per cent convinced, to the point where he'd even asked Anna-Maria if she thought it was a problem to anybody that not only was a new family member about to materialize out of nowhere but that the new relative was homosexual. "Not at all," she had reassured Shamus. "You'll have something in common with at least one cousin. And Armando will think it's cool. My father's biggest problem is that you're English — anything else pales by comparison."

When Will had brought up the fact that Armando didn't seem to have noticed Shamus's striking resemblance to his beloved Uncle Carlo, Anna-Maria pointed out that her son was twenty-seven-going-on-fifteen. "All he notices is himself," she said.

Around midnight, Will and Shamus had bid Anna-Maria goodbye. She had embraced them both warmly and told them she was looking forward to seeing them the next day, and to meeting Edith. Her father had inched open the kitchen door to shout *"Buona notte,"* which Shamus took as a portent of acceptance some time in the future.

Apparently, the old man had told Anna-Maria when she'd asked him about Edith that he remembered the brothers' mother as being *"molto simpatica."*

But Shamus wasn't sharing Domenico's good opinion of Edith. In fact he was so angry he could strangle her, right there and then, in front of all the boat passengers. And even though Shamus and Will had agreed to give Edith at least twenty-four hours to confess before they tackled her, Shamus hadn't been able to restrain himself for even an hour.

"Well," he asked his mother loudly, "was Carlo my father?"

There was an outbreak of giggling from the English schoolchildren. "Sad bastard," one of them said, in a voice obviously designed for Shamus to hear, followed by peals of laughter from the rest of the kids. Shamus whipped around and glared at the smirking adolescents sitting behind him.

"Why don't you go back to your pathetic little lives in whatever boring suburb you've been allowed out of," he yelled.

"That's completely uncalled for," protested one of the teachers.

"Really?" demanded Shamus, blood pounding in his temples, lips tingling with rage. He stood up to his full, intimidating height and glowered at the skinny man who'd protested. "I tell you what is called for. Sterilization of all the brain-damaged parents of this gang of morons to make sure they don't produce any more. And if you don't keep the little bleeders quiet, I'll be forced to do it myself."

The teacher ushered the kids out of their seats to sit in some empty places a few rows farther back. As he sat down again, Shamus glanced at Will.

"What the hell are you grinning at?" he demanded of his brother.

"You can take the man out of Liverpool, but you can't take Liverpool out of the man." Will quoted back the line that Shamus had used on him the day before.

"Not now, Will, for Christ's sake," growled Shamus. Then he turned his attention back to Edith. "Well?" he insisted.

"For God's sake, calm down," urged Edith. "You're making an exhibition of yourself." She looked away in an obvious attempt to dismiss Shamus. She stared pointedly at a crumbling building to one side of the boat that resembled an old dockside warehouse on the Mersey.

"You can't pull that one on me, not any more," retorted Shamus. "And I don't give a shit what anybody thinks, and neither should you. It should be me you're considering, not them."

"I planned to tell you," Edith pleaded, "but not like this. Not on a boat full of people, for heaven's sake."

"I don't care!" said Shamus. "Why should you care what all these strangers think?"

Some of the "strangers" on the boat were deliberately not looking at the bizarre trio of distraught older mother and two middle-aged sons. Others were paying careful attention, obviously struggling to follow the soap opera unfolding in front of them. Edith glanced around. Then she took a deep breath. Between gulps and an occasional tear, Edith told Shamus and Will the whole story.

First she described her promise to Joe.

Once she got going, her inhibitions melted away and even Shamus was taken aback by the way she poured her guts out. She explained that she'd meant to tell Shamus after Joe died, but by then he'd had his hands so full with Luke she didn't want to bother him. And she wanted them both to know that it hadn't just been a roll in the hay with Carlo — which was more information than Will wanted to hear. Edith told them primly, but in no uncertain terms, that they had no idea whatsoever what times were like when she and Carlo were "together." Then, when Carlo died, she continued, she'd felt so awful, knowing that Shamus would never know his real father, that she couldn't bring herself to say a word. But when she found out Shamus and Will were both going to be near Venice at the same time, she'd had the bright idea of planning the trip so that she could tell Shamus at some point while she and Will were with him, so they could support him, if he needed it.

"How did you find out anyway?" she asked, pulling a tissue from her handbag. Will explained about banging into Armando and going to Da Baccanello. "But you weren't to go to that restaurant without me," she scolded. It had never occurred to Edith that her sons might go into Domenico's restaurant before she arrived. She knew it was close to the hotel — she'd requested that of the travel agent — but she had no idea it was the only one on the stretch of street where the hotel was situated, let alone directly opposite. Edith's tone reminded Shamus of being told off for crossing the main road when he was a kid. He felt his blood beginning to boil again.

"Why didn't you warn Domenico we were coming?" asked Will. "Can you imagine what a shock all this has been to him?" When Edith made some excuse about not having thought it through, that perhaps she should have planned things a bit better, Shamus couldn't contain himself.

"It's so typical of you and your half-cocked ideas," he protested. "It's like your Greenham Common episode all over again." It occurred to him then that he was yelling at an old-age pensioner in front of a boatload of people, but he still didn't care.

Edith was indignant. Although clearly upset, she seemed determined to hold her own against Shamus's tirade. It struck Shamus as fortunate that, even though she was eighty-three years old, his mother was obviously as tough as old boots. He hoped the passengers overhearing their altercation had come to the same conclusion as Edith told Shamus in no uncertain terms that she'd only ever had his well-being in mind and repeated that she would have told him all about Carlo once she got settled in Venice. He simply hadn't given her a chance.

"You seemed so lonely after Luke died," she concluded. "I really wanted you to meet your Italian relatives. I was just waiting for the right moment."

His mother's appeal was so heartfelt that Shamus relented. Besides, the emotion-charged atmosphere, coupled with the mention of Luke's name, brought him close to tears. He was incapable of talking.

Edith and Shamus had been so engrossed in their heated exchange they hadn't noticed that the vaporetto had reached San Marco. As the group of objectionable English children disembarked, a ginger-haired boy turned and threw Shamus a V-sign, then gave him the finger for good measure. Will and Shamus caught each other's eye and broke into guffaws of laughter, which, judging by the frown on the teenager's face, rankled more than any rebuttal would have done.

A revivifying breeze had sprung up and the sky was lightening. Mother and son sat back, relieved at an unspoken truce. Shamus could see a few patches of blue sky. As the boat veered away from the quay, a couple of rays of sun pierced the cloud cover. The huge church of Santa Maria della Salute, which towered over the entrance to the Grand Canal, was illuminated in blazing sunlight. Thrown into sharp relief against grey skies in the background, the massive domes of the church appeared even more imposing than usual.

Suddenly, Shamus was hit with the ramifications of what he'd discovered about himself in the previous twelve hours. While wallowing in his own petty preoccupations, not to mention simmering with resentment of Edith for having duped him for sixty years, Shamus had completely failed to recognize the incredible opportunity the situation offered. He was half Italian, for Christ's sake! The fact gave him permission to do all sorts of things: have a tantrum, confront anyone he disagreed with, cry without embarrassment in public, tell people he loved them. Why not? He'd already succeeded in venting his anger at the English brats and their teacher without feeling guilty. He didn't care what his Italian friend Vince thought. There was absolutely no reason he shouldn't embrace the stereotype of an outgoing, pain-in-the-ass, effusive Italian. Shamus laughed out loud.

Edith was more alarmed by this maniacal display of mirth than by the rages and anger he'd shown earlier. "I'm sorry, dear. I'm sorry," she soothed in an attempt to calm her son, who appeared to have come unhinged.

Shamus turned to his brother. He'd understand. Hadn't Will been banging on for the last twenty-four hours about Shamus making an effort to be more outgoing? As Will claimed he'd been during the period the two of them had spent together in London all those years ago. But Will was staring at the scrolls and buttresses of Santa Maria della Salute, every sensual curve and fluid arch beautifully illuminated in brilliant sunlight. "Looks like a picture on a bloody jigsaw puzzle," he said, but with such awe and admiration in his voice, he might have been comparing the scene to a masterpiece by Canaletto.

Shamus turned to his mother with the intention of telling her everything was all right, that she was forgiven. But, prompted by Will's comment, her attention had been diverted to the panorama of palazzi and imposing buildings that lined the canal in front of the vaporetto. She was experiencing a sensation of lightness. If she hadn't known better, she might have thought she was pleasantly tipsy. Edith felt less world-weary than she had in years. She looked around, eyes dry and bright. "I thought it would be like the Mersey but different," she said wonderingly. "I never dreamt it would be as beautiful as this."

The last vestiges of Shamus's resentment and anger evaporated in the brine-laden Venetian air, replaced by an exuberance so intense he felt high as a kite. He suddenly realized he was so hungry he could eat a horse. Or at least a dozen *dolci,* with lashings of cappuccino made with full-fat milk. And not decaffeinated either, Shamus told himself. He threw his huge arms around his mother and his brother. But in spite of his resolution of just seconds earlier to be more demonstrative, Shamus couldn't go so far as to express himself in English. So he spoke in Italian. He pulled his mother and brother to him. *"Ti amo,"* he whispered. Then he said it louder, looking first at Edith, then at Will, then back to Edith. *"Ti amo, ti amo, ti amo."*

Will brayed with laughter when a teasing Italian voice echoed from two rows ahead, *"Anch'io! Ti amo! Ti amo!"* I love you too! I love you too!

Edith's heart had given a lurch when Shamus spoke those familiar words. She automatically dabbed at her dry eyes with a wad of tear-soaked tissue. Will looked away from the jigsaw-puzzle-picture-perfect view to wink at his brother. Shamus returned the wink as their vaporetto chugged its way up the Grand Canal, without a doubt the most beautiful thoroughfare in the world.

Edith faltered when she was confronted by the two large signs at the customs gate in Liverpool airport, one red, one green. Should she declare the old cigarette case that Armando had given her? She'd staunchly refused to purchase any of the Venetian souvenirs that Will and Shamus had tried to make her buy. She had too much "stuff" as it was without carting home gruesome carnival masks or brightly coloured glass gewgaws. She decided gifts probably didn't qualify for any import duty and marched, with only slight pangs of guilt, through the green, nothing-to-declare channel. As promised, a young friend was waiting to drive her home. The friend was fifty-three years old, but Edith called everybody "young" who was born after the end of World War II.

Edith had felt strangely unaffected when she met Domenico Baccanello again. She couldn't equate the tall old man with the damaged young boy she'd last seen more than sixty years earlier in a damp tent on a rainy day in Arrow Park. Domenico was reserved but polite. The closest he came to being amiable was when he told Edith he'd always wondered why Carlo had never remarried. He tapped the side of his forehead in a gesture she took to mean that the penny had finally dropped, and then he smiled.

Young Armando, on the other hand, had embraced and kissed Edith when they first met. The only occasion when Edith lost her composure was when Armando pulled out the cigarette case and presented it to her. Even after Will explained it all to her, she simply couldn't comprehend that it was Carlo's. But once she saw his initials, the fact of the silver case, totally unchanged since last she had seen it, had sunk in. The slim rectangle of metal acted like a potent talisman on Edith. When she closed her eyes and stroked its silky patina, it propelled her back to the war years with Carlo.

At a lavish dinner at Da Baccanello — which reminded Edith of Anna's meals — Will recounted that it was when Armando explained what the initials C.B. on the cigarette case stood for that his tantalisingly vague suspicions had taken a definite shape. He remembered the name Baccanello, which was, of course, Anna-Maria's maiden name. Then a closer inspection of the restaurant photographs, and the undeniable resemblance of Shamus to Carlo, had given Will the push he needed to browbeat Domenico into confirming everything else.

The next afternoon, after Will had referred to Domenico as "a miserable old bastard," Edith had told him and Shamus every detail about the internment and the sinking of the *Arandora Star.* She was glad when Will had the good grace to look shamefaced. "Is that why you were once so gung-ho about going to that war memorial in Bardi?" Shamus had asked. Edith was amazed he remembered. Will suggested they all take a trip to the memorial the following spring. "After all," he'd said, "this little holiday has been such a roaring success."

At the airport, before Edith left Italy, Shamus was talking animatedly about seeing his brother and his mother again soon. Apparently, he and Will had cooked up a scheme for Shamus to stay with Will and his girlfriend in Mrs. Maguire's old house in Shrimpley over Christmas. Edith was relieved there'd been no suggestion of his staying with her. She couldn't have been more satisfied with the outcome of her trip, but her sons had been so rambunctious for most of the time in Venice, Edith had found them rather tiring.

Nevertheless, she was looking forward to seeing Shambhala again. Will had mentioned that the house seemed unchanged, even run-down. She wondered if the wartime photo album might still be up in the attic, where Mrs. Maguire had hidden it after Joe laid down the law about never wanting to hear Carlo's name again. Edith knew that Mrs. Maguire had forgotten all about it when she moved and left the album in its dusty hiding place under the rafters. Edith wasn't sure whether it would do Will harm or good to see photographic evidence of how happy he'd been as a baby.

She'd made it very clear to her sons that she didn't want anyone in Liverpool knowing about what had been revealed in Venice. "It's my business and nobody else's," she insisted. "You can tell all your pals in London and Toronto whatever you want, but I don't want it discussed around my own house."

So when Edith's friend asked, as she hoisted Edith's bag into the car, how her trip had been, Edith simply replied, "Very nice, thanks. It's a beautiful place."

It was like the answer she'd given to people in the '40s and '50s when they asked, "How was your war, then?" It wasn't unusual in those days to hear statements like, "Phil's war was terrible; he was torpedoed twice," or "Jill's war was hard; she worked as a Land Army girl on a farm in Yorkshire."

More often than not, Edith simply told people that her war had been uneventful.

Acknowledgements

Heartfelt thanks to WWII Italian internees Luigi Rafaele Beschizza, Nicola Cua and Gino Guarnieri, whose first-hand accounts via the archives of the Imperial War Museum London were both affecting and invaluable.

Thanks to my mother for stories of 'her war.' Thanks to my brother for prompting reflections on fraternal interaction and for a lifetime of support.

I can't measure the value of the gift of 'time-to-write' given to me by my good friend and business partner, Joseph Gisini.

Many thanks to *Descant* magazine, particularly editor and friend, Karen Mulhallen, for publishing the short story Barnabotti Brothers, which was the genesis of *Edith's War*.

To copy editor Sheila Wawanash, many thanks for the alchemy performed on the manuscript. *Mille grazie* to Armando Pajalich and Michelle Alfano for checking the manuscript with Italian eyes. Thanks to social media guru and publicist, Ruth Seeley, for all her expertise and hard work.

Thanks to my friends who patiently tolerated my obsession with the writing and publication of this book. Much gratitude goes to the people who have followed my blog throughout the process, and to those who commented. Thanks to Jack David of ECW Press for his sage advice.

Last but most important, my undying gratitude to editor, Jennifer Day; her suggestions, guidance and support were inspiring and transformative.

Books

Many thanks to the authors of the following books, which were invaluable sources during research for *Edith's War:*

Divided Loyalties: Italians in Britain during the Second World War, Lucio Sponza. Peter Lang AG, European Academic Publishers. Bern. 2000

'Collar The Lot!' How Britain interned and expelled its wartime refugees, Peter and Leni Gillman. Quartet Books Limited, 1980.

The Night Blitz, 1940-1941, John Ray. Cassel and Co., 1996

Art Behind Barbed Wire, Jessica Feather. National Museums Liverpool, 2004

Isle of the Displaced: Italian-Scot's Memoirs of Internment During the Second World War, Joe Pieri. Neil Wilson Publishing, 1997.

Web Sites

Hundreds of web sites were consulted and cross-referenced during the research and writing of this book. Here are a handful of the most meaningful:

http://www.chrisgibson.org/arandora/

http://www.thearandorastar.com/as-italian-list.htm

http://www.bbc.co.uk/history/worldwars/wwtwo/

http://www.liverpoolmuseums.org.uk/maritime/exhibitions/blitz/blitz.asp

http://www.nationalarchives.gov.uk/education/

http://www.theirpast-yourfuture.org.uk/

Historical Notes

There is a claim by Bridget Hitler, the wife of Alois, Adolf Hitler's half-brother, that young Adolf visited the couple in Liverpool as a young man, arriving in November, 1912 and staying until April, 1913. Unfortunately there are no other accounts of his visit and experts are divided as to the veracity of Bridget Hitler's memoir. Mike Royden has an excellent account of the claim and other related material on his web site: http://www.btinternet.com/~m.royden/mrlhp/local/ hitlerinliverpool/hitlerinliverpool.htm

Within hours of Mussolini's declaration of war against Britain and her allies on June 10, 1940, Winston Churchill issued the command to arrest and intern all Italian males living in Britain. He is reputed to have said, in his inimitable style, "Collar the lot!" Hence the title of the book by Peter and Leni Gillman (see book list). Almost all the men and boys taken into custody were later taken aboard the ships *Arandora Star* and *Ettrick* to be taken to Canada. The ships were not marked by the conventional use of a red cross to warn enemy vessels that the passengers were civilians. The *Arandora Star* was torpedoed and sunk in the morning of July 2, 1940 by a German U-boat. Some 446 Italian internees were drowned. The following web site lists their names: http://www.thearandorastar.com/as-italian-list.htm

Many of the bodies of the *Arandora Star* victims washed up in subsequent weeks and months on the north-west shores of Ireland. An excellent amateur four-part series outlining the tragedy as it relates to Ireland can be found on YouTube at: http://www.youtube.com/watch?v=EeuZ6ft6pYw

A large number of the men who drowned as a result of the sinking of the *Arandora Star* were from families who hailed from Bardi in the Emilia Romagna region of Italy. A memorial chapel in Bardi has been dedicated to the victims. For more information see: http://www.chrisgibson.org/arandora/bardi.htm

In May 1940 the Huyton Alien Internment Camp in Liverpool admitted its first internees. Liverpool was targeted as the temporary destination for many aliens and internees during WWII for its convenience as an embarkation port to the Isle of Man, Canada, and Australia. The camp was situated on the site of the recently built Liverpool Corporation Woolfall Heath Housing Estate. In 2004 the Walker Art Gallery, Liverpool mounted an exhibition of works produced by artists during the time they were housed in the camp. Two of the artists whose work appeared were Hugo Dachinger and Walter Nessler. *Art Behind Barbed Wire,* by Jessica Feather is the catalogue to the exhibition and contains much fascinating information about the camp.

The direct hit on the large underground shelter in Durning Road, Edge Hill, was the worst single incident in the Liverpool air raids of WWII as regards loss of life. This occurred in the early hours of November 29, 1940. About 300 people were tightly packed into a shelter in the basement of Edge Hill Training College in Durning Road. When a parachute mine hit the building, it collapsed into the shelter below, crushing many of its occupants. Boiling water from the central heating system and gas from fractured mains poured in. Raging fires overhead also made rescue work extremely dangerous. In all, 166 men, women and children were killed. Many more were badly injured. See National Museums Liverpool web site: http://www.liverpoolmuseums.org.uk/maritime/exhibitions/blitz/blitz.asp